LEVIATHAN

Printed in Australia
First published April 2025

Cover design by It's Made By Brooke
Internal design by Jessica Chaplin

Paperback ISBN 978-1-7637529-5-5
eBook ISBN 978-1-7636529-6-2

More great titles can be found by visiting www.matthewcirsonauthor.com.au

 A catalogue record for this
work is available from the
National Library of Australia

LEVIATHAN

Matthew Cirson

Also by Matthew Cirson

The Depths Within: Part One
The Depths Within: Part Two

MAWSON
AUSTRALIAN ANTARCTIC DIVISION RESEARCH STATION
ANTARCTICA

1

THE WIND BUFFETED the heavily insulated walls of the Emergency Power House and the structure seemed to tremble as if a cold shiver had run up its spine. This was perfectly understandable, knowing the location of the EPH and the torrents of wind and ice it was subjected to on an hourly basis. Such extreme cold, to make a Sydney southerly and the chill that it carried from this land seem like a cool shower on a summer's day. Such winds that would make even the harshest of Sydney's hailstorms seem like a shallow exhale. Even the shattered roof tiles, the endless debris that seemed to pour from the cladded houses, the damage that always seemed to leave the inhabitants exasperated. Whereas the winds that now buffeted the Australian Antarctic Building System's structure, which those at Mawson knew as the Emergency Power House, were a cool and easy 170 kilometres per hour. The storms of Sydney were nothing but pups to the wolves of the Antarctic winds.

The blue, yellow, red and green structures that all stood around Mawson base camp stood these winds time and time again, and seemed to shrug them off like they were but only the first hint of the Southerly that signified the end of summer.

Mawson was home to up to 120 staff in its peak period. Over the winter however, the numbers dropped to thirteen key and essential members. Amongst the marine biologists, the cosmic ray analysts and the glaciologists, Danny Myers was apt to call himself the most important man on Mawson. He was a diesel mechanic. Not only did the entire camp run off the power generated from the four main Caterpillar generators, but the inhabitants of Mawson also survived off the heat that was generated from the cooling systems. Yes, Mawson did also have a windmill which generated some power, he was forced to admit time and time again when reminded by Marie Swan, a young marine biologist. Nevertheless, Mawson would be brought to its knees if it wasn't for Danny's four kings and his ice queen.

Danny ran his hand over his brow. He'd been in Mawson for six months now. He had experienced the Antarctic night, which was a period in winter where the sun would turn the sky a murky red. He had experienced the winds and colds, yet he just couldn't get used to wearing so many damned clothes inside and still not breaking out in a sweat. He ran his socket over the ice queen's left rocker cover bolt by bolt, to check the torsion of each. On the road trains he had trained on, he never really seemed to care so much as to go into this amount of effort and detail, but the difference between 400 kilometres isolation and 4000 kilometres meant that he would take as long as he needed to make sure she would purr like a kitten.

Danny's ice queen was a V12 Caterpillar turbo diesel generator; she generated a whopping 385 kilowatts of power per hour and was Mawson's emergency backup generator. The main power supply came from Danny's kings: four 3306 Cat turbo diesels that ran in a bank. Only one or two kings ran at one time together, until the strain on the alternators became too great. They were set to switch on automatically to spread the load over the generators. Danny worked throughout his time to swap the load over onto different engines to ensure that each and every motor ran for at least a day here and there. Now the time had come for the ice queen to take her turn.

For an environment so cold and with winds so damned fast, Mawson staff were particularly cautious of fire. The Emergency Power House that housed the ice queen was on the complete other side of the camp to the Main Power House where the four kings sat, just below the wind turbine, which Danny heard whirring forty feet above his head.

He wiped at his brow again, as if just the thought of working on an engine should break him out in a sweat. He checked the torsion of the bolt heads on the transfer adaptor case and the alternator. He checked the fuel lines for age and cracks. He even checked the co-generative plumbing that linked the ice queen's cooling system to the lines that ran throughout camp when she was running. As always, she was in A1 condition. The only thing left for him to do was to power her up and rest the kings for a day or two.

He paused at the control box; his hand hovered over the switches. He lowered his head in contemplation and smiled as he sat next to his queen. Danny pulled his phone from his pocket. The screen lit up and his smile broadened as he looked into the eyes of his partner. It had been six months since he had seen her, felt her. Yet, it had only been three months since she had given him the news that he was going to be a father.

That night had been one of mixed emotions for Danny. He had smiled and laughed as to follow the cue from his partner Louise, but secretly he had been scared shitless. Before he had left Sydney, he had spent a night on the town, wining, and dining Louise in the city. They both knew it would be just over twelve months until they could be in each other's presence, and so they spent every second how they should've. The hotel room was lavish for what they needed, as realistically they had never left the king bed once he had laid her down upon it.

Twelve months, he would be away for. Twelve months of hard, government paid work so that they could buy a house upon his return. Now it seemed like a house might require a further twelve months of work just to have enough for the bloody deposit, let alone the money the kid would need. The smile washed away from his face as he ran his gnarled hand through the stubble on his chin. His eyes went from the beautiful blue of Louise's eyes to her hand, which was placed over her stomach. She had sent him the photograph three months ago along with the ultrasound images.

Danny had kept the news to himself. She'd told him while he was in his "Donga," which is what most of the Aussies called their bedroom. Only after a few weeks of Danny slipping further into his own mind had the Australian Government's guidelines come rushing in to save the day.

'Are you ok?' Jonty McIntyre had asked.

'You right?' Gary Hansen had pried.

'What's wrong?' Marie Swan had soothed.

'Come on, you can tell me.' Gary again.

'What happened?' Corinth Butler, the cook cut in.

Bombardment after bombardment of questions and concerns for their team member that seemed to be withdrawn. Each inquiry, each question plucked at the strings of his temper and the more they asked, the more he wanted to be alone. Finally, after the third night of his team mates trying too hard to include him in everything that they were doing, he snapped and told them all that his partner was pregnant and he didn't know how he felt about it.

Their reaction made him laugh, and Christ he had needed that laugh. Jonty, the camp leader and glaciologist, was disappointed that Danny's sour mood wasn't anything serious and that they had wasted their attempts at cheering him up. Gary, the helicopter pilot, clapped his hands and called for a celebration, he then exited the main mess to retrieve something from his Donga. Marie Swan had kissed him full on the lips in her joy, then had blushed and had likewise left the room. Sean Wilson the electrician and Craig Hollins the cosmic ray analyst, began to sing "Cats in the Cradle," to the humour of the rest.

Gary had returned with three large bottles of Glenfiddich. He roared as he entered the mess and held the bottles high in the air so that they almost touched the ceiling tiles. Music was played, songs were sung, and even Jonty didn't seem like the total prat that he was by the end of the night. Even Marie had likewise reappeared at some point, her red cheeks back to their usual complexion.

Danny had felt better after that night of release but he still hadn't addressed the problem, which was the fact that he wasn't sure if he was ready to be a father. Of all the people that had come to him, of all the people that had given him advice, it was the youngest person of the entire expedition that had made him see some sense. Marty Milonis, a nineteen-year-old film marketing intern, had taken an opportunity to get paid a hell of a lot more money than an intern would generally expect, to spend a year on Mawson and document the life of the inhabitants, the aurora of the Antarctic night and the wildlife that surrounded them. Due to his job, everyone found Marty in their life at one point or another, yet he never intruded and was always interested. Even Jonty seemed to warm to him.

It was few days after the party, when Danny was working on one of the Hägglund's – a large capable tracked, transport vehicle – that Marty had shown up to do some filming. They had gotten to talking as Danny replaced the destroyed bearings in the drive axle. He didn't know if it was the fact that he was working that put him at ease, or whether it was Marty's uninterrupted listening, but Danny put everything out on the table. He spoke about his fears of being a father, his fears of raising the kid in Sydney, which was near too damn expensive to support himself let alone a newborn kid. He spoke about his own father who had supported him until his death and how alone he felt in the world now that his old man was gone.

Marty smiled at him as he adjusted the lens of his camera and focused on some seals out on the rocks to their north. 'Are you proud of your dad?' he had asked.

Danny paused underneath the chassis of the Hägglund and turned to the young cameraman. 'Yeah, of course I am.'

'That's what your kid will think of you, man. You just need to let it have a chance to know you. You guys will be fine, worst comes to worst do another year out here. We all know the money's good enough, otherwise there would be no-one to put up with Jonty's shit.'

For the second time since he had been told about Louise's unexpected bundle of joy, Danny had thrown back his head and laughed, and Christ he had needed it.

The second piece of advice that Marty gave him was to create a video log as letters to the kid. 'When I get worked up about something, I talk to the camera as if they were the person or thing I was concerned about. I'd lay it all out on the line and if I want to, I can go back and watch over it. Sometimes, I look back at what I've said, and I think I was so stupid to be so worried about something so small. Hey, maybe you'll have the same luck?'

Marty had gone as far to set up something he called a 'safe box' on Danny's phone so that each time he created a video, it would automatically save it there and in the internet, not just on his phone. Wonders would never cease.

So, there Danny sat, alongside his ice queen with his phone in his hand as his thumb hovered over the record button. He considered the features of his own face, his coarse blonde stubble over his angled jaw. His crooked nose that hadn't seemed to stop running since he'd arrived in this damned place and his blue eyes that seemed greyer the longer he peered into them. Christ, he looked cold. Even though in the EPH the temperature was a respectable ten degrees, he still wore his beanie, hooded jacket, and thermals. He swallowed a dry mouthful of air and pressed record.

'Hey, kiddo…' His voice was coarse but soft, although he spoke loud enough to be heard over the winds that continued to push about the EPH.

'It's now been three months since I was told by your beautiful mother that you existed and…' He took his eyes from the camera to focus on the V12 by his side, he smiled. 'And I couldn't be happier.'

He groaned as he stood and held the camera on his face as he did so. 'I know you'll still be too young to realise that I wasn't by your side for the first three months of your life, but I'm sure your mother will remind us constantly when she finds reason to. Anyway, I just wanted to apologise about that because the truth is…' He looked to the generator again as if to build up his resolve. 'The truth is that I would never have gone away if I had known that your Mum was pregnant with you. I can't wait to meet you and I'm sure you're going to be the best kid anyone could hope for. I just need to work for another six months here on Mawson and then I'll be home with you and Mum.'

He smiled at the camera and thought, *that kid Marty is a hell of a lot older than nineteen, I don't care what anyone says.* His attention moved to the generator, sighed and returned his eyes to the camera. 'There's just one thing you need to know, and I'm sure your mother won't ever forgive me for this. I... I laid my hands on another woman, I just couldn't help myself because the heat she generates, gives all of us here so much warmth.'

He turned the camera so that the generator was visible over his shoulder. 'This is her. I called her the ice queen after your mother,' he paused and added, 'now that's something that your mother definitely won't ever forgive me for.' He laughed as he walked over to the generator's control box. 'Anyway, this big girl is our backup generator and I've been getting her ready to run for us. So, I'll give you a bit of a show, of the big queen running. Now it'll probably be too loud in here for you to hear me say goodbye so I'll do it now.' He leant forward and kissed the screen.

'Ok big girl, let's go,' he said as he held the camera in a position so that his future child could see the V12. He powered up the pump, and the room was filled with a high pitch mewling as the primers reached pressure. He held the switch to heat the plugs for a few seconds and then pushed the big red button. The EPH was filled with noise and power as the ice queen came into life.

Danny laughed as he leant the camera in closer, to give his future child a better show. He returned the camera back to his face and shouted as loud as he could the three simple words he couldn't wait to say face to face: 'I love you.'

2

AT MID—MORNING, the camp came alive as people returned to the Red Shed from their various start of day duties. The Red Shed was the largest of all the AANBUS structures on base and was situated near enough to the centre of camp to be thought of as its epicentre. It held not only all the winter crews' rooms, or Dongas, but an entertainment area, a mess area, and most importantly, the kitchen.

"Woollies," an abbreviated slang for Woolworths, a supermarket chain on the mainland, held most of the camps rations and snacks. As per anything in Australian vernacular, the nicknames seemed to appear and stick at some point in time and everyone was helpless but to follow them. Nevertheless, this didn't stop Jonty, their fearless leader, in holding a meeting during the peak of summer to decide whether the pantry's name should be changed to Coles. Needless to say, the motion didn't carry.

The short walk from the EPH to the Red Shed took Danny only a few minutes, yet the preparation for the journey took five times as long as the journey itself. No matter the time an individual spent outside of the warmth of the AANBUS structures, they needed to be swaddled up in their full, extreme cold outfit. Each individual was expected to wear around three layers of clothing beneath their final waterproof layer. This morning, Danny had long Merino wool thermal underwear, a t-shirt, track pants and a warm woollen hoodie. Two pairs of Hard Yakka socks, knee-high gumboots, woollen gloves under ski gloves, a balaclava, and then over everything a matching insulated pants and jacket combination that seemed to be made out of the same spray material that was so popular in the nineties. The fact that a person's clothing was such an important part of life at Mawson meant that a lot of time was spent inspecting the clothes for disrepair. It also meant that the crew considered each outing carefully and planned even the shortest journey as if their life depended on it.

The wind hissed through the gap in the jamb as Danny forced the door shut to the cold porch behind him. The doors into the structures were tremendously thick with insulation and required some force to move them, especially when the wind was up. As he shut the door he stepped back and noticed a new sign had been stuck to the door: *Please push with both hands to close the door QUIETLY.* Danny shook his head as he turned to enter the facility – there was only one person that came to mind when he read that sign and he was the last person he wanted to think about.

In most places of rest and relaxation, there tended to be "cold porches" before the main entrance to the facility. This was a basic, heated room where the expeditioners could remove their wet outer clothes and store their gumboots or work boots before they entered the rest of the structure. It took Danny another few minutes to carefully remove his outer few layers and stash them in his compartment. He rolled up his balaclava so it sat in a rumpled mess on his forehead. He replaced his gumboots with ugg boots and left the cold porch for the bustle of the mess.

The noise struck him as he walked through the lower rooms of the facility. The smell of coffee was the next thing to hit him and instantly his stomach gurgled. Helicopter pilot Gary Hansen leant against the serving counter to the kitchen. In one hand he held his steaming coffee mug, the one with the US G.I drinking a cup of Joe, with the caption: *how about a nice big cup of shut the fuck up.* Gary's other hand kneaded his eyes as he rested his chin on his chest.

Danny rested against the serving counter next to him as he laughed.

'Ten a.m.,' he said to the pilot and his closest friend on the base. 'The international recognised time for smoko.'

Gary grunted, his eyes bloodshot and bleary. 'Yeah, now all we need are cigarettes.'

'You can say that again.' Danny sighed. If any of them were smokers before they left, Mawson had a good way of making you quit upon arrival thanks to the cold, coupled with government regulations, plus the fear of fire that Danny could never quite grasp. There were no designated heated smoking areas in Mawson. If a person wanted one that bad, they were welcome to step into the weather and smoke as many as they wanted. 'And how long do you reckon you'd last this time?'

'Long enough to get Jonty's damned voice out of my head, Gary grumbled as he gestured to the other side of the mess hall.

Danny turned to see Jonty moving towards them, a stern expression plastered across his face. Jonty was a tall, slender man with blonde wavy hair that swept back around his head. He was always clean-shaven and many of the other men joked that this wasn't due to his grooming, but a lack of testosterone. His voice was of a higher pitch and had nasal undertones, as if he was always battling hay fever. There didn't seem to be just one particular thing that annoyed most of the men about Jonty; it was the sum of everything. His stricken urgency, the way he patronised everyone, the way the women seemed to blush when he looked at them.

'Good morning gentlemen,' Jonty said in a strict tone as he approached them.

'What's so fuckin good about it?' Gary grumbled without making eye contact.

Jonty seemed to ignore this; a small frown that accentuated the lines at the side of his mouth was his only reaction. 'We have a very important meeting this morning, so please make yourself available in fifteen minutes.'

'Hey, I'm available,' Danny said, 'as long as the coffee's on the house and the grub is good.'

'Hey available, I'm Gary.' Gary held out his hand and Danny shook it.

Jonty pursed his lips and walked off to the cold porch. Danny slapped

Gary on the shoulder and walked into the kitchen to fix himself a coffee.

Corinth Butler or 'Ma' as Danny called her, stood to the far side of the kitchen; Danny greeted her as he approached the urn. Corinth was a woman of about fifty, she was a little heavier set than most of the people at Mawson. Her black hair was scraggly and etched with greys, that ran down from her scalp like peppered snow across the nunataks of the peaks. Her face was likewise etched with faint lines that seemed to multiply as she smiled, which was all the time. She was a great human being, and given the old proverb "the way to win a man's heart is through his stomach," Corinth Butler had everyone at Mawson in the palm of her hand.

Danny approached her with a steaming coffee in hand. 'How's it going, Ma?'

As if on cue her lips spread into a smile as she worked. 'Just checking my babies.' Her babies were the four dozen eggs that remained of the February shipment. If anyone had told Danny that eggs could last eight months with the proper care, he wouldn't have believed them. Yet here they stood, September the 26th in the year of our lord, 2019, and there before Corinth were four trays of eggs that had lasted eight months so far. As the whole camp relied on Corinth for most of their meals, and there was nothing better on earth than eggs for breakfast, everyone was heavily invested in the longevity of Corinth's babies.

Eggs didn't just last eight months because it was cold. Every two weeks they needed to be flipped to ensure the yolk didn't stay in contact with a piece of shell for too long. The shells were also oiled to prevent air ingest. All of this was part of Corinth's duties, but every night a person was set to assist her in whatever she needed help with. Of course, this was organised by Jonty and his work roster.

'And how are the babies?' Danny asked as she ran an olive oil-soaked cotton ball over an eggshell and placed it upside down back into the tray amongst its gleaming brothers and sisters.

'They're doing alright.' She sighed. 'It's a long time to nurture these things. I think we should eat them soon; I don't like holding them past eight months.' Everyone had their own job through the winter, but Danny couldn't think of anything more tedious than flipping what seemed like endless dozens of eggs every fortnight.

'Hey, why don't you surprise us all and make eggnog? You might even make Jonty seem bearable.' Danny laughed.

'If you can get Gary to give me some of his stash, I might take you up on that.'

Danny rubbed at the stubble on his chin. 'I'm sure he'd take some convincing, but maybe it would be better if the persuasion came from someone of the other sex, huh, huh?' he asked as he poked her in her side.

Corinth jumped at the poke and she almost dropped the egg in her hand. She took a deep breath of air as she blushed and she feigned her anger. 'Oh you. Danny Myers.' She placed the egg down carefully in its tray and then swung a tea towel at him. 'Go on, shoo, you dirty-minded little boy.'

Danny fled from the wrath of her tea towel swings as he laughed in imitation of a shrill child. He left the kitchen to browse Woolworths, where he snagged a packet of freeze-dried trail mix. As he returned to the mess, he saw that most of the crew had appeared.

Sean Wilson sat cleaning his glasses, his cheeks flush from the cold of his short walk. Marty sat next to Marie Swan with his hands back over his head as he tried too hard to be interested in what she had to say. Craig Hollins sat playing an Italian card game called "Briscola," that had been taught to most by the resident doctor, Anne Castelli, who sat with Craig. Charlie Muscat, a geologist in his mid-forties, stood over Anne's shoulder and tutted while he shook his head. Soon after, Craig threw a card down and yelled, 'Setto Bello!' as he laughed and dragged the won hand over to his pile.

Danny saw Gary, who sat at a table with Wendy Phillips, who handled all the plumbing whether it be high pressure fuel or low-pressure wastage. Alongside them was James Sutton, who was an ok guy for one of the nerds. The word "nerd" seemed a harsh name for the scientists that inhabit Mawson, however it was spoken with affection by the "blue collars" as they were dubbed by the nerds. This tit for tat between those at Mawson seemed to help everyday life go by even faster and James, the entomologist, contributed more so than Gary himself.

'So, what's this meeting about?' Danny asked as he sat down. 'Speaking of which, where is Jonty?' He remarked, realising the only member of their tribe that was missing was their head, apart from Bob Taylor, who ran their communications array, plus everything else in that corner of the world.

'Who cares?' Gary mumbled into his coffee cup.

James raised his eyebrows, and gestured with his head to the corridor. Sure enough, Jonty came through, a briefcase in his hand and his usual stricken appearance. What surprised Danny was that Bob entered the room right after him. Being in communications, it was rare for Bob to leave his office unless it was an emergency, like replenishing his food stores. For Bob to be in the room now, something big must have happened.

It seemed that everyone had caught onto this as the mood of the room changed with Jonty's entrance and the chatter of voices soon fell to silence. Jonty understood he held the entire room's attention yet still he looked around and asked ever so politely, 'Can I have everyone's attention, please?' He paused while he made eye contact with everyone in the room. 'Corinth, could you join us please?'

After a short pause, old Ma came into the mess and sat down beside Sean. With that, Jonty smiled and opened his briefcase. 'Thank you for joining together this morning, I understand you all have your duties but this is very important, so I will jump straight in. The first thing on the agenda is the placement of these new signs.' Jonty held up a laminated piece of A4 paper. His hand covered most of the text but Danny was still able to read the word "QUIETLY" in its large, bold font. A few people shifted in their seats and Gary groaned.

'We need to keep other's comfort in mind while we stay here and the noise some people make within the mess area while others are sleeping is abhor–' He stopped as James raised his hand. 'Yes? Mr. Sutton?'

'I'm sorry to interrupt,' James said in a very serious tone. 'I was certain that you said that the meeting this morning was very important, because I'm sure everyone else has a very busy day in front of them.'

Gary snickered and slapped his leg.

'Yes, well James,' Jonty rebuked. 'I'm sure you all are very busy but our team members' comfort is a very important part of our working relationships.'

'Yeah Jimmy, stop being so rude,' Marie bristled.

Gary laughed again and leant in close to James. 'Now we know who complained,' he whispered loud enough for entire room to hear.

'Yes, I'd thank you all to be silent while whoever has the floor is speaking.' Jonty paused again while the room settled down and Marie shot Gary a distasteful glance. 'Yes, please be sure that when you move through the cold porch that you are mindful of the noise you make. Is everyone in agreeance to this?'

Jonty pursed his lips again as he looked around the room, only to be answered by grunts and small begrudging nods. 'Ok, thank you. Our second motion is regards to the roster. We will need to add another chore heading, as the verandas from the cold porches are becoming swamped with snow.'

'Look Jonty,' Charlie Muscat sighed as he stood up. 'If this is what you have for us then fine, but I have a deadline coming down on me quicker than Blitzkrieg, so if you don't mind, just continue without me.'

Charlie began to leave the room. Gary and James both stood up, as did Anne Castelli, who to Danny's amusement had also seemed to have lost her patience.

'Ok. Ok.' Jonty held up his hands. 'I can see you're impatient so I'll cut to the chase.' Everyone, including Charlie stopped to hear what else he had.

'Amery's loose tooth broke free last night.' The room stayed silent. Danny had no idea what the hell he meant, but Charlie Muscat's jaw dropped. Jonty rustled through his briefcase and pulled a few pieces of paper out. He walked around the room and began to hand them out to the groups as people began to retake their seats.

'It has been designated D-28, it's the largest break from the Amery Ice Shelf in history.' Danny finally understood. The Amery Ice Shelf was an enormous frozen glacier that was basically captured in an inlet. Being six hundred feet thick it was more than just frozen water, and for decades researchers had taken journeys out to the shelf from Mawson to take core samples at varying depths. Danny himself had even driven a crew out there once, early on. Being more than sixty kilometres from base, the trip required the attendance of a mechanic just in case.

'Six hundred feet thick, early reports are that it is about 1600 square kilometres and weighs about 347 billion tonnes.' Danny whistled as Jonty continued around the room.

'*Titanic*, eat your heart out,' Gary said as he peered over Danny's shoulder at the diagram in his lap.

'We estimate that roughly 65 kilometres of new ice frontage has been revealed and the responsibility falls to us to inspect the break point.' Everyone in the room looked up at Jonty, then at each other. 'Amery is in Australian claimed land. It's either us or the guys over at Davis, but don't forget the Chinese have a base in-between Davis and ourselves and for the time being we want to keep this inhouse; who knows what we're going to find out there.'

'More ice?' Gary asked.

'Yes, but it's what's in the ice that teaches us so much.' Jonty spoke with breathless excitement. Being a glaciologist, Danny prepared himself for a lecture but thankfully Jonty was never given the chance.

'I'll go,' Charlie announced.

'What about your deadline?' James enquired.

'This could have some major breakthroughs for my field, so pardon my French but fuck the deadline.'

Gary laughed and held up his coffee mug. 'That's the spirit, Charlie.'

Marie Swan also stood up. 'I'll go as well, as you said we could find anything out there.'

'Ok so that's four of us,' Jonty said as he clapped his hands together. 'I think we should leave in an hour. That will give us enough time to prepare the supplies.'

Danny stood up as he began to speak. 'Four of you? So is Gary flying you or are you taking the Hägglund?' As Jonty turned to consider him, Danny's shoulders slumped. He should have known the answer to his question as that was the reason why he had to go the last time.

'Ahh, you're one of the four Danny, and you're driving.'

3

THE FOUR–CYLINDER FORD ENGINE whirred away happily beneath them, as the rubber tracks of the Hägglund churned over the ice, snow, and rock. Back in Sydney, Danny had been a diesel mechanic, so long hours of sitting behind the wheel never bothered him. One never knew what the day would bring, whether he would remain local to the Sydney basin or whether he would travel north, or south, or worse yet, west over the Blue Mountains and beyond. It wasn't that he didn't enjoy the drive over the hills, but the shoulders were narrow and the people that drove those windy roads generally didn't know how to drive a greasy stick up their own ass. That, coupled along with the fact that once he had found the broken-down hauler, he would literally risk his own life on the side of the New South Wales highways, trying to find what was wrong with the bloody thing. It was a sad thing to say when the safest place to work on a truck was under it. Those days were behind him now, but the further he drove the Hägglund, the more Jonty spoke and continued to speak, making Danny wish he was back on the side of the highways in the dirt, grime, and heat.

'Hey, watch out.' Jonty interrupted himself as he shot a finger forward to the flat plate windscreen.

The world snapped back to reality in Danny's mind and he saw that the left-hand side tracks were dangerously close to a fissure in the ice and snow.

Danny planted the accelerator and swung the wheel hard to the right. The body of the large machine twisted and whined as the linkages between the two cabins oscillated and slowly the cabin directed itself back to safety.

'Gee whizz, Danny, I thought you were going to drive us right off the edge there.'

Danny pulled the Hägglund to a halt and swivelled in his seat to face Jonty. 'It has been three hours Jonty. Three very long hours that you have not shut your damned trap, and to be honest, I've had enough.' His whole hand shook with rage as he pointed his finger at Jonty's face. 'There's another two and half hours to go in this shit, so if you want to keep talking, I suggest you and whoever wants to talk with you get into the back compartment with the diesel and the tools. Because if I hear one more goddamned word out of your goddamned mouth, it's going to get fuckin ugly.' The whole cabin remained silent; the seconds that passed seemed like hours. 'Alright?'

'Someone got up on the—' Jonty began in a sulk.

'What did I just say?' Danny roared in his face. 'Literally two seconds ago. Just shut up for the rest of the trip, that's it. They can talk.' Danny pointed to the two wide-eyed passengers in the back compartment. 'I'm sure they'd have plenty to say because you haven't given them a chance to talk!' He took a breath. 'Haven't you?'

'Ok. Ok.' Charlie leant forward from the back seat and patted Danny on the shoulder. 'It's all done now big fella; you've gotten it off your chest and everyone feels a lot better.'

'Yes, everyone feels great,' Marie continued. 'Now let's keep going, as I'm sure Jonty is feeling very tired now. Isn't that right, Jonty?' She spoke like a mother to a child and nodded her head very slowly.

Danny took a breath; the four-cylinder diesel still rattled beneath him as the hot air from its cooling system churned through the cabin. 'Yeah,' he said solemnly, 'sorry about that.' The Hägglund's tracks churned back to life and the cabin fell back into silence.

Twenty minutes passed with only the slight fluctuations of the Ford diesel and the howls of the wind against the brick-like edges of the

Hägglund to entertain them. Danny watched as snow billowed up in front of them and he tracked his way over hills and around nunataks. Slowly but surely, they made their way to the Amery Ice Shelf.

Gary had been the lucky one; he was to meet them out there in another four hours with Marty, to see if they could offer any assistance. Their flight would only take them about an hour, yet Danny had five hours to sit in this tin can as it crawled over the ice and snow. The painful part was that the Hägglund could go faster – it was safety protocols that prevented Danny from taking the beast over thirty. In reality, it could be doing fifty to sixty, although it wasn't meant to. In the end, he had another half an hour worth of fuel left and then he would have to pull up and fill the tanks from the reserve cans in the back. None of this was ideal, but diesel was a hell of a lot cheaper to run than the Robinson R44 helicopter that Gary piloted. Also, the Hägglund could carry a lot more weight than the bird could ever dream of. If they needed to bring back any samples or core drillings, the Hägglund was the only choice.

'Red Brick, this is Mawson. Do you copy? Over.' The radio crackled.

Danny sighed as he unhooked the radio's microphone from the dash and depressed the button. 'Yeah, Bob.' There was a long silence, until Danny depressed the microphone again and said, 'Over.'

'It's been over three hours with no progress report, are you guys ok? Over.'

'Yeah, Bob all good mate. We will be on Amery in another two hours. Tell Gary he can take off in another hour. Over.'

'Will do, Red Brick. Safe drive. Mawson out.'

Danny frowned as he hung the microphone from its hook once more. He turned to the two in the back seat. 'I'll need a hand in a minute, I need to top up the tanks.'

'I'll help you out,' Charlie said; he never took his eyes from the window to his right.

Marie smiled sleepily at him, then laid her head back on a rolled-up jumper so that she might fall asleep once more.

'No time like the present then,' Danny said as he slowed the vehicle to a stop. He shot a distasteful sideways glance at Jonty before he vacated the vehicle. Their leader sat there with his back to the driver. Danny shook his head and opened the door. The cold rushed in like a cancer. Marie gasped and then buried her face into her jumper pillow as Charlie likewise opened his door and snow swirled through the cabin.

Danny pulled his scarf up around his face as the wind hammered into him. He trudged to the rear cabin of the Hägglund and reefed the doors open. Charlie came around the other side; Danny had never seen a man look so cold. He walked like a tree trunk that had sprouted legs and had donned a spray jacket. Charlie was a tall, slender, Maltese man in his forties. His hair was peppered black with grey shot through and he had startling blue eyes that stood in contrast to his olive skin. None of this could be seen through his many layers, and Danny had to laugh as the older man came into view.

'Do me a favour and grab that funnel!' he yelled at Charlie to be heard above the wind. Together they walked back to the front chassis to fill the tank. Danny opened the flap and struggled with his gloves to remove the filler cap. Once he had it off, he faced Charlie and moved his mouth close to the side of his head. 'Put the funnel into the spout and hold it there. When I start pouring, the second you can, put your head close to the funnel and listen for the gurgles. If it starts getting full, then pat my leg; we don't want to spill a drop of this.'

Charlie nodded and they went about it. The work was cold and without conversation, as there was no point trying to shout over the howling winds. Once he was about three quarters through the second can, Charlie patted Danny on the leg with a heavily gloved hand and they packed up. Shortly after, they were back in the warmth of the cabin of the Hägglund and continuing on to the shelf.

About another hour of silence had passed when Charlie finally spoke up. 'I'm sorry to pry Marie, but you're a mother, aren't you?'

Marie laughed as she yawned and stretched. She was a woman in her mid to late thirties. It was difficult to tell with the number of layers that people wore down here, but Danny was pretty sure she hid an amazing body beneath all of that cotton.

'If I had a child Charlie, it would be a bigger miracle than the birth of Jesus Christ.'

Both Danny and Charlie laughed, while Jonty pretended to be asleep. Something about Charlie's face must have urged Marie to continue. 'I don't have a uterus.' She asserted with a soft smile.

'Oh, I... I'm sorry,' Charlie said softly as his attention drifted out of the window, abashed.

'Don't be, I'm happy.'

Charlie turned back to her with a new look of confidence on his face. 'I suppose you could always adopt, couldn't you?' He smiled back.

'I don't need kids to live my life, Charlie.' The smile had vanished from her face.

'Hey, sorry to butt in,' Danny interrupted, feeling the tension. 'You're into marine biology, aren't you? Why would you want to come and look at an ice shelf?'

This was the right thing to do and Danny saw it immediately in her reaction. As the smile returned to Marie's face, she met Danny's eyes in the rear-view mirror and settled back into her seat. 'I think Jonty was right when he said we don't know what to expect. Who knows how old the ice is within the centre of the shelf? As the D-28 tooth has been loose for as long as we have known it to exist, we haven't been able to test the ice for fear of forcing it to dislodge.'

'That's right,' Charlie joined in. 'It's the same for myself – now that the face of the ice shelf has changed, there could be unearthed specimens dating back thousands of years. Whether they be rock or life forms buried in ice that thick is anyone's guess.'

'Or there could be nothing?' Danny asked.

'Hey,' Marie laughed. 'No-one needs that kind of negativity.'

Danny and Charlie laughed again while Jonty continued to pretend to sleep in his sulks.

'Alright, so how do you guys think you're going to get to the face if we're going to be standing on top of the shelf?'

Charlie leant forward, grinning. 'How heavy is this vehicle?'

Danny frowned. 'Four tonnes. Why?'

'Well then two small bodies shouldn't worry it when we use it as an anchor to abseil over the edge, should it?'

4

'YOU GUYS ARE INSANE,' Danny said as they pulled onto the ice. Amery reminded Danny of a lake – vast, flat and calm. The shelf seemed to stretch for an eternity. Somewhere up ahead, it ended in a cliff of ice and fell over two hundred feet to the ocean. Although they had said that the newly created iceberg D-28, Amery's loose tooth, was six hundred-feet thick, the majority of that lay under the water level. As with any icebergs, including the one that had sunk the *Titanic*, the majority of their mass lay below the depths.

'We aren't insane. The definition of insanity is attempting the same thing over and over and expecting different results. As this is the first time we're trying this, you can't call us insane yet.' Marie laughed back at him.

'Yes, maybe. Whatever. If you guys fall, you're goners.' Danny came back.

'Yes, that's right, that's why we will use every precaution available to us so that we don't fall,' Charlie answered calmly.

Danny couldn't believe what he was hearing. 'Jonty,' he said as he pushed their leader's shoulder. 'Are you hearing this horse shit?'

Jonty sat up straight and gave Danny a flat expression. 'Are you talking to me now, are you?'

Danny rolled his eyes. 'Oh, for Christ's sake, if you're going to be like that you can go back to pretending to be asleep. Did you hear what they are planning to do?'

Jonty's expression of flat disappointment didn't change. 'Yes, we all came up with the decision while you were doing the final checks over the vehicle. What did you think all the rope was for?'

Danny was exasperated. He stared at Jonty as the words processed. He was defeated, it was three against one. 'At least wait for Gary to come and use the chopper to look at the wall.'

'From forty feet away? We need to be able to touch the wall Danny, how else are we going to take samples?'

'Christ almighty,' Danny moaned as the Hägglund continued to chug toward the horizon. 'The winch on this thing has never been used, I'm not sure it will even work.'

'It will be fine,' Jonty said, relishing in the fact that he was allowed to talk again. 'Once we get to the edge, we'll have something to eat and drink, set up and wait for Gary. I won't allow anyone over the edge unless we have the bird in the air to act immediately.'

Danny grunted in astonishment. 'At least that is some form of consolation.'

The cabin fell back into silence as the vehicle trudged along the ice shelf, almost as if in anticipation of the greatest thing they were ever to see. The wind continued to howl and snow lashed the windscreen. Danny slowed the vehicle down in his hesitation; the last thing any of them needed was for him to drive the bloody Hägglund over the edge. The speed fell away as all of them seemed to lean forward. The late afternoon sun blared red across the sky in front of them, the snow partially blocking it out as it whipped across the ice beneath them. Finally, Danny let the vehicle come to a stop and killed the engine. He spoke softly as he clasped the door. 'Welcome to the end of the earth.'

The sound of the wind and the snap of the icy air cut through them as all four doors opened simultaneously. Danny stepped out of the vehicle and slammed the door behind him. Thick rubber seals made it hard to close the bloody doors sometimes and, sure enough, he needed to help Marie with hers. Together the four of them walked in a line to the edge of the shelf and they all gasped.

D-28, the Amery shelf's loose tooth, was gargantuan. It looked large enough to be another continent of its own as it sat in the distance. 'Jesus Christ,' Danny whispered to himself as he gaped at the massive wall of ice. It stretched further than he could see.

'There it is!' Jonty shouted as he pointed.

Once more Danny's annoyance flared, but he held his tongue as he continued to gaze at the massive section. Danny edged closer to the edge and looked down, eyes wide, at the water below. A number of smaller chunks of ice floated between themselves and the monstrous berg. Although smaller, these chunks of ice were still larger than Boeing 747s, yet in comparison to the monster that was the loose tooth, they seemed insignificant. Danny pointed down to them. 'Is it breaking up?' He hollered to be heard.

The others peered over the edge as well and Jonty shook his head. 'Think of all that as mortar to a brick wall: when you remove a brick, the mortar crumbles.'

'Just instead our brick is three hundred and forty billion tonnes!' Charlie shouted into his ear. 'The mortar is going to seem as big as suburbs.'

They were right – beyond D-28 Danny couldn't see. The section was so large that it was as if the earth had broken between Albury and Wodonga and he was left to stand on one side to look at the other. To his left the berg came as close as to touch the shelf, but over to his right the vast distance between shelf and berg was phenomenal. It seemed as though the ocean had picked up the massive block and thrown it in a long arc that stretched hundreds of kilometres. As the berg and shelf disappeared off into the distance, they did so at almost sixty degrees apart.

'Well, the people with low-lying houses on the western coast will have the shits.' Danny laughed.

This brought another shot of disapproval from Jonty, who turned to him with his hands on his hips. 'I think we had better start preparing for the rappel; we will have more time to look at this later.'

With that they headed to the rear of the Hägglund, except Marie, who remained on the edge of the abyss, much to Danny's discomfort. He walked cautiously behind her and as he neared her, it seemed as though she was saying something but he couldn't hear it under the wind. Her head tilted from side to side and her body was rocked by a spasm. Her hands wrung together in front of her and she took another step toward the edge, gazing further down into the depths.

As he wrapped a gloved hand around her arm, he could see that her mouth was moving beneath the layers of cotton that covered her face, as if deep in conversation, but no sound came out.

'Hey, you ok?' he asked in a shout.

It seemed to take an age for her to blink and consider him. When she did, it was as though she had no idea where she was and what she was doing there. Then slowly, her eyes filled with recognition.

'Oh my, I don't know what happened,' she said almost inaudibly as she allowed herself to be led away from the shelf's edge.

Panic swelled in Danny's stomach. He put her arm over his shoulder to take her weight and was alarmed at how easily she allowed him to support her.

'Hey guys,' he called to Jonty and Charlie, neither of which acknowledged him. 'Oi!' he bellowed again, and he saw Charlie's head appear from around the side of the Hägglund. 'We have a problem.'

Charlie and Jonty rushed to his side and assisted in getting Marie back into the cabin. Danny fired up the engine to get the heater running, while Charlie went into the back to fetch a thermos of coffee.

'I'm alright you guys,' Marie assured them as they covered her with blankets and handed her a steaming hot cup of black coffee.

'I'll feel better once you've drunk that cup,' Charlie said as a frown creased his brow.

'It's nothing really, I just felt like…' her words trailed off as her eyes became unfocused.

'Here comes Gary.' Jonty interrupted as he leapt out of the cabin. 'As soon as he lands, we'll get him to take you back to Mawson.'

Danny took a last glance at Marie. She raised the thermos cup and took a sip. Danny turned to Charlie. 'Mind looking after her?'

Charlie nodded and Danny left the warmth of the cabin. As soon as he opened the door, he heard the *whup, whup, whup* of the powerful rotors of the R44 Robinson. Jonty stood close to the edge of the shelf and waved his arms. Gary obviously had seen him; he was headed straight for them. The Robinson came from along the coast from Mawson; this brought it over the section of iceberg that had nestled back up against the shelf.

Danny joined Jonty in waving his arms. He wanted Gary to hurry up and land so that they could pile Marie into the back of his bird and he could piss off back to Mawson. He could take Jonty with him for all it mattered. The whole plan had been half-cocked from the get-go; not even two hours remained of sunlight and they had only just gotten here.

As the Robinson that Gary had named 'Big Red One' after some American show came closer, he started to make out the people in the cabin. He saw the big black jacket that Gary wore and he could make out the smaller, almost childlike size of Marty to his side. When the chopper came over the gap that had been created between the berg and the shelf, he saw movement inside the cabin and to his horror, the chopper plummeted below their eye line.

'Holy shit!' Danny screamed as he heard the engine roar as the chopper rushed toward the ocean.

'What does he think he's doing!' Jonty yelled as they both rushed back to the Hägglund. They panted as they struggled to move as fast as they could to reach the red cabin of the tracked vehicle. Danny tried to look through the glass but it had become fogged by the heater. He yanked the door open and saw Charlie's surprised face before he lunged for the microphone, but Jonty had beaten him to it.

'Gary, what the hell do you think you are doing?'

Silence. Danny held his breath, and listened as hard as he could, but below the wind he could not hear the rotors any more. 'Oh shit, don't tell me,' he muttered.

Jonty moved the microphone back to his mouth and pulled his scarf away from his face with the other hand. 'Gary, you answer me right–'

The chopper roared above the crest of the shelf, and the world was thrown into a cloud of snow and silt driven by the power of its rotors. He didn't know what his friend was doing, but it looked as though he had nearly clipped the edge of the ice shelf. Danny raised a hand to protect his face from the swirl, while Charlie yelled at them to shut the doors.

'Jesus!' Danny roared as he climbed into the driver's seat and slammed his door shut. He rammed the fan speed of the heater up to high and directed it onto the windscreen while he rubbed at the glass with his elbow.

'Goddamn it, Gary!' Jonty screamed into the microphone once more. 'We have a sick person down here.'

'Jonty, I'm ok,' Marie insisted over her thermos cup.

'It's beside the point,' Jonty snapped at her, then back into the microphone. 'Would you at least answer me?!'

The crackle over the radio came loud and clear and Danny had to laugh at his friend's sense of humour, as a poor attempt at an American accent filled the cabin. 'This is Big Red One calling all survivors of the Red Brick Shithouse. Do you read me?'

'Cut the shit Gary, we read you. Can you hurry up and land?' Jonty retorted unamused.

'Before I land, you might want to hear what I have to say.' The American accent was gone.

Everyone in the cabin was forced to sit in silence and listen to this back and forth while the heater fan cranked and the view beyond the windscreen slowly became more than just a blur.

'Gary, Marie isn't well and I'd like you to land and take her back.'

Gary's Big Red One came back into sight and it hovered directly in front of them, only thirty feet away. Although Danny had heard the humour in Gary's voice, from what he could see of his face, he wasn't laughing.

'That may be Jonty, but the fact of the matter is that you guys were too slow getting here.'

Everyone in the cabin exchanged a glance. Jonty's eyebrows were furrowed and from what Danny could see, this may be the closest he had seen their leader get to swearing.

'What do you mean we got here too late?' The irritation poured out through gritted teeth.

Through the windscreen, the chopper continued to hover. Next to Gary, Danny could see Marty, but he didn't look at them; his gaze was down at the ocean off to his left, out to where the distance between berg and shelf was the greatest.

'What I mean by that Jonty, is that someone beat you here. We are not alone.'

5

'I SAY AGAIN, RED BRICK' – the radio crackled in the cabin of the Hägglund – 'we are not alone'.

Everyone in the Hägglund all exchanged a glance.

'You must be mistaken Red one,' Jonty tried. 'It isn't possible.'

'Yeah,' Gary laughed. 'I hear you, Jonty. But what you're telling me and what I'm looking at are two different things.' The R44 bobbed in the air as Gary swung its tail around so that the nose of the cabin followed the face of the Amery shelf.

'And what are you looking at Gary?' Jonty said flatly.

'Well, it's an old ship of some sort, doesn't seem rusty so it can't be too old.'

'A ship?' Jonty said without activating the mic. 'Who the hell could've made it here by sea before us?'

'It has to be the Chinese,' Charlie said in a gruff tone from the back seat. He adjusted the blanket he had thrown over Marie.

Jonty nodded slowly at this and Danny understood why, realistically, Charlie was correct. The Chinese had a base of their own closer to the Amery shelf than Mawson, however it was internationally understood that Amery fell in Australian claimed research area. This meant if the Chinese wished to enter the direct proximity of Amery, they needed a signed agreement from not only the head scientist from Mawson, but from the Davis camp as well.

'Gary, can you identify which country the ship belongs to?'

'Well, that's a big ten-four.' Gary's American accent was back. 'They even made it is easy for me with the Japanese flag painted across its hull.'

'Japan?' They all echoed.

'But Showa station is…' Marie started; she had begun to regain the colour in her face.

'A long way away, yes…' Jonty finished for her as he lowered his head to his chest. After a period of silence, Jonty exhaled a long sigh and raised the microphone once more. 'Copy Big Red.' He placed the mic back on its cradle and sat back. Danny watched him silently along with Charlie and Marie. It seemed as though time was standing still as the R44 hovered noisily in front of them and the wind howled and buffeted the cabin of the Hägglund, while Jonty just sat there.

'You alive in there, Jonty?' Gary's voice crackled over the radio.

Jonty calmly retrieved the radio once more and spoke without any emotion in his voice. 'Piss off Gary, I'm thinking.'

That comment brought Jonty up a few rungs on the ladder of Danny's opinion. A small smile crept over his face as he turned his head to look out of the side window.

'Take your time thinking,' Gary cracked back. 'This bird only costs a thousand dollars an hour to keep in the air so take all the time you want, captain.'

Jonty sighed again. He muttered something about Bob Taylor under his breath and straightened himself in his chair. 'Red One, can you land on the ship?'

'That's a negative, Red Brick,' Gary came straight back, his US military grunt voice beginning to merge into a southern drawl.

Jonty's eyes narrowed at this. 'Can you communicate with them?'

There was a slight pause and Gary replied, 'It looks pretty quiet on deck, Jonty. I can try scanning the radio but I flew only a hundred feet or so away from it; surely someone would've heard me.'

'Try again, we'll wait here.'

'Ten-four Red Brick. Stand by.' Gary had lost his battle to succumb to a full southern drawl. The R44 roared and disappeared below the ice shelf. Shortly after, a stone-cold army G.I. voice came across the radio, as Gary made his best attempt to act serious.

'Unidentified Japanese vessel. Unidentified Japanese vessel. You have entered Australian waters without permission. I say again, you have entered Australian waters without permission. Identify yourself, over.'

Although he saw the humour in how his friend spoke, Danny didn't laugh. Neither did any of the others as Gary's message repeated over the various bands.

'They won't reply, sons of bitches,' Charlie grunted.

'Why would they not?' Marie asked him.

'Probably trying to rob us of first findings. It's not every day you get to examine ice first hand that could be millions of years old,' Charlie answered.

'That's enough,' Jonty snapped. He still hadn't met anyone's eyes; he remained focused on the point of the shelf where the R44 had vanished. 'Can't you all see this is serious? I need to concentrate here and none of you are helping.'

Just when Danny had started to gain a little respect for Jonty, it all went down the drain.

'We are taking the situation seriously,' Marie said.

'Well, take it seriously in silence.' His short, gruff words seemed to sting Marie more than anyone else.

Charlie had just begun to open his mouth; his eyebrows were furrowed beneath his beanie as Gary came back over the radio. His voice seemed quieter beneath the rotors as the R44's engine powered somewhere below them. 'All quiet down here, Red Brick.'

'Can you see anyone on board, Gary?'

'That's a negative sir, she looks like she's been quiet for a while. Everything seems to be froz–'

A voice sounded next to Gary and he stopped talking. Everyone in the cabin of the Hägglund leant closer to the dash of the vehicle to try and hear what Marty was saying.

'Hey yeah, you're right,' Gary came over shortly after. 'Red Brick, our young cameraman has good eyes for a virgin.' At this Danny did laugh.

'The ship appears to be moored.'

Once more, confusion spread through the cabin as the three passengers in the conversation exchanged another glance.

'Explain, Red One.'

'Well, there is a chain… no, a steel cable running down into the ice from the bow. I… I can't see properly from here but it looks to me as though it goes straight into the ice shelf.'

'That's fine Red One, return to us and put down to our west. Wait there for further instructions.'

'Ten-four Red Brick. Out.'

Jonty considered his team as his lips developed that annoying purse once more. He glanced briefly from soul to soul as he let out another terrible sigh. 'Marie, when Gary lands I want you to go back to base. We will make camp here, and prepare to descend to the vessel in the morning.'

'That's a long time to wait Jonty, and it is not why we are here,' Charlie complained.

'The Japanese vessel may not be why we are here, but it has become a priority.'

But Charlie wasn't finished. 'I can't see how it's a priority when there is so much more to see just down the face of the shelf, and what would you have us do? Climb right past where we want to examine just so that we can go look at a Japanese ship? It won't matter, come night fall the crew will try and escape anyway; they won't stick around to get prosecuted.'

Jonty looked at Charlie with pure contempt. 'The priority of this expedition, whether you like it or not Charlie, are the expeditioners. My first concern is to get Marie back to Mawson.'

'Jonty, really, I'm fin–' Marie tried to interject but Jonty cut her off.

'That may be, but I'm not taking the risk,' he said with finality. 'Once Marie is back at Mawson, I will then consider a descent along the face but I will not risk your life, your life' – he pointed at Charlie and then Danny –'nor my own. We will wait till morning when Gary can return with enough fuel to remain in the air for some time. He may even be able to think of a way to lower us onto the ship without rappelling down two hundred and fifty feet of ice. The ship may contain people that need our help, and no matter how old a piece of ice is, ice is ice, and humans are humans.' He took another breath and sighed again as he gazed out the window and watched as Gary brought the 44 down, only thirty feet away. As the R44 landed, Danny considered Jonty and tried to read the expression on his face. He wondered if, deep inside, he was hating himself for the decision to put Marie or other possible souls before his research.

'Until then Charlie, I don't want to hear any more of it.' Jonty frowned and his face seemed to age twenty years. He considered Danny for a while. 'Do you have anything to add?'

Danny simply shook his head. To be honest, he didn't blame Jonty for his attitude in the last few minutes; he was in charge and he didn't appreciate being questioned. The man was easy to dislike but, in this situation, the best way that Danny could help was to shut his mouth and do what he was told.

Jonty grunted softly as if in surprise. 'Would one of you gentlemen please assist me in helping Ms Swan to the helicopter? I will also need to speak to Mr Hansen.'

Danny held true to his final thought and volunteered.

The snow whipped around the cabin more fiercely as the rotors continued to spin. Danny wished that Gary had shut the chopper off, but if he didn't plan to be grounded for long, he knew there wasn't any point. Marie stood between Danny and Jonty, wrapped tightly in the blanket that Charlie had thrown over her. Her eyes were almost covered by the beanie while her nose was buried into the cotton blanket she clutched to her face. Danny had an arm around her, as did Jonty, and they trudged with lowered heads towards the R44.

As they neared the chopper, the doors flew open and Gary and Marty climbed out of the cockpit. Marty ran over to help them, but couldn't and ended up just walking back with them awkwardly. Gary, on the other hand, threw open the rear door and helped Marie enter the cabin. He barked at Marty to go in through the other side and help her get settled.

It was amusing to watch Gary speak to other people, especially Marty who had obviously not been around Gary, nor helicopters, for long. After he had given the instructions, Marty had started to walk off, but to the rear end of the idling helicopter. Gary calmly placed a hand on the shoulder of the departing cameraman, pulled him close and pointed to the whirring tail rotor. He then deliberately turned Marty's head so that they looked each other in the eye, holding it still while he shook his own head slowly from side to side in an exaggerated 'no.'

Once Marty had left on his new course, Gary smiled to Danny as they bellowed to greet each other. 'Nice drive out, mate?'

'You know it. Any ideas on how we're going to get down to this ship tomorrow? I don't fancy climbing.'

Jonty joined the conversation, seemingly nonplussed that Danny had asked the question.

Gary rubbed at his chin for a while. 'Let me think about it. You're not going to try and get down tonight, are you?' he said this as he looked over to the setting sun, which had already started to cast a bleary red fire across the sky.

'No, we planned to camp tonight and meet you back here at sunrise.' Jonty took over.

'As long as you sign the overtime card, I'll do whatever you say, Jonty.' Gary smiled.

'Ok, well head back to Mawson now. Get Anne to give Marie a looking over, whether she thinks she needs one or not. Come back alone in the morning and bring some extra fuel, if we need to leave the Hägglund here tomorrow we will. No point dragging it back and forth when we have this.' He gestured to the R44.

Danny frowned. 'We shouldn't leave it out here too long,' he said as he thought about all the work that would be created by the machine's short holiday in the elements. Extreme cold can do many things, and not just to humans.

'We will only take it back once we have finished our assessment of the shelf, and that won't take long. I've already spoken about priorities once today, Daniel.' With that Jonty left them. Danny watched with Gary as

Jonty walked off into the swirling snow toward the Red Hägglund.

Gary patted him on the back and Danny turned to hear him over the chopper's rotors. 'Well, looks like you guys are in for a great night.'

'Thanks, don't remind me.' Danny considered his friend. 'Fly safe man, I'll see you tomorrow morning.'

Gary smiled back. 'Sleep well, Daniel,' he mocked. 'I'm sure you two will have fun working out who's the big spoon.'

6

SINCE HIS ARRIVAL AT MAWSON, Danny had spent countless sleepless nights staring at the pitch black that loomed around him. This had seemed to triple since the news of his soon-to-be child; the new responsibilities and life that awaited him back in Sydney. All those nights that he had lain there, were nothing compared to what he experienced that night on Amery. The winds ripped along the ice shelf to hammer the Hägglund, howling around its blunt angles. The tracked vehicle weighed an easy four tonnes, yet it shook and trembled in the fierce onslaught as if it too feared the ominous wails that the wind carried.

Danny lay in the rear compartment of the vehicle with the two other men. The thermal tent that they had dragged out of the vehicle to set up remained in its PVC bag out in the elements, along with all the spare diesel Danny had brought along. Their sleeping bags were piled all around them as the three men lay side by side, as by the wise words of Jonty, 'the body heat of three men, is better than one.' Danny was fine with this, but to keep warm a human body needed energy, and the rations that were packed for this trip were high in protein. Energy bars, freeze-dried meats and the shakes that reminded Danny of the gym freaks back on the mainland, all did a wondrous job in supplying the body with energy. The biggest negative that he could see, or worse yet *smell,* was the flatulence.

'Sorry.' An apology, when it came from the heart and was truly meaningful, could mend bridges, unite men and rebuild relationships. Yet when it was on the tail end of a five-second thunder clap that seemed to shake the ice beneath the four-tonne tracked vehicle that sheltered them, it didn't have the same effect.

Sleepless nights like this made a philosopher of Danny. He imagined that the same could be said of most men – either that, or they turned into a councillor for themselves or an archaeologist of the mind, left to dig up long-forgotten conversations from years past. Yet, Danny focused on the 'what ifs'. He thought about the ice shelf that they sat on, the vehicle that sheltered them, and the only comparison he could think of was a body fighting an infection. If the Amery Ice Shelf was the body, then the men inside the vehicle were the foreign matter. A cancer that latched itself to the flesh and implanted itself further into the roots of each cell, compromising more of the body with each day that they remained. The winds that hammered them and the silty snow that came up into their eyes, were the anti-bodies that tried to reject them, to no avail. But that was just all bullshit.

Then his thoughts fell to the ship below them, if it was still there, and the questions flowed over and over again. What were they doing there? How could they have beat them here? What were they going to do tomorrow?

In the end, he couldn't answer any of them, and after what seemed like a day's worth of dreaming, his thoughts drifted to his family and he was left to consider his next instalment to his log for his future child. Sometime between the faint and bleary thoughts of names and what to say in his video log, he fell asleep amongst the sheep skin furs and the musky air.

The next morning came hard to Danny. Hägglunds were a sizeable vehicle and in terms of their capability, they had no match. Yet, when considered as a bed or a bunk, Danny thought that a heap of gravel spread out over the ground would have made a more comfortable cot than the hard steel of the base floor. He struggled out of the cabin as the sun burnt into his eyes. He held his hand up to shield his face as he approached the front cabin to retrieve his sunglasses. Through the deep polarised lenses, he marvelled once more at D-28. The iceberg just looked like another land mass; he struggled with how to describe its size, then smiled as he pulled his phone out of his pocket.

As the video began to record, his smile widened as he spoke once more to his future child.

'Hey there kiddo. Another cold day here in Antarctica, but it's a special day.' He positioned the Hägglund over his right shoulder. 'After a single night's camp out in this big old rig, I have to help a few of the scientists dive into some stuff.'

In the screen, he saw Charlie emerge from the cabin behind him and stretch his back. 'Here's one of them now. Hey Charlie, come say hi to my kid.'

Charlie saw the phone in Danny's hand and came over. 'The only thing I can offer you, are my deepest regrets for having this man as a father.' The two men laughed and Danny repositioned the camera to face himself.

'As you can see, your Dad gets to work with a bunch of comedians while he's away from your Mum. But hey, this is the coolest thing that you'll get to see today, this is the real reason we are here.' Danny switched the phone to use the forward-facing camera and panned over D-28. 'This here isn't just another block of land, this is a new iceberg. It broke away from the shelf I'm standing on only two days ago, and look at the size of it.' He panned the camera along its span. 'Look how big it is, huh kiddo.'

Danny moved closer to the cliff face to film over the edge. 'See how thick it is,' he said in an awe-inspired voice. He panned the camera to show his future child as much as possible, but each moment on the edge was like daggers in his guts. He grimaced as he stepped back and switched the phone back to the rear camera. 'Now, when we watch this together, I'll have made you a bet that you have never seen anything cooler in your life. Did I win?' He left time for his future-self to respond. 'Yeah, I thought I did.'

Just then a sound rippled across the winds that made him gaze into the distance. With another smile he returned his attention to the camera. 'And I have one more surprise for you, kiddo.' He switched the camera once again. 'Here it comes.'

As the camera rolled, the R44 hurtled into sight and sent a flurry of snow and ice into the air. Danny held the camera high and zoomed in to the best of his ability as Gary landed the bird. Finally, he spun the camera around again and yelled to be heard over the helicopter. 'Funny how I have to yell this each time to be heard, huh? I love you, kiddo. I'll see you soon.'

He shut the camera off as Gary cut power to the R44's rotors.

'You're getting right into this whole father thing,' Charlie said from behind him.

Danny gave him a small smile. 'I made my own bed.'

Charlie smiled back as he switched on the small camp stove to brew coffee. 'Time to lie in it, am I right?'

'Yeah, you know it,' Danny replied distantly as he watched Jonty emerge from the rear of the Hägglund and arch his back in a similar fashion to Charlie.

'Want a coffee?' Charlie asked Danny.

'Mate, I think I'm going to need one today.'

Danny left Charlie with his jet boiler and headed over to Gary, who had thrown open his cabin door. Jonty, likewise, headed him off to join them.

'Sleep well gents? Or was there little to no time for that?' Gary winked.

'You're just jealous you didn't get to watch,' Danny said flatly.

Gary laughed and handed him Marty's camera from the passenger seat of the chopper. 'Yeah, well the next time you guys want to play *The Bold and the Beautiful*, throw this in the corner so we can all get a glimpse.'

Danny took the camera from Gary's hand and held it up in question.

'After Marty saw that big bitch yesterday, he told me he would give you guys his camera so you could film the boarding. He said it would be good to prove that we did the right thing, in case this gets brought up in court.'

'You mean the ship's still there?' Danny asked.

'Yeah.' Gary seemed puzzled at the question.

'You seemed surprised, Danny.' Jonty finally spoke. 'Did you expect them to run off in the night?'

'Well, yeah I kind of did. But anyway, court?'

'It's a good idea,' Jonty remarked as he took the camera from Danny's hand. He opened the LCD monitor screen to check something. 'This is our research territory; the Japanese have broken quite a few international laws by breaching our borders. I was up most of the night thinking about it.'

You were up most of the night dropping your guts, Danny thought.

'Yes, we should record our boarding and what we find; no doubt it'll come up later.' He closed the screen of the video camera and handed the device back to Danny. 'That can be your job today.'

'Great.' Danny sighed as he slid his hand through the strap on the side. 'Hey, I almost forgot. How's Marie?'

Gary nodded. 'She's fine mate, just needed a warm shower and a dose of her own bed I reckon. I offered her the warmth of mine but sadly no takers.'

Danny shook his head as he saw Jonty's look of disgust from the corner of his eye. 'Alright, so how do we want to do this? Are we going to rappel or do you think you can drop us off safely with the bird?'

Both men looked to Gary as Charlie brought over a steaming thermos and four mugs. The question hung in the air as everyone was eager for the warmth of the coffee.

'Don't waste your time rappelling,' Gary said as he took a swig of coffee and gasped at the heat. 'Christ, Charlie would it kill you to use some sugar?'

'Not everyone likes sugar,' Jonty remarked.

Gary laughed. 'You know what Jonty, that's you.'

'What?'

'A sugarless coffee: bitter and leaves a taste of disappointment.' He laughed to himself again.

Danny smiled but his eyes returned to D-28 again. All of this because some block of ice floated away.

'Anyway,' Gary continued. 'I can drop you at the bow. I had another look this morning, swell's down, so there's no trouble there. Just do me a favour, don't jump off the chopper. Step off, otherwise you bastards will send me straight into the ice shelf and you'll have another one of those mongrels on your hands.' He pointed to D-28.

Everyone agreed as they drank their coffee. Danny sighed as he drained his cup; he didn't even want to do that, the coffee had already gone cold, and Gary was right, it needed sugar. The sad part was he wasn't even allowed to tip his coffee on the ground. Away from camp, even if a guy needed to take a piss, he would have to do it in a bottle of water and take it back; work that out.

'Are we doing this?' Danny said as he handed Charlie his now empty mug.

Gary and Jonty drained their mugs and handed them back to Charlie. 'Let's blow this pop stand!' Gary barked.

7

IF DANNY THOUGHT D-28 was impressive from Amery, it was more so in the air. When given the perspective from a hundred feet off the ground, a person saw its true size as if seeing an image in the third dimension for the first time. Danny, Jonty and Charlie sat in awe as Gary took them up in the R44. Not even Gary had anything to say as he took them up to show them the secrets of the ice. The sun kissed the surface of the berg, which was once the Amery shelf's loose tooth. A silent giant as it floated in its place, Danny scanned to his right where the berg had come away from the shelf and saw that the gap had increased. It was hard to tell with something so large, but D-28 was on the move.

'We will need to record D-28's movements and try to estimate its course,' Jonty said as they hovered there for a short while.

Charlie leant forward from the rear of the cabin to point to their left. 'Looks like it's caught up over there on the shelf's mass. If you can see, it's the southern section that's swinging hard. If I could put a wager on it, I reckon it will swing about then come to rest just up there on the coast.'

'$100?' Gary held his hand back.

'Sure,' Charlie said as they shook.

For a moment longer they sat in the air and watched the blues, whites and greys of D-28. The way the sun hit the cliff face and cast shadows against the ridges of the ice created a face as weathered and aged as one that seen the elements for a thousand years, not just three days. Then as the R44 shifted slightly, the shadows changed and once more there was the new aged beauty, a clean-skinned grape that was fresh from the vine.

All the beauty and wonder were lost to them the moment that Gary took them below the level of the cliff top. The further they descended between the two cliff faces, the less the sun was able to penetrate down into its depths. Instead of bright and glistening walls, as they had been in the sun, the cliff faces became dark walls of slate and, in some sections, black amethyst that hinted at their ancientness in their silence. The further they descended toward the ocean floor the colder it became and the darker the world got, until finally the entire reason they had come down here became visible before them.

The ship was old, that much was apparent to Danny the moment he laid eyes on it. The way it was shaped, designed, was not something he had seen before. It was not something he expected to see here at all, to be honest. The ship was very long and stood taller at bow and stern than in its centre. Three tall 'H' frames rose up from its decks, one directly in the ship's centre and two more where the decks rose up to the fullness of its height at each end. A flag was painted on its side – a white rectangle with a red dot in its centre. Forward of the flag were five characters that Danny assumed were in Japanese. If anything, he got the same impression from the ship that he got from seeing a car that had sat in a field for countless years; it looked forgotten. Long scratches were etched down the sides of the ship and as Gary took them around to the bow, Danny saw heavy damage, as if the ship had been involved in a front-end collision.

'Hey, hold her steady so I can get a photo of the markings.' His voice echoed through the headsets.

He held Marty's camera steady and pressed the still image button. He took five photos to be safe and waved Gary on.

'Hold on ladies,' Gary said as he took the R44 closer to the bow of the ship. 'I'm not going to set her down, I'll just rest the left skids on her front rails there.' He gestured with his head as he swung the R44 around to face the front of the ship. 'Be steady now, one of you off at a time, don't all rush. Danny, you grab that handheld so you can tell me when to pick you up.' The pilot again gestured with his head and Danny grabbed the yellow radio and jammed it into his spray jacket.

The closer they got, the more Danny saw the age in the ship. There was no movement on deck, nor in the windows that lined the bridge in the tall section that bordered the bow. Gary set the skids to rest on the rail and the cold hit them as Jonty pushed his door open. With a grunt and a gasp, he stepped out gingerly and shut the door. Danny opened his door and once more the cold hammered him. He stepped down onto the skid and then dropped the rest of the way onto the bow of the ship. He helped Charlie out the rest of the way, and then slammed the door of the R44 shut.

The moment the door closed, the chopper bellowed and rose into the air. Danny took the radio out of his pocket and turned it on. 'You on channel, Gaz?'

'Yeah mate, sing out when you need me, I'll go back up top and wait.'

'Righto, out,' Danny said and nodded to Jonty. The head researcher raised his eyebrows at the gesture and Danny handed him the radio. 'Here, hold onto this for me; my pockets are full.' Jonty glanced at the radio in his hands, while Danny moved further onto the deck.

As the R44 ascended up to the ice shelf, Danny noticed the bridge looming above them.

The three men advanced down the deck; the glass windows were intact but frozen over so that they couldn't see through. Danny ran his gloved hand down one of the rails; the metal seemed frozen too.

'How long do you think this ship has been here?' he asked.

'Two days,' Jonty remarked, without a second thought.

Danny hit record on the camera in his hand and hissed his doubts. 'I just don't know about that mate.'

Charlie went to move down the starboard side and Jonty called him back. 'Until we know what the full story is with this ship, I would prefer if we all stuck together.'

There was no doubt in Danny's heart that Jonty had said this more for his own safety than theirs, but nonetheless he agreed. The three walked slowly starboard as they searched for any signs of life. The light was low, and their footfalls echoed off the cold steel, ice and water. Nothing was comforting about where they were; nothing reassured Danny at all about any of this. He felt as though he stood on a ship that had just resurfaced after it had disappeared into the Bermuda Triangle some thirty years ago.

'Hello?' Charlie called out and the echoes came right back. '*Ello. Ello. Lo. Lo. O.*'

'Jesus,' Danny hissed. 'Cut the shit, Charlie.'

'Why, what's wrong? We are here to see why they are here, are we not?' Jonty crossed his arms and pursed his lips once more, which made Danny want to remove it with his fist.

'Yeah, but fuck.' It was at that point that Danny realised he didn't know why he had cautioned him. When he thought about it, the only reason he could put forward was that when he got right down to it, he was terrified.

'We will want to find the bridge,' Jonty said with a surprising amount of bravado in his tone. 'If there's no-one there, then we should at least find something of use.'

'That's right,' Charlie agreed, 'it should be up here. Follow me.' Charlie moved forward and began to climb a set of white, cross-backed stairs. As soon as he placed a foot on the steel he swore and grabbed the rail. 'A lot of ice here guys, be careful.'

Danny filmed as they all carefully climbed the stairs. As they mounted the first landing they got a glimpse of the full length of the vessel in all of its silent, frozen glory. There was no rust, but even in the low light they could see the glimmer of the ice that had formed over the metal. Larger chunks of glacier that must have come from the ice shelf above them, littered the deck in places. In the rear galley Danny saw that a large portion of the raised structure had been torn away by something.

'This ship has not been here three days, Jonty,' Danny said in a small voice as he gazed at the world through the small screen of the camera.

'You won't know that until we find the bridge,' Jonty muttered.

'Well let's find the damned thing so we can get the fuck out of here.' Danny hissed through chattering teeth, though he wasn't sure if it was from the cold or the panic stirring in his stomach.

Jonty and Charlie both looked to Danny then shot each other a stern glance. Danny felt better the moment they turned to climb the stairs in the other direction. With the view of the deck behind him, he felt his chest loosen up and took a few steadying breaths.

'Ok,' he said to himself. 'Ok.'

'Are you alright there, Danny?' Charlie had stopped halfway up the second flight and was looking back.

'Yeah, I'm ok. Sorry guys, keep going, I'll be fine. I'm just having a moment.'

'We're almost there. C'mon.' Charlie gestured with his head and Jonty followed.

Danny stared up after them, raised the camera once more, and continued.

The upper deck was slick with ice and they needed to slide their feet across the walkway rather than lift a sole. If Danny had squeezed any harder with his left hand, his felt his fingers would have left imprints in the rail.

Finally, they came to a steel hatch. Charlie pushed on the door and his feet slid backward. A smile spread over Danny's face as he watched the older man struggle.

'It's locked I think,' Charlie said sheepishly.

Danny's smile cemented itself on his face as he held out the camera to the older man. 'It's alright mate, you guys stand back and let the wrench swinger work.'

Charlie took the camera and moved to the side while Danny took hold of the hatch's wheel and put his whole body into turning it. His feet let him down. With no grip underfoot, he was unable to lock his body into position and it took most of what he had not to fall. Danny gritted his teeth as his brow furrowed. He pushed each foot into the corner of the hatch's frame and pushed hard, then with his hands he twisted. His gloved hands slipped slightly on the frozen metal, but then found their grip. Inside the apartments, a groan of old steel rang out and the ship seemed to shriek with it as the wheel started to turn. Finally, there was a solid clunk and the wheel stopped. Danny shifted his feet, braced himself against the rail behind him and pushed his way into the apartments.

8

'CHRIST, HOW LONG YOU THINK this tub has been here?' Charlie gasped as he stepped through the hatch.

'Something tells me a little longer than a day or two,' Danny murmured beneath his breath again.

The short hallway was dark and brutally cold. If he thought that the temperature outside of the apartments was bad, just the first step inside was enough to correct him. Ice ran up the walls and gave them a blurred appearance. Where steel had once made a sharp angle, the ice had formed to soften it into a gentle curve. In other places where flat, smooth sheets of steel were riveted to one another to form a wall, water had frozen in a way to give the wall a texture that sent an easy chill up his spine. Small bumps and ripples lined either wall to the point that it seemed that even the hide of the ship itself had erupted into the same gooseflesh that ran across Danny's body as he stood there.

Jonty gasped as he stepped into the hall and Danny saw in his peripherals that both of his arms had wrapped around himself, as if to protect him from the cold death that seemed to emanate from the vessel. Their breath carried steam from their mouths as their bodies were racked in shivers and the exhalation dribbled from their lips. The three of them stood only a few feet inside of the opening, the light that rushed inside the open door behind them only managing to illuminate a further five feet from where they stood. Beyond the line of light, the cold seemed to lurk and swirl, as if ready to swallow them if they dared to step beyond.

'Ok,' Jonty said almost too loud, and the words bounced back at them over and over. They all looked forward to the darkness as if another man had spoken back to them. 'We've come this far,' he continued as he stepped past Charlie and dropped his voice to a whisper. 'Let's find the bridge.'

Jonty moved up to stand beside Danny and then stared blankly at him, as if waiting for the mechanic to move forward. *That would be right,* Danny thought. *Let the grease monkey go first.*

'How the hell are we going to see in this shit?' Danny whispered, cringing at the echo of his own voice.

Just then a light came from behind them, but it wasn't daylight; this was harsh and artificial. Danny and Jonty looked behind them and saw Charlie. Marty's camera was in his hand, a small light positioned to the side of its lens shining like a beacon.

'The wonders of technology, huh?' Charlie quipped in a soft voice. 'I'll take over filming, you guys can lead the way.'

'Great,' Danny mumbled as he dug his gloved hand deep into his right pocket and retrieved his phone. 'The wonders of technology,' he mused as he ran his rubber-tipped thumb across the screen of his smartphone. The gloves were a must in this environment – to have to remove your gloves to be able to use your phone could mean a number of things out here, and remaining warm and safe wasn't one of them.

Soon the small light from Danny's phone joined the heavier beam from the camera, and shortly after another beam emitted from Jonty's hand as well. The lights raced across the darkness and tore into it like a bullet through meat. Beyond the darkness lay the rest of the hallway and directly opposite them was the starboard side hatch. Its edges were made soft by the ice that caked it, while its frame remained blurred and undefined in the poor light. In its centre, the wheel that operated its lock was twisted and deformed. In places, the steel that formed the ring had snapped under some obscene force.

'Let's find this bridge so we can get the fuck out of here,' Danny hissed as his light washed over the wall to his left. He crept forward. In places the white walls that glistened under the film of ice that they bore, were stained red. The colour was deep and in places almost had become black. The contrasting red ran lines, as if smeared across the walls underneath the icy ripples. As Danny ran his hand across one of the smears, the ice ground beneath his gloved fingers and a powder listed to the floor. 'Fuck me, I hope this isn't what I think it is.'

'I think I found it.' Jonty's voice came from behind him. Danny's attention was drawn in his direction in time to see him disappear through an opening halfway up the hallway. Meanwhile, Charlie still had the camera trained on the red smears they had found and was adjusting the lens to focus in the low light.

'Come on,' Danny said to Charlie. 'I think he's right about sticking together.'

'Yeah,' Charlie whispered. His eyes were wide and unblinking, focused on the digital viewfinder that came out of the side of the camera. Danny moved his light across the floor to see if there was anything to trip them up and then moved forward to the opening.

Jonty's flashlight sent odd waves of light across the wall on the opposite side, which formed dark lines of shadows from the outline of its door and hatch-wheel. The way the light moved, it reminded him of a time when he had visited the Sydney Aquarium and the way the light had danced through water. It had rippled and swirled up the walls around them; just that in itself was fascinating and beautiful. The light in this hallway did not give him the impression of beauty; it didn't make him smile in awe. Instead, the hairs on the back of his neck stood on end and his heart quickened in his chest.

All of a sudden, the light froze in one spot. The swirling motion and the ripples vanished as Danny closed on the doorway. 'Ahh, guys?' Jonty called from inside the room. 'I've found the crew, or at least one of them.'

Danny and Charlie rushed into the room behind Jonty and froze as their eyes were drawn immediately to the focus point of Jonty's light.

A man sat in a chair in the corner of the room, his head thrown back over the rest. His clothes were almost white from the ice that had formed on his lifeless body. The flesh of his bare hands was white, verging on blue. He wore brown, knee-high boots that were dulled by the frost that had covered them. Likewise, brown leather straps crossed his upper body and led to a large pouch that sat empty at his side.

'Holy shit,' Danny murmured as Charlie moved closer to the body. 'Hey, what are you doing?'

Charlie ignored him. He moved the camera and the light focused harder on the lifeless form. Danny squinted as he looked at the peculiar way the corpse was dressed. Although washed out by the years of frost that had caked on his limbs, the man appeared as though he was straight out of a museum. The green of his uniform sat flat against the dark brown of his belt, and straps that laced itself across his chest. Even still, the brass of his buckle gleamed softly in the artificial light, as did the ice that had crystallised on his face.

'I don't believe this,' Charlie muttered as he moved the light of the camera away from the body.

Danny followed the beam of the light with his eyes. Consoles, gauges and crap were littered here and there. 'What are you looking for Charlie?' he asked, mesmerised by the frozen equipment. It was only at that point, that Danny took in the whole room that he stood in. The entire bow section of the room was lined with glass, though it was nearly impossible to tell this as the windows were covered with that much ice that almost no light whatsoever seemed to pass through them. Danny imagined that out on a sunny day at sea the entire bridge would have been lit beautifully by just sunlight alone. Now, however, it remained in the dark.

'I'll know when I find it,' Charlie whispered as he walked from console to console.

Danny saw small brown porcelain jugs, blankets and smashed glass in one corner. In another, piles of papers and maps were strewn across a table.

As Danny walked over to the body, light danced across the wall behind him as Charlie and Jonty moved on to search the rest of the bridge.

Danny moved around the chair and shone the light of his phone onto the man's face.

'Ahh shit,' he grimaced and angled the light away.

'What?' Both Jonty and Charlie had stopped their search and had trained their lights onto him.

Danny raised his hands to shield his eyes. 'I just saw old mate's face; can you lower your lights?' The others didn't comment, just returned to their search as if they knew what he was talking about.

Danny moved his light back over the man's face, and felt his stomach roll at how it was horribly disfigured. His eyes had sunk back into his head, while his skull had blown outward at the crown of his forehead. In the power of the blow, the man's nose had twisted and bulged outwards, while his cheekbones had sucked in. The way his head hung back over the chair, Danny saw a small blackened hole under his jaw; the flesh all around it seemed as dark as the hallway behind him.

'Jesus,' he hissed again as he moved the light to the wall behind the man. He shuddered as he saw that the brain matter that had come out of his head and spread itself across the wall, still remained beneath the layers of ice. As he moved the light across the wall, he squinted as he noticed a pattern below the matter.

'Hey Jonty, can you give me some more light over here?'

'What have you found?' he replied. The light from Jonty's phone joined his own.

'Bring your phone closer and I'll tell you.' He shifted himself around the body. 'Sorry big feller,' he said as he bumped the man's head with his hip; it had become stiff in its position. It took everything he had to focus on the wall. Running his hand over the frozen surface, sheets began to tumble to the ground to shatter. He brushed harder and harder and then even Jonty came to help him. Eventually, enough ice had crumbled to the ground that they would be able to see, so they stepped back.

'And what do you think that is?' Danny asked the other two.

Charlie joined the light from his camera to that of the other two and laughed. 'Exactly what I was looking for.'

Beneath the remnants of the ice and the brain matter from the man in the chair, the entire wall had been painted with an insignia. A red circle was painted across a white field and red lines etched their way across the white, like the rays of sun stretching outward from its fiery centre. It seemed like the flag of Japan, but the lines that ran outward were wrong.

'That's the rising sun of the Empire of Japan,' Charlie supplied after no answer from the other two.

'Empire?' Jonty questioned. 'The Japanese haven't been an empire since…'

'The forties. That's right,' Charlie said; both of their voices had risen back to normal level. It was easy to see the excitement in Charlie's face. 'No-one beat us to the ice shelf, guys.'

'You can't be serious,' Jonty said.

'It has to be right!' Charlie exclaimed. 'Look at the rising sun, look at the way this guy is dressed, I bet he's an officer. Even the ship looks old, you have to admit that much Jonty.'

Danny shifted in his stance and he felt something hard under his boot. He moved his light to see what it was.

'Well, if what you're saying is true Charlie, how come no-one has seen it before?' Jonty went back at him while Danny bent over.

'Maybe it's been inside the ice shelf for all this time, maybe–'

'Hey, look at this.' Danny interrupted and both men faced him. 'Get your damned lights out of my eyes.'

Both of them lowered their beams to his hands. The fierce artificial light made the pistol appear boxier than it was. Its handle was narrow and rounded at the bottom. It had a large looped trigger guard that looked strange against the small frame. Its upper was short and rounded with a circular ridged handle at its rear, which Danny assumed was the charging handle. Overall, the pistol gave Danny the impression it was a poor man's space ray gun or an overdone water pistol.

'Reckon it's his?' Danny gestured to the dead man. 'Would make a lot of sense, wouldn't it?'

'That would make him an officer if he carried a pistol.'

'I thought Japanese officers had swords? Like a samurai?' Danny asked, still holding the pistol in his open palms.

'I'm sure a lot of them did, but that still doesn't prove that the ship has been here since the forties,' Jonty said flatly.

Danny blinked. 'Woah, wait a minute.'

Jonty and Charlie looked blankly at him.

'Where have you been for the last five minutes?' Charlie asked him. 'That's what I've been saying. There's too much proof here Jonty, you can't discredit it.'

'We need to find the ship's log. That's the only way we'll know for sure what's happened here.'

'Right!' Charlie exclaimed as he slammed a gloved hand against his forehead. 'The ship's log, how could I forget, that's perfect.'

'Where do you think it would be?' Danny asked as he gingerly put the pistol down on the table next to the dead officer. 'Wouldn't this dude be the guy to write it?'

'Either the officer or his first mate, generally,' Jonty said.

Danny examined the contents of the table – it was littered with empty brown jugs, maps and papers, but all the writing was in the lined characters of the Japanese. Then beneath a steel helmet Danny found a leather-bound book. He pushed the helmet aside and it clanged hard as it fell to the ground. Everyone jumped at the sound as if it was a gunshot; Jonty opened his mouth to say something but quietened when he saw the binder in Danny's hands.

'That has to be it.'

The leather was brittle with age and once again covered in frost, but as Danny unwound the leather tie that held it closed, he saw that the pages inside were unharmed by the moisture. As he expected, he was unable to read the literature that lay within the stiffened pages as all of it was written in the vertical Japanese characters.

One the first page beneath the vertical lines of scrawl, was a yellow flower lined out in a stamp. Whereas to the left side of the page was a bright red square with four separate characters inside. 'Whatever it is, it looks bloody official,' Danny said as he flicked through some other pages.

'Be careful with that,' Jonty hissed as he rushed over. The binder was snatched out of Danny's hands before he was allowed too much of a further glance. He leant on the table and watched as Jonty and Charlie poured over the binder, the two men engrossed in the text.

'I thought you told me to be careful with that thing,' Danny complained as he scanned the room once more with his torch.

'We are being careful; you look around for anything else,' Jonty snapped.

'Asshole,' he muttered under his breath, as he walked to the instruments that lay below the glass frontage of the bridge. He passed two banks of gauges, all of which had displays for various instruments. The chairs that had been once bolted to the floor for the users of the consoles, had been torn out and strewn across the other side of the room. The floor had buckled in that place and Danny only noticed because he almost tripped on the warped metal. *They get me to look around while they pore over the log. I bet neither of them can even read Japanese,* the bitter thought crossed his mind. He shone his light further down the bridge and saw where one of the chairs had wound up. It sat in an odd position on top of something in the furthest corner away from the officer. He walked towards it while Jonty and Charlie continued to tut and mutter to each other behind him.

As he continued over to the chair, Danny shone his light across the rest of the room. On the portside of the door they entered from, old clothes hung from hooks frozen into sheets that sat squat on their fasteners. More shit, junk, and wasted food lay scattered along the floor below them. Papers and what appeared to be bloody rags were piled in a corner next to another console.

What the hell had happened here? Danny understood the blood on the wall behind the officer; that the bloke had shot himself was without question. But there weren't any wounds on his body and there was no answer for the blood in the hallway and the rags that he'd just seen. So many scenarios rushed around in Danny's head: mutiny, a failed boarding by another army. If the ship was supposed to be from the forties, maybe the crew had a scrap with some Americans, who knew?

He figured that in the end, if they could work out what was in the binder then all of their questions would be answered.

His foot struck something hard and cold; he swore in pain as he tried to catch his balance. His other foot slipped on some slick portion of ice that had formed over the floor and he felt himself fall. The sound he made when he hit the ground drew the attention of Jonty and Charlie and soon, their lights scoured the room for him.

'Danny! Danny, where are you?' He heard Jonty calling as the lights rushed from wall to wall.

'I'm over here,' he called as he tried to get up. His arm bumped something hard next to him and he complained as he raised himself to his knees.

'Are you ok? What happened?' Charlie said as the two men's footfalls approached.

'I just tripped over this damned stool,' Danny complained again as Jonty's and Charlie's combined lights washed over him. 'It's stupid because...' Danny stopped as he raised his phone's light to the faces of the two men. 'What's wrong? Why are you looking at me like that?'

Jonty and Charlie were frozen to the spot. Their eyes were the size of the bases of the brown jugs that littered the officer's table. Neither of them spoke. Jonty raised a trembling hand, and pointed. Danny realised that their eyes weren't on him. They were on something behind him. Slowly, he began to turn. Each moment took an age and he took in everything that the light washed over. Then finally, he saw it, and began to scream.

9

HIS VISION REELED as he struggled to maintain his consciousness. At the same time, he fought with everything he had just to get away from that damned thing. Images of blood and torn flesh whipped through his mind even though his eyes were closed. Its mouth open in a scream that was frozen in time, not by the cold but by the death that had come upon it as suddenly as the fall had come to Danny. Still, he screamed as he pushed with his legs and sent his phone spiralling across the metal floor. Then finally, darkness, darkness, darkness.

'Daniel?' A voice, far, far away.

'Danny? Come on man, wake up.'

'Daniel, come back to us.'

'Ahh shit, Jonty. Do you think he hit his head?'

'No, he's fine. I think he just got a fright. Got any water?'

'No, I didn't think to bring any. Christ, how the hell are we going to carry him?'

'You won't have to,' Danny said, as he opened his eyes and then closed them against the savage light from the video camera.

'Danny!' Charlie exclaimed as he gave him a shake. 'Good to have you back amongst the living.'

'You gave us a real fright there,' Jonty said almost distractedly, his eyes already scanning the bridge as if he had lost interest.

'You got a fright? Well Christ, I'd hate to hear what I got,' he said as he clambered to his feet. His legs felt horribly shaky beneath him and he doubted whether they'd hold his weight. He leant heavily on a console to his side and felt his head spin again. 'Ahh Jesus,' he muttered as he put a hand to his forehead. 'Where's my phone?'

'Here,' came Charlie's voice. Danny looked up at him. He grabbed his phone from Charlie, then sunk down the side of the console and rested his head against the cold metal, panting heavily.

'What the fuck was that thing?' he said almost in a whisper. The swirl in his head had begun to slow and he slowed his breaths.

'Ahh…' Jonty began as he scanned over to the scene of horror. 'As far as we can tell, it used to be a man.'

'Didn't look like any man I've ever seen,' Danny shot back as he glared through bleary eyes.

'Well, if it's been here for seventy years then I imagine there would be some rot and decay,' Jonty said.

'Then why does the kamikaze officer over there look as though he only just shot himself?' Danny snorted; his senses had pretty much returned. He felt ill, but he was confident that he wasn't going to faint again. In fact, he was quite embarrassed that he had fainted whereas the nerds hadn't. *It was just the fright, nothing more*, he told himself over and over as he regained his feet.

There was no answer to his final rebuttal – no-one had any idea. 'I think it's time we left,' Charlie said faintly after a pause.

'Not before I look at this one last time,' Danny said with certainty. 'I need to see it properly.'

'Are you sure, man?'

'Charlie, leave him,' Jonty said as he placed a hand on his shoulder. 'We will leave when you're ready, Daniel.'

Saliva had built up in his mouth. He wanted to spit, but the training of leaving absolutely nothing behind in the Antarctic zone was too strong his mind and he swallowed. He hated being called Daniel. He was sure Jonty knew this and that was the sole purpose for his insistence in calling him that. 'It won't take long.'

He thumbed the flashlight icon on his smartphone and the light washed over his feet. With gritted teeth he began to walk over to the scene of horror and for the first time in so long, he felt himself begin to sweat. He saw the chair he had tripped over, now thrown further away by his thrashing. He saw what appeared to be a leg, but even that was a stretch. The only thing that made him come to that conclusion was the remnants of fabric that covered a portion of it that seemed somewhat like trousers.

The creature's abdomen was rippled and lumpy like the ice that shimmered over the steel walls of the vessel. Its flesh was grey and blue-black veins traced every inch of it, where it had remained intact. Slashes and gouges covered the flesh; in some places long strips hung back to reveal the dark, aged meat beneath. The sword that had supposedly inflicted the damage was lodged in its chest, and stood upright. The fabric that was wrapped around its handle was red with the blood from either its wielder or its victim. The blade was likewise red with blood, frozen to the steel before it had a chance to run its way down.

The body's arms lay back under itself and its joints seemed all wrong, as if every joint the man had in his arm from shoulder to wrist had been reversed. It had no hands to speak of; its wrists were nothing but the nubs of the forearms that were splintered into sharpened points. The worst part was its head, which had been severed from its body. It lay only a few feet away, its face frozen in a snarl of demonic rage. Its lower jaw had separated at its centre, either by the force of the sword's blow or by some other unnatural force. The two halves lay flayed out beneath its mass, its upper jaw frozen above the floor with teeth that looked as though they belonged in a dog's mouth. The teeth were yellowed and the gums were black with rot. Between the two lower halves of the jaw, a long, brown tongue lay frozen in state. Where a nose had once been, two slits ran up its sinus to where two eyes sat squat and staring to either side. If the head was the worst part of the body, then the eyes were the worst part of the head. They weren't human eyes, but more that of a serpent. The irises were yellowed and faded, whereas the cornea were long slits that ran vertical through the colour.

'Fuck me drunk,' he hissed as the sharp light from his phone ran across the features one more time. 'Let's get out of this place.'

He couldn't remember the walk out of the apartments. All that surfaced in his mind when he thought back on it was the wave of fresh air that seemed to hit him as he walked through the final hatch. The other feeling was an odd sensation; despite the sweat he had broken into up on the bridge, when he stepped onto the deck of the ship, he had felt warmer than he ever had in his life.

'Red one, Red one. This is Jonty, do you read me?' The sound rolled back at him from the cliff face but Danny barely heard it. He leant over the railing that bordered the bow and peered down at the icy calm water beneath. Each breath steamed through his face mask and wisped across his eyes as he stared blankly into the blue.

'You feeling alright?' Charlie had leant up next to him and Danny hadn't even noticed.

The middle-aged Maltese man looked at him under large white bushy eyebrows. Likewise, every breath he took was visible through the cotton of his scarf that he'd pulled up to cover his large nose.

'Yeah, just happy to be out of there.'

'Tell me about it, that damned place freaked me out.' Charlie held his eye contact, as if curious for a reaction. 'Tell me something?'

Danny raised his eyebrows in answer.

'What happens now?' The question was a good one, and Danny could tell that the elder man was worried about the answer.

'I was going to ask the same question.' Truthfully, he had no idea how they would treat this ship and what they had found on that bridge.

'Translating the log, I suppose that's the first step but… do we tell the Japanese?' Charlie seemed to be talking more to himself at this point so Danny turned his head back to Jonty. 'Who knows what the log will tell us, but it can only tell us so much, can't it?'

Danny watched Jonty pace back and forth in front of the large bulk of the apartments as he spoke to Gary up above. He squinted as he peered down the deck beyond the portside of the apartments.

'If we want to know more, we would have to look further, wouldn't we?'

There were no military armaments that Danny could see. There were no guns or anything else that would make him believe that this was a military vessel. So, if it wasn't a military vessel, then what the hell was it?

'But there's no way I'm going any deeper into this ship without some… some… I don't know, something more than a damned video camera.'

Danny ignored Charlie as his rant seemed to get more hysterical by the second.

'I mean we have no idea what could be down there. If this ship has sat here for the last seventy years, then surely nothing could remain alive below, but diseases? Who knows what could be in stasis in this bloody cold?'

Then Danny saw something interesting that panged at his memory banks. He saw a steel wire of enormous gauge run through a channel and over to a winch drum. The cable was nowhere near thick enough for an anchor, but for hoisting something it would be fine.

'And if anyone thinks that I'm going to be a government guinea pig then they've got another thing coming, haven't they?'

He ran his eyes back in the other direction. The steel cable ran towards the nose of the ship, through a pulley and then it disappeared over the bow. How he hadn't noticed it before he could never answer; he would've had to near step over the channels to get to the apartments. Then he realised there were two channels for cables, one portside, one starboard. To match at the apartment end was another winch drum; this one was fully wound, its cable retracted.

He looked over the portside, the side that faced the open water, and saw a heavy circular baseplate where something had been mounted. When he compared the starboard side, he saw it, the thing that would answer most of his questions.

'Charlie Muscat isn't going to be the first person to suffer from some bloody, forgotten flu or who knows what these bastards had back then, that they didn't tell anyone about. Probably explains what happened to that… Hey, are you even listening to me?'

Danny had left Charlie where he stood. He moved to the starboard side rail, toward what he had seen. There, mounted proud as anything, was a long cannon. Danny started to laugh.

'What is funny about all of this?' Charlie snapped behind him as he threw a hand on Danny's shoulder and whirled him around.

'What is one thing that the Japs keep getting in trouble over?' Danny asked him.

'I… What are you talking about?'

'Come on, it was even on the news a few years back. Put the Greenies on the map.' The laughter still sat in his throat and he smiled more because he had worked something out. A mechanic/detective, his future spawn would be proud indeed. But if a detective were to follow their nose, then the next question would be…

'Whaling?' Charlie got it right in one. As the smile vanished from Danny's face and the first sounds of Gary's R44 could be heard above them, he nodded. He turned his back to Charlie and moved away from the harpoon cannon.

'You might be interested to know what's below the deck,' he said to Charlie as he leant over the bow. Just as Marty had said, the steel cable was visible, taut but not strained at it disappeared into the ice shelf at a forty-five-degree angle. 'But I want to know what's on the other end of that cable.'

10

THE R44 POWERED THROUGH THE AIR with a fury matched only by the snow swirling below them. Once more Danny was astounded by the power the wind carried in this place. The force of nature scared him just as much as the ocean did, but it was only when he was in the air that he felt this fear. If there was something to say about any of the main forces of nature, whether they be the sea, lightning, the earth, or the fires that lay below, it was that you could at least see what did the damage. If a freak wave were to lunge forth from the depths of the ocean in a swift invasion of water and silt, an individual would feel wet. They would hear the water rush toward them as Danny was sure many did in the tsunami of Indonesia in the previous year. Most of all, they would see their doom coming for them. The same could be said about every other force of nature; even lightning could be seen tracing its ragged arcs through the air. What Danny disliked about the wind was that it was a ghost.

Sure, an individual could trace the wind's movements by noting the direction the leaves on a tree swayed. In the same notion, a curtain's movement in a gust-less room would raise the attention of its only inhabitant, and raise the hairs on their necks. Some would argue that in the case of tornados or cyclones, the wind could indeed be seen, but that is only the same notion that could be afforded to the invisible man when his flesh was burnt. Cyclones were visible only by the debris they carried.

If there was a cyclone in a world free of dust, dirt, debris or structures, would an individual even know that it was there? Would the only alert be the sound of the onrush before an individual was sucked from the ground and hurled to their death?

The Robinson lurched in the air and Danny's guts rolled. His legs closed together as his balls ran for the safety that seemed to lie in the nestle of his throat. Beside him, Charlie seemed to be going through his own internal battle as the R44 was thrown here and there by the invisible force. In the front of the cabin, Jonty's face was hidden mostly by his clothes, but Danny could see that his eyes were clenched firmly closed.

Gary, to his credit, laughed and threw the R44 into the movements that were forced upon it. The sound as the rotors ripped through the opposing gusts rocked through the cabin and the light body surged with the fight. Later Gary may even admit that they shouldn't have been in the air during that wind storm, but it would never be during his fight with it.

They hadn't bothered to land next to the Hägglund, because as soon as the three expeditioners were safely back aboard the Robinson, Jonty had told Gary to return to Mawson. No-one had objected. They had been in the air for half an hour when the wind had picked up. As the flight from Mawson to the Amery Ice Shelf took about forty minutes by air, they were pretty much back to base. Through gritted teeth they watched the land below them as the R44's cabin jostled in the air. The sounds the cabin made didn't help the situation; below the odd warning beep and red-light flash that Gary seemed to ignore, the cabin clattered like an old four-wheel drive traversing corrugated dirt roads.

Finally, Mawson came into sight. Their home amongst the rocks, snow, ice and seals. The AANBUS buildings were the first thing that came into view; the blue, green, yellow and red squat structures were a welcome break from the monotonous white and greys of the Antarctic landscape. Amongst the buildings, Danny saw the singular, motionless windmill, which ironically had to be locked down in windstorms so it didn't self-detonate. Then finally the diesel tanks, and smaller petrol tank that sat almost like the vanguard to the seawall.

Danny had to laugh; it had been a decent amount of time since he had seen the camp from the air. It looked like a hoarder's backyard. He imagined a bush block property, with sheds scattered here and there. Each shed housing a wreck of some description while the others held boxes upon boxes of tax receipts from businesses that had long since closed.

He sighed. Being lost in his own mind was a kind respite from the thoughts of the whaler, although the sight of the leather-bound log that sat on Charlie's lap was a dim reminder. Jonty would call a meeting that night after dinner, that much he knew. Along with the fact that he would have to relive the whole thing again as the entire camp decided what to do with the mess they were in. He had six or seven hours to fill before the meeting was called. The funny thing was that it wasn't even the thought of the meeting that seemed to worry him, it was finding something to keep his mind and his memories at bay for the next six hours.

As Gary brought the R44 down to land, Danny gazed over to the big Red Shed. He thought about his bed, and how nice a warm shower would feel. He thought about the feeling of resting his head on the pillows and how that he knew he would spend the next six hours staring at the dark roof of his Donga. Then as the chopper settled upon its concrete square, Danny noticed two figures making their way to Main Power House. They stopped in their tracks as the chopper's rotors began to power down and then headed to landing zone.

When Danny lifted himself out of the cabin, his legs wobbled dangerously and he had to steady himself on the frame.

'Woah there, big feller. You alright?' Gary said as he stepped out and clapped Danny on the shoulder.

'Yeah, I'm sure you're used to seeing people in this state given the way you fly,' Danny replied as he collected his phone from the seat and slammed the cabin door. 'I'm in the right mind to report you to the bloody Civil Aviation Safety Authority.' He said this with tongue in cheek, knowing full well Gary had actually been reported once before.

Gary smiled but said nothing. The day had finally come where the pilot didn't have a comeback; he would have to remember that. As Gary left him in silence and Charlie followed him, Jonty moved to his side.

'Don't forget, seven tonight. I'll arrange that everyone is there and we can discuss this as a team.'

'No problem,' he replied as he held his stance next to the chopper and let his attention drift to the Red Shed.

'Are you ok?' Jonty asked, in the similar condescending tone Danny recalled from when he had been depressed about his family's new addition.

'Yeah. How about you?' he asked, not really caring.

'I'm ok, now,' he said in a soft tone and looked down at his feet. 'Get something to eat, you'll feel better.'

Jonty trudged off to the Red Shed. Danny remained, as if in wait for something. He didn't really know what to do. He felt great, now that he was away from the ship, almost like he could breathe again. Once he had landed on the ship, claustrophobia had settled over him, beginning with a tight chest. After the faint, he had wanted nothing more than to just get out of there. Now that he stood back at Mawson, he wanted to bend down and kiss the rock beneath his feet.

He felt like something had happened but nothing really had; he had gotten a bit of a scare but that didn't account for the way he felt. It didn't account for the lack of conversation on the flight back. Now that he thought about it, he couldn't remember anyone speaking but Gary. Jonty had said a few words when he had clambered back into the cabin, regarding the meeting, but once the bird had flown above the ice shelf again, the passengers had fallen silent. Charlie hadn't even said a word when they had landed. Christ, when he was on the ship he wouldn't shut up.

'Hey Danny,' the voice shook him out of his daydream.

Danny spun around; Wendy Phillips and Sean Wilson stood side by side at the nose of the chopper. He stared at them as if in shock that someone had spoken to him, but the truth was he couldn't find the words to answer them.

'Did we interrupt something?' Sean asked.

'Ah, no,' was what Danny found.

'Ok,' Wendy said with a sideways glance to Sean. 'Look, we were just going to check the co-generative system, we thought we should ask if you want to join us. But if you're too busy...'

'No, that's a great idea,' Danny answered her properly this time as he shook his head and rubbed at his eyes with his fists. 'Sorry, just had bugger-all sleep last night and I'm struggling a bit today.'

The two laughed and the three of them continued to the Main Power House. They chattered about the chore roster for some time. Mawson was a decent sized camp, and a lot of little jobs needed to get done that weren't in line with people's main role. Hence a roster had been put in place some years ago that gave everyone a different job to do and a rotation of when they had to do it. During the summer periods when there was near a hundred people on camp, the roster didn't really worry anyone so much as there were more people to go around than small jobs. Yet in winter it seemed that every night there was another small job that needed to be done and with only skeleton staff it was rare that anyone got a night off. Wendy had been the unlucky one to draw the new detail of de-snowing the Red Shed's steel veranda. She made the mistake of telling the pair of them how crap the job was and then tried to see if they would swap for their own rostered chores.

'I don't even know what I'm rostered on for tonight,' Danny said with his hands up against Wendy's demand to know what his roster was.

'I'm pretty sure you're on cook duties tonight,' Sean came back. 'I'm in the greenhouse,' he said with a soft smile.

'Either of those are fine, I copped the veranda shovelling three nights in a row!' Wendy barked. 'Come on, swap with me – I'll owe you one.'

'From what it sounds like, you'll owe me three, and I'm not convinced that you'll have anything to pay that one back with, little miss. Sorry but sounds like you're on your own,' Danny said empathetically.

'Hope you scald yourself in the kitchen,' she replied flatly as they entered the Main Power House.

Danny laughed as he removed his waterproof jacket. He went about checking on his four kings as the other two continued to barter on chores over the rattle of king three and four. While he checked the bolt tensions on the first king's alternator, he let their conversation wash in one ear and out the other. He just hoped that the two didn't ask him about what had happened that morning. He hoped that Marie or Gary hadn't talked.

'Well, you're just unlucky to have received that same chore three days in a row. It's not often that a third of the staff need to go away overnight,' Sean said in response to something that Wendy had said. Danny could have hit him.

'It's not my fault that the three musketeers wanted to have a boy's night in the snow,' Wendy barked back as she checked the radiator plumbing and its coupling into the co-generative system. 'What was that all about anyway?' she asked Danny.

Here we go, Danny thought. His shoulders slumped. 'You were in the meeting Wendy, they wanted to look at the ice shelf, it's got a new face after the iceberg broke off.'

'Yeah well, why did Marie have to be rushed back?' she replied bitterly.

'Marie.' The name slapped him in the face. He had forgotten all about her. He thought about the way she stood on the edge of the ice shelf, obviously talking to herself as she peered down at the depths below. Her mouth had moved beneath her scarf. There was something about the way she'd stood there, the way her eyes slowly came back to life as she gazed at him, as if she had come out of a coma or something.

'Hey Danny, where are you going?' Sean asked.

'I... I need to check something,' he mumbled as he threw his spray jacket back over his jumper and stormed out into the winds. He needed to see Marie, he needed to see if she was ok, to see if she had felt the same way he had felt. Something was up with that damned ship, and it wasn't just that thing that they had found either.

He climbed the steel steps of the Red Shed's veranda and burst into the cold porch. Mindlessly he undressed again and left his gumboots below his locker. As he moved through the mess, he saw Corinth Butler in the kitchens once more. She smiled at him as she noticed him bustle through. 'See you in a few hours?'

'You know it.' He tried to sound chirpy, but he felt as though he failed.

He felt bad for that, Corinth was one of those people that you hated to upset. He would make it up to her tonight when he helped her before dinner.

Marie's Donga was along the same corridor of rooms as his own. Three doors up from the safety of his own room and on the right-hand side. He knocked on the door. The sound that his fist made as he pummelled the heavy door startled him and he stepped back. The door opened halfway and Marie Swan stood in the doorway. Her blue eyes widened, surprised to find him at the door. As her smile parted to reveal her glistening white teeth, a lock of blonde hair fell across her face.

'Danny, well aren't I a lucky girl?' she said playfully as she rested her shoulder on the door jamb, allowing the lock of hair to remain across her face as she spoke.

Danny didn't know how to answer her as she crossed her arms and smiled coyly at him. Her arms folded beneath her breasts, which were much more visible beneath the pink sweater than the multiple layers she wore on Amery.

'Why do you say that?' he asked finally.

'Well, to have two of my fellow expeditioners come and make sure I'm ok. You boys do know how to flatter a girl,' she laughed. 'Come on in.'

Lines creased Danny's brow as her words ran through his mind, but as she pushed the door open, he understood what she had meant. Charlie Muscat sat in the room in a low-backed couch, a steaming cup of tea rested loosely in one hand.

'Danny,' Charlie acknowledged him. Danny nodded back as he stood by the small coffee table that sat between the couch and another low-backed chair.

'Sit down, please. I just boiled a pot of tea, do you want some?' Marie beamed at him; she appeared about ten years younger than she had out on the shelf. Maybe the cold had gotten to everyone?

'Yeah, sure,' he replied as he sat down next Charlie. While Marie fussed about with the pot of tea, Danny looked at the elder man. 'So, how are you feeling?

'Oh, I'm fine. I probably didn't eat enough or something.' Marie said as she brought the tea over and set it on the coffee table. Danny peeked into his mug; she had put milk into it. He hated when people did that.

She sat down on the chair across from them, behind her, her neat bed lay made with a bright pink doona cover and about a thousand pillows that surely would be thrown to the floor each night for her to pull back the covers.

Marie's gaze shifted from Charlie to Danny and back again. 'So what happened out there?'

Danny glanced at Charlie with flat eyes. 'Ahh look, were going to go through that tonight and I don't know if I can go through it twice today.'

'Tonight?' she enquired.

'Yes, Jonty will call a meeting for tonight at seven. Everyone will be informed at what we found and we will need to discuss what to do about it as a team.' Charlie backed him up. Danny looked at him, the elder man must have felt exactly the same way.

'Marie, look,' Danny started, 'I don't know about Charlie, but the reason why I came here was to ask you a few questions.'

'Ok, well sure.' Her smile faltered ever so slightly but she remained polite.

'When you were on the edge of that ice shelf, something happened to you. I want to know what that was.' He spoke slowly and firmly.

'Nothing happened, Danny.' Her smile faltered on her lips. 'As I said I probably didn't eat enough and I got a bit faint.'

'That doesn't explain why you were talking to yourself out there.' He pushed harder.

'I wasn't talking to myself.' Her tone sharpened as it had done in the Hägglund.

'Marie, I was standing right there. Your eyes were unfocused, your mouth was moving beneath your scarf and you were moving closer to the edge.' He paused as he gathered himself. 'If I hadn't grabbed you, I think you would've gone over.'

She seemed shocked. She sat back on her bed and Danny saw her jaw push out. *Here we go again,* the thought washed through his mind as he prepared to cop an earful.

'And here I was thinking that you two came to see if I was ok,' she said almost to herself. 'Gentlemen, I feel tired and as we are just going to discuss this situation tonight at seven, as you said yourself, I don't want to bore myself with repetition.'

'That's not what I said, Marie.'

'You may as well have. I thought you were just going check in on me but I don't need you coming in here telling me that I'm suicidal, thank you very much.'

Charlie leant forward. 'Marie, we were all concerned for you.'

'Concerned enough to push me to the side so the men could take all the credit. I know how it is.'

'That's not how it is at all,' Danny said, putting his hands up in a calming gesture.

'Oh, don't you try and calm me down, you're the one that made out I was the damsel in distress.' Her cheeks now flushed.

'Marie, I don't think he did that at–' Charlie tried to interject.

'And the rest of you had no problem at all believing that the only woman in the expedition had an *"episode"*.' She emphasised the last word with her hands. 'I'm sure you'd just as soon prefer me to come back into the kitchen. Isn't that right?' She turned on Charlie like a tiger defending its kill.

Danny put his tea down on the table without taking a sip. 'Look, I think we got off on the wrong foot. I think you're right, we will discuss it tonight at seven. If you feel like discussing this then, then that's fine, but I'll let you bring it up and you can answer the question to why you came back.' He stood up and faced Charlie. 'I think we may have overstayed our welcome.'

'Yes, I think you have,' Marie said, flipping the hair out of her eyes now and crossing her arms. 'To think I wasted my good tea on you. I can't just go and replace that, you know.'

She walked almost on Charlie's heels as the two men retreated to the door. Once they were outside, Danny opened his mouth and went to face her but could only step back when her door slammed in his face. Once more, the two men looked at each other.

'I need to speak to you privately,' Charlie said softly as he leant close to him.

'Come to my room, it's just here.' Danny gestured.

Danny led Charlie three doors down the hall and to a door on his right. He turned the knob and stepped into his Donga. Unlike Marie, Danny had not put much effort into personalising his own bed room. Dirty shirts and small clothes lay scattered here and there. He kicked them to the side and picked up a bunch of clean clothes to make room for Charlie to sit. He threw the clean atop of the dirty and nodded at the chair as he sat down on his bed. Charlie closed the door behind him and went to the chair.

'That didn't go well,' Danny said, 'sorry if I ruined something you had going there.'

Charlie smiled softly as he considered his right Ugg boot, which was crossed over his left leg. 'Look, I think we went there for the same reason, you were just a little more forward than I was.'

Danny noticed that Charlie's speech had slowed somewhat since they had left the ship; the older man seemed much more in control.

He uncrossed his leg, leant in close and clasped his hands together. 'Danny, how did you feel on that ship?' His eyes were grey and full of interest as they locked onto his own.

'I felt as though I was trapped and that I needed to get out of there, like the world was closing in on me.' He had no problem saying this, he had already come to terms with it as he'd stood next to the R44.

'Anything else?' Charlie never blinked.

'Cold.' He continued, 'I felt so damned cold. Colder than I've ever felt here.'

Charlie leant back on his chair; his lips twisted into a frown.

'What about you?' Danny asked as he continued to stare at the older man.

'I felt exactly the same.' His frown transitioned to a sad smile. 'I felt like I had emphysema and that all of the light had gone from the world. Like I was under that damned ice shelf.' He raised a hand and coughed into it. 'When I got back here all I wanted to do was talk to Marie to see what had happened to her but even she seems different now. She seems nicer. She would never have offered us tea. Nothing here is easy to replace.'

'Yeah, I noticed that too.' Danny rubbed his hand through his stubble and took his beanie off. 'What about Jonty?'

Charlie's large white eyebrows furrowed as he looked up at him. 'What about him?'

'Well, I can't see that he changed at all. I mean I fainted, you…' He pointed at Charlie who raised his eyebrows. 'Hey, come on, you know you went a bit weird on the deck before we left. And Marie, something happened to her but I can't say that Jonty changed at all.'

Charlie leant forward again. 'Maybe we should talk to him tonight?'

'I think that would be a good idea, but we need to watch Marie as well, something isn't right there.'

'I don't know, Danny. I think you might be thinking that because you hadn't received a dose of her wrath until now. Don't forget we all got a serving on the way out to the ice shelf. Not as bad as today granted, but I think that feminist part of her has always lurked just below the surface.' He scratched at his chin as he stood up. 'I think she's disappointed that she missed out. She blames you for that because you saw her weakness.'

'Well, I was just trying to help out,' Danny said.

'She's a woman, Danny,' Charlie said with a blank expression. 'You'll always be wrong; God help you if you have a daughter and you haven't worked that out.'

<h1 style="text-align:center">11</h1>

THE MESS HALL remained silent for the most part, one of the few times in Danny's memory where the entire camp had sat together in a meeting. The camera that had accompanied them down onto the ship sat on one of the tables while the images from its memory were displayed on the flat screen. Even Gary managed to keep silent as the ghostly images of the old Japanese whaler were cast onto the screen. At first, only Charlie and Jonty were visible on film, then after they had ascended the great, frozen stairs to the bridge, he saw himself. Danny watched as his past self reefed open the hatch and stepped into the freezing darkness of the whaler's apartments.

Marie gasped and held a hand to her mouth as the camera panned across the frozen blood on the walls. Anne Castelli frowned as she leant forward to get a closer look. Corinth Butler closed her eyes and held her face in her hands, while Wendy Phillips buried herself into James Sutton's shoulder. Danny and Charlie remained silent through the video. That was until the Japanese officer was discovered, and the artificial light from camera and the two phones washed over the man's pallid, grey skin. Danny's stomach rolled when the camera purposely zoomed into the bullet wound, at this even Gary hung his head with an uncourteous remark.

As Danny turned away in disgust, he noticed Marie Swan. She sat in the furthest possible chair from him, with her arms folded neatly across her chest. Her jaw was set, and her eyes seemed drier than the ice had been. Her expression remained infallible even as the ice was torn from the wall and the three lights combined once more to expose the rising sun of the Japanese Empire. Even on the large, flat screen mounted on the wall, the way that old flag seemed to be exposed from the ice sent shivers trembling up his spine. He forced himself to watch as he waited for the next scene to be displayed.

'That's what we found,' Jonty said, as he paused the video on the icy flag.

Both Danny and Charlie looked to each other at the same time, while Jonty offered them all a short pause. When Danny returned his gaze to Jonty, he found that the head scientist's eyes were fixed on him, as if to dare him to bring up the elephant in the room, or in this case the horribly disfigured creature.

'The ship belongs to the nation of Japan. This much is obvious,' Jonty started again as he closed his eyes in an exaggerated blink and rested his ass on one of the tables behind him. The image of the rising sun loomed behind him like a kraken from the past. He folded his arms as he opened his eyes once more and swept the room to address their entirety. 'We managed to recover the ships log, but of course its text is in Japanese and we are unable to read it. The crew of the ship met a grizzly end; that much is evident through the remains of an officer that we found, but a few other questions were raised by this.'

This must be it, Danny thought, *he will have to mention the creature now.*

'Charlie is of the opinion that the ship belongs to the Empire of Japan,' Jonty said flatly, as Charlie repositioned himself in his chair. 'This of course seems to be apparent by the flag, the way the man was dressed, and the armaments that we also found in the room.' Once more, Jonty's eyes burnt into Danny's as he finished his sentence. 'But I am reluctant to say here nor there, until I can read the ship's log.'

'Armaments?' James Sutton asked.

'Isn't Japan a democracy? How can there be an empire?' Craig Hollins ran over the top of him.

'I can't believe a research station can be full of so many fools,' Anne Castelli muttered to herself, then sighed. The questions stopped and everyone's focus was hers. 'Japan still has an emperor but its Imperial Empire ended after the Second World War. So yes, Japan is a democracy but it still has an Emperor, Craig.'

'Thank you, Anne,' Jonty tried to regain control of the meeting.

'And as for you Jonty,' Anne continued right over the top of him. 'You have alluded to a nation state that was overthrown seventy years ago but that flag is symbolic and means more than just the actions of the nation during the Second World War. That is exactly like saying that the Buddhist Swastika only relates to the Nazis even though it has been around for thousands of years.'

'Here, here,' Gary said, clearly with no idea what the woman was talking about.

'Anne, the only political argument I want to get into right now is about who owns the rights to the ship, not who designed the wall art,' Jonty fired back.

Danny laughed as he settled back into his chair. Jonty was a weird cat, but in moments like this, he would be happy to have the guy as a friend. The hard part was that Danny knew that even with the very next sentence Jonty would destroy any ground he had made and send himself straight back down the social step ladder.

'Anne, do you mean to say that the ship is from the Second World War?' Sean asked.

'As I was just saying,' Jonty raised his voice, 'it would seem that way, but I am not ready to say here nor there.'

'Well how else could it have beaten us there?' Gary asked with raised eyebrows.

'There are stories of Japanese soldiers still in service decades after the war had ended, because they were never told that Japan had surrendered,' Corinth said.

'Or they didn't believe it,' Charlie agreed with her.

'Has anyone ever thought that this could be a big hoax?' Craig asked.

'A hoax?' Charlie's face screwed up. 'What planet are you on?

They'd dump an old ship on us with a dead Japanese guy dressed up as an officer and sit back and wait for the laughs?'

'Yeah, well, it was just a thought,' Craig grumbled.

'If that's the best thought you can come up with, keep the next one to yourself,' Charlie snapped.

Danny put a hand on his shoulder. 'Hey, settle down man, it's a group discussion.'

Charlie gave him a withering look and then trained his eyes on Jonty. 'Tell them about the real question Jonty. If you won't, Danny will.'

Jonty looked like a deer in the headlights. 'What question?' he said through gritted teeth. Danny saw the creature in his eyes and for a moment he thought that maybe Jonty was right not to talk about the monster; all it would do is scare everyone here. Maybe there were other important things that needed to be settled first. Danny considered Corinth. What would it help poor old Ma to know about that thing?

'Stop, Charlie.' Danny gripped his shoulder again.

Charlie brushed him off, his cheeks reddening beneath the stubble on his cheeks. 'Come on man, tell them about the cable.'

'The cable?' Danny said almost at the same time as Jonty. 'I thought you were...'

'The cable that goes into the ice,' Charlie said again as he stood up. 'Didn't you take a photo of the ship when we were on the way down?'

'Yeah,' Danny said vaguely, finally remembering the steel cable going into the ice. So many things had happened in the last few hours that he had forgotten the entire conversation on the deck before they had left. To be honest, he couldn't even remember the flight back. Danny stood and went to the camera but Marty beat him to it.

'It's all good, Danny.' He smiled up at him. 'I'll find it if it's right at the beginning.'

Danny sat back down as the image on the screen went back to the menu. His heart stopped in his chest as he thought he saw an image of the creature, then Marty scrolled away and it was gone. He scanned the room to see if anyone else had noticed, but the room had erupted into a low buzz of conversation.

'Here,' Marty said as he looked up to the screen. 'Just like I remember. See it?'

Marty walked up to the television screen and ran his finger over a section forward of the ships bow. It was hard to see in the light of the photograph, but just visible was a faint, dull line of steel that came from the ship's prow, then ran through the air and directly into the ice shelf.

'It's just a bit of light or something mucking up the lenses.' Craig dismissed it.

'It's not.' Danny stood up and walked to the front of the room. 'We all saw it. The ship used to be a whaler from what I can tell. Here.' He pointed to the mounted harpoon cannon that was visible in the photograph and the massive winch to its rear. 'The cable runs along the prow and then vanishes directly into the ice. I saw it with my own eyes Craig, I was there.' Craig rolled his eyes.

'It's just a joke or something,' he dismissed once more.

At this, Charlie joined Danny at the front. 'The ice shelf broke only three days ago now. When we arrived, the ship was there. Gary and Marty saw it before us. We have been aboard that ship, it has not moved under its own power for a long time, that much is certain.'

'Well then, why isn't it rusty and covered in barnacles?' Craig came back with a scowl.

'Steel doesn't rust when it's frozen.' Anne came to their defence. 'The same can be said for barnacles, it's too cold down here for them.'

'If the cable had been shot into the ice, or driven into it, then we would see chunks missing around it.' Danny traced the line of the cable across the screen with his finger. 'The cable goes straight into a wall of ice, there's no gaps around it. Can anyone explain to me how they would insert a steel cable into a block of ice without leaving any visible damage?'

'There's no way that the ship has been moved in the last three days,' Charlie said firmly. 'If we can all agree on these two things, then the simple answer is that the ship was there before the ice shelf broke free.'

Jonty threw up his arms. 'And you finally come out with it.' Everyone went silent. 'You have been dancing around this since we walked onto the ship. I thought that was what you meant but I didn't think you were that insane. How could the ship get so far into the ice shelf?'

'How could it have arrived after the break?' Charlie rebuked. 'If it couldn't have arrived after, then it must have existed before.'

Jonty rolled his eyes. 'An educated guess.'

'Isn't that what science is?' Danny asked, 'Aren't all of you "white collars" scientists?' He pointed to all of them. 'I can't see a better explanation.'

'I'm still yet to hear an explanation to how a seventy-year-old "whaler" was found behind three hundred and forty billion tonnes of ice.' Jonty folded his arms again.

'That's easy,' Charlie said with a smile. 'The answer is at the end of that cable. The question is how do we find out what it is?'

The entire room looked to the photograph. The ice shelf needed to be protected. If the steel ran through the ice, then whatever it was would lay below the ice shelf. There was no way that they could survive swimming beneath it. Nor would they want to damage the shelf to inspect it, not since three hundred and forty billion tonnes just fell off it; they wouldn't risk further damage.

'I have a way,' Bob Taylor said. This was the first time that Bob had moved, let alone spoken, so everyone lent in to listen. 'During the summer I often relay requests to other government departments to ask for services or supplies that our researchers might want. One thing I ask for is satellite thermal scans that the meteorologists need to explain one thing or another. I've seen these scans; they may be able to help. If I got the coordinates of where you would want them to scan, I could ask for it to be done.'

Jonty nodded. 'Gary, could you provide Robert with those coordinates?'

'Yes sir,' Gary answered in an American accent.

'Ok well that's one question,' Jonty said as he began to pace. 'The second one is what are we going to do about the log? Does anyone know how to read Japanese?' The room remained silent. Everyone stared back with blank expressions. 'I really think the information that we need lies within those pages. I am reluctant to send it to someone as I don't want any of this to get out but…'

'Give it to me.' The voice was soft, sweet and confident. Danny watched Marie; her hand was outstretched as she looked up at Jonty.

'Do you speak Japanese?' Charlie asked.

Her eyes moved beneath their lashes as cool as anything and a soft smile came over her face. 'No, but I know how to use the internet. I should be able to translate, it just might take me a while. Besides, I feel like I let you guys down out there and here I'll be able to help out.'

Charlie and Danny exchanged a glance as Jonty clapped his hands. 'Fantastic! Now there is only one more troublesome thing about this whole situation, which we all need to discuss before we close the meeting.' He held the tips of his fingers together, almost as if he was ready to take a dive. 'Unless, anyone here has read up on their international law, I am currently uncertain to who has the rights to this ship. If it had surfaced in Botany Bay, the answer would be something different and the problem wouldn't be in my lap. But as we stand, we are in Australian claimed land for the purpose of research. That does not mean that this is Australian land, as no country may own land in Antarctica. While I am researching what legal rights we have to that ship, I do not want anyone to talk about it, I don't even want anyone to talk about the loose tooth. If it comes up in conversation, as no doubt the news may report it back on the homeland, just say it's really neat or something like that.'

'Neat.' Gary rolled his eyes.

'I'm being serious here,' Jonty said with distinct anger in his tone. 'We don't know what we have found here, not yet. Until we know, keep it a secret. Otherwise, we will have not only the Japanese on us, but don't forget that the Chinese have settled a small base in-between us and Davies. Are we agreed that word of this is not to leave Mawson?'

There were unanimous sounds of agreeance throughout the mess and a look of relief spread across Jonty's face. 'In that case, let's bring this meeting to a close. Gary, please pass on those coordinates to Robert. Marie, the log is in my Donga, can I have a quick word with you in there?'

'No time like the present, isn't that right Bobby?' Gary said as he gained his feet.

The whole room seemed to fill with conversation instantly as people started to get up. Danny stood there as everyone left; he watched Wendy and James leave together in the direction of the Dongas, lucky guy. He watched Craig and Sean walk off laughing; the two would spend the remainder of the evening discussion how bullshit the entire meeting had been, of that there was no doubt.

Danny considered the photograph of the whaler once more. Another shiver ran up his spine as he traced its lines.

'Hey Danny,' the soft voice came from behind him.

'Hey Marie,' he replied without facing her. His eyes remained on the cable.

'I just wanted to apologise for how I acted before, I know you must have had a long day.'

'No apology needed,' Danny said as he glanced back at her. He didn't want to stare but it seemed that she had become more beautiful by the moment since her return. Her cheeks glowed, her eyes were so piercing, even her hair seemed to shine bright in the fluorescents. 'You look like you've recovered well. You look great.'

She smiled as she blushed. 'Hey, don't try and flatter me mister, don't forget you have a woman at home.'

Danny smiled at her. 'We're all good then?' he asked. It was an honest question; he was still concerned about what happened out there, but he didn't want any trouble on base. There was nothing worse than when two people had an issue with each other in an isolated environment; everyone was dragged into it. He imagined they would all get a dose of that in a couple of weeks when Wendy woke up to herself about James.

'All good,' she said with a smile as her eyes hid behind her lashes for another second. Then she walked away, and instead of looking at her face, Danny was left to watch her ass move from side to side as she left to visit Jonty in his Donga.

Danny frowned as he turned his attention back to the ship. He ran a hand over his stubble again. Maybe Charlie was right about him not understanding women. If he was a betting man, Marie had just flirted with him only hours after throwing him out of her room. He scanned the room to see if Charlie had been present, to see if he wasn't alone in what he thought, but there was no sight of the older man. In fact, there was no sight of anyone.

He frowned again as he looked back to the camera. Marty had left it there, maybe he thought that Jonty wanted it. Danny picked it up and navigated into the menu. He would take the camera to Jonty's room as he missed his chance to talk to him after the meeting. Charlie was supposed to join him and he had vanished too.

'Damn you Charlie,' he mumbled to himself as he walked to the Dongas. Charlie had lost his temper for a while there and then had carried on fine as if nothing had happened. Was it just him or had everyone gone stupid since their return? If anything, he felt like having a drink but Gary had left to help Bob Taylor. He needed to talk with Charlie, but he was gone. If he couldn't talk to Charlie, Danny knew that he should talk to Jonty, but he was occupied with Marie. So much to do, yet nothing could be done. He walked around the corner and into the hall that led to the sleeping apartments and stopped.

Charlie was knelt next to one of the doors about halfway up the hall, his ear up against the wall. His back was to Danny so he didn't notice him walk into the hall. Danny just stood there; he didn't know what to do. It appeared as though he was eavesdropping on someone but that didn't seem like him. He went to take a step toward the door when Charlie rose to his feet. In panic, Danny backed out of the hall so not to be seen, but Charlie slunk his way up the hall and disappeared through another door.

Danny squinted in confusion as he leant back into the hall. The door that Charlie had crouched outside of opened and shortly after, Marie exited, the ship's log in hand. She smiled back into the room and shut the door. The second the door was closed, her smile vanished. She turned her back to Danny and entered her room, part way up the hall.

Danny's frown spread to his eyes. With the camera still in his hand, he walked up the hallway, feeling stupid as he crept along like he had become involved in some espionage thriller. It looked as though Charlie had gone into his own room and Danny was happy for that; at the moment he wanted to trust only himself and that meant he needed to speak to Jonty alone. The minute he knocked on the door, he felt like an even bigger idiot. What was the point of sneaking if he was going to knock? The door opened shortly after, and Jonty welcomed him in.

12

IT HAS BEEN SAID, that if you give an individual a space to call their own, then after a period the space will start to reflect their owner. Even if it is subconsciously, the owner will decorate or leave mess lying around here and there. No matter how much someone may disagree with this statement, a lot could be said for the way a person kept their room. Marie's was warm, plush with pillows and small nick knacks. A kettle to make tea with and even a small tea set where she could entertain as she had done with Danny and Charlie. Danny's room was a mess of clean and soiled clothes, a laptop and charger cables all knotted together. Where Marie's Donga smelt of perfume and different kinds of teas, Danny's smelt of differential oil, another sickly-sweet smell that seemed to sit at the back of one's throat. Danny was sure that if he walked into any person's room, he would probably be able to work out who it belonged to after some fashion, but as he sat in Jonty's donga, he thought that everything that could be said about psychology was a load of shit.

Every inch of the walls were covered in posters, whose contents ranged from heavy metal bands such as Amon Amarth and System of a Down, to video game likenesses of demons and men in strange armour. One particular poster stood out to him: a single man who wore green armour stood in a field of fire as demons of all sorts surrounded him. In one hand he held a demon by its throat, if you could call it that, in the other a double-barrelled shotgun. In the background, rising up like a monolith of ancient worship, was the skull of a giant, with large curved horns that sprouted from each side of its head. Danny shivered as he turned away from the poster and saw that Jonty was staring at him.

'I…' Danny started. 'I like your room.' He felt like a child that had just gone over to a new friend's house for the first time.

'Thanks,' Jonty replied flatly. 'How can I help you, Daniel?'

Danny searched briefly for somewhere to sit and saw that there was nothing. A small computer desk sat against one heavily postered wall; he expected to see it littered, but there was not even a speck of dust on its top. Just a closed laptop, a notepad and pen nestled beneath it. Danny rested his ass on the corner of the desk and folded his arms awkwardly, as he struggled to work out what to do with the camera he still held onto. Jonty on the other hand stood in the centre of his room, his arms straight down by either side while his eyes burnt into Danny's.

'How's Marie?' Danny finally asked.

'Marie?' Jonty questioned. 'Fine. She was just here a second ago.'

'Yeah, I saw her leave,' Danny confided. 'How was she, we had a…' He ran his hand over his stubble as he stumbled for the word.

'Altercation?' Jonty finished for him.

Danny looked at him. What had he been told, and who by? 'Yeah,' he said flatly. 'I went to her room to see how she was.'

'And how was she?' Jonty asked this time.

Danny felt the conversation being turned on him. 'Well, she was ok…' he tried.

'But you had an altercation?' Jonty asked again, his face remained set in stone.

Danny frowned as he dropped his hand to his lap. 'She seems on edge, she started fine, she welcomed us in.'

'Us?' The question interjected Danny's train of thought. Had he walked into an interrogation?

Danny considered him closely. 'Am I ok here? Do I need a lawyer?'

A ghost of smile appeared on Jonty's face, then it was gone again. 'No need for that, I'm just trying to understand the situation.'

Danny's mind went to Gary, and what he said in the meeting when they were told about Jonty's new signs. 'Now we know who complained.' *Marie, Marie, Marie*, he thought. 'What is going on here?'

'And that's exactly what I'm doing here, trying to work out a situation.' Danny stood up from the table. 'Four of us went out to that ship, Marie didn't even step on it and we had to send her home. Charlie seems paranoid, every time I turn around, I seem to see him either watching me or Marie.'

'And how does that make you feel?' Jonty asked, calm as still water.

'How does it make me feel?' Danny asked incredulously. He placed a hand to his chest and raised his eyebrows, yet the man who questioned him had not even tilted his head. 'I don't fucking know how I feel, Jonty. To be honest I'm starting to freak the fuck out.'

'What are you scared about?' Jonty asked calmly again.

Danny shifted away from him, still holding the camera in his hand. He frowned again as he contemplated his answer. 'Ever since I passed out,' he mumbled low. He looked Jonty in the eye. 'I haven't felt right since. It's like something happened to me when I passed out and I don't know what. But whatever it is, I think Marie and Charlie are the same.'

Jonty didn't say anything, he just stared at him.

'And the reason why I'm coming to you, apart from the obvious, is that you were there too. Surely you've seen it.'

Finally, Jonty broke his eye contact. He sighed a long terrible gust of air as he sat down on his bunk. 'It's not easy being in my position,' he confided. 'Being the head researcher, during the winter in this... this place. It's not like you can just decide that you want to have a day off and someone else can take over.' He considered the wall, maybe one of the hundred posters that lined his Donga. 'You can't ask for help, because help is thousands of miles away and even in an emergency, they would be two to three weeks away at best. So, it's just me.'

Danny figured it had been a long, long time since Jonty had gotten anything off of his chest to anyone. Maybe it was his time to take one for the team and give him a shoulder to sob on. He moved back to the computer desk and rested his ass on the corner once more.

'The ship is a concern,' he continued. 'That I grant you, but I stand fast to what I said on top of Amery that day. My main concern is for the lives of the expeditioners and at the moment, yourself, Charlie and Marie are right at the top of that list. I feel that the next few weeks are going to be the most important – the more we act as a team the easier it will be.' The way he started to talk it was almost as if it was to himself, as if Danny for that moment, didn't exist to him. 'But the way things are going…'

Jonty stopped for a second and considered Danny.

'Daniel, can I trust you?' All of a sudden, he looked as though he had aged ten years. His face had become pallid, lines creased his brow while bags suddenly appeared under his eyes.

Danny was at a loss, is there ever any other answer to this question? 'Of course,' he said, intrigued at what was to come.

'Great. That's so great to hear,' Jonty said softly as he shuffled toward Danny and leant toward him. Jonty glanced toward the door. 'We better talk quietly; you never know who may be listening.'

Danny's mind went straight to Charlie and his heart started to beat a little faster. 'What's happening to us Jonty?' he whispered.

'I don't know but I think you're right with what you've said, Daniel.' He placed a sweaty hand on Danny's shoulder. 'It started to happen before we even got onto the ship, first to Marie, then to Charlie. Even I feel it. It feels like I'm closed in, like I'm claustrophobic, and that's probably why they're acting out, the poor people.' He placed his face into his hands and started to knead at his eyes. When he looked back to Danny again both of his eyes were red and bleary, as if he had been crying. 'What I am about to ask you is very important.'

'Sure, anything.'

'I need you to watch Charlie and Marie. You're right, they've changed, and I'm concerned their condition will continue to deteriorate.'

'What do you mean deteriorate?' Danny asked, genuinely shocked by the statement.

'It's hard to say,' he almost hissed. 'But at the moment I don't trust them, do you?'

Danny thought about this for a few seconds. Given Marie's outburst and Charlie's current attitude, it was hard for him to truthfully say that he could trust either of them. 'No, I suppose I don't.'

'See, we are both on the same page. I knew we were.' Jonty nodded to himself as he said this. 'In your daily work, keep an eye on them, ok? I'll do the same, but we can't make it obvious.'

Danny nodded in agreement.

'Now I want you to know, there's no need to panic, ok? More than likely, nothing will happen at all, but I'd rather have someone I can trust keep an eye on these two while we are all making up our minds on what to do here. You've always been a well-liked guy around Mawson, people go to you with problems and all are always happy to be in your company. So, let them come to you, hear what they have to say and let me know if there is anything you're worried about. We will keep the camp together, you and me.'

'What about the ship?'

Jonty didn't even take a breath. 'The situation will be a delicate one when it comes to that ship, so I'll need to divert a lot of my attention there, especially where it comes to dealing with the home land. So, Danny I really appreciate your help on this.' He stood up and offered him his hand.

Danny straightened and the two men shook. 'Thanks for having trust in me I suppose,' he replied. He hated being in the situation where people thanked him and complimented him, he never knew how to take it.

'Come on, go and get some rest. We've all had a big day.' Jonty clapped him on the shoulder and once more Danny was struck by the thought that this guy wasn't so bad after all.

Danny allowed himself to be led out of the Donga. The two men wished each other good night and then the door closed between them and latched. Then Danny was alone in the long, silent hallway. He glanced from side to side, feeling all together exposed. He thought about Charlie and how he had slunk off to his own room before Marie had exited. He considered the door that he had disappeared through, it was shut tight.

He stood there for another few seconds in anticipation of him cracking the seal. In his mind he could imagine the eye in the darkness, staring at him through the slit. But the door never did open, not even an inch.

Feeling paranoid and stupid, Danny headed to his own Donga. He didn't realise how tired he was. The day had been enormous and in all of that he had only had one coffee in the morning and one of Charlie's damned protein bars. Now that he thought of it, he was damned famished. He walked beyond his own door and continued back to Woollies. The mess was deserted as before and the entire Red Shed seemed to be plunged into silence.

He frowned at this, because all of the lights had been left on. If it was one thing that pissed Danny off more than what Jonty did, it was when people didn't turn the lights off. Everything here was diesel. If you left the lights on for ten minutes more than you needed, that was diesel you'd just poured down the drain. Danny went to make himself a cup of coffee and it was only then that he realised he still had Marty's camera in his hand. He stood there for what seemed like an age, as the kettle boiled and then clicked off. He stared at the camera; the images that lay within it rolled through his head. The images that had been left unshown, unprojected up on the wall, and Jonty had managed to elude him again on the subject.

Danny made himself a strong coffee. Even though he wanted to go to sleep, he had one more job for the day. While in the mess, he took a few muesli bars from Woollies, plus a Snickers, and stuffed them all into the pocket of his hoodie before he carried his coffee and the camera back to his room.

As he sat amongst the strewn clothes on his bed where the covers were all messed up, the smell of the diff oil penetrated his sinuses. He knew that after a while he wouldn't even be able to smell it and that was fine. He ate and drank, then ate, all the while the video rolled on the small side screen of the camera. He had just watched himself force open the hatch once more and step through into the darkness of the apartments, when something caught his eye. He looked to his door, at the line of light that penetrated beneath it. There were two dark spots.

As the video continued to play, he saw the two dark spots become one. Quietly, he got to his feet. He took his time with each step so not to make a sound. He kept his eye on the door knob the entire time. For a room that was roughly nine metres deep, it seemed to take him an eternity to cross it. One step, then another, closer and closer he came. Behind him, in the video he had left playing on the bed, he heard them talk about the dead officer and he heard Jonty mention the log. Closer and closer, he focused hard on the door knob. To his horror, it started to turn.

Not in bravery but in pure fear, he leapt for the door and twisted the knob hard before he pulled it open. His breath was hot in his chest and his heart hammered hard in his throat. He opened his mouth to demand to know what he was doing there. The words started to come then died on his tongue. There was no-one there.

Danny stepped into the hallway and scanned back and forth, but it was empty. The lights that were set to sensor were off. They came on now in such a dazzling brilliance that Danny was forced to shut his eyes. His expectation to see Charlie had been so great, he had almost even seen him there as he burst through the door. He shook his head and rubbed at his eyes with the heels of his hands. It had been a long, long day.

Back in his room, on the camera, he heard himself find the log and he shuddered. Once he had found the log, the next thing was the monster. That was the last thing he wanted to see right now. The door clunked as he closed it behind him, and he made sure to latch it this time. He sat on his bed and held the camera as he heard himself fall on the tape and watched the video as Jonty and Charlie rushed to his aid.

He saw his own face as he lay there and attempted to gain his feet. He saw the monster to his side and his stomach rolled as he watched his reaction to the sight only mere feet from his face. The way the light made shadows across that thing's face and body made it even more horrific in the small screen than it had been in the flesh. He watched himself flail and fight, and then he was gone. Out and still, and the camera kept filming.

'Oh my God,' he heard Charlie say.

'Quick, help me get him away from there,' Jonty said. He watched as Charlie placed the camera down on one of the instrument panels. Unfortunately, the way Charlie placed the camera the visual was useless, but he heard everything. He heard them struggle with his weight as they dragged him away from the thing.

'Over here. Yeah.' He heard Charlie's panting.

'Ok.' Jonty, then a sigh and soft clunk. 'God, he's heavy.'

Then there was nothing for a short time, maybe only a few seconds where all Danny could hear was the pair struggling to catch their breath. Then there was a sound as if someone with very light footfalls was running across a steel floor.

'What… what's happening?' Charlie's voice, distraught again.

'Oh my God,' Jonty this time. 'Quick get the camera's light.'

The soft rapping continued beneath Charlie's heavy footfalls, then the camera was moving and swirling and the images were impossible to make out.

'Fuck.' He heard Charlie swear and the image focused and became still.

He was looking at himself again, on the floor and pale. Paler than he had ever seen himself. He was having a seizure. Jonty took his jacket off and rolled it up roughly and jammed it under his head. He then knelt and lightly supported his head at either side so that Danny didn't smash himself to pieces.

'Christ, what's happening.' Charlie again, distraught.

'It's ok,' Jonty tried to calm him. 'He's having a seizure.'

'Great, if anything else can go wrong then please, let's have it.'

'Jesus Christ, Charlie,' Danny said to himself as he watched the video. 'Thanks for the support.'

Then his body stopped shaking and his eyes opened. *Well, at least that's one thing.* He thought to himself, *I wasn't out for very long.* On screen, his mouth opened and he spoke, but the words that came out of his mouth were not the words that Danny remembered speaking.

'Free.' A long rasp. 'Me.' Just as long and horrible.

'Oh my God.' Charlie again.

'Free me.' Just as long and painful.

'What's wrong with him?' Charlie cried to Jonty again.

The seizure seemed to start once more; Danny's limbs began to thrash again like they were part of their own being. 'Free. Me.' Shorter this time, almost guttural.

'Damn it, Charlie help me.' Jonty called up to him. Once more, the camera was placed down in a horrible angle and Danny was left to watch nothing but his own feet tremble and kick while the two men held his body down.

'Free me.' His voice had become almost a sob. The desperation poured out almost like tears as the words ran from his mouth in a higher pitch than before, 'free me.'

Danny put the camera down and he held his hands to his mouth as if to stop a scream but there was nothing coming out.

'Free me.'

Finally, his body stopped fighting and the words, those damned words, stopped coming. Once again, he was left with silence as the two other men tried to catch their breath. Charlie stood up after a while and retrieved the camera. His breath was heavy in his chest and even Danny could tell he was close to a panic attack. Christ, he didn't blame him.

As he came closer to the camera, Danny heard the words he was saying under his breath, 'Oh Christ, Oh Christ.'

The image whirled as Charlie picked the camera up, then as it settled it shook with the tremble in his hands and Danny had to look away as it was making him sick.

'Charlie, listen to me.' It was Jonty, and it sounded as though he was right on top of him. 'Listen to me.' Almost aggressive. 'Don't panic. Keep your head ok, Charlie?'

'Ok Jonty.' The older man's voice trembled as it came.

'Look at me Charlie.' The camera didn't move but obviously Charlie obeyed because the next word that Jonty said was, 'Good. Charlie, can I trust you?'

Danny's eyes got large with the words.

'Can I trust you Charlie, because the next few things we need to do are very important.'

'Y... Yes Jonty. You can trust me.'

'That's good. That's really good to hear, Charlie.' He heard him pat the older man on the back. 'We need to stick together here ok. Something is happening and I am going to need your help. Ok?'

'Ok Jonty.'

'Marie… Something is wrong with Marie, I got her out as quick as I could but… I think it might be too late, and now Danny… we can't trust either of them, Charlie.'

'N… No.' Charlie sounded as if he was about to burst into tears. 'No, we can't.'

'It's just you and me Charlie, for the moment, until we work out what to do. Ok?'

'Yes Jonty.'

'When he wakes up and when we get back, you watch him, ok? And you watch Marie. If anything happens, you let me know, ok?'

'Y... Yes'

'That's good to hear. Now we aren't panicking, are we?'

'N... No.'

'We're good?'

'Yes, Jonty.' His voice had started to calm.

'Quick, he's waking up. Come here and act like none of that happened otherwise we will have a problem, Charlie.' The two men walked side by side to stand above his body once more. He saw his eyes blink a few times and then open. 'Daniel?'

'Danny? Come on man, wake up.'

'Daniel, come back to us.'

'Ahh shit Jonty. Do you think he hit his head?'

Danny stopped the video. He sat there for a long time, looking at his body on the ground. He wanted to pick the camera up, to throw it across the room. He wanted to slam it into Jonty's lying, fucking face. Everyone seemed to be playing a game, and everyone seemed to want him as their pawn. He picked the camera up once more, his face hot with the rage and the fear inside of him. He moved back to the gallery and selected the file.

The title came up with the question of all time: 'Are you sure you want to delete this file? Yes, or no?'

Danny hit 'yes.'

13

'HEY KIDDO,' his voice was flat. 'It's been a few days since I have done one of these for you.' He yawned. The face that stared back at him wasn't his own. The bags beneath his eyes were the size of the dormant steel cogs of the Hägglund, the vehicle that at this very moment lay forgotten on Amery, somewhere above that damned ship. His yawn finished in a growl and he blinked his weary bloodshot eyes. 'Sorry about that, it's been a full-on few days here and your old pop is tired, but hey you don't care about that, you want to see something cool.'

Danny had thought that each video he completed for his unborn child should contain something of interest so not to bore them. In the end, what he wanted was not for the child to see the boring sides but the beauty that lay behind the work. He switched the camera to feed from the lens on the back of his phone and he saw the image change on the screen. The weary, aging man was gone, replaced by the beautiful rocky shore in front of him. The ocean was calm enough today, as was the wind, and for first time in what had seemed like a decade, Danny found that he didn't have to shout to be heard. He could even hear the water break as the seals dove in and out in a playful motion amongst themselves.

'See, now look at that.' He yawned again. 'It's not every day you get to see something so cool, not even at a zoo would they play so freely kiddo.' He said this with a soft smile on his face as a big bull scal leapt out of the water and slid across the rock on its belly. Its mouth was open and it barked in a playfully ferocious bellow to its pack mates. The smaller seals likewise opened their mouths and barked as they fled before the rushing bull, leaving it the king of the rock for a short period of time.

Danny laughed as he switched the camera back around. 'There you go kiddo, something fun to start the day. Anyway, just a quick one today, I'm dead tired and the day's only just begun. Love you, kiddo. See you soon.' He kissed the screen and smiled as he finished the recording. As soon as the camera application on his phone closed, the smile vanished from his face. He gazed at his reflection in the black of the glass and he blinked. His eyes felt like they had gravel beneath their lids, every blink was six hundred grit paper against the softness of his eyes.

He would have been lying if he'd said that he had slept well the last few nights. Hell, he probably would've been lying if he said he had slept at all. When one's body became this exhausted it was hard to tell most things; reality became a blur and even basic things like the light of the day didn't seem real. It was almost as if he saw the light as it was in a scientific diagram, beams of colours in a refracted state, spread out before him like on an artist's palette. Time meant nothing, days were just made up of periods of light where he trudged about, and the periods of dark where he stared blankly at the roof of his Donga, while his mind raced about from one thing to another. But even that had started to slow, even the thoughts that skipped from one fragment to the next had become blurred. And now he didn't even know whether the voice that echoed in the depths of his mind was his own, or whether it was something else, something foreign.

'Free me.'

Sometimes when he heard it, it sounded like himself but then at other times it was so far off, so distant, it could have come from anyone or anywhere. He had even spoken to his partner via video call, either last night or the night before, but of the conversation he could remember none of it. He remembered seeing her face, her beautiful smile, and even the bump of her belly where his unborn sprog was growing. Then it seemed the next moment he had looked over to the screen and all he could see was his own reflection behind the words 'call disconnected.'

Sleep would not come; hunger was a myth. He couldn't remember the last time he had done anything. He had avoided contact with anyone and tried to busy himself with his mechanical work but even that had become a risk. He couldn't trust himself to torque a rocker cover bolt, let alone maintain and handle the four kings that kept everyone here alive. And now he stood atop the diesel tanks, on the mezzanine walkway, with no idea how or when he had arrived here. Something had to give.

Danny's face twisted into a frown as he looked around. The day was beautiful and he felt the warmth of the sun bite into him, even through his many layers. He turned to the Red Shed, where his bed lay within. He stared longingly at it for some time, then his eyes drifted further to his right; beyond the communications, was another Red Shed, smaller by far than the main mess hall.

The smaller red building was just another AANBUS structure, identical to the others, but this one housed the labs. It struck Danny, while he headed toward the labs, that any person that considered these structures might believe that they had entered a redneck housing estate. He thought of countless examples in Sydney alone – Ropes Crossing, Jordan Springs, even Oran Park Town for Christ's sake. Street after street of identical houses, perhaps reverse imaged just to break it up. Here at Mawson all of the structures were sheds. Even the original, a throwback to the early days, was just a shed, brown now with rust. At least they had coloured them differently, which is more than what he could say for the Sydneysiders.

The lab was quiet when he entered, yet he could tell from the cold porch that at least three people were in here. Coats, gumboots and gloves were gathered below three of the name tags. Amongst James Sutton and Craig Hollins, was the woman who he had been searching for. The one that might hold the answer to his current prayers.

He knocked on the glass of her open office door and feigned another smile. 'Hello Anne, you got a minute?'

Anne Castelli was into her fifties but had looked after herself well enough to pull off early forties. Her hair was silver with shades of black, which almost gave it a hammer tone impression in certain lights. It hung above her shoulder in a short bob that revealed her age more so than her body.

Her green eyes gazed up at him from behind horn-rimmed glasses, her expression was stern as always but that meant nothing to her mood. 'Come on in Danny, take a seat.' She glanced over to the large whiteboard calendar on her wall. 'You're not due for your check up for another two weeks, what's wrong? You haven't been into Gary's scotch again?'

Danny felt like shit and he sure as well figured that he looked like shit. Anne was not one to walk on eggshells for the sake of another's feelings. 'You think I need Dutch courage to come and see you?'

'Well, it wouldn't be the first time that a man has felt intimidated by me. It says a lot about a man when he is frightened by a strong, independent woman.'

'If you keep going like this, I may not need to ask you for the tablets, you might just put me right to sleep,' Danny said, unamused.

'Sleeping tablets?' Her thin eyebrows raised above the rim of her glasses as her lips twisted on her slender face. 'Explains why you look like you've been on a six-week bender. How many nights has it been?'

'Only a six-week bender? I'll have you know I was aiming for eight weeks.' Danny yawned as he threw a hand over his mouth. 'A couple of days I think, maybe more, but zero sleep. I can't even catch twenty minutes.'

Anne sat in her chair and eyed him for a while. 'What happened to start this? You've never had a problem your entire life.'

'How do you know that?' Danny asked quickly. She was right, but she didn't need to know that.

'Look at where you are Danny, you're thousands and thousands of miles away from any hospital.' She folded her arms as she rested her back against her chair. 'If anything went wrong you think I wouldn't have a copy of every single person's medical history? Everything is life and death out here, now you tell me, Daniel Myers.'

Danny should have known better than to play stupid games with Anne Castelli. 'Anne.'

'It's to do with that ship, isn't it?'

'Anne, its fine.'

'Is it, Danny? Why can't you sleep then?'

'I have other things going on in my life other than what happened on that ship,' he said flatly.

'And what happened on that ship?' The questions came hard and fast.

'Anne.'

'I only ask as it's my duty of care.'

'Anne.' The tones of annoyance poured out in his voice. 'Nothing happened on that ship.'

'That's not what I've heard.'

Danny examined her. A slip? Could the stern old bitch have slipped? 'What do you mean by that?' Anger in his voice now.

Anne looked away and shrugged her shoulders.

'Nah, don't give me that bullshit. What has Charlie told you?'

'Why did you jump straight to that name?' Her eyes pierced straight through him.

'Well Marie then, Jonty doesn't seem to be aff…' *Too tired*, he thought. *Too damned tired to be playing these damned games.*

Anne's eyes glinted as her eyebrows raised and she sat back in her chair once more.

A slip or a trap being set, Danny thought. *Probably the latter, and I think I just felt its jaws close around my legs.*

'I think "affected" is the word you are looking for?' The triumph was clear on her face.

'Would that be a record for you?' he said indignantly. 'How many moves was that? Already at checkmate, huh?'

A ghost of a smile crept across her lips but it was her eyes that laughed at him. 'I think I had you in five, the other few were only for your sake.'

'Uh-huh.' Danny rubbed at his eyes and yawned again. 'I wouldn't call that a fair game.'

'Life isn't fair, Daniel. But as we are keeping you up.' She rested her elbows on her desk and rested her chin on her intertwined fingers. 'What would be affecting the three of you, but not Jonty?'

'Nothing.'

He needed to remember her expression for when he was a parent. The look said 'you just lied to me. I know that you did and if you know what is good for you, fess up.' She didn't say anything and it added testament to the fact that a good parent uses silence more than words, when it comes to confrontation.

'I can't speak for anyone else, but I fainted.' There was enough of the truth in the statement to get her off his case, he knew that as soon as he said it.

'Fainted?' she repeated. 'Please explain what happened.'

'Well, we were on the bridge, you saw the video. It was just after that I went over the other side away from Jonty and Charlie and when I got there I…' He paused for half a second to think. 'I felt light-headed and there you go. Next minute, I'm on my back with Jonty over me and Charlie off to the side.'

The parental expression of disbelief had edged back onto her face again. 'Did Charlie still have the camera on record?'

'I checked last night.' He yawned again and hoped that this made the story more believable. 'He must have stopped because it wasn't there.'

'Why are you lying to me, Danny?' Blunt and cold.

'I'm not!' He held his hands up. 'Not really.'

'And if I asked Charlie or Marie the questions, in concern for your health, which is the right that I have. They would corroborate your story, would they?'

Danny thought about Jonty's last words to Charlie on the tape. *Act like none of that happened otherwise we will have a problem, Charlie.* Charlie's silence depended on how great his fear of Jonty was. Marie knew nothing about the bridge, of that much he was sure, unless Charlie had told her before he had walked in on them.

His eyes widened. 'Yeah, why wouldn't they?' Danny shrugged. 'Anne, look all bullshit aside, I feel like shit and I need to sleep, can you help me or do I need to break into Gary's stash?'

Reluctantly Anne had handed over two small, white tablets. She made him sign for them before she would release them from the canister and ordered him to take them and go straight to bed. Danny didn't need to argue with that. He caught a glimpse of James Sutton in the lab leaning over a microscope as he left. He gave a wave as a just in case; the last thing he needed was for people to start bitching about him because he didn't say hello. Jimmy Sutton wasn't bad, but nothing would surprise him when it came to camp bitchiness.

He dressed himself in the cold porch, the tablets stored safely in his hoodie's pocket, and left for the Red Shed. He undressed again in the next cold porch and was well and truly exhausted by the time he reached the kitchen. Corinth Butler smiled at him when he saw her.

'Hey there boyfriend,' she winked at him. 'You ready to start dinner prep?'

Danny groaned, the damned chore roster. 'Ahh Ma. I'm off to bed with doctor's orders.' He patted his stomach where the tablets lay. 'Reckon I could call in sick for once?'

She looked concerned for him but at the same time there was an annoyance that she was going to get left without help. 'Yeah sure, as long as you find someone to do your job. You know the rules Danny.'

He didn't know what to say, he could barely stand, let alone go and beg someone to take his place in the kitchen. Besides, there was no-one nearby. 'Come on Ma, I'm not faking it.'

'Rules are rules, Danny. If we made exceptions for one person, we would have to make them for everyone.'

What was it with every woman in this place that they acted like his mother? He had nothing to say. He wanted to just take the pills and go to bed, but if he did that without finding someone to help, he would pay for it for the next month. One learnt pretty damned quick not to piss the person off who made your food.

'Hello Corinth.' The voice sounded behind him.

Danny spun around, eager to beg for his life, and was shocked to see Anne. 'Anne, I have a favour to ask.'

'You need me to do your dinner service?' She said it flat and expectantly.

Danny nodded. He figured he would take a leaf from her book and try some silence on for size. If it made him do what she wanted, then perhaps it could work the other way around.

'I noticed that you were rostered on tonight just after you left,' she said as she unfolded a roll of fabric that was under her left arm. 'I figured you wouldn't have had the sense to arrange someone to help poor Corinth, so I better help.'

Danny could have kissed her. He would've, but he wasn't sure what would've happened, so he decided to hug her instead. When he pulled away her face remained stern as she gazed up at him through her glasses once more.

'What are you thanking me for? I'm doing this to help Corinth, not you.'

'Same-same, Anne. Thanks.' Danny walked to the tap, popped the two tablets into his mouth and bent under the tap to drink them with water.

He smiled mentally at the sound of disgust from his rear and he felt the wallop of the tea towel on his back. He left the kitchen with a wave as the two women clucked and fussed about his actions and complained about the insensitivity of men.

As he laid down on his bed fully clothed, he felt the weight fall off him. He felt the grogginess overcome him and as the tablets wave of intoxicating sleep rushed over him, he imagined his mind as a hostage against itself, as if the subconscious had risen above its level in the depths to hold his body to ransom. He imagined a stone ring wall with himself in its centre, bedridden and sickly. Other versions of himself manned the ring wall, rifles in their hands as they barked orders to one another. Each time the sickly version of himself started to fall asleep, one of his clone guards would rush forward and sink the butt of their rifle into his ribs or his stomach to wake him once more.

Then one of his clone guards screamed and pointed into the distance. A wall of white rushed toward them. As it came closer, Danny could see that it was as if the white wall rose from the earth as it progressed and rushed upward into the air.

It's the medicine, come to put me to sleep, the thought rolled loosely around in his head. The clone guards screamed to one another as they fired on the wall but its onrush continued. The sound that it made as it came closer was like that of the ocean, but as if someone had pulled the plug out of the ocean and it rushed forth out of a spout.

Closer and closer, the firing became more frantic, more sporadic. It breached the outer ring wall, almost here. He saw clone guards sucked upwards, disintegrating as they were swept from the ramparts. Rifles and men lost to the sea of healing sleep. Then it was over the inner ring wall and it was on him. He felt it take him like a savage beast took its dying prey, the mercy in it. The peace.

He felt as though he was falling, falling but tumbling, as if the sea of medicine he was in was pushing him over and over and over. His arms flailed and his legs tried to kick but he was helpless; the mercy had come but now he was in its grasp. He was helpless but to do what it wanted.

Then the swirling stopped and he felt as though he was treading water in a dark pond. The place around him was cold, but he was ok. He didn't feel anything, which was a godsend. He didn't feel tired, he didn't feel weak, just alone.

Before him a shape was coming out of the darkness, a huge bulking shape that stood more than fifty feet tall. It didn't make a sound as it listed toward him, it just crept slowly through the water as he treaded and tried to push himself away from it.

He knew what it was, he knew where he was.

The Japanese whaler came out of the darkness, its prow buckled and damaged just as it had been when he had seen it from the air. A long, stiff cable ran down from its starboard side and into the water, he saw the line it made and the spray from the water as the cable rushed past him.

Danny followed the cable's path with his head, and then he turned back and started to scream. The ship was going to run him over. He tried to kick and paddle but he couldn't move. He fought with his whole body and spat and swore as the monstrous hull came down on him.

He took a deep breath and kicked as hard as he could and then it was on him. Once more, he felt himself swirling and falling, pushed deep beneath the surface. He fought to rise again but the force of the ship passing above him only spun him harder in its wake. His lungs screamed for oxygen; he felt his eyes want to pop out of his head. His heart hammered in his chest; he needed to breath but he couldn't rise, he just couldn't get there fast enough. He opened his mouth and felt the water rush into him. He sucked, and felt it flood his lungs. The internal explosion was immense but still, he did not die.

The pressure in his head subsided. His eyes relaxed and settled back into their sockets. Yet he didn't move, he just remained below the surface, in stasis. The ship was gone, its wake had settled yet the feeling of being alone was gone. Something lurked below him, deep down there. Well below the light. It eyed him, that he knew. It was coming for him but his body couldn't move. His body couldn't help him now, only his subconscious could, but it had turned against him.

'Free me.' The voice was deep, eternal. Not from his own body. Below him, two amber lights appeared. They burnt into him, almost through him, as they locked onto his lifeless, floating body.

'Free me.' It came again. The water shook with each word, each syllable. Then the water began to rush as if something enormous, something unfathomable was moving through it. 'NOW!' The amber lights became larger, larger. The water rushed around him, pulled him downward toward it. Danny opened his mouth to scream, but you needed air to scream and his lungs were filled with water.

'Free me!' Again and again, he sensed below him a mouth that could have swallowed his whole house back in Sydney, open wide in a maw of razor teeth and death.

The rushing became harder and faster and he could see it coming. The rows and rows of teeth that folded back like sharks, but these were long and piercing like a cat's. Each one fifteen feet in length. All of those teeth, the upper bank and the lower, and the dead centre of the darkness in its middle. The ever-hungry throat, the desire to feed. It all came over him, the teeth rushed past and he could smell the rot of the old flesh that was caught in the gums, chunks that were larger than him, caught there for decades in stasis below the surface. The darkness rushed up to meet him, closer and closer. Danny closed his eyes…

He sat up in bed, wet with sweat as his heart raced in his chest. Getting out of bed, he rushed to the mirror on the wall. Despite the fright, he looked a hell of a lot better. The bags under his eyes were mostly gone, the grogginess in his head was still there, but he figured it would disappear as he woke up. He slowed his breaths and forced them to become deeper and deeper. With each breath, his heart slowed and he felt the blood cool in his veins. He sat down on his bed and put his hands in the pocket of his hoodie. He frowned as his fingers brushed something.

'What the…' he muttered as he pulled a piece of paper from his pocket. 'I didn't…' He unfolded it. He stared blankly at the words for some time. He didn't have any paper in his pocket when he went to sleep; it was the same pocket that he had stored the tablets in, so he was sure of it.

The handwriting was not his own, that was another certainty.

He read the note again then glanced to the door. He had not latched it. A feeling of violation came over him as he examined the paper once more and forced himself to read it again.

Meet me in the hydroponics lab, when you wake.

14

EVERYTHING WAS FOREIGN, the world was at a disconnect with reality. Danny's hands felt wrong on his face, and he felt as though he was wearing someone else's clothes. The thoughts in his mind felt like intrusions of privacy, while the vision that was projected into his brain from his eyes, seemed to be awash with sepia tones. Every command that was sent through his nervous system was rife with mutiny and sloth. Even when his stomach grumbled in its discontent, Danny had thought that a small creature had entered the room, one of those small, bastard dogs that growled every time someone came into sight.

He held the note in his hand as he groggily made his way through the mess. Unaware of how long he had slept, he didn't know whether he needed to eat, shit, or vomit, but imagined that any of the above would aid in the position he was in. However, when any man is tired, hungover or ill, coffee will always be the first thing that he seeks. As the coffee ran down his throat, a pain shot through his guts, and he doubted whether he could keep it down.

He held the note up to his face again and considered the handwriting. The lines were almost childlike in their roundness and inconsistent spaces between letters. In his befuddled state, the first thought he had was of primary school and pen licences. How the teachers would come short of striking their students to instil the methods of slanted lines and loops. Cursive joints and fluent contact, all of the things a hopeful young apprentice would need to learn to be able to adopt the almighty ballpoint pen. Somehow, he doubted that the individual that authored this note wielded such a pen with a licence.

He took another sip of coffee and cringed as it burnt him all the way down. *Meet them in the hydro lab*, he thought with irritation. He didn't even know how long he had been asleep for, how they hell would they know to meet him now? The thought sloshed around in his mind like the coffee in his mug and as with the liquid, the longer it sat there the worse it tasted. He tipped the rest of his coffee down the drain, grabbed a muesli bar from Woollies and left through the cold porch.

The hydroponics lab was set off mostly by itself. As with the rest of the camp, the designers had refrained from building AANBUS structures too close to each other, as they were afraid of fire. This had always confused Danny; he couldn't understand why people would be concerned about fire in the coldest place on earth. But he supposed when air conditioners ran almost all the time, and a lot of heat ran through not only electrical wires but insulated pipes, anything was possible. When it came to concern about preserving their only source of regenerative food, the designers and research heads took absolutely every precaution.

The lab was situated right on the coast rather than inland. If someone were to stand back and look at the white, container-like structure, Danny wouldn't blame them for thinking it was a fridge. Perhaps in a past life it had been a fridge, but when one stepped inside the lab they were hit with heat and humidity that could be found nowhere else on this damned continent.

In line with further precautions, if the main powerhouse were to fail, and Danny's ice queen was unable to be started, at least the hydro lab had its own genny to run the lamps and the pumps. He had often taken the walk to the lab's spare generator to ensure that it worked and to 'exercise' it, but rarely had he stepped foot inside the structure itself.

The main reason for that was that it was a pain in the ass. The head researchers and the brain's trust had taken further precautions than just placing the structure out by itself. Each person that wished to be admitted had to go through the checklists; had they smoked or eaten then they would need to change clothes and wash vigorously. Even coming in contact with food before entering the garden could risk contamination with spores or spiders. How anything could survive in the bloody cold was beyond Danny, but nonetheless, he was not about to be paraded in front of everyone because he didn't follow the rules.

The cold porch for the garden labs was smaller than most, as generally there weren't too many people in the structure at one time. But as he entered, he saw something that made him pause. Another person's jacket, beanie, gloves and spray pants were folded on the stool. He didn't recognise them at a glance but already the questions rolled through his head. Danny muttered to himself through gritted teeth as he took off his over pants, jacket, beanie and gloves. The entire time he disrobed, he couldn't take his eyes from the clothes that sat there already discarded by their owner.

As he pushed through the door and into the garden, the heat hit him like a brick wall. Seventy per cent humidity and a constant twenty-five degrees of heat was like stepping into a sauna compared to the outside world. Green vines hung from the roof, looped over chords that had been run from edge to edge. Large rungs of tomatoes stood to attention at his left while cabbage, snow peas and fennel clung to their Rockwool cubes. Danny had once asked why they used fake cubes to grow stuff when they had such a great setup – if they used soil and fertiliser then they could make some monster 'Ganga'. He couldn't even remember who he had asked, maybe Wendy or James, but they had told him that even soil was prohibited on base and no foreign material was to be brought in.

As sweat started to line his forehead and Danny loosened the collar around his neck, he heard movement behind the tomato stalks. The one who had come into his room while he was sleeping came forward and revealed himself.

The figure was shorter than he had expected, and he wore a bright red jumper with some sports logo plastered across it that he didn't recognise. He wore tracksuit pants that were the grey type that Danny hated, mainly because when you had a piss everyone knew about it.

Bob Taylor's bald pate glowed red under the light and his flesh glistened with the sweat that ran down him.

'I… I was hoping that you'd come sooner,' he stammered, almost as if he was intimidated by the man he had summoned.

'Bob,' Danny said with disbelief. 'What the fuck are you doing?' He asked this for a few reasons, not only was he pissed off that he had been summoned here, but Bob was one of the most important people in this place – he was their link to the outside world. If Bob was away from his post, then any emergency contact, anything at all, would be missed until he returned.

'It's ok,' he said as he held both of his palms out in a calming motion. 'I got Gary to cover for me. He knows how to use everything so it's fine.'

Danny shook his head. 'How did you know I was awake and why did you come into my room?' He said this last part through gritted teeth.

Bob moved over to a section of snow peas and plucked a pod from the vine. 'In case of theft, there is actually a camera in each dorm hallway.' He threw the entire pod into his mouth and continued to talk as he munched away. 'We don't like to let that one be known.'

'And…?' Danny remarked, unamused.

'I came to talk to you, because I feel like you're one of the ones I can trust.' He spoke to his feet more than to Danny. 'Gary says the same.'

It was news to Danny that Gary hung around with Bob Taylor. To be honest, it was news to Danny that anyone did. Yet, he recalled that Gary was the one to work with Bob and offer him the coordinates of the ship.

'Trust me with what, Bob?' he said it irritably, and then felt bad when he saw the smaller man cringe at his tone. 'Look, I'm sorry. Anne gave me some tablets that kicked the crap out of me and now I feel like I've got a hangover to end all hangovers.' He took a step closer to him. 'What's up?'

Bob scanned the room again. His mouth moved as if he was talking but nothing came out. 'Do you remember… how I said I'd ask for those scans to be done?'

'The thermal scans of Amery?' Danny questioned, but he knew.

'Y... Yeah.' He made eye contact briefly, then looked away again. Someone that operated radios needed to be quick and sure-minded, but with the way Bob acted in front of him, Danny had no idea how he'd ever got into that position. 'Well, I got the results.'

Danny's eyebrows raised. 'Why are you telling me? Haven't you told Jonty?'

'Well, no, I haven't. I haven't told him, because it scares the shit out of me.'

'Bob, you're talking like you're about to confess to something. What's wrong? What did it show?'

Bob walked closer to him. As he moved, he pulled some folded pieces of paper out of his back pocket. It was then that Danny saw how his hands trembled. His thumbs struggled with the edges of the paper, and then he dropped them onto the floor. Danny sighed as he squatted to help the man. He picked up one of the papers and his eyes locked on the image.

That he was holding an aerial view of Amery, he had no doubt. He could even see the gargantuan D-28 in the left-hand side of the scan. The greys and the deep blues were one thing, but the line of the ice as it had separated was something distinct and something that he would remember for the rest of his life, so when he saw it on paper, he knew it at once. There was no way he would have been able to tell that the ship was there, as even a ship of that size was nothing when compared to the ice shelf and the size of its loose tooth. However, there was one section that drew his eyes to it, and as he thought about it more and more, it had to be where the ship was, it just couldn't be anywhere else. Through the dark blues, the greys and the blacks, a red spot glowed brilliantly on the page.

Danny put his finger to it. 'What the fuck is that?'

Bob had leant down next to him. He was a little too close for Danny's comfort but, given the shocking news, he didn't complain. Bob's eyes were wide. 'That's what I was worried about.'

Danny stood up and then rested his back against the framework that held the tomatoes. He held the scan in front of his face as he continued to examine it, gobsmacked. 'It has to be the ship or…'

'It can't be any ship,' Bob said flatly. 'Even the *Queen Mary* wouldn't show up that big, and steel isn't hot. If anything, the steel would come up black rather than the deep blues that you're seeing there. It's something else.'

'Nah.' Danny shook his head and handed it back to him. 'It's wrong man, run it again.'

Bob held it back to him. 'I did.' He looked deep into his eyes. 'I got them to run it three times, over a few days too.' He handed each different one over. 'If anything, it looks like it's getting hotter.'

Danny had to admit it. With each different scan, each different image, the red spot had grown in size with each consecutive date. The only thing that remained the same was the location. 'What could it be?'

Bob shrugged as his mouth made that soundless motion once more. 'The only thing it could be, well… from the reports anyway… is organic material. But to be able to be visible on a thermal scan, below six hundred feet of ice… I don't know how hot it would need to be.'

'Pretty bloody hot from the sounds of it,' Danny said as he looked at the images again.

'I… I even managed to get a scan that had perchance been taken a few weeks ago, and there was nothing.' He held out another piece of paper.

Danny took the page and rested it atop the others. Instantly, he saw the tell-tale outline of Amery. The way it shrank the further it came inland, but this was different than the rest. 'D-28?' Danny looked up at Bob. 'The tooth hadn't broken off?'

'No, not yet, the date that happened was the 25th.' He leant over to examine the page. 'This scan is from the 18th.'

'A full week before the break, and no heat signature?' Their eyes locked. 'You don't think that this heat caused that break?'

'Well, it's been loose for a long, long time,' Bob said.

'How long?' Danny asked as the pages fell to his side in his hand.

'I knew you'd ask this; I had the same thought.' A soft smile appeared on his face. 'The last time anything happened with Amery was in the sixties. They call it calving. It released another monster iceberg back then. It was over a hundred and forty kilometres long.'

'Christ,' Danny said. He lived in Western Sydney, for him to drive into North Sydney took him about an hour and half in traffic and it was only thirty kilometres. The distance he was talking was near enough out to Lithgow, and that included the entire Blue Mountains. 'Christ,' he repeated.

'You guys were worried that there was something attached to that cable.' He pointed at the spot again. 'Well, the answer is yes.'

Danny sat quiet, and looked at Bob's finger against the stark lines of the thermal scan. 'What now?'

'That's what I wanted to ask you,' Bob said in a tone that showed his disappointment. 'I've come to you for help here.'

'Mate, what do you want me to do?' He raised his voice and waved the papers. 'I'm a bloody diesel mechanic, not the head of this place. Why haven't you shown Jonty?'

Once more Bob's mouth moved as if he was talking, but nothing came out. 'Jonty... Jonty's been weird these last few days.'

Few days? Danny thought to himself as he rubbed at his eyes with the heels of his hands. *Jonty was born weird.* 'Weird, how?'

'He's been booting me out of my office to take calls,' he said in a stricken voice, as he peered over Danny's shoulder to make sure no-one had joined them in the room.

Danny screwed up his face. There was no need for Jonty to use Bob's office for communication; the only communications that came through Bob's office were from the government that owned the facility, and other bases stationed around the continent. For his own personal communication, Jonty, like everyone else, had their phone which used base wi-fi and he had his laptop for video calls. 'Why?'

'He wouldn't say.' Once more the short round man shrugged his shoulders; the sweat had continued to run down his face and had started to darken the neck of his hoodie. 'He just said it was confidential and related to the government and if I press it with him, he gets angry.

I've never really seen him angry before.'

Danny frowned. He thought about everything that had happened over the last few days. He thought about his conversation with Jonty, the talks about trust and distrust. Then he thought about the video camera, he thought about the conversation that Charlie had with him.

'Jonty wants everyone to trust him and to distrust everyone else. He wants Marie, Charlie and I at each other's throats while he works behind the scenes. And now this?' Bob waited expectantly for him to continue. *And this one is probably one of his, sent by the man himself to test my loyalty.*

'Tell him,' Danny said as he stood up. 'He's under a bit of pressure, old Jonty.' He forced a smile. 'I'm sure he'll be fine in a few days, tell him and he will work it out.'

Bob looked at him blankly, as if he'd been expecting a different answer. Danny considered him for a while, then slapped him on the shoulder. 'All good?'

Bob blinked as if the slap awakened something in him. 'Yeah, thanks for reassuring me.' Bob offered a brief smile and then gathered his papers and scurried for the door to the cold porch.

Danny let him go. He gave him a bit of time to get through the door and dress as he didn't want to be in that small room with him. Once he was sure that he was gone, he entered the room himself and dressed back into his outside wear. He thought about their conversation as he headed back to the Red Shed. He was sure that Jonty had sent Bob to test him, he was positive. His face screwed up into an angry snarl as he thought about the action of that treacherous bastard. *He was probably expecting me to run straight to Charlie. Maybe I should, would fix that mongrel and his schemes.*

The thoughts rolled over and over in his head. The anger that had settled in his stomach spread throughout him like a cancer. His fist clenched in their heavy padded gloves, his mouth a snarl of rage behind his balaclava, his eyes small hateful beads. He burst through the heavy insulated doors and slammed them behind him, hopeful that he pissed someone off. He sat down on the bench in front of his locker and reefed off his gumboots.

'How's it going, Happy?' The voice came from his side.

Danny snapped his head over as he pulled his other boot off and saw Gary sitting in front of his own locker, as he put on his own boots. 'Fan-fuckin-tastic,' he grumbled through his balaclava.

Gary laughed at his friend's mood. 'Bobby must have had a beauty for you then.'

Danny stopped. He turned his head slowly back to Gary. 'Bob?' The seeds of mistrust bloomed in his mind as the name rolled off his tongue. How had Gary known about their meeting? If Gary had known, who else had? Who else had Bob gone to before he had finally come to me? Who else had gone to Bob, before he had come to him? A thousand thoughts all at once.

'Yeah, he found you, didn't he?' Sincere as anything. Gary didn't wait for an answer, he just continued as if talking to himself. 'Seemed to be in a bother, said he needed to talk to someone he could trust and someone who could help him. So, I said you, you're the main man. Aren't you, Happy?'

Fuck. The thought was loud and clear in his head. Poor Bob had been genuine in his concern for all of them, and he had sent him right to the bloke he was afraid of. *Well done, Daniel.*

'Yeah mate, he found me,' he said in a sombre tone, the fight all at once taken out of him.

'That's good, he's not a bad bloke after all,' Gary said as he stood up and pulled his arm through one of his outer jacket's sleeves. 'Good to get another one on our side.'

Danny sat there off in his own world. 'Yeah, you know it man.' His voice seemed dreamy, almost not his own. 'You know it.'

15

'BABE, ARE YOU OK?' Her voice came to him like a siren's song. Through the fog of his mind, he was helpless but to follow her sweet sounds. 'Earth to Danny. Are you there?' With each sound, he was pulled further from the muck of his own mind, pulled back to reality. Back to her. 'Babe, seriously you're starting to scare me.'

'Huh?' He blinked and shook his head. The tears in his eyes made the light stretch out before his vision, like the old childhood superstition of spirits reaching for the sky. 'Oh, sorry chook.' He rubbed at his eyes, which only made the watering worse. He knew that when he opened his eyes again and faced the camera, they would be red as well as watery, Louise called them his 'bong rat eyes.' Each time he became tired or rubbed at his eyes, they would go the brightest red, replicating the eyes of a person who habitually smoked marijuana. He opened his eyes and looked at the blurry image of his partner, the woman he was soon to be attached to forever.

'Just finish punching a few cones?' The smile appeared at the corner of her mouth. Ever the lady, Louise Bastianich had been his staunchest supporter in this race of life. No matter the decision that needed to be made, he could always count on her to be by his side. Yet, if he thought that he would get through life without all of her little jokes, he was sorely mistaken. Maybe that was why he loved her.

'You know it.' He yawned through his smile.

'Alright, so what's going on?' Her face had taken a serious, stern look. 'You haven't been "here" lately Danny.'

Here we go, the thought rolled through the back of his head. *Time to get your knuckles rapped.* 'Yeah, I know, sorry chook. Just been pulling some big hours out here.'

'On what?' Her eyes were expectant, like she knew he was full of shit and she was waiting for him to put his foot further into his mouth.

'Oh, you know,' he shrugged. 'Just mechanical stuff. This and that. Bits and pieces.'

'Uh-huh.' Flat and indignant. She hadn't bought it. 'I've seen you work hard Danny; I like to think you are a hard worker, but this isn't it.'

'Come on babe, it's not that bad. I've just been tired, coupled with having trouble sleeping.'

'Trouble sleeping?' she repeated. She had a few tells when she wanted the conversation to go a certain way; he had already seen two of them. The first one was that she would give him a compliment, like he was a hard worker. Now started the repetition, she would let him run and give him all the line he wanted, like she was a pro game fisherman and he was the juicy trout, all puckered up and ready to bite. She would let him come in, with only the odd repetition here and there to entice him further into his story and then…

'Yes, I have been having trouble sleeping. But it's ok, Anne gave me some pills.'

'Pills?'

'Yes, I took some sleeping pills, that's probably why I have been zonked out. But its ok, I've stopped taking them now and I'm fit as fiddle. Anne says she's happy.'

'Well, I'm glad "Anne" is so happy.' And then came the strike. 'Is she there now? Is that why you're so distant?'

When a fish is hooked, there isn't anything left for it to do but fight, thrash and play the game. Sometimes he'd get off the hook, other times he wouldn't and he'd be sucked right into the maw of the fisherman's net. 'Well actually, she's under the table right now, that soft tapping is actually her head hitting the table top.' Sometimes it pays to know you're living in a catch-and-release pond. The silence was thick and volatile. Her eyes burnt into his face.

Two seconds, five seconds.

He watched her face intently. The corner of her mouth twitched, and then the sound he had been waiting for, finally came. She laughed.

Their conversation flowed a lot better after that. Her jokes came back quick and sharp, she said that even if he had another woman under there, the joke would be on them as she had given him herpes before he left. Beyond it all, it was the best medicine he could have gotten, having talked to her. She lit up his days with her smile, her eyes were like torches in the dark. He frowned at that thought, as it made him think of the eyes in his dream and the way they loomed below him. The way they looked through him, like the eyes of an ancient and powerful predator. He thought about the thermal scans, and that menacing red dot that had appeared on a scan that should have only shown the deep, dark ice.

'Babe?'

'Sorry chook,' he started again.

'This seems to be becoming a common occurrence,' she muttered to herself but loud enough for him to hear. Another one of her tricks.

'Lou, it isn't.'

'Well explain the other night then?' Her mouth tensed as she brushed a line of her dark hair away from her eyes.

His face screwed up as he tried to work out what she was talking about – one thing was for sure, he hadn't come onto the call to get interrogated. 'What do you mean the other night?'

'Oh, don't remember that one?' Another trick, but this one was a dangerous one. 'Maybe it's just my imagination then, is that what you're saying?' Sarcasm meant that she was getting angry; if she were a rattle snake, it would be her rattle, her warning.

'Babe, I don't know what you're talking about,' he tried to watch his tone but failed.

'I came onto this call to talk to you because I miss you.' She almost yelled this last part. 'I don't want to see you zone out on me and stare at the screen for half an hour.'

'What?' He screwed his face up even more. 'Nah, I didn't do that.'

'Babe, half an hour I sat here trying to get your attention, like just now. But I couldn't wake you up.'

'So, I fell asleep?' Now he was curious.

'No, you just… zoned out. I would've thought that the line just dropped out and the screen had frozen, like it always does, but I could see you breathing. You just sat there, eyes open, staring at the screen and nothing would touch you.'

He had no answer for this, no explanation. He thought about his seizure on the ship, he thought about the film he had deleted, now this. Nothing good could come of this.

'Like I said,' he tried, 'I've been really tired. No joke, when I took those pills, I think I slept for a day straight.'

Her eyes had become sad. Her lips hadn't begun to quiver and he didn't think she was going to cry on him, but he could tell that she wasn't happy. Not in an angry way; she wasn't like that. Truthfully, she wasn't. 'Are you sure?'

'Yes Hun, I'm sorry. I'll make sure not to punch cones before our calls and I'll have a few cups of coffee instead.'

'Promise?' Both sides had raised the white flags, it was time to sign the treaty for a night.

'Promise.'

For the briefest of moments they admired each other. Confident in their relationship and their love for one another. The soft smiles on their faces the only thing that showed their content, their happiness of just being able to see each other.

'How are the videos coming along?' she asked, changing the subject away from him and onto their child. Danny was happy for this respite of constant bombardment of his own mental health. As everyone on camp had already demonstrated, the best way to make sure someone is not ok is to constantly ask them if they are.

'They're coming along,' he said happily, then sighed. 'It's been a few days since I've done one though.' He rubbed at his chin and felt the gravel of his stubble bite into his hand, it always itched when it got to that crossover point between being stubble and being a beard. 'I'm trying to have something of interest in each video, you know? Like something cool to show the kid.'

Louise nodded as the smile reappeared on her face, and she turned her face.

'Have you watched any of them?' he asked curiously.

She returned her eyes to him and shook her head. 'No, I just…. I feel weird watching them, they're meant for the baby, not for me. I don't feel like it's my place.'

He laughed as he let his face fall into his hands. *Bloody woman*, he thought, *spent the last half an hour prying into my wellbeing but won't watch a video made for her unborn child.* 'Chook, can you just make sure they're there? Marty set up this thing on my phone so that once I record one it goes to the folder online.'

She nodded enthusiastically. 'Oh yeah, they're there. I get notifications every time you do one.'

'Alright then,' he sighed; he didn't care. In the end he probably would be embarrassed if she had watched them anyway. The way any man felt when he openly displayed his feelings. 'Before you go, let me see your gut.'

'Don't call it that,' she said crossly.

'Come on, whip it out.' He laughed.

She stood up and even under her oversized hoodie he could see the size of her. Still, when she lifted the hoodie over her girth, he gasped. She looked as though she was ready to burst, even her belly button seemed to be inverted. 'Oh baby,' he said in a perverted voice.

'Yeah, you like that?' She egged him on in a seductive voice. 'How about these.' She pulled her hoodie up a little higher so that he could see the full roundness of her breasts. She held the fabric just shy enough so that he couldn't see the brown ripeness of her nipples but that was ok. Even from here he could see that even they had grown.

'Look at that,' he whispered as he felt himself become hard.

A knock came from his door, three sharp rasping beats, then the door opened and a man's head leant in through the crack. 'Danny, you in here?'

'Jesus Christ,' Danny said as he shoved his laptop screen to the side so Jonty couldn't see Louise. 'Don't just barge in here man.' Through the computer he heard Lou scream and in the short second before he lost sight of her, he saw her body drop down out of view from the camera.

The expression Jonty gave him in the instant before he pulled his head back was of pure loathing. His eyes flat and depthless, his lip curled at the edge in the beginnings of a snarl. Then the door slammed shut and his face was gone.

'Motherfucker,' Danny said as he slammed his fist down on the desk, not caring that Jonty would've heard. 'You ok Lou?' he moved the computer and saw her face once again.

'Yeah, what happened?' She truly was beautiful. He loved the way her big eyes looked at him through this damned screen. In that instant, he would've given anything just to be back with her.

'Fuckin boss walked in. Anyway, he's probably still standing there waiting, so I better go. Love you.'

'Love you too, get some sleep,' she said with a smile, as she smoothed her hoodie over her body.

'Yeah, you know it.' He hit the disconnect button and stood up. The speed at which her face disappeared from the screen could only be matched by the speed at which his erection had died in his pants. Irritated, he stormed to the door and tore it open.

Jonty stood there, almost too close to the door. The sight of his face enraged Danny again. 'Listen here man.' He pointed his finger in his face. 'Don't you ever barge into my room again, you understand me?'

'Calm down, Daniel.' Flat and indignant, not even a speck of emotion.

'Don't you fuckin' "Daniel" me,' he said through gritted teeth. 'I could've been in there with Marie fucking Swan for all you know. In future, you knock and wait for me to answer before you walk into my room. You may be the head researcher here and my boss, but that doesn't give you the right to everything. Understand?'

'I need you to go and pick up the Hägglund that was left on Amery.'

He didn't even react to the words that Danny had just blasted him with. 'Gary will be leaving in an hour to take yourself and Charlie Muscat up there.'

'What, why?' Danny came back, the fight sucked out of him.

'You said it yourself Daniel, you didn't want that machine left on Amery. It has been over a week now and the time to bring it back is now. Weather reports for the next few days aren't looking great.' He blinked for the first time since Danny had opened the door. 'I suggest you get your things. Unless Marie has any objections?' He made to peer over Danny's shoulder and into his room.

Danny didn't say a word as Jonty's eyes returned to him and lingered. Caught almost in a childish game of staring, where neither party wanted to show their weakness by blinking, each man held their gaze. Yet, the game didn't continue for long; Jonty blinked, and started to walk away. Danny watched him go down the long corridor, back to the mess hall, back to communications. He thought about the red spot on that thermal again. He honestly thought that would've been what the conversation was about, but once again he was proven wrong. Once again, he was being sent to that damned place, where that damned ship was and whatever lay below.

16

EVERYTHING SEEMED A BLUR. Everything he saw seemed skewed. Everything he heard seemed like it came from a television that was in another room. The blades of the R44 beat the air overhead, but when Danny closed his eyes, that wasn't what kept them afloat. As if in the palm of a giant's hand, the chopper moved up and down through the air, like in the motion of each step.

Gary sat at the controls and swore while red lights illuminated his face. The sky outside was as hostile as the sea below them, and as the cabin of the chopper pitched and yawed, it became more and more difficult to tell the two apart. Lightning struck at them from the heavens, as large reaching waves clawed up at them from the depths. Ice showered down around them; large chunks blown to pieces by some unnatural force. Sweat lined Gary's brow and his beard was caked in blood. Each time the red light flashed and illuminated his face, the years seemed to advance, until nought was left but skull and gaping pits where his eyes had been.

That's what we are, when you get right down to it, Danny thought as he waited for the doom. *Just an empty cup, with nothing left to pour out.*

Yet, when he opened his eyes, everything was calm, everything was fine. So, with each lingering breath that his body drew, he found himself pondering yet another philosophical conundrum. What was the dream and what was the reality? That was the basis of his question, but as with so many things, when the door had been opened to let in a welcomed visitor, other things had slipped through the crack. Things that weren't as welcome as the smiling guest, things that lingered and festered. Those with black fingers that clawed at the dreamer's mind. Those with eyes larger than anything, that sat low in the depths of the mind waiting for their moment, waiting for their freedom.

He opened his eyes and yawned as the sleep left his mind. He scanned the cabin and saw his calm friend by his side. The sun sat low in the sky, but it always sat low to them. Nevertheless, no cloud stood before its warmth, nothing blotted out its light. The cabin shook and shuddered sporadically as bursts of wind hammered into its side, but otherwise the R44 sailed through the air like a kite guided by its string.

'Catch them when you can, huh?' Gary's voice came through the headphones, audible above the wind and the whistling blades.

Danny took in the scene and saw his friend behind the controls, as he had been in his dream. Gary's face was focused on him, which left Danny feeling uneasy, just as he would've felt uneasy in a car where the driver's attention wasn't on the road. However, a Sydney highway and the skies above the Antarctic coast were two very different things.

'What's that man?' Danny asked as he blinked and rubbed his eyes. He yawned again as if unable to stop. Christ, he was tired. Never in his life had he been this run down.

'Sleep,' Gary said. The smile remained on his face. There was something to be said about men that didn't really care about anything, who always seemed to be happy. 'You've been out since Mawson.'

Danny looked around, he had no idea where they were, how far they had come or how long they had spent in the air. 'Yeah,' he sighed. 'You know it, man.' To be honest, he couldn't even remember getting on the chopper in the first place.

He peered into the back of the cabin and saw Charlie there. The last time he'd seen the man was when he had squatted outside of Jonty's room. Even then he hadn't really gotten a good look at him. Charlie had aged ten years since he had stepped foot on that ship. Maybe Charlie had been having the same problems with sleep that he had.

Danny blinked as he considered the older man. His eyes felt dry and old. Christ, his whole body felt dry and old, and if his appearance was anything like Charlie's, as he slept against the cabin door, then he could understand why he felt the way he did.

'That's good you're getting some sleep, man. Hell, it looks like you need it.' Gary kept the conversation going.

How the hell was he supposed to answer that? Each time he slept, the dreams would stir in the depths of his mind. Horrors that swelled beneath a shadowy surface, or lurked behind a smoky screen, to the point where it wasn't even the dreams that kept him awake, but just the notion of them. Rest was what he needed, but it had been some time since rest could be found when his eyes closed for the night.

'What are you on about?' Danny rebuked as he pressed down on the open mic button with his left foot and shot a sideways glance at their pilot.

'You look like hammered shit,' Gary said, laughing. 'Even Charlie looks like shit. Jonty has always looked like shit. I'd say that going out to Amery has done something to you guys, but Marie is looking hotter by the minute.' He took a breath and shook his head. 'Christ, I saw her yesterday with these tight little yoga pants on. If I was a married man like yourself, I would seriously think about the value of half my shit.' Gary shuffled in his seat and moved his legs and laughed. 'I'd have to have a hell of a lot more than I do now to pass that up.'

It had been some time since he had seen Marie. To be honest, he didn't know how long. It had struck him as odd when Jonty had told him that it had been a week since their return from Amery. The best he could work out, it had only been four days. He knew that he had lost time to the tablets, but that long?

'Hey what's the date?' he asked.

'The date?' Gary asked him. 'Don't know, don't care,' he said this in an American accent. 'Date makes no mind to me, only the time of the day and hey its five o'clock somewhere in the world, right?'

Danny gave him a blank expression. 'Piss head.'

'Hey don't be jealous now.' Gary laughed again. 'It's not my fault you didn't bring enough.'

To some extent, this had been true enough. Once the last supply ship docked around February or March, there was no way to get anything on the continent. If you didn't bring enough to sort out your own habits, then that was your own problem, no-one else's. In one way, this problem combined with the cold was enough to make Danny give up cigarettes, but a drink of scotch every now and then, was no-one's enemy. Gary on the other hand had brought ample supply of the good stuff. It was said that when his green F100 had pulled up at Melbourne's port, the entire back was full of liquor, only a single duffel bag that contained his clothes had been strapped to the top.

The conversation died. Danny pulled his phone from his pocket in an attempt to satisfy his curiosity of what the date actually was. He thumbed past the phone's home screen and hovered over the picture of his beautiful Louise for half a second before he moved on. His eyes locked on that small tab, the seven that seemed to haunt him with every passing second. If that was right, then it had been a week and half since they had been to that ship. How many tablets had he taken? How many did Anne give him in the first place? How many days had he lost? Hell, he couldn't even tell how many days he could account for, let alone how many he had lost.

He looked back to Charlie, who sat there almost collapsed against the cabin door. Was he in the same boat? How many days had they lost together? What picture could they make together? Could he be trusted? All thoughts that stemmed back to the ship, back to Jonty and that game that they were intwined in.

'There she is,' Gary said chirpily through the radio once more. 'Red Brick, safe and sound.'

The Hägglund they had driven out to Amery sat in the same position that he had left it in. The glass had turned to the same icy frost that remained on the ship countless feet below. Snow had built up around its tracks but nothing seemed serious about its position, only that it would be bloody cold and he figured the batteries would all be flat; the cold seemed to have a knack for sucking the life out of any battery.

The way the vehicle sat there, almost abandoned in the centre of the ice shelf, reminded Danny of that damned scan that Bobby had shown him. It even looked like the red spot on the map. Danny didn't know what to expect. Part of him thought that the ice would've heated so much that the Hägglund itself would've fallen down into the centre of the shelf, never to be seen again. But here as they came up, it didn't seem like anything had changed whatsoever. D-28, still as magnificent as ever, sat off the cliff face, perhaps a few hundred feet further away at its furthest point, but it seemed as though its progress was as slow as anything. He supposed that when something was a few hundred years old, it wasn't in a rush to get anywhere.

'Want to check out the ship?' Gary asked, his eyes locked on Danny's.

'Man, no thanks. I just want to get that piece of shit running and get back to Mawson.'

The expression that Gary gave him was one that suggested that he didn't believe his ears. He shook his head slightly as he raised his eyebrows and looked back out the windscreen. 'Righto boss,' he said in an American accent as he gave the cyclic a twist and the R44's engine changed its pitch. Gary took them closer to the Hägglund and performed a dramatic circle around the vehicle.

'Just don't piss off on me as soon as you land,' Danny said. 'I got make sure I can start this thing first.'

Gary nodded without a word in reply, as he brought the chopper down to a gentle rest on the ice shelf. He powered it down, and they all sat and waited for the brake to engage and halt the rotors before they stepped out. The cabin shook as the brake pulled up the motion and Danny saw that Charlie had woken up.

'You right?' he asked.

Charlie stared at him as if he was unaware where he was or what he was doing there. Danny knew how he felt. 'Yeah,' he answered with a yawn and he stretched his arms. 'All good.'

Danny caught Gary's eyes as he shook his head. Gary smiled at him, his headphones were now pulled down around his neck. 'Two peas in a pod, huh? Don't fall asleep driving the slow boat, ok?'

A ghost of a smile appeared on Danny's face. He popped the cabin door and shuddered as he stepped out into the cold.

He was right about the batteries and the way they lasted in the cold; the turn of the key only emitted a low growl as the starter struggled to turn. Danny frowned beneath the folds of his balaclava as he made his way back to the R44 where his tools were. He pulled his lithium jump pack from his bag and took it back to the Hägglund. A few minutes later, the Red Brick was rumbling away and the frost on the windscreen faded beneath the heat of its demisters.

As Danny packed his tools, Charlie and Gary loaded the spare fuel they had dragged along in the chopper's side baskets, into the back compartment of the brick. There was enough diesel there to get to Mawson and back to the shelf again, but more than enough fuel was safe, not enough fuel was death, and a little extra weight never hurt anyone. Once the last of his tools were loaded in amongst the fuel, Danny looked back to Gary and shrugged as he clapped his hands together. 'All good?'

'Yeah man,' Gary said as he headed over to them. 'Stay safe, huh? I'll get Bobby to check on you guys every hour, ok?'

'You know it. Fly safe man.'

Danny and Charlie watched from the warmth of the cabin as Gary fired up his R44 and it lifted into the air. They had barely spoken a word to each other, and still they remained in silence until the last speck of the chopper was gone. The diesel rattled beneath them as Danny swivelled in his chair to face the older man. They considered each other for some time before Danny threw the brick into gear and they began their long trip home.

Their trip remained somewhat silent. Danny for the most part swore continuously as they first began to move, as the location that they had entered the ice shelf from was gone. The landscape looked different, and where Danny thought he had driven down the snow-encrusted rocky slope to reach the shelf, there was now a large rift between land and ice. He even stepped out to see if anything was familiar to him, but he couldn't be sure. He returned to the warmth of the cabin and continued down further toward the narrowest point of the inlet and the ice shelf.

Eventually he found a section that seemed flat and stable enough for him to drive the square vehicle off the ice and back onto the land.

The diesel laboured as it carried them up the incline and further away from the ice. The higher they climbed, the better he felt and the more he felt like talking. Charlie however sat motionless, his eyes fixated on the windscreen. The Hägglund took them along the ridgeline that bordered Amery, down by the nunataks that Danny had almost run the tracks up on their journey here. For two hours it laboured and continued to drag them across the snow, ice and stone back to Mawson.

'Red Brick. Red Brick. This is Mawson, do you copy?' Bob Taylor came through over the two-way.

Danny's eyes went to the microphone and he began to reach for it but Charlie beat him to it.

'This is Red Brick. We have you loud and clear Mawson. Over.' His voice was surprisingly alert. Danny had thought that the older man had been close to being unconscious, yet his voice could not have sounded more aware.

When Bob came back, he was almost as shocked as Danny was. 'Oh. Charlie hey. Just checking in and making sure you're all good. Over.'

Charlie still didn't look at Danny. The microphone went to his mouth; his voice sounded cheerful but there was no smile on his face. 'We are fine, Bobby. Everything is fine. Over.'

There was a short pause, and Charlie had obviously expected for Bobby to come back as he hadn't hung up the microphone as of yet. Sure enough, a few seconds later: 'Danny, you ok?'

Once more the mic went to Charlie's mouth. 'Danny's fine, Bobby. We're ok. Over.'

Once more there was another pause, as if Bobby was thinking what to do.

'Hey can I have that?' Danny asked Charlie. 'I want to see if Gary got back ok.'

Wordlessly and without eye contact, Charlie handed the mic over to Danny. Danny took it, and raised it quickly to his mouth. 'Hey Bobby, its Danny. Gary get back, ok? Over.'

Almost instantly Bob came back, the sound of relief in his voice was obvious. 'Yeah Danny, yeah he's fine. He's here now with me. Over.'

'Hey Bobby, how did you go with your problem. All good?' He tried it on for size. Curious to see if he would get a rise out of anyone on either end.

'You'll see when you get back,' Bob said, sullen. 'How long? Couple of hours? Over.'

Danny stole another quick glance at Charlie, his back was still straight and his eyes had not moved from the windscreen. 'Yeah. At least. Over.'

'Ok. There's a camp meeting in a few hours, Danny. But that doesn't matter.' Once more his voice was flat.

'What do you mean?' He cut through the transmission.

'I… I can't talk now, but the decision's been made, Danny. It's already happened.'

Danny let the Hägglund come to a halt. 'Ok Bobby, you stick with Gary, ok? We will talk when I get back. Over.'

He shifted in his chair to face Charlie as he hung up the mic and Bobby's voice came back. 'Ok, Red Brick. Out.'

'Charlie,' he said in a firm voice. 'Look at me.'

Charlie's head didn't move, his mouth twitched and eyes rolled around in his head but he didn't look at Danny.

'Charlie,' he tried again, 'what do you know?'

His mouth twitched again, and his body almost spasmed as if he was fighting against himself, half of him with the order to move, the other half to sit still.

Danny began to reach for him. Charlie spasmed again, and his eyes rolled around in his head as his mouth spread into a grimace.

'I can't stand it,' he said through gritted teeth. 'I can't stay here anymore.' His voice was a high, harsh whisper, as if he was about to cry. 'I don't want to anymore. I just want to get out.'

His hands went to his collar and began to loosen the jacket ties that clung around his neck. 'I can't breathe. I just want to get out.'

'Hey,' Danny said as he pulled his hand back slightly, 'it's ok, man.'

'I want to get out. I want to get out. I want to get out.' With each repetition his voice became higher and faster. 'I want to get out.'

Danny opened his door and stepped out as Charlie began to sway back and forth with his hands around his own throat. Danny slammed his door shut and raced around the front of the Hägglund. Through the windscreen he saw that Charlie had begun to thrash about wildly. Even through the wind that had started to pick up, he could hear him howl. He reefed open his door and had to step back as Charlie's arm swung out at him.

'I want to get out. I want to get out,' the man wailed as his eyes rolled back into his head. Danny reached forward and tried to get a hold of him through his flailing arms. He copped a smack to the side of his head and his feet slid in the snow slightly, but he still had a hold of Charlie and that prevented him from falling.

'Charlie!' Danny screamed at the top of his lungs. 'Fuck. Calm down man!' He struggled out as he fought to restrain him.

'I want to get out!' the older man bellowed as his legs kicked and thrashed.

'Alright!' Danny roared as he dragged Charlie out of the cabin and into the snow.

Charlie screamed as if he was on fire as his face touched the snow. Danny pushed himself away from him and sat up as he watched Charlie Muscat flail and thrash. His gloved hands clawed at his throat and his eyes as he rolled around on the ground and gasped for air. 'Lemme out, lemme out, lemme out.' In his hysteria, the words had formed one inconsolable wail until not even the singular phrases could be understood.

Charlie kicked the body of the Hägglund hard with his shin and Danny heard something crack but Charlie didn't falter in his movements; he continued to roll and thrash and scream and fight. His eyes bulged from their sockets and his tongue came out of his mouth too far. He clung to his neck and strained in a final gurgle and then his body fell limp and laid still there in the slush.

'Fuck me drunk,' was all Danny could say, the same thing he had said when he had seen the creature. Danny got to his knees and crawled to

Charlie's side. He grabbed the collar of his jacket with both hands and shook him. 'Come on man. Not like this, come on!' He shook again and again while Charlie's head lolled about. His mouth hung open and nothing came out, no breath, no scream, no sigh. His eyes moved in their sockets but he could only see the whites and the veins that seemed to bulge out of the surface.

'Charlie, man. Come on.' Danny shook him again. 'Fuckin' wake up!' he screamed into his face. Then the eyes snapped back, they rolled around the right way, and focused hard on Danny's. Two hands came up hard on either side of Danny's face and gripped him with a strength that surprised him. Charlie leant up out of the slush and pressed his face hard against his own, their eyes were so close they were almost touching.

His mouth moved, but Danny couldn't see it, he could only feel the whiskers of his beard rub against the older man's as he screamed in his face. 'Free me!'

17

DANNY PULLED HIS HEAD BACK with all of his strength, but it was not enough. Charlie's two hands crushed down on his skull from either side while he screamed into his face. He could smell the thickness of peanut butter on his breath from his breakfast before they had left. He felt the hot breath and the spit against his lips as the crazed man put every ounce of air into screaming those two words that had haunted him from the small screen of Marty's camera. 'Free me!' They stretched on and on and on.

Danny pushed both of his gloved hands into Charlie's face and pushed back with everything he had. Inch by inch, he felt the heat of the man dissipate as the distance between them increased. He shifted his hands while his arms laboured against his attacker's. Charlie's fingernails bit into his skin through the gloves that padded them. Danny shifted his hand again and somewhat muffled the continuous stream of shrieks that hammered his ears. He pushed up hard with one hand under Charlie's chin while the other remained on his face and then finally, the screams stopped. The relief on his ears was one thing but not only did the pressure on either side of his head double, he also felt Charlie's jaws close on his fingers.

At once, screams filled the air again but this time they were his own.

Pain shot up his wrist, down his neck, and a pulse had started in the middle of his head. His scream of pain turned slowly to one of rage as he summoned his strength and pushed back on the older man with all that he had. Years of heavy lifting, hard work, and tough bolts to break had made his body into one of iron and grease; when he called on his strength, it was ready and waiting. The grip around his head struggled at first and then broke as strips of flesh were torn from his cheeks by the fingernails that had now cut through the fabric of the gloves.

The chill struck anew at re-exposed flesh as blood started to stream down his cheeks in ribbons to form at the ball of his chin. Danny swore. His first reaction was to hold his face, but as he pulled the gloves away and he saw the blood stain his cotton palms, the anger swelled in him and his eyes raised to Charlie.

Charlie was clambering to his feet in the slush as he muttered hysterically to himself. Every now and then he would bark a short sharp shriek of horror, as his teeth gnashed and his eyes bulged from their sockets. Danny rose to meet him, his fists clenched.

As the two men came together, both of Danny's hands came up to seize Charlie by his throat while his flailing arms and thrashing legs caused an onslaught of glancing blows and near misses. Danny deflected Charlie's attack as he stepped in the other direction and the older man rushed past him to collapse into the slush once more.

His breath had become hot in his lungs and the pounding had become an incessant drone in his mind. Steam rushed from his mouth with each exhale as Danny closed in once more. He felt like a powerful bull, unstoppable and undeterred. Charlie had half risen when Danny's first blow struck him hard in the face. Before his body went back into the slush, Danny felt Charlie's nose crumple. As he fell back, he saw the blood on Charlie's chin that had spurted from the ruin that he had left. Charlie screamed in rage and desperation as he rolled in the slush, leaving blood streaks through the snow as he went. He regained his feet and considered Danny with eyes as empty as a rabid dog's.

'Free!' he wailed as he threw his head back and charged.

Danny stepped back and felt the heavy steel of the Hägglund at his back. His foot slipped in the slush and one of his legs went out from under him.

'Me!' Charlie roared as he closed the gap. Danny struggled on one knee to evade the blow.

There was a tremendous hollow clump as flesh slammed into metal. One of Charlie's knees hit Danny high in the chest while a fist slammed hard into the side of his face. Danny felt another rush of anger fill his head while blood ran down his neck and pooled at the lip of his hoodie. Charlie staggered back; his ruined nose had smeared across his face in his impact with the steel side of the Hägglund. Blood ran down his upper lip and pooled in his mouth where two rivers of overflow ran down either side of his gape. He tried to scream and instead coughed a large cloud of bloody mist into the air. He tried to breathe in and must have taken more blood on his inhale as he was reduced to a coughing mess.

This was the respite that Danny needed to get to his feet. He spat a bloody splotch of snot and sinew into the snow at his feet.

This time, he charged.

He drove his shoulder into Charlie's gut and lifted him high into the air. With a roar, he drove Charlie down into the slush. The air that remained in the man rushed out in another cloud of blood that rose into the air and settled on Danny's back.

Danny lifted himself and pinned Charlie's arms down to either side with his legs.

His fist slammed again and again into the older man's face, and with each sickening thud, more blood spread from his nose to run across his lips and down into the pits that held his eyes. With each fist fall, he lost himself further to the rage that had built up inside of him.

Danny screamed and screamed and screamed. Louder and louder, with each punch, pain worked its way up his forearm and deep into the rotator cuff of his shoulder. But he didn't stop; he couldn't stop. Fuelled by the fire within him, his anger had taken control and he was helpless but to watch as Charlie's features spread out over his skull and his gasps for air became strangled by the blood that Danny had spilt.

Finally, with one last tremendous, crashing blow, Danny brought his whole body down on his old friend and sucked air in as the rage within him passed on.

Danny leant back, while his knees remained on the older man's arms. His breath was hot and steam seemed to arise from more than just his mouth. A haze sat above Charlie Muscat, waves and swirls of steam came from his face, or the blood that covered it. A cloud of it hung around Danny as if it were scavengers waiting for their turn. His face was hot with the wounds that Charlie had given him, but all the heat and all the blood was low on his face, so his eyes were clear enough to see what he had done.

Charlie lay below him, motionless.

Danny would have liked to have thought that he had just knocked him out, but the puddle of blood that streamed down from the cavity where his nose had been, suggested otherwise. If he had tried to breathe, he would have to cough. Either that or succumb and drown in the blood that had once coursed through his veins.

Danny's chest heaved as the rage cooled. 'What have I done?' His voice trembled, almost stumbling over the steam that it carried. 'What have I done?' He held out his hands so that he could see the blood that covered the cotton underlays, bright reds mixed with the heavy, dark clots.

He fell off Charlie. 'Oh fuck. Fuck. Fuck,' he whimpered as he covered his face with his hands, then quickly recoiled from the mess that covered them. Danny didn't know what to do, he didn't know what would happen. He needed help and he needed it now.

He clambered back to his feet, his breaths short and sharp as his body began to shake. Slowly, he staggered back to the Hägglund. His legs began to cramp and pain shot in all directions through his body and his head. Leaning through the already open passenger door, he clutched for the microphone of the UHF.

'Bobby!' he screamed through the mic. 'Fuck me.' He struggled with himself off the air, as he almost slipped again. 'Bobby, goddamn it, are you there?'

The voice that came back was cold and flat. He knew it at once. 'Hello, Daniel.'

Instantly fear shot back up through Danny's spine. Half propped against the door, with one hand clasped on the dashboard to steady himself, he stared at the mic in his hand.

'Are you there, Daniel?' The voice came again.

'Fuck!' He screamed into the open air without depressing the button. Should he wait to talk to Bobby? Would Bobby ever come back? It didn't matter, none of it did. What had happened had happened, and he had defended himself. He depressed the button and this time when he spoke, he was a little calmer. 'Jonty? Is that you?'

'Yes, Daniel,' he came back, cool as ice.

'I… I…' How was he supposed to say it?

'Yes, Daniel?'

'Charlie went… Charlie went insane, Jonty.' He took a breath and shook again as his heart climbed up to nestle in his throat. 'He attacked me.'

The silence was murder, a strangling force that crippled him into submission. Each second that passed was another tonne of weight on his chest, another inch that his lungs could not expand.

'Where is Charlie now?' There was no emotion in that voice, no concern for Danny's safety.

'He's dead, Jonty,' Danny said flatly. There was no point in denying it. 'He kept coming at me, he wouldn't stop. I killed him.'

Silence. The wind started to rise around him and the howl came long and low through the air. The sound of it sent more shivers up his spine. He was alone. Alone, with the man that he had killed.

'Jonty?'

'Yes, Daniel?'

'What the fuck do I do now, Jonty!?' He screamed into the microphone.

'Can you bring him back, Daniel?'

Danny stared at Charlie's body. The way he just laid there; his eyes no longer visible under the pools of blood that covered then. He turned away in a grimace. 'Yeah, I… I can do that.'

'Good, Daniel. Good.' Silence again.

He stared at the mic for a full minute, waiting for more than just 'good.'

Nothing came. 'Jonty?' He yelled into the mic as the wind's howl had become more ferocious.

'Yes, Daniel?' The voice was cool to the point of cold again. Not even shaken by the loss of one of his team members.

'Where's Bobby?' he asked, fear for the entire camp running through him now. It wasn't just him that was in danger. It was everyone now.

'Bobby…' the voice repeated, almost in an attempt to recall who belonged to the name, 'he is having a rest; I gave him the evening off.'

'Bullshit you motherfucker,' Danny swore to himself aloud without depressing the button. There was no point in asking him more. He threw the mic back into the cabin and didn't even bother to hang it up on its cradle. He slammed the passenger door shut, so that at least when he was ready to leave this damned snowy outcrop, the cabin would be warm. He returned to Charlie and sighed. 'Come on, man. Let's get you home.'

The exchange with Jonty had left Danny cold. He refused to call whatever that was a conversation. The panic was gone, but a stone of anger and dread sat in his stomach. Scenarios played in his mind over and over as he stood there and considered Charlie's body. He was over two hours away from Mawson. He didn't know what frightened him more: two hours alone with his own thoughts, or two hours knowing that a man he'd just killed – his friend – was in the back compartment.

He gritted his teeth as he knelt next to Charlie and pushed his head to the side. The blood ran from his depths of his eyes and left a smear of scarlet across the side of his face as it ran to the slush below. After that image, Danny figured that anything red and liquid would be off the table for him when it came to food, he just couldn't get the image out of his head. He couldn't understand how something so thick and so vital could merge with the snow that quick. How could it stick to his face to create a hot, sticky mess and then just melt away and be nothing more than food colouring in the next.

The distance between the back end of the Hägglund and where Charlie lay was only a mere few feet, but in the slush and the ice, it may as well have been a few miles. At first Danny tried to do the right thing by the body and pick it up, but as he took more and more of the weight in his arms, it became harder and harder to keep his balance. At one point, he fell and came face to face once more with the older man. Danny's nose touched the place where Charlie's had once been. He felt the warmth, the stickiness and he saw the redness remain as he pulled his face away. His stomach rolled and clenched. He managed to turn his head enough to avoid vomiting on Charlie's body, however he was not able to save himself from the same fate.

Dirty, sticky, and with a horrible feeling in his stomach and head, he looped his arms beneath Charlie's pits and dragged him the rest of the way. If getting him to the vehicle was difficult then getting him into it seemed impossible. The man weighed roughly ninety kilograms, which was Danny's equivalent. Although Danny had more muscle than fat to his body, it made little difference when he tried to lift Charlie's dead weight into the rear compartment. Finally, exhausted and near the end of his tether, Danny had dragged Charlie in. Danny's wish to try and save Charlie's body from further damage had finally been superseded by the need to get moving.

He stood at the back of the compartment. Charlie's body lay over the tent and blankets that they had slept in together not even a fortnight ago.

Danny shook his head. It felt like years had passed, to see a photograph of them back then to now, he was sure that anyone would've agreed. 'I'm sorry man,' he said to Charlie. 'You needed help. Now I need it.' He closed the door and entered the cabin.

18

HE WOULD'VE LIKED to have said that he had driven the entire way back to Mawson in silence. He would have even preferred to have slipped into another transient state, to rock back and forth and mutter to himself as Charlie had done, before... nevertheless, he sat there behind the wheel of the Hägglund and sobbed, as tears rolled down his battered face. Each tear that touched his open wounds stung as if they had been loaded with salt. The throbbing that ensued came in heavy waves like an electro magnet powering up. He could feel the waves, he knew when they would hit him and how much they would hurt. Part of him wished that was why he was crying, but of all the people he thought that he might lie to, himself wasn't one of them.

He didn't know whether to scream in anger or pain. Whether to lash out in a primal fury or to curl up in a ball. Whether he should feel sorry for himself or for Charlie. So, in his frustration, he cried. Like a child who had fallen off his bike and skinned his knee, with no idea what to do but to return home and let someone else clean up his mess.

Even that had been hard, a task that had been his own and one he could've done blindfolded: drive the Hägglund back to Mawson. Hell, he didn't even know if he could do that. He had driven on and off now for what seemed like hours. Driven while his eyes had been clear, then as the headlight beams splintered into refractions through the tears that blinded him, he was forced to stop time and time again. He sniffed as snot ran down into the hairs on his lip, and wiped at his bloody face with his ruined gloves as he took a deep breath and tried to calm himself. His body spasmed with his grief and he tried to sigh. He didn't care if he froze to death just outside of the camp limits, there was no way he was going to enter the camp in this state. There was no way he was going to let anyone see him like this.

It wouldn't be far now. Minutes had turned into hours, and hours seemed to pass like years, but he knew it couldn't be far now. The ice and the snow dominated the land less and less toward the coast. Waving slopes of white where only nunataks stood proud, gave way to stone and grit, revealed by the headlights. Not only this, but the rubber tracks of the Hägglund became noisier the closer they came to camp, and now they sounded as though he had near been driving on gravel.

Soon he saw the windmill, then a hint of green or blue, colours of life in a land of desolation. The AANBUS structures stood stark against their background. He drove through the camp that had sheltered him and Charlie. The camp that would either welcome Danny back in, or turn on him in the next moments. The camp that he was forced to come home to, as he had nowhere else to run.

As the headlights illuminated the Red Shed, he saw that the heavy door to the cold porch stood open. He almost felt a parent's annoyance, in the same respect his father might have yelled at him for holding the fridge door open, but then he saw the figure step through. It was impossible to tell who it was at this distance, but it didn't matter as after that one came another, then another. Soon the entire steel veranda of the Red Shed was lined with the bodies of his camp mates. Ten or more, he couldn't tell. He figured that it would be all of them, that was if Bobby was alright.

The Hägglund came to a halt as he looked out at the figures on the steel steps. In turn they stared back at him. Dread filled his gut as he took a final breath before taking the plunge and opening the driver's door.

He didn't say anything as he stepped out of the vehicle. Nor did he say anything when the first of the figures approached him. The footfalls were light in the snow yet the sound they made were like avalanches of dread in his mind. Smaller than most, thinner, yet it was hard to tell with the many layers they wore.

'Oh Danny.' Her voice was sad but soft. 'What did he do to you?' Her touch was warm on the rawness of his face and the warmth seemed to spread throughout him from the first place she touched him. 'I was so worried when Jonty told me. Are you ok?'

'Yeah, Marie,' he said softly as he took a staggered breath. 'I'm fine but… Charlie.'

'I know. I know,' she soothed. She shushed him and drew him into an embrace. 'We all know, it's alright.'

'You all know?' he asked, genuinely surprised that Jonty would have told them.

'Yes, Danny. We do.' She smiled softly at him as she placed a hand on his chest. 'Come on, let's get you inside and get you something warm to eat.'

Marie Swan led him toward the crowd. Gary, Anne Castelli, Sean, Craig and Wendy stood in front. Behind them he saw Jonty, Bobby, Jimmy and Marty. Nowhere did he see Corinth and to him that was the nicest thing as Danny knew she would be over her stove, fixing him a bowl of soup. Gary laid a hand on his shoulder and squeezed as Marie led him past. Anne examined his face closely and then joined in beside him. The rest of them just stared at him. Their mouths grim on their face, their eyes sullen and deep.

'Charlie–' Danny said to Anne as she stepped into the cold porch with him.

'I can't help people that are dead, Daniel.' She looked at him with a stern, expression. 'You, on the other hand, have had the Grand Canyon carved into you face. I can be more help with you.'

'I don't want to leave him there,' he tried again, as he sat in front of his rack.

'Shh, Danny,' Marie said again, soft and soothing. She placed a hand on his thigh. 'The others will take care of him.'

'Where?' he asked.

Marie raised her eyebrows in question to him.

'Where will you take him?' Now that he didn't feel as though he would be thrown out of the camp, he felt a partial ownership over the body. Not in the primal sense, but rather that he felt it was his responsibility. More and more he felt like a child; Anne would clean his wounds while Marie tutted over him. Corinth would make him soup and the three of them would stand over and watch as he ate. Meanwhile Gary, Craig, Sean and the others would pull Charlie from the back of the vehicle and do whatever they would with him.

'We don't have a morgue,' Anne said solemnly. 'We don't expect people to die while they're here.'

'Where?' he asked again.

'In the freezer.' Jonty's voice was cold. 'Alongside the sausages and steaks.'

Danny stared over Marie's shoulder at Jonty McIntyre. It was impossible to read the man's facial expression, yet he stood there with his arms crossed at the entrance to the cold porch. Danny didn't reply, just continued to stare at him.

After a while Jonty continued, 'Each time you eat a meal, I want you to think about that Daniel.'

'Jonty!' Marie exclaimed but Danny put a hand on her shoulder.

'It's alright Marie,' he said as he stood to his full height. 'If he wants to say something he has his right.'

'You killed him,' he said.

'I told you what happened over the radio.'

'I know what you said, but you could have restrained him,' Jonty snarled back.

'Could I just?' Danny came back as he took another step toward him.

'Danny,' Anne said in a low voice.

'Could I just restrain a guy that had suffered a full mental breakdown and was thrashing so hard he near broke his own bones? Could I?' Danny laughed as he took another step closer. 'Restrain a man that pressed his fingers into my face so hard that his finger nails went through two layers of cloth and then did this!' He pointed to his face as his laughter turned to rage. He took another step.

'Danny,' Anne again. 'Stop.'

'Nah, fuck him,' he snapped back. 'He put me out there with him.' He pointed in Jonty's face. 'He knew that Charlie hadn't been right since. He knew what happened out there but he didn't want to tell any of you. He didn't want–'

'Danny!' Anne yelled.

'You knew that he was going to go over the edge, didn't you?' Danny laid hands on him and pushed Jonty hard into the lockers. 'You fucking knew it, didn't you?' He felt hard hands on his shoulders and he twisted. 'Fuck off me.' His eyes burnt into Jonty's and that smug smile.

'That's why you sent Bobby away, you were waiting for something to happen. You mother fucker.' He tried to throw a punch but his arm was stuck on something.

'Danny!' Another man's voice. 'Calm down man.'

'Get off me!' he roared as he twisted and tried to get his hands back onto the prick.

'So, now we can all see your temper, Daniel,' Jonty said smugly as he slipped away from Danny's grasp. He took a few steps and pressed a finger to his lip to check if he was bleeding.

Anne Castelli walked between the two men. She stood with her back to Danny and she eyed their lead researcher. Jonty looked at her, his smile cemented to his face. 'Anne, we will ne–'

The slap cracked through the air. Jonty's head swung to the side and a red handprint became visible on his white cheek. The same hand he had used to check for blood a moment before returned to his face, and his eyes were wide with hurt and shock. The cemented smile was gone. Jonty's eyes narrowed as they fell upon her.

'Get out,' she growled at him. 'How dare you say what you did.'

He opened his mouth as if to say another word but she cut him off.

'I don't want to hear anything else come out of that venomous mouth. You've done what you've done, now leave. Let the rest of us clean this mess up.'

Jonty, defeated and at a loss, laid his eyes on everyone in that room, as if weighing the consequences of their actions. Without another word, he left.

The second Danny heard the other cold porch door slam, he was released by the man that stood behind him. He instinctively turned to see who it was. Gary stood there; the soft smile that usually resided on his face was gone.

'When did you decide to come in?' Danny asked his friend.

'When I saw jackass come in after you.' He nodded to the door. 'I figured it would be up his alley to start shit, so I thought I better come in. Never thought it would be me stopping you from hitting him though.' He laughed and the soft smile returned.

'Yeah,' Danny agreed. 'Do me a favour? Next time, don't.'

'That's enough,' Anne said crossly. 'We aren't about to laugh about this situation.' She moved over to a medical bag she had sitting to the side and began to remove some cotton balls. 'Sit down Danny so I can clean your wounds.'

Danny sat down as the anger drained from his body. Marie sat down right next to him and took his hand in hers. Gary shot him a look as he sat down opposite and raised his eyebrows. As Anne pushed Danny's head back and stood over him, he felt Marie remove his cotton glove liner and toss it aside.

'Is this where you tell me that this won't hurt a bit?' he asked Anne.

She stared down at him, her face stern. 'Would I ever lie to you Danny?' And she ran an alcohol drenched swab down the lines carved in his face.

The pain was horrendous. He groaned as he felt the cotton drag through his flesh. He squeezed his hands and clenched his teeth and almost forgot that Marie held his hand in hers. He automatically released his grip and looked toward her, but only her concern for him lined her face. She ran her other hand up and down his arm as Anne continued. If he didn't feel like his face was about to get up and walk out of the room in frustration, he might have managed an erection. The feel of her breast as it rubbed against his arm, while the back of his hand laid flat against her thigh. He dared not look at her. Anne stood above him and so he concentrated on her and the focus in her eyes.

When it was done, he collapsed back against the lockers. He didn't want to talk; he didn't have the energy to remove his boots or his jacket. He needed a shower badly, but the idea of water touching his wounds was too much.

'Come on big feller,' Gary said as Anne packed up her equipment. 'Time to get you inside.'

Gary helped him remove his boots and put on his Ugg boots, while Marie unzipped his jacket for him. Together they stood him up and one on either side, they led him out of the cold porch and into the mess. Gary sat him down while Marie disappeared. When she returned, she held a steaming cup of coffee and some hard bread while old Ma brought over some soup.

'Try and eat please,' Marie urged him. 'It'll help.'

They stood over him, Marie, Gary and Corinth. They watched him closely as he ate and he blew softly on the rim of the soup cup to cool the liquid. Anne Castelli had already left, no doubt to tend to Charlie and the others who had to move him. He was thankful that they were here; not only was he grateful for the help they had given him but he was happy they hadn't seen Charlie. He felt sorry for Wendy, Jimmy and the others; they were good people, they didn't deserve to see things like that.

By the time he had finished his soup, the others had started to return. Wendy didn't even seem to notice him as she walked in, she just headed straight for the dorms. Craig and Sean said they were happy to have him back safe and then entered the kitchen together. Marty and Bobby remained and sat down with him at the table while Jimmy was said to remain with Anne while she examined Charlie's body. They all sat in silence as Danny moved onto his coffee and mopped the hard bread in the remnants of his soup bowl.

'I was really worried about you,' Bobby said finally. 'We all were.'

Danny lifted his eyes from his food to see them nod in agreement.

'We couldn't work out why he would call a camp meeting the minute you guys had left,' Marty continued. 'It didn't make much sense to us but he said that you two were part of the decision-making process because you guys were there.'

Danny furrowed his eyebrows. 'Where?'

Marty looked to Bobby. 'You were right. He doesn't know, does he?'

'Know what?' Danny continued.

'Danny,' Marie placed another soft hand on his arm and Danny saw Gary's eyebrows raise once more. 'Jonty has called in help regarding the ship.'

'Help?' He questioned again. The throbbing in his head was making him sick and he was worried that he was at risk of throwing everything back up again.

'I showed him the scans,' Bobby said. 'Everyone here knows.' He scanned their faces. 'But Jonty didn't really care.'

Danny's face screwed up again. 'I can't believe that he didn't care.'

'Well, I don't know that he didn't,' Bobby continued. 'But I think his mind was already made up.'

'Ok.' Danny put his coffee cup down. 'Can someone just tell me what's happening?'

Gary shifted in his seat. 'He's got a private salvage crew coming,' he said flatly. 'Where he found one, I don't know, but they'll be here in five days.'

'Five days?' He exclaimed. That was too soon. 'How long ago did he call them?' It took about two weeks from Melbourne to get to Mawson. If the crew would arrive in five days, then it meant that he had either called them a week ago, or they were already south of Australia. He knew which he had figured on.

'Well, who knows? But he's saying they were close by when he got in contact with them,' Gary finished.

'They're bringing supplies as well to top us up before summer,' Marty jumped in. 'We wouldn't have enough to feed their whole team while they set up.'

'Set up what?' Danny asked again.

'Christ,' Marty said as he slapped his shoulder. 'I keep thinking you know all of this. That's what Jonty said. They are setting up a camp on Amery. The deal he made with them was that they will create a tunnel for us so that we can take samples of whatever that heat signature is.

Once they've done that, they can have the ship and whatever is on it.'

Danny stared at him. He couldn't fathom what he had just heard.

'That's why he got you and… and…' Marty tried.

'Charlie,' he finished for him; the name felt like daggers in his heart.

'Yeah… to bring the Hägglund back. He said we needed it here to take out their gear when they arrived.'

'They're going to tunnel into the Amery Ice Shelf?' he repeated. 'Isn't it protected?'

Those that stood before him exchanged glances with one another. A short period of silence followed where each of them searched for someone to step up and continue the story, while others looked down to their shoes or over to the kitchen where a glint may have caught their eyes.

In the end, it was Marie who continued for them. 'Well, it was decided that the thermal signature of a heat source was worth investigating.'

Who protects something from the people that were sent to protect it? Danny thought.

'This is something pretty amazing,' Marie continued. 'Who knows what we'll find down there.'

Those were the same words that were said before we went to the shelf, his suspicious mind rattled off again. The world had gone mad and nothing made sense. Things that seemed obvious to him were now pushed aside in the search of something else, and what confused him more was that everyone was aware of it and were ok with it, as far as he knew.

'And you guys are ok with it?' he asked before he rammed the last piece of sopping hard bread into his mouth.

'Looks like we're going to have to be,' Gary said as he laughed. 'Because it's happening.'

'There's a lot more to everything here than what's just on the surface,' Marie stated. 'Imagine what will happen if we find something new. Something that no-one has ever seen before.'

'Imagine what will happen if you don't get some rest,' Anne Castelli said as she walked into the room. 'It's good to see that your entourage has fed you but it's past time that you showered. I need you clean before

I bandage your wounds and I'm ready for bed myself.'

Danny would like to have thought that he had almost forgotten his wounds but it was impossible to forget the winding throb. That, and it had gotten to the point where the people that surrounded him wouldn't look him in the eye. He could only imagine what his face must look like.

'Yeah,' he said as he pushed his coffee cup away. 'Good call, Anne.'

'I'll do this for you,' Marie said with a smile. 'You go and get cleaned up and have a good rest.'

'Thanks Marie. I appreciate it,' he said to her.

'I'm sure you'd appreciate something else too,' Gary mumbled under his breath.

Danny shook his head then started to head to the showers. He stopped and turned to face them all. 'Guys, I just wanted to say…' He paused. 'Charlie…'

'It's ok,' Bobby said. 'You don't have to say anything.'

'That's right,' Marty agreed. 'We all know things aren't right at the moment. We aren't blind.'

Gary pushed back his chair and walked toward him. 'We know you're not a murderer, man. No matter what cock head says, it's not your fault.'

'If you want to talk to us about it, then you can.' Anne stepped forward, for once her stern expression seemed softened. 'But don't feel that you have to.'

Danny considered all of them. Each one of them stood there with concern in their eyes and trust for him, he could feel it. 'Thanks guys. Really.'

He left them there and headed for the showers.

A hot shower had never hurt so much and had never felt so good. Danny held his face away from the hot spray and let the water run over his shoulders and down his back. All of the guilt washed away and swirled down the drain along with the dirt, blood and grime. The blood mixed with the water; their two streams became one and then he couldn't tell the difference. Eventually the waters ran clear and he was clean, or as clean as he was apt to get. He needed to sleep, again.

He towelled himself off and grimaced when the white fabric was left with red splotches after he cleaned his face. He got another towel from the rack, and dried the rest of his body before he finally gathered the courage to look at himself in the mirror. Deep gouges were cut into each cheek. They started as far back as his ears and coursed through to just before his nose. At the very tips they came down to needle points and Danny thought he was damned lucky he didn't lose his nose.

Just then there was a knock at the door and Danny jumped. He put the towel around his waist and opened the door slightly to see who it was.

'Anne went to bed,' Marie's voice was soft and kind. 'She was tired so I said I would put your bandages on.'

'Ahhh…' Danny said as she placed one of her smooth, long fingered hands on the door and began to push it open. 'I'm sure I can do it.'

'Don't be silly.' She said playfully as she made her way in. Her blue eyes lingered on him as she passed. Her lips formed a soft smile before she broke eye contact.

'Marie, really I…' He tried again as he made sure his towel covered his unmentionables.

'I said its ok.' She asserted as she put down Anne's bag from before and unzipped it. Danny watched her pull out a few wraps of bandages, ointment and gauze. 'Now you just grin and bear it.'

Danny leant back on the sink basin as she approached him with the ointment in hand. He screwed up his face as she applied the ointment Anne had given her, but he couldn't help but stare at her as she did so. Her little upturned nose, her perfect round little mouth. He forced himself to look away as he felt himself stiffen.

She laughed softly. 'I'm glad you're ok, Danny.' He didn't look back at her. He thought about Louise, he thought about the child she was carrying. 'I just got so worried when Jonty sent you two out there… all alone.'

Danny remained silent. Louise, their kid. The videos that he was making, all of it. Still, his manhood betrayed him, her and the rest, as it pressed hard against his towel.

'It must have been so terrifying being out there all alone with… you know.' Marie was talking softer now and had stopped applying the ointment.

He felt her fingernails run down his bare chest, and down the flat of his stomach. 'You must be so brave.'

Louise, their kid, the videos.

'So, so brave.' He felt her tug at his towel.

'Marie,' he pushed at her shoulders. 'I have a partner.'

'Oh, come on,' she said playfully. 'All this way out here and so long, everyone needs a bit of comfort.' She smiled as she stepped back and began to unbutton her blouse.

'Oh Jesus,' he said as his cock began to throb in time with the wounds on his face.

'I know you've been thinking about these,' she said as she popped another button. 'And I've just been dying to see…' She moved forward and reached for his towel again.

'Marie I can't!' he said firmly as he sidestepped out of her way. 'I'm sorry. You're beautiful and all that and any man would be nuts to turn you down.'

'Then don't,' she tried again as she popped another button. The curves of her breasts were all but hanging out now. He could see the darkness of her nipple just below the line of the fabric. They were almost there.

'I'm sorry,' he said hurriedly and he turned and ran out of the bathroom, leaving his clothes, Ugg boots and everything else behind.

He ran, naked but for the towel, that damned towel, to his Donga. He slammed his door shut behind him and rested his back against it. He breathed heavily while his cock and his face continued to throb. Without another thought he quickly turned around and snapped the lock home.

'Ahh man,' he said to himself. 'Louise, I may have done some bad things today, but being unfaithful wasn't one of them. At least I can say that.'

19

HE HAD HELD HIS FAITH with his partner. He had thought about Louise often, especially in that moment with Marie, and the thoughts of her had warmed him somewhat. He thought about stories that he had heard, that everyone had heard at least once or twice. The mountain climber or the Amazon explorer, one or both or neither… who cared in the end anyway. Some idiot would get lost, most of his team would die but he survived, and the reason why he survived was because he had a photo of his girlfriend, and he would gaze at it each night to stave off the cold or to endure the intense hunger or whatever other bullshit. Then he was found, and when he came home the first thing he would do, would be to find the girl and tell her how she had saved his life. How her photo had been his one thing to hold onto.

In reality, the dude had probably shown every other man on the expedition the photo and bragged how he had fucked her in one way or another. Or he had conveniently forgotten about that 'one thing,' when he was chatting up some other broad that 'meant nothing to him.' All of it was bullshit and part of him looked forward to his next talk with Louise so he could tell her exactly how bullshit it was. She would frown at first, then she would smile when she heard of her partner's faith. But would she? Danny didn't think so somehow.

Somehow, the conversation would steer in a certain direction. Danny thought about the *Titanic* and its treacherous course that led to its final destruction. There was no telling what dangers lurked down that path of conversation. Wisely, despite his pride, he would eventually decide to never speak a word of the matter again.

For the meantime, the wounds of his faithfulness were rawer than the flesh on his cheeks. The stupid thing was, he wasn't upset because he didn't get his night of lust; he didn't care about that at all and would never have considered doing that to Lou. Danny was so pissed off because he had lost his Ugg boots, his favourite pair of track pants, and his best hoodie.

In his mad escape to hold onto his virtue, he had left everything behind. Instead of using his hands to hold onto his belongings, he had used both hands to hold the towel over his stiffened member. The next day, once he had realised his error, he had searched the bathroom, he had searched the laundry, he had even gone so far as to search in the rubbish stores that had yet to be incinerated. Nothing. Nothing. Nothing.

The more he looked, the less he found and the sourer his mood became. His face pained him; Anne had scalded him the next day for not bandaging his face up. How could he explain? He sighed and took her abuse as she called him a stupid man then proceeded to lecture him on how men weren't as invincible as they thought.

He sighed and thought about how cold he was. He had tried multiple things to fill the void the loss of his possessions had given him but nothing worked. No matter how many socks he put on, he always felt the chill in his toes. No matter what pair of long johns he put on under his work pants, they weren't comfortable to lounge about in, and they reeked of diff oil. Finally, no matter how many shirts and other jackets he tried in a mangled ensemble, he never felt quite right.

He was sure Louise would laugh when he told her and he would hold this deed over her, like he had in his head. Then he sighed once more and his shoulders slumped even further than they had. He wouldn't tell her a damned thing. The very first thing she would say was one of two things. First, 'come home now,' and he heard her go off in his head. 'I'm not having you there for another three months while I'm about to burst and you're "trying"' – he knew she would emphasise that word –'to keep your cock in your pants.'

The second one was the one that he feared. The old 'don't come home at all.' Women were fickle beasts sometimes. Even if a man had done the right thing in the situation, which Danny thought that he had, they would get blamed for it. Even if no words of anger were directed at them, even if they were told by their loving partners, 'you did the right thing,' the eyes would tell another story. That, and their mouth. The woman's eyes would look upon their man with the distrustful eyes of a lady that was two seconds away from paying someone to follow them, just to prove their 'innocence.' Their mouth would sit on their face somewhat the way that Anne Castelli's sat on hers.

'Jesus,' he said to himself as his mind fell onto Anne. He instantly felt sorry for any poor bastard that would've dated and seen this side of her. Louise could blow her stack but Danny actually preferred it. He called it the Maltese blow-off valve. Most Maltese he knew were like it, mainly the men, but Louise was lucky enough to get it. A person that was equipped with it was very quick to temper, but once the blow-off valve had opened the pressure was released in a storm of a furious outburst. Once the pressure was gone however, they were fine. It was like ripping a Band-Aid off: short sharp pain, then five minutes later you forgot all about it.

Anne Castelli on the other hand… Danny figured that a man would need more than just Ugg boots and matching set of track pants and hoodie to weather that cold.

He sighed as he pushed his collapsed meat pie around the plate in front of him. Although Danny wasn't ashamed of it, he was one of those people that turned perfect meat pies into mush before he ate them. However, in this instance he had turned the perfect shape into mush and then realised he had not been that hungry. He hated eating with half of his face covered in patches and gauze.

After Anne had finished berating him, she had reapplied the ointment, and had covered his wounds with strips of gauze and then patched over the top. She told him that as the wounds were on his face and a stupid man like himself couldn't stop talking that she would need to apply new wrappings each night and day. That was all well and good, but as the ointment dried and the gauze became hard, each movement of his mouth became uncomfortable. Each time he smiled, it pulled at one thing or another, and chewing was the worst. He may as well rub his face up and down a linishing wheel it irritated him that much. But each time he mentioned it to Anne, she just told him he was stupid.

If he had thought that the worst part about the wrappings was eating, then he soon changed his mind once he had tried to put his washed balaclava back on. On perhaps the third day of his return he decided that a quick check of his kings and of course Anne Castelli's namesake, the ice queen, was in order. In truth, putting the balaclava on wasn't too bad. It was a little uncomfortable wearing it, as it felt weird not having it touch his cheeks, but the problem came when he had to take it off. Being as Anne would call, a stupid man, Danny forgot about his wounds and pulled his balaclava off as he normally would. With it came the patches, the gauze and half of the scar tissue that had begun to form. After twenty minutes of trying to contain his agony while he swore and spat and threw shit around the power house, he re-swaddled himself as best as he could and then dragged his sorry ass back to Anne.

He had expected the scalding from that one to be epic. As his mind always did, he played certain scenarios out in his head, like a child when they were worried about getting in trouble from their parent or teacher.

What disturbed him was that he didn't get a single rise out of her. It was like when a parent was beyond being angry with their child and they were just disappointed. He even apologised and told her that he would more careful in future. She replied that she would believe it when she saw it. Straight through the heart…

Today was the fifth day since his return and he was fine. The flesh on his face itched as it reknitted itself. If anything, it was probably worse on his face due to the fact his stubble was growing through the scabs. But in every respect, he was better than he'd been five days ago. Even the pain in his chest about what had happened with Charlie was gone. He had spoken to Louise, but had refrained from telling her about the events related to Charlie and Marie. When she asked about his face, he just told her that the ice queen bit back at him one day and that he was lucky not to lose his sight. He laughed at his words, like any stupid man who'd had a close call with death usually did. She believed him, that much he knew, and that was all that mattered.

The hardest part about the last few days, even harder than putting up with cold and not having his favourite clothes, was the awkwardness between himself and Marie. Danny resorted to silence and kept to himself. Marie, on the other hand, spoke loudly around him and laughed almost too much. Maybe she wanted to be the centre of attention? Maybe she wanted people to know something had happened? In any case, it didn't take long for people to see the tension there and as curious humans did, they asked the questions.

Gary was the first. Danny saw no harm in telling his best friend so he told him, in confidence, everything that had happened. Gary's mouth hung open in disbelief.

'You turned down that?'

Danny had to laugh. Firstly, at what she would have said if she had heard Gary refer to her person as 'that.' Secondly, that a man like Gary couldn't understand the choices that people in relationships had to make. 'I would crawl naked all the way to Amery and back just to suck the cock of the last bloke who fucked her.' Were his next and last words on the subject.

Of course, Danny's hopes of their conversation remaining in confidence were about as good Gary's chances with Marie. James let it slip when Marie walked past one time and his eyes followed her ass. 'And to think he passed it up,' he mumbled beneath his breath when he was sure she was safely out of ear shot, yet loud enough for Danny to hear. Men weren't afraid of other men in those situations, they were afraid of the woman hearing what they had said.

The situation with Jonty hadn't been fantastic either, however Jonty had maintained his silence as well as Danny had on that front, which was something. Gary, having more interest on the subject that included Marie, had forgotten all about the altercation with Jonty in the cold porch. Anne Castelli was not the type to gossip either, so realistically no-one bothered him at all. Bobby, on the other hand, had started to come out of his shell. A man that usually remained confined to the incessant noise of the communications room, more and more Bobby had reached out to Danny, to inform him of one thing or another.

Bobby had become increasingly obsessed with the ship and what lay below the ice shelf. Having not been to either he constantly asked questions, which was fine, Danny didn't mind. It wasn't a bad thing to have Bobby on side, as everything went through him. Although he'd little to do with the ship situation, he was now arguably the most knowledgeable person at Mawson about it. Jonty used his equipment to talk to the salvagers and whether Jonty liked it or not, Bobby knew a lot more than he needed to.

'The guy he keeps talking to is called Rheinmarsh,' Bobby had told him the previous night, as he accompanied Danny to Anne's lab. 'Sounds German but the guy's English is fine.'

'Rheinmarsh.' Danny repeated the name. 'That's a new one.'

'Yeah, you don't get ones like that back home much, huh?'

The first name it actually made him think about was Nathan Hindmarsh, a footballer that Danny had followed in his youth, but a Rheinmarsh he had never met nor heard of.

'All I know is they arrive tomorrow,' Bobby said as he surveyed their surroundings. The way Bobby slunk about and checked over his shoulder made Danny laugh. It was as if he was in an old, hard-boiled crime show from the fifties. Every dark alleyway held a well-dressed gangster ready to mow you down while under a street light, somewhere in the distance a man smoked a cigarette and watched. Except here, at Mawson, there was none of this. Only ice, snow and stone, and a harsh breeze that threatened to give you a chill.

'What time?' he asked.

'They'll get here in the evening at some point as far as I know. He didn't offer too much. Just that he refers to them by the name of their ship, the *Baroness*.'

Danny gave him a confused look.

'Oh, like the *Baroness* will be at Mawson the following evening,

Yeah, he's one of those guys.'

Danny nodded. 'When he gets here, I'm sure he'll refer to himself in the third person as well.'

Bobby laughed too hard then entered an embarrassed silence. His face lit up as he remembered something else. 'There's one more thing,' he said, elated, before he glanced over his shoulder again. 'Tomorrow night there will be another camp meeting.'

'Another one? Christ.' Danny swore as he rolled his eyes. Jonty and those damned meetings were beyond pissing him off; it seemed that any drop of the hat or any change in the wind called for a meeting these days.

'Yeah, I think Marie has finished with the translation of the log,' Bobby said with a smile.

Danny had forgotten all about the log. The book that would contain everything they needed to know about that ship. 'She finished it? Like, all of it?' he asked incredulously.

'Yeah, can't wait to find out what's inside of it,' Bobby couldn't contain his excitement.

'I can,' Danny mumbled as his mind went back to that creature. The creature that none of them knew about, not even Marie. Only Jonty and himself now that Charlie was gone.

Bobby had stopped. It took Danny a few steps to realise and he looked back at him.

'I thought you'd be just as excited as I am,' he said with a saddened expression. 'Like, when has anything like this ever happened before? We will go down in history with this,' he said, the excitement creeping back into his voice.

'Don't get your hopes up, Bobby,' Danny said as calmly as he could. 'I don't think it ended well for them on that ship. I don't want the same for us.'

'Oh, we'll be fine, everything's dead,' he brushed it off.

'Not by the looks of those scans you showed me,' Danny rebuked. 'Don't get too close to this Bobby. I appreciate you telling me what's happening, but even I don't want anything more to do with this.'

Bobby was horrified. 'How could you say that?' he gasped.

'Bobby,' Danny started then paused. He didn't know what to say. 'I need to get inside man, I'm too cold to stay out here and talk. You just be careful. Don't get too close.'

Bobby didn't offer a reply.

Danny entered the lab and endured his gauze change in silence.

The next day he remained in solitude as he worked and did as much maintenance on the generators as he could. He wanted to keep his mind off everything, but the announcement of the meeting had come the next morning. Jonty had informed everyone in person so that there were no exceptions. In his own case, Jonty had said it loud enough in the mess so that he knew Danny would've heard, and that was that.

So here he sat, ten minutes before the meeting. He kicked around his broken meat pie that had long since gone cold, as he waited for the rest of them to come and sit around him. He thought about what was to come, about Bobby's excitement, and he couldn't decide how he felt. He knew it was going to be awkward to sit there in front of Marie while she read aloud what she had found but the feeling that had settled in his gut was more than just that. He didn't want to know. It wasn't that he didn't care, of course he did. It was just that everything had gone wrong since that damned ship and the last thing he wanted to do was to go deeper down that rabbit hole.

As the minutes dragged on and the meat on his plate began to congeal, the rest of the camp came in. James Sutton sat near Danny, they didn't exchange any words. Gary came in and sat next to him, Corinth walked in from the kitchen, saw his plate and took it from him.

'If you're not hungry then don't cook it, Danny,' she said with a gruff voice. 'It's not like we can run down the road if we run out.'

He sighed.

Soon after, Jonty had come in, as well as Bobby. Wendy arrived, seeming particularly disgruntled. James moved to give her a space to sit down; his face fell as Wendy went and sat in the furthest possible seat from him.

Danny's eyebrows raised. Maybe others were having lover troubles too. He hoped secretly that Gary had noticed, so that someone else could be the centre of his gossiping sessions. Craig, Sean and Anne came in together. Then, finally, Marie. She didn't meet anyone's eyes; she held a basket full of papers in her hands and headed straight for Jonty, her head down.

Danny scanned the room; he was sure that they were missing someone. He counted and counted again and again.

'Is everyone here?' Jonty asked and Danny wanted to speak up. They weren't all there but who was missing?

Then his shoulders slumped as he hung his head as he realised.

'Yeah, all here,' Danny said in a solemn voice. Charlie definitely wouldn't be joining them.

20

'OK, WELL LET'S MAKE A START THEN,' Jonty said with a calm look around the room. 'I think it's rather obvious, the reason why we are gathered here today,' he said in a solemn tone. 'Our discovery out at Amery has been on the forefront of everyone's minds since we returned. It seems that each day that progresses, something new surfaces and something else seems to go wrong.' He lapsed into a short silence. 'Anyway, Danny.' Jonty turned his attention to him. 'You were the only one absent from the meeting the other day. Given what transpired, I felt it unnecessary to bring you up to speed on recent events. If you like, we can recap the events of the previous meeting so that we are all on the same page?'

Danny cleared his throat. 'That's unnecessary, Jonty.' He felt smart for mocking the previous statement. 'Some of my fellow camp mates have already brought me up to speed.'

'Is that so?' Jonty said as his eyes washed over Gary, Bobby, James and the rest. 'Well in that case we won't linger. Marie, would you like to continue?'

Marie Swan cleared her throat as she shuffled through a pile of her notes. 'Hi everyone.' She raised her head and smiled briefly at the small group in front of her, before she buried her face in her papers once more. Danny couldn't understand why she acted so shy. She had never seemed shy, but since the other night she had acted in different ways to different people around camp. To some she would seem almost boisterous, yet to others, like now, she could barely maintain eye contact. 'As some of you may remember, I volunteered to translate the ship's log, that Jonty, Danny and Charlie…' she paused after she said the name and looked directly at Danny. 'Found,' she finally finished.

Danny shifted uncomfortably in his chair, before he averted his eyes and resorted to fiddling with his face coverings.

'Anyway, it took me a while, I know. But I think I've pretty well done it.' A soft smile was on her face, as if waiting for everyone to stand up and clap. It didn't happen.

'Well, what does it say?' Craig Hollins said impatiently as he shifted himself in his chair and swapped his cross-legged position from one to the other.

Marie gave him a disapproving look before she returned to her sheets once again. 'Ok so firstly the name of the ship is the *Nisshin Maru*.'

'*Nisshin Maru?*' Anne Castelli sat up. 'That can't be right. That's the name of the whaling ship that had that run in with Greenpeace not long ago.'

Marie looked at her blankly. 'Yes, Anne.' She said it in a tone that reminded Danny of a teenager being asked if they had done their homework. 'I'm aware of that, but that doesn't change the fact that it's what is written here.'

Anne fell back into silence, and Danny saw the line of impatience crease the corner of her mouth.

'Anyway, it's called *Nisshin Maru* but more than that, the way it translates is like it's the second one. So, *Nisshin Maru 2*, like a sequel to a movie or something.'

A few of the people in the group raised their eyebrows and nodded their heads in interest. This seemed to encourage Marie, so she continued.

'Anyway, Charlie was a lot of things,' she said solemnly, 'but he was right about the ship.'

Once more, people exchanged glances and Marie waited to see people's reactions before she continued. Danny was getting sick of hearing that damned name; each time it was like a dagger in his guts.

The worst part was that each time someone said it, at least one person glanced in his direction. He'd had enough.

'The ship is indeed a whaler and was commissioned by the Japanese Imperial Navy in 1937. The flowery thing in the beginning of the log is actually the Imperial seal of Japan.' She smiled around the room, as if this was something of great interest. Then sighed and lowered her head to her notes again. 'Anyway, it was built in Japan, gross registered tonnage of about 17,500.' She read these things aloud as if she was reading someone's resume, one that she didn't find interesting at that. 'A lot of it was just guff about the war.'

'Does it tell you how it wound up here?' James Sutton interrupted.

'Yes, I'm getting there.' Once again Marie offered another impatient look. '1943, February 7th it was torpedoed twice. The ship was thought to be lost but was actually towed to Ishigaki Island for scrapping.'

'Scrapping?' Sean Wilson laughed. 'Christ, they didn't do a good job of it.'

'Instead, it was repaired and put back into service later that year,' she continued.

It became evident to Danny pretty quickly that very few people actually cared about the ship's full history, they just wanted to know the ending. James Sutton had started to huff and shake his head. Sean had started to clean his glasses, while Craig just stared off in another direction.

'Anyway, where it gets really interesting is about May 6th of the following year.' She picked up another note and started to read it aloud. '*Nisshin Maru 2* coursed for the Philippine coast carrying war supplies, armaments, machine guns, artillery and depth charges. Torpedoed by enemy submarine, location: East China Sea.'

'Bear with me here as it sounds like some of this was written in panic.' She scanned her notes before she continued. 'Torpedo, Torpedo,' she said as she furrowed her brow and sped up her pace. 'Flooding in lower decks but explosions missed armaments. I think they were hit more than once,' she offered as context. 'Hatches are closed, bulkhead is holding, ship listing but not sinking. Manage to escape using shallow primed depth charge to shield from further pursuit as we made our escape. Two casualties lost in flooding were unable to escape before hatch's closure.'

The room had gone silent with this retelling. Although the translation was obviously far from perfect, it was easy to understand everything that had happened so far.

'Main course to Philippines, too dangerous,' she continued. 'New course charted to Okinawa to make repairs.' She took a breath. 'It looks like they managed to make it there. They repaired the ship again and took sail for the Philippines in early to mid-October of that year.'

'Wow, they must have been hit pretty good if they were put out of commission for six months,' Marty said. 'Seems like a long time.'

'Anyway,' Marie continued after a short glance in Marty's direction. 'These guys had some pretty bad luck from the sounds of it. They left Okinawa on the 10th of October that year, same cargo machine guns, rifles, depth charges etc, etc, reprovisioned. Then I had to look this part up,' she said as she shuffled to another page. 'The US Army invaded the Philippines on the 20th of that month so they must have had some naval power in the area.'

'What does it say?' Craig urged her on. He leant forward, eagerly waiting the next part of the story.

'Encountered American destroyers off South coast of Philippines, had to flee to safe distance. Destroyers remained in chase. Suffered minor artillery damage to foredeck from destroyer fore gun. Unable to fend off. Unable to defend, must run. Getting closer.' She shifted to another page. 'Crew tied buoys to the depth charge and used timer detonator to ignite. Depth charge floated…' She paused as she poured over her notes once more. 'It looks like the destroyer took damage from the explosion.'

'Crafty bastards,' Gary said in a laugh. Danny looked at him in confusion; he wasn't sure of what he meant. Gary sighed. 'A depth charge is set to explode at a certain depth, I gather they used it like a pressure fuse. If the fuse is set but the charge never reaches the depth it won't explode but it remains armed.' A few people around nodded. 'So, Marie said they used timer detonators, they worked out how long it would take for the destroyer to reach their current location, set the timer and threw them off the edge. Pretty clever.' He finished with a grin and sat back in his chair.

'Thanks Gary.' Marie offered him a smile then reconsidered her notes. 'American naval power too great, cannot return to Philippines. Submarine threat too great, cannot return to Japan. Papua New Guinea is under attack. We have nowhere to go. We are alone.'

'Shit,' Wendy Phillips murmured. Surprised at her input as she had remained silent until now, her comment drew everyone's attention.

'They didn't have much luck at all,' Corinth agreed with Marie's earlier statement.

'That's what brings them down here I suppose,' Marie said with a frown. 'They couldn't go anywhere else. I'll continue.' She found her place in her papers again. 'This next part I've summarised. Lightly provisioned for short journey, forced to put ashore in Palau for fresh water and food supplies. Picked up small force of twenty infantry led by a Lieutenant Ishimura. Crew happy to have soldiers for protection but food stores didn't last. It took them only a few days to get desperate.' She ran her hands back up her notes; she had obviously made a timeline. 'Looks like they ran into trouble off the Philippine coast on the 16th, they picked up Ishimura at Palau by the 20th, and by the end of the month they were out of food.'

She took a deep breath and let it out in a long stream as she repositioned herself on the desk. Taking up the next page, she read on. 'They tried to go ashore at Nauru and then at Tarawa but were attacked. Soldiers were able to repel forces with the weapons that were meant for the defence of the Philippines, but they left empty handed.' She sighed and put the page down. 'The rest I don't need notes for,' she said with an expressionless face. 'With nowhere else to go, and not enough man power to force a landing, they headed south and south, where they wound up here,' she concluded.

The silence was almost deafening.

'Come on, that can't be it,' Danny said. 'That doesn't explain what it's been doing for the last seventy years. That doesn't explain the… the rest of it.' He almost let slip about the creature but remembered that no-one else knew. Now wasn't the time to speak about it.

'Well, I thought that much was obvious,' Jonty said implacably.

'You explain it then, because I didn't get that part,' Gary backed him up.

Jonty rolled his eyes and sighed. 'Well, they were low on food, the ship was an old Japanese whaler which was recommissioned to be used for the war effort. Tell me this, if you were starving and you were on a whaling ship, what would you do?' He pursed his lips. 'I'd go fishing.'

'So, what are you saying here? They go fishing and wind up halfway inside of the Amery Ice Shelf?' Danny questioned.

Jonty palmed that one straight off to Marie. It was funny to watch and all he had to do was turn his head and give her the same 'what do you reckon' look he had been giving Gary and him for the last few minutes. Marie opened her mouth, shut it, then composed herself and started again. 'Of how they get in there, it doesn't really say. The last entry translated to pretty much what Jonty said.'

'What did they get on the hook, Marie?' Danny said as he crossed his arms and sat back in his chair. 'I know it says it.'

Marie turned to Jonty, who just dropped his eyes to the ground. Marie was on her own and she knew it. 'The word that they used to describe it was, "Leviathan",' she said flatly. 'They called it a monster whose girth almost matched the height of their ship.'

No-one stirred until Anne cleared her throat and spoke up. 'A leviathan is a sea monster,' she said, her eyes narrow. 'That's exactly what the word means, "sea monster."'

'Uh-huh,' Danny said as he leant over his knees and stretched his back. 'Enough bedtime stories; how did it get into the ice shelf?'

Marie crossed her arms and looked at him fully for the first time since the other night. 'It doesn't say exactly. All that it mentions is that the men on board were that starved that they decided to try and kill the beast but the ship was too small to subdue it. Instead, when they harpooned it, they were dragged. The rest is clouded. They mention something about a heavy fog that they were forced inside, but it gets hard to understand in their panic.' She unfolded her arms and rested her ass on the table once more. 'Maybe the "leviathan,"' she made quotation marks with her fingers as she exaggerated the word. 'Was living under Amery and when they harpooned it, it tried to go home and they were just dragged along with it?'

'Dragged through an entire suburb worth of ice wall?' Gary said in doubt. 'No creature alive would be strong enough to drag a ship through that much, the chains would snap before that happened.'

'Good point,' Danny said. 'Either that or the ice shelf was already weakened, I don't know.'

'Still, the sea monster part is bullshit,' Gary muttered.

'Yeah,' Danny agreed, 'I think you're right'.

'Yep.' Craig, then Sean, even Jimmy Sutton began to stir. Wendy even stood up and went into the kitchen.

'I suppose it doesn't matter anymore, does it?' Bobby said. It was the first thing he had said in the entire meeting.

'What doesn't matter?' Danny asked him.

'Whether we believe what Marie just told us,' he said softly. 'A crew is coming to dig down there, because whatever they caught is still there and it won't be long until we find out what it is. Whether we like the answer or not, we're going to find out.'

He was right. There was no point bickering or carrying on. Everything that had been set in motion was what it was.

'It's not too late you know,' Bobby continued. 'We don't have to find out.'

'Excuse me?' Marie got off her perch and approached him. 'Maybe one of the biggest finds in the history of marine biology falls in our laps and you say "let's just not find out"?'

'I don't like what it's doing to this place.' Bobby came back at her, his usually frightened eyes gleamed with passion. 'Danny's right. Ever since you guys came back none of you are the same.'

'So, it's you that's putting these ideas into his head, is it?' She turned on Danny. 'It's you that's trying to sabotage everything that I'm trying to do.'

Well, he thought as he stood up, *she picked her moments and now she's all in.* 'Just let them take the ship and let's forget about what's under there. Enough is enough.'

'Don't give me that shit,' she snarled. 'You couldn't get your way with me and now you're trying to screw me over.'

'Wow,' Craig said.

'You know that's not what happened Marie.' He pointed at her. 'You know damned well, and I think everyone else here does too.'

'I don't know, but I'd sure like to,' Craig said as he put his hand up.

Everyone turned on him. 'Shut up.' He lowered his hand slowly.

'If you want the real revelation, if you want to fucking play games mate,' Danny said in full anger. 'Why don't you two little connivers tell them about the creature on the bridge?'

Jonty seemed confused. He looked to Marie, then back to Danny. 'Ahh, what are you talking about, Daniel?'

Danny glared at him. 'Don't you start now. The creature, the one I fell on. Remember, I fainted and you threatened Charlie?'

'I threatened Charlie?' Jonty said with a soft laugh as he placed his hand across his chest. 'I did no such thing.'

'He recorded it, dipshit!' Danny yelled. 'Charlie had the camera on record the whole time. I watched it.'

'I think you might be under a bit of stress, Daniel,' Jonty started again. 'Nothing like that ever happened.'

'I know it happened and so do you,' Danny snarled.

'Look, this is an easy fix.' Marty stood up. 'I kept all the data; I'll just go get the camera.' He started to walk off.

'Don't bother.' Danny growled. 'I fucking deleted the footage.'

'You deleted it?' Gary said.

'Oh, how convenient,' Jonty said with a laugh. 'I guess it's also convenient that the only other person that could back up your story is unable to?'

Danny didn't say a word. He just glared at Jonty. Regret flowed through him, why had he deleted that tape? He was so tied up with being worried about everyone's motives he never thought it might be wise to keep it, even if it showed him talking in his unconscious state. He had no choice, he had to come clean. 'I deleted it, because–'

His words were cut short by the sound of an air horn. A horn so deep and so loud that it could only come from a ship. Bobby stood up. 'It's the *Baroness*! She must be here.'

At once, everyone lost interest in Danny's confession, except for Jonty. Craig stood up along with Sean, Marty, Jimmy and the rest and began to head for the cold porch.

'Shit,' Bobby said. 'They've probably been calling me and I've been sitting in here. Shit!'

As everyone left the room, Jonty stood there and held his eye contact.

'Don't you want to meet your long-distance boyfriend?' Danny snarled at him.

Jonty smiled but stepped closer, waiting for everyone to leave. Everyone, except for Marie that was.

'Don't fuck with me, Daniel,' he said so low that if it wasn't that his face was only an inch from Danny's, he wouldn't have heard him. 'Mind your place and keep out of my fucking way. You're nothing here, keep it that way.'

Danny pushed him away. 'Fuck off me,' he snarled again.

Jonty laughed, he turned to Marie and nodded towards the door. Marie shot Danny a hateful look as she followed Jonty out of the door. Then he was alone.

He sighed as he sat down again, he rubbed at the sores on his face and swore to himself. 'What have I gotten myself into. You stupid, stupid, stupid…'

He heard the sound of a package crumple and the tell-tale noise as someone bit into a potato crisp. He raised his head and saw Wendy standing there. She looked around confused. 'Where did everyone go?' she said through a mouthful of crumbs. 'I was only gone for a second.'

A laugh escaped him as he got to his feet. 'You'll never be a lady, Wendy,' Danny said with a smile. He gave her a wink and headed for the cold porch, to join the rest.

21

THE EARLY MORNING AIR bit at him. It sunk its teeth through the fabric of the balaclava that covered his face, through the many layers that lined his body, and drove itself deep into his bones. A shiver ran up his spine and a soft voice in the back of his head said in a weak, defeated voice, *'I will never be warm again.'*

Perhaps the voice was right. Sure, he could have a hot shower and let the steam open his pores and sting at his frozen fingertips. He could lay beneath the covers of his bed, curl up into a foetal position and pray to never see the light again. His body may be warm, but not truly. He knew what that weakened voice meant. It was the same whenever he had gone camping down on the Moonbah River, down at Jindabyne.

He'd spend hours down on the river in the late afternoon sun, if you could call it that. The sun at Jindabyne didn't seem to warm anything, it was like it just hung back above the ozone and peered down at the gullies and said 'fuck that. Too cold down there for me.'

What always struck him as peculiar was how the cold slowly soaked into a man when he didn't move. Everything felt fine while he sat there, but the moment the man would try and get his body into motion again, everything would fall apart. The shakes would take him, he would lose his speech and all clear thought. A hot shower couldn't even completely dispel the cold that had worked its way into the fabric of his being. Not until he had moved to warmer climates did he ever get the feeling of being completely defrosted.

Danny felt the same here and now; only when he was back in Sydney would he feel the warmth again, but would that ever happen? He doubted it more and more with each passing day. The feel of this place had gone sour. If people like Bobby could feel it, then… he didn't think it would take much longer for whatever was 'going' to happen, to reveal its nasty head. Something told him that the arrival of the *Baroness* was only the beginning that would bring about its bloody end.

It had been almost nine months since Danny had seen a ship off the Antarctic coast. Not one that had come close enough to anchor up and send landing craft. He had forgotten how surreal their presence was in the environment. How intrusive. *Far be it from me to judge,* he thought, *the crew of the ship probably had the same thought about Mawson. If they gave two shits at all.*

They had all journeyed out into the cold the previous night, yet all they saw were the lights that illuminated the plate glass of the ship's apartments. The shape of the vessel loomed in the darkness, like a monster in a child's closet. He saw enough of the thing to know it was there, but not enough to know the real shape or the real size of the vessel. They stood there, in the freezing cold below the tanks that had the camp's name painted on them in stark white, seven-foot letters. Yet nothing happened. It wasn't until Bobby had decided to come down and tell them that they wouldn't leave the ship until morning, had they all decided to turn back to the Red Shed.

Now, the sun had cast a bleary tear across the sky and the darkness had slowly started to yield its hold on the sky's canvas. Danny leant against the pylons for the tank that was labelled 'W' of the camp's welcome sign and wished he had a cigarette. Yet, as the sun ebbed away at the darkness and the world itself began to spring out of the gloom, more and more of the ship was revealed to him and those that stood by and waited.

The *Baroness* was a monster of a sea liner, with only two colours making up her scheme. Her apartments, as well as the weight marker on her hull, were a bright red. A red so rich that it could either be associated with the wealth of royalty or the danger of blood. Her hull on the other hand was as black as night itself. The railing that ran all around her decks and apartments was painted in the same thick paint, but the hull seemed different. The steel of its prow shaped up and rose to a high point above its foredeck, as if to armour it. Even at a glance, the steel seemed thicker than usual, and it almost had an edge to it. He had heard the word 'icebreaker' before, but never had he seen a vessel so worthy of the name.

Although the lights still illuminated the ship's apartments, he saw a lot of movement on deck. Danny watched as they lowered a skiff, not unlike one his friend had used for fishing back in Sydney. The hull was placed gently into the water and then detached. Then four figures, who were dressed in clothes so dark that it looked as though the hull of the icebreaker had swallowed them as they descended a ladder to the skiff below.

It was said that noise travels over water, but Danny couldn't believe how well he could hear. He heard their small talk, heard one of them slip on the running boards of the small skiff and he heard the rest of them laugh. The sound seemed to come in waves, as if someone was playing with the volume knob on a television. At first, he could hear words as clear as day, but only fragments not full sentences. Then there was nothing but the water sloshing against the heavy steel hull of the icebreaker.

As if on cue, the entire camp ventured out onto the veranda, as the small skiff fired up her engine. Water churned behind her as the coxswain adjusted the trim. The motor's pitch changed as the tension on the propeller became greater and the skiff hurtled toward them. Gary purposely bumped Danny's shoulder with his own and Danny glanced at him. The pilot winked as he took a bite out of an apple and smiled while he chewed open-mouthed. 'Hold onto your hats, huh?' Gary said.

'Yeah, you know it,' Danny grumbled as he stood back. He didn't know whether to feel relieved or scared. Everything to do with that damned ice shelf was a problem. The ship was a problem, the creature was a problem, and he was sure that whatever it was that lay below the ice was going to turn into one big fucking problem. This crew was going to take a problem off their hand, that problem he knew and part of him felt ownership of that. The problem they were going to get in return was one that Danny wanted nothing to do with, it was one that he was most afraid of.

One by one, the members of Mawson moved away from their tanks to head down to the closest thing they had to a moor. Snow, ice and stone ground under their feet as they walked to the water's edge. Danny watched as the figures turned into men and features began to appear on their faces, the closer they came.

'Christ,' Gary said almost to himself, 'they'd have to be freezing.'

Danny hadn't noticed it before, but none of the men on the ship were dressed for warmth. They all wore long-sleeved shirts that seemed to cling to them, and beanies that were rolled up on their heads. The thing that shocked Danny most of all, was that none of them wore face masks when the wind chill on that boat would be enough to freeze the beard on a man's face. Danny shook his head as he watched them, but none of them seemed to shiver. None huddled low in a ball in a desperate attempt to hold onto their body heat. In fact, they were rather the opposite; they stood tall and faced straight into the wind that must be blasting into their faces. They all wore polarised glasses, so they couldn't be that stupid, and all had stern, hard-lined jaws.

Danny stood at the water's edge along with Sean, ready to help the newcomers disembark from their skiff, as there was nowhere to tie the small boat up. As the engine dropped its revs, the skiff's prow fell forward in the water. Small waves sloshed ashore and wet Danny's gumboots. He squatted and held out his hands. One of the crew members tossed Danny a rope, he caught it and began to pull in their prow as the engine died. Another crew member threw a rope to Sean and he brought the stern about, while another crew member threw over some inflatable fenders. Eventually, both Sean and Danny held the skiff's weight against the sharp line of their makeshift moor, while Gary and Jonty stepped forward to help the crew off.

The first man off the ship was tall, slender and straight backed. His jaw was covered with a thin white beard which made the thin slit of his mouth barely visible. He extended his hand and Jonty took it to help him ashore.

'You must be Rheinmarsh.' Jonty smiled magnanimously. 'I'm J. McIntyre.'

'Jay?' Danny heard Gary say behind him. 'Really?'

'Mr McIntyre,' The slender man said in a reedy accent that Danny struggled to pick. It was a washed out European something or other. 'The pleasure is all mine,' he said this without a smile. 'I am Gottfried Rheinmarsh, but please just refer to me by my surname.'

Jonty pumped Rheinmarsh's hand up and down vigorously, almost too happy to meet the man. 'We are really pleased to have you here Mister Gottfried.' He said either purposely to slight or unknowingly, either way, neither man made an attempt to correct the error. 'I hope your journey was safe and fast and that you have our supplies?'

Rheinmarsh looked around at the other Mawson camp members. The more he saw, the more unimpressed he seemed. He said not a single word to any of them in greeting. 'The trip was what it was Mister McIntyre, and yes we do have your supplies, however I suggest we conclude our negotiations before we allow ourselves any further pleasantries.'

'Oh,' Jonty said. 'Of course. Would you and your men like to join us in our mess for some coffee and we can nut the rest of this out.'

'That would be just fine.' Rheinmarsh faced the three men who had begun to step forward for assistance off the skiff. 'These three will accompany me, to ensure you haven't lured us down here for some Australian foul play.'

Jonty laughed, almost too loud.

This will be an interesting few days, Danny thought. *Good old Jay will be in the fight for his life to hold onto the power of this place.'*

'No foul play we assure you.' Jonty spoke through his smile.

'We will see.' Rheinmarsh gestured to the first man who was being helped off the skiff by Gary. 'This is Matthew Thompson, my electrical engineer.' The man was broad-shouldered, thick-armed and had a patchy beard. He didn't make any greeting except for a nod to Gary once he was ashore.

The next man stepped forward. 'Paul Stathis, our structural engineer.' This man was shorter than the rest and probably the broadest over all. He appeared to have little to no neck whatsoever but he had a certain amount of strength to him. At least this man looked Gary in the eye and offered him a gruff 'how you going?' in a very strong Australian accent.

'Finally,' Rheinmarsh sighed. 'I'll allow you to meet the most paranoid of our crew, Kee Peters.'

Danny almost didn't believe his eyes. This last man, thin and almost sheepish looking, had a rifle slung over his shoulder, and a big one at that.

'Woah mate,' Gary said as he took his hand away. 'We don't let any cannons on land at Mawson mate.'

'I assure you my friend–' Rheinmarsh stepped forward and offered his own hand to Peters '–my colleague here is quite harmless, even with his ZKK. Please inform our kind hosts why you felt the need to bring along your rifle.'

Kee Peters glanced around at them as he stepped ashore. 'Polar bears.' He said it as if it was the most obvious thing in the whole world, like the way someone answered the question, 'what colour is the ocean?.

Rheinmarsh sighed again. 'As you can see Mr McIntyre, good help is at times very hard to find. Despite my constant assurances that he would not need this firearm, he insisted on bringing it. Perhaps one of you could explain to him why it is unnecessary? I am unfortunately at the end of my wits.'

'You're on the wrong end of the earth, man,' James Sutton said in a laugh. 'You literally could not be further away from a polar bear than you are right now.' He bent over and shook his head as his laughter shook him. The rest of Mawson began to laugh and for once Rheinmarsh smiled.

'See, my friend?' He slapped Peter's on the back. 'It is unnecessary, anyway you have it now. Let us all get out of the cold and have some coffee.'

'Yes,' Jonty rubbed his hands together as if all of a sudden feeling the cold. 'Don't worry about the rifle, it will be fine. Let's get inside.'

With that everyone headed up the short slope to the Red Shed. Danny couldn't believe it. One quick joke and everyone didn't care that this man had an elephant gun on his shoulder and were happy to let him bring it in.

'Hey bud.' Danny turned his head to see the coxswain still behind his wheel. 'You can throw the rope back in, I'll head back now, the boss will call if he wants me.'

'Ok man, safe drive,' Danny said as he and Sean threw their ropes back in and headed up behind the mass.

Inside the mess, everyone from Mawson stood around while the four men from the *Baroness* sat and drank coffee. The rifle sat on the table with its action closed, a sight that Danny never liked to see. Wet footprints had been tracked through the place where the newcomers had come in; not having their own set of boots to change into Jonty had obviously allowed them in on an exception.

'We would like to see the ship,' Rheinmarsh said in-between sips of his coffee.

'I can get Gary to take you up there in the R44,' Jonty said. 'That will give you a look at the ship and also give you an understanding of the ice that you will need to drill through.'

'I want to get onto the ship,' Rheinmarsh said flatly. His eyes never left Jonty's.

The room went silent for a short time, at the instant growth of tension. 'Our agreement was that you would excavate the ice shelf to allow us access to the heat source and only then would you be able to take the ship.'

Rheinmarsh smiled his false smile once more. 'Did I say I was going to take it? I want to inspect what I have bought before we seal the deal.'

'We can show you photos of the interior of the deck,' Jonty tried again and pointed to Marty. 'Marty has the camera.'

Rheinmarsh stood and began to approach Jonty. 'I don't think photographs will cut it, my friend.'

'Well, what's stopping you from just taking the ship without doing what you promised?' Jonty added angrily.

Rheinmarsh placed a hand on his shoulder then patted his face softly. 'Nothing, Mr McIntyre. Absolutely nothing.'

The room went very quiet. *What have you brought into our camp Jonty?* Danny thought as his eyes fell onto the closed breech of the ZKK. *What have you done?*

'Just as there is nothing stopping you from seizing us right now,' Rheinmarsh said as he regarded the rest of the camp. 'That is why I left my second in charge back on the *Baroness* along with our most important person: our diesel mechanic.'

Danny could've laughed at that. He even saw Gary, whose mouth had dropped open at this display of chest beating, glance at him at the mention of a mechanic.

'But we have travelled a very, very long way, Mr McIntyre. A very long way, based off a word that came from your mouth.' He tapped Jonty's chest at this. 'So would you begrudge me a look at my prize before I spend any more time or money on your word?'

'You don't believe me?' Jonty said indignantly. 'Is that it?'

'If I didn't believe you, I wouldn't have brought two full teams, two full weeks down to this block of ice. The *Baroness* is a magnificent ship, and very strong, but she doesn't run on good intentions Mr McIntyre.' He placed his open palms before him. 'Your word brought me here. I have shown my hand, I am here. Now it is time for you to do the same.'

'The R44 only holds four people,' Jonty said. 'So not all of you can go.'

'Mr Peters can stay behind,' Rheinmarsh allowed.

Jonty shook his head. 'One more will have to stay, I'm sorry. That ship still belongs to us, so if you're going to go aboard, I want to be there too. Only four seats, Gary takes one as the pilot, there is no room to land safely.' He held up one finger. 'I make two. So, you get two seats: one for you and someone else, or two for your engineers.'

Rheinmarsh smiled again, however this time, it didn't feel fake. It felt about as real as anything this man had done so far. 'You drive a hard bargain, Mr McIntyre,' he said as he sighed. 'Two it is.'

22

DANNY WATCHED THEM pile into the R44. The rotors slowly built up their pace and the snowdrifts slowly stirred below the sleek hull. Bit by bit, torrent by torrent, snow was driven from where it had settled as the rotors hurtled past overhead. Soon the R44 was making its own blizzard in the heavy snowdrift that lay around it, white fans flew up in front of it as if to shield it from the outside world. Waves upon waves, until finally, the pitch of the turbine changed and everything blew outward as if an explosion had occurred at the epicentre of the flurry. Danny could almost see the invisible wall as the snow pressed flat against it, in the moment before it was blown away.

He watched as the R44 rose into the air. She steadily beat down on them with her might and grace. Gary banked her and she began to pick up speed, the turbines changed pitch again and now he heard the *whup, whup, whup* as the air broke around her. Then she was gone, off over the AANBUS structures, away beyond nunataks and off to that damned ship again.

Danny sighed as he lost sight of the R44. His hand rubbed at the stubble on his face. He started to head back to the shed; it was still very early and his stomach had begun to complain that it had not been fed yet. As he started to move, he noticed that he wasn't alone. One of the crew members that had remained stood about twenty feet to Danny's right. He had turned broadside to Danny, as he stood in the same direction that the chopper had flown off in. Large white plumes of smoke erupted from his mouth as he exhaled a nicotine-riddled breath.

Being an ex-smoker, instantly Danny felt the urge to ask him for one. He felt the hunger in his gut, the eagerness in his head and the yearning that lingered just beyond the tip of his tongue. As any ex-smoker should, he started to walk away. Yet he wasn't even twenty feet further on when he heard the sound of boots crunching through snow behind him.

'Hey,' the unfamiliar voice called out. 'Hey, you.'

Danny stopped and regarded him. It was the squat man, the structural engineer. He glanced up at Danny as he approached. The breath was heavier on his lungs, either from the cold, the fact that he had almost had to run to catch up, or the fact that he was a smoker and should've known better. Danny looked at him, uninterested. He didn't greet the man.

'What do you want me to do with this?' The man asked as he held out his open palm. A crushed cigarette butt lay in his out-stretched hand, the bent over tobacco end dark with ash. Instantly the smell hit Danny full in the face.

Danny was caught off guard. He didn't know what the man wanted, whether he was taking the piss out of him or not. 'What?'

The man's face was expressionless. He pushed his hand further out to offer Danny a better look at the crushed-out butt. 'What do you want me to do with this? I don't like to just throw them on the ground. Smoking is a filthy enough habit as it is, let alone the bloody pigs just throwing them about.'

'Yeah,' Danny said, almost shocked that the guy would care to ask. 'Yeah, especially for the poor bastard that has to pick them up.'

'You know it,' the man replied. 'Maybe that's why I don't like to do it. Maybe I had that job in another life.'

That fucker stole my line, Danny thought, then laughed. 'Yeah, hold onto it for now.' He nodded in the direction he was walking. 'I'll show you where to toss them.'

'Thanks,' the man said as he fell into step alongside him. 'I'm Paul, by the way.' He extended the butt-free hand to shake Danny's. 'I think our bosses are as bad as each other when it comes to introductions.'

Danny shook his hand as he smiled beneath his balaclava. 'Danny Myers. You hungry, Paul?'

'Always,' he replied with a grim smile as he pushed both of his hands into the pockets of his parka.

They walked together to the Red Shed. The wind picked up to deliver a single burst of indignation that the sun had reclaimed the sky. The flurry stung at Danny's eyes and he lowered his head while the man behind him turned his back to it and shrunk his almost non-existent neck further down below his collar.

'Aren't you guys cold?' Danny asked as he rubbed at his eyes with the backs of his knuckles. 'You aren't dressed for the weather; I know that much.'

Paul shrugged. 'It's not too bad. We have some pretty hi-tech gear on that ship.' He gestured back to the *Baroness*. 'Not all of it stays on the ship either.'

Danny gave him a confused look.

Paul laughed. 'Yeah, my face is a bit cold.' He pointed to the balaclava that Danny wore across his own face. 'Next time I leave the ship, I'll bring my own, but otherwise I'm warm as toast.' He pulled at the back of his sleeve to show Danny the layering he wore beneath. The garment beneath his dark parka was almost like the spandex that the push-bike riders that everyone hated back at home wore. It was thin, but multilayered, that much was obvious. Lines that were almost like metallic crosses checked their way up his arm in a diagonal pattern. Paul let his arm fall back to his side. 'I don't know what this stuff is, but Christ it's better than anything I ever bought from Kathmandu.'

Danny frowned. 'You don't know what it is?'

Paul shook his head as he rubbed his cheeks. 'Nah, none of us do. Maybe Rheinmarsh, but he didn't say. They were given to us just before we got the job. Something to help us or some bullshit, I don't know.'

Danny raised an eyebrow as he pushed his way into the cold porch. He wanted to interrogate this guy, ask him as much as possible, but he didn't want to cook the goose too quickly. Jonty and the others would be a few hours, that much he knew. So, he had a good while to wine and dine this bird before he threw it on the griller.

'Come on in man, welcome again to the mess.'

Paul watched as Danny sat down and disrobed. Danny took off his entire top layer off. His balaclava, his gloves, jacket, wind-proof pants and gumboots. Paul, on the other hand stood around, still holding the cigarette butt. 'Oh, fuck,' Danny said. 'I forgot about the damned smoke. Give it here and I'll show you where the incinerator is after a bit of food.'

Paul smiled and handed it over. Danny took it and put it on the toe of his gumboot. It would last fine there. Danny peered down at Paul's wet engineer boots and frowned. 'You should take your boots off; we try and keep it as dry as possible inside.'

Paul shrugged. He sat down next to Danny and took off his boots. Danny led Paul inside and gave him a tour of their kitchen and food stores. He made him another coffee, white with two, the way any man has it. He fixed him some toast with peanut butter and honey, his own particular favourite, and afterwards they sat, both without boots, at the table where the rifle had sat only twenty minutes before.

Paul took a sip of his coffee and placed the mug down gently on the table. Colour had begun to flush his cheeks and a line of sweat followed his hair line. He blew out a gush of air as he leant back and unzipped his parka. 'I tell you,' Paul said as he pulled one of his arms out through the sleeve. 'This underwear is great for out there but I'm burning up.' He let the parka hang over the back of the chair and Danny saw for the first time the full garment.

It clung to his body in the same likeness as spandex. Paul was a fit man and from the looks everything below was hard as iron so it wasn't unflattering for the poor man. Danny knew that in his soft and chubby youth, he would have rather died than wear something like that. The metal cross hatchings ran over the entire garment. The thing that perked Danny's interest more than anything was the brand name that was embroidered on the left breast: R.A.G.E.

Danny's eyebrows furrowed again. 'Weird brand name, never heard of that one before.' He said as he pointed to the word.

Paul stuck his bottom lip out as he looked down at it. 'Yeah.' He shrugged and left it at that.

'I'll have to look it up.' Danny said, trying another tactic. 'If the shit's that good, I might have to get a couple of pairs sent down. You saw how much of a pain in the ass it is to get ready to go outside.'

A smile flickered across Paul's face. 'Tell you what,' he raised his coffee mug. 'Keep making coffee like this and I'll give it to you before we leave.'

Danny smiled. 'Blend 43 mate, there's nothing else. You sure they won't get the shits?'

Paul shrugged again and turned his attention to the kitchen. 'It's just a shirt. Who cares about a shirt?'

Danny dropped it. He could tell the man wasn't interested in discussing the weave of his fabric and he didn't want to lose him. Danny followed his gaze over to the kitchens. 'Do you want me to get you anything else?'

Paul yawned. 'No. I'm fine thanks, just looking about.' He raised his coffee mug again and took another long drink. 'Just happy to be on the ground again.'

'Long trip huh?' Danny tried to keep it natural.

'Long enough.' He shrugged again. 'Was supposed to be up in the Northern Territory right now, sweating my ass off.' He laughed. 'Never thought I'd be sweating my ass off down in Antarctica.' He pulled at the collar of his shirt again.

'What were you supposed to be doing?' Danny kept it going, he wanted the man to feel comfortable.

'Fishing,' he said flatly, obviously annoyed that he missed his trip. 'But that's alright. Work is work and that's what pays for those trips.' He took another swig of coffee.

'So based in Melbourne?'

Paul shook his head. 'No, based in Perth, at the moment anyway. The *Baroness* was about to head to the Solomon Islands when we were told about this job. Now here I am.' He shrugged again and drained the last of his coffee.

'Told?' Danny asked. 'Jonty didn't contact you directly?'

Paul shook his head again as he stood up and picked up his parka. 'Nope. We got the tip off by some other mob that wanted us to go and do it. They offered us a shitload of cash and gave us all this gear.' He pointed to the garment again. 'Even if the ship turns out to be a financial dud, we should still be ok.'

Now Danny was completely screwed up – some other company knew about the ice shelf and wanted these guys to manage it? 'Man, that sounds pretty weird.'

'Of course, I could be bullshitting you,' Paul said flatly as he considered him. Then he laughed and slapped Danny on the shoulder, the impact making him spill his coffee on himself. 'Just joking with you, but don't go advertising that crap, you'll get me in trouble.'

Danny smiled as he stood up and took both of the mugs back to the kitchen to wash them up. He took a tear of paper towel and mopped at the coffee stain on his hoodie.

'Want to show me where this incinerator is?' Paul called out from the mess hall.

'Yeah, yeah,' Danny replied softly as discarded the paper towel in failure. 'Come on, I'll show you now.'

They headed back through the cold porch. After he had slid his feet into his boots once more, Paul stood and waited while Danny got dressed again. In another few minutes, they were back out into the cold and the steam from Danny's mouth was almost as great as the new cigarette plumage that erupted from Paul's. Danny took him around the back of the Red Shed, up the slope further toward the great white wilderness, where they kept the incinerator. Paul crushed out the other cigarette on the sole of his boot before they entered the small shed.

Almost like an indoor combustion heater, their incinerator had a flu that ran up through the top of the shed's roof and had a small chamber where fires could burn up to six hundred degrees. 'Toss them in there, man. Next time someone has a bunch to do they'll burn them up at the same time.' Paul tossed them in there and thanked Danny.

As they exited the shed, Danny slapped him on the back. 'Feel free to just come up here and throw your butts in whenever you're in camp. It'll get a bit boring for you if you're here for a bit, so I hope you brought a few packs.'

Paul nodded as he laughed. 'Yeah, thanks mate. But I don't think we'll be in your way very much.'

'No?'

Paul shook his head. 'We never mingle with those outside the crew, this is a rare chance for–'

A report cut him off. It wasn't so loud to mean an explosion but the sound rolled and rolled and bounced back off the slope to fill the emptiness that Mawson was known for with a brief explosion of power. Danny and Paul looked at each other.

'The rifle,' Danny said.

'No, surely…' Paul murmured.

Then they heard a woman's scream and they both broke out in a run.

23

HIS FEET POUNDED THE SNOW and the stone below it. He almost slipped countless times, but either he caught himself or Paul was at his side to steady him. The sound had come from beyond the communications array. Even now Danny still heard the rolling effect the gunshot had in the open wilderness. How long had it been since this land had heard such a noise? Had it ever? The animals that dwelled on its rocky shore had probably looked around in confusion, unaware what that noise meant. Unaware that every time that roar ripped and rolled through their ears it could mean the end of another life.

Danny remembered reading something back in school that related to Hawaiian or Tahitian indigenous. That in the age of colonisation, the revelations that island natives faced when the European settlers had landed were beyond belief. In their age of sticks and stone spearheads, to see their friends or their enemies blown to pieces by the Europeans' cannons, could only be explained by sorcery. Ideas that balls of lead could travel faster than any man could see, did not exist in their minds. Nor did the notion that small granules of powder could burn, and the gasses that they created could push such projectiles to such speeds. It is a shame that this history is lost to us. How could one describe a native's first experience with such weaponry? Danny thought it was easy: horror.

Again, the gunshot tore through the air and its report hammered back at Danny over and over as the sound rolled off the snowy hills. Once more he heard the shrill scream, this time shorter and higher pitched.

'That motherfucker,' Danny hissed as he came about the side of the Red Shed at full pace, Paul only inches behind him. *How could he come to land and turn that cannon onto them, they're researchers!* The thoughts screamed through his mind. His fists clenched into balls of iron and his teeth clenched hard against one another. He heard voices ahead, low and casual, but below his heavy breath he couldn't understand.

He was only a few feet away from the communications array now. He saw the legs of people on the other side. They stood still, no-one was running, no-one was screaming. He came about as the third shot ripped through the air again and the sound near deafened him at that distance. His hands went to his ears as the pain shot through the centre of his head. He slipped and felt himself going. His legs went in one direction and his upper body went the other. He saw a shallow red puddle, and knew it could only be one thing. Next, it would be his turn.

The air rushed out of him as he hit the deck. He opened his mouth and tried to suck in another breath but found that his chest had closed up on him. He spluttered as he rolled over, and then accidentally sucked in a mouthful of snow. He coughed and tried to breathe as he felt the heat rise in his face. His eyes watered and his chest screamed with pain as he tried to lift himself. He felt hands on him, raising him up out of the snow, and then finally, he felt the air reach his lungs and he began to settle as he heard a woman's laughter below the roll of the rifle fire.

He tried to see where the noise was coming from but the hands spun him the other way. He saw Paul's face. 'You ok Danny?' he said, but Danny didn't care about him. He needed to help the woman. He tried to push him off, but the hands were too strong. Then all of a sudden, they released him, and he was falling again. He felt the wetness of the ice and snow on his face and he began to slide. Through the ice and snow, he saw the red puddle get larger as he approached. He saw it coming and the last thing he wanted was to become soaked in another person's blood. He tried to push himself but it was no use, he closed his eyes and shut his mouth tight, and then he felt it touch his face.

It was fabric that touched him, not blood. He pulled the red spray jacket off his face and examined it, it was a woman's. 'Jesus, Danny,' he heard another man say. 'Sure, know how to make an entrance.'

Danny raised his head and saw Craig Hollins above him. He held out his hand and helped Danny to his feet. The pain in his chest was almost gone, yet the ringing in his ears lingered slightly. 'I heard gunfire,' he said, dumbstruck.

'Bit hard not to huh?' said Sean Wilson, who had been standing next to Craig.

'But the screams?' Danny was still confused.

'Yeah, she's been having the time of her life,' Craig said as he pointed off in front of him.

Another gunshot ripped through the air and Danny jumped at the noise. He spun towards it and saw Wendy Phillips. She had the man's rifle to her shoulder; the recoil had almost knocked her on her ass. She howled with laughter while the *Baroness*'s crew member held her in place with one meaty hand.

'God, she has a real kick to her!' Wendy screamed. 'I think this'll be the sorest I've been for a long time.'

'There's still one left in it. Have another go if you like,' Kee Peters said as his hand moved to the small of her back.

Wendy looked up to him, her smile bright on her face. 'Nah, its ok. I don't think my shoulder could handle another one of those.' Her eyes dropped then met the young man's once more. 'Thanks for letting me try it though.'

Kee smiled and moved his hand up her back once more. 'Anytime. Here, better pass her over.' He left his right hand on her back and reached out with his left, managing to move his face even closer to hers. She didn't pull away.

'Looks like Wendy's found herself a new guy,' Craig said flatly. The only thing the three of them needed now was a can of beer.

'Uh-huh,' Sean uttered.

'Yep,' Danny agreed.

'And what do you think you're doing?' Another voice came in.

Danny looked to his left and beyond Paul, who had lit another cigarette, was Jimmy Sutton.

'Oh shit,' Sean muttered, 'this won't be good.' He started to move toward the enraged young man. 'Jimmy, don't.'

'Get your fuckin' hands off her man.' Jimmy was pulling his gloves from his hands, his face red with anger.

Kee turned around, confused. The hand that had been on Wendy's back was raised in the air and he held the ZKK with the other, the muzzle raised vertically. Jimmy's fist caught him full on the jaw and both men went down. The rifle clattered into the snow and ice; bare knuckles grazed naked cheeks while Kee's gloved hands pawed at Jimmy's face. The two rolled over in the snow while Paul, Sean, Craig and Danny rushed in to stop them.

'Stop it you pair of clowns!' Craig bellowed.

Sean slipped as he ran in and fell on top of them, which enraged Jimmy even further.

Wendy went red with rage. She knelt down as Craig struggled with one of Jimmy's arms and Paul wrestled to contain Kee's strength. She grabbed a hold of Jimmy's ear and twisted it into a similar shape that her mouth had become. 'How dare you,' she hissed into his ear as everyone stopped fighting simultaneously. 'You know what I hate more than sore losers?' She grunted into his ear as she lifted him by it. Jimmy had slowly gotten to his feet, his head tilted at a hilarious angle while Wendy held onto him. 'Jealous ones!' she roared as she lifted her knee into his crotch.

The wind went out of Jimmy as his balls rushed up to nestle in the hollow of his throat. He crashed back down to the ground in a mess of agony and self-pity.

'Don't come and get the shits with another man because you're jealous it's not your gun I'm playing with!' Wendy yelled down at him and stormed off.

Paul, Craig, Sean, Kee and Danny were all still sitting in the snow together as she left. They all watched her go, all five feet and two inches of iron femininity.

Craig was the first to start laughing. He kept his as guffaws, low and as discreet as possible, but when Sean let out the crack of his own failing resistance, the rest of them went. All of them bar Jimmy that was. Jimmy clambered to his knees; tears of his embarrassment were hot in his eyes. The hatred for the men that had laughed at him, the one that had semi-succeeded in stealing his lady. He knelt there for some time, with his hands between his legs, as if waiting to catch his balls when they decided to drop again.

Craig got to his feet, as did Sean and Danny. Paul chuffed to himself as he helped Kee upright.

Kee rubbed his jaw, 'Hey, you throw a good right, man.' He extended his hand to Jimmy. 'No hard feelings?'

James Sutton glared up at the newcomer with bleary red eyes. He didn't look at his hand for a long time, but then when his eyes dropped, Danny thought he saw the retreat in them. Jimmy took his hand, and Kee helped him up. Once to his feet again, James met Kee Peters eyes again as his face twisted in anger and he threw another punch. This time Sean was fast enough. He caught Jimmy's looping right in his own arm and threw him to the ground again.

'Might be better if you two head back to the ship,' Danny said flatly as Craig bent down and picked up the rifle that Jimmy had started to crawl for. 'I don't think Jimmy is himself today.'

'Yeah, too many weeks with blue balls, now she went and popped them on him,' Craig laughed as he raised the rifle to avoid one of James's half-hearted swipes for it. The rest of them laughed and Paul agreed.

'Hey,' Paul said in a gruff voice again as he patted Danny on the back. 'Thanks for showing me around today.' He extended his hand again.

Danny shook and nodded. 'No dramas man. Sorry for flaking out on you before, I just thought the worst.'

'Don't mention it.' He looked over to Jimmy. 'He'll be ok?'

'Yeah, you know it.' Danny smiled as he went to went to help Sean.

Craig handed the rifle over to Kee, muzzle first, which was a horrible way to hand someone a firearm. Danny shook his head as Kee gingerly took the ZKK back into his possession, dusted the ice, snow and grit from its action and slung it over his shoulder. Before he walked off, he took another look at Jimmy. 'It's not worth it, man. If you calm down and want to have a beer, let me know.'

'Get fucked,' Jimmy spat back.

Sean whistled, as he forcibly led James to the Red Shed. 'Maybe not just yet.'

Danny walked with the other two back down to the crappy moor while Kee used a radio that was hooked to his belt to talk to the ship. A man named Reicher acknowledged the call and barked a quick 'ok' when Kee asked for the skiff to come and retrieve them.

There was little enough to talk about while they waited. They watched together as the Coxswain climbed back down the ladder to the skiff that had been moored at the *Baroness*'s side. They heard the engine fire up and soon enough they saw the water churn white as the skiff propelled itself forward toward them.

'Home sweet home, huh?' Danny asked.

The other two nodded. 'Won't be long until he will have to come back for Rheinmarsh and Thompson.' Kee laughed. 'He'll have the shits when he finds out he's going to get interrupted twice in one afternoon.'

As Kee moved, Danny saw that he was wearing the same undergarment that Paul had been wearing. He noticed the metal cross hatching stretch up the fabric that laid against his neck. *R.A.G.E*, he thought and as the skiff pulled up to collect the two newcomers, Danny pulled his phone from his pocket to video them as they left.

'Hey kiddo,' he said as he placed the *Baroness* over his shoulder. 'Have I got some things to tell you about,' he said with a smile, and lifted his balaclava to expose his scarred face. 'But first, how about that view?'

24

DANNY WAS AT A LOSS for the rest of the day. He had nothing to do and no-one to share the time with, so he sat and he waited for the R44 to return. Minutes turned to hours as the sun fortified its stronghold in the sky, until it reached its highest point, which in Antarctica wasn't really that high at all. Still the skies remained empty. The only sound that buffeted his ears was the gentle lapping of the sea against the stone bed they all sat on. The wildlife even seemed to desert them today, perhaps they had considered the sound of the gunshot and realised that it couldn't mean anything good for them and decided to move to quieter outcrops. Perhaps the sight of the *Baroness*, almost majestic as she lay dormant off the coast, was enough to strike fear in their hearts. Maybe it was something else. Something more threatening.

Danny would've like to have remained outside and enjoyed the little warmth that the sun had to offer but he just couldn't handle the cold. Forced to return to either of the powerhouses intermittently, Danny's nose had begun to run at the constant shift in temperatures. Flash frozen into a crisp by the breeze that rolled off the slope to their south, then basted slowly in a warm bath generated by the heavy diesels co-generative systems. He sniffed and wiped a long glob of snot from his face. If he kept this up, he was apt to give himself a chill. He retrieved a hanky from his pocket and blew his nose, then wiped his face as best as he could before covering up again under the safety of his balaclava.

This is it, he thought. *If you're not back now Gary, I'll have to go inside.*

When he stepped back into the frozen atmosphere for what seemed like the twentieth time that day, he did so with ears trained for sound. He strained his hearing and screwed up his face as he struggled to listen below the woosh of the windmill's slow and steady rotations. There was something there. Something, just off in the distance. Danny headed back down to their makeshift moor and looked out. In the distance, far off, he saw the tiniest of specks in the air and all of sudden he felt as if an enormous weight had been lifted from his shoulders.

'Thank fuck for that,' he said as he took in a breath as if for first time. He waited patiently then, unperturbed by the cold winds that buffeted at his spray jacket and pants. He thought he had never heard a sweeter sound than the almost rippling effect the R44's rotors made as they broke the air around them.

Gary brought the bird in low and fast. The sharpness in which he brought the nose up and washed away the speed made Danny's guts roll; he could only imagine what it would have felt like for the passengers.

Gently, the skids were placed on the ground and Danny heard the turbine die. The doors of the cabin burst open before the rotors had been brought to a halt and Danny saw Gary react to the sudden onrush of cold air. He applied the rotor break and the cabin shuddered under the force.

Rheinmarsh was the first to exit the cabin. His face was set in stone and he offered Danny neither a greeting nor insult as he walked past him to the shore. Thompson, their structural engineer, followed him. Like his boss, he paid Danny no attention. He figured that Kee and Paul must have been the only talkative members of the entire crew, but then he remembered what Paul had said about their usual jobs. The crew of the *Baroness* was not meant to mingle with the members of other teams. They were there to do a job and that was it. A smile crept over Danny's face. He must remember to tell Jimmy that – it would be sure to lighten his mood.

Jonty vacated the cabin and their eyes met. From the instant Danny saw him, he knew that he was about to get another job. Jonty stood there, half in the cabin, half out as he put his gloves on his hands and squinted against the light flurry that the wind had blown in his face. Then he approached, a ghost of a smile on his face.

'I'll need you to help the crew of the *Baroness* bring some supplies ashore,' he said flatly.

'Uh-huh,' Danny replied. He wanted to ask about the ship but before he could open his mouth Jonty ran over the top of him.

'They have four thousand litres of diesel, another ten drums of Avgas. Plus, food and sanitary supplies for us.' His attention drifted to the Red Shed. 'I'll need to get Jimmy and the others to help as well. We will need to use our skiff and punt to assist in the unload, and that doesn't answer the question of the drill.'

Danny looked back over to the *Baroness* and saw that the skiff was already on its way back to pick up Rheinmarsh and Thompson.

Danny sighed. At least he would have something to do for the rest of the day. For that matter, all of them would have something to do. Danny considered Jonty, who was still staring up at the Red Shed, his back to him. 'What happened with the ship?'

Jonty paused, then looked back at him over his shoulder. 'Nothing.'

'Come on, more than nothing would be nice.'

Jonty turned back around with a smile. 'Don't worry Daniel, no doubt you'll see for yourself when you go back out there.'

It was as though a wire shorted in his head. 'Back out there?' He pointed behind him. 'Fuck off, not happening.'

Jonty laughed. 'That's the job, Daniel. I need you to take the Pioneer out there for them with a load of their gear. Once you've helped them set up, I'll send Gary to bring you back.'

Danny opened his mouth to argue but Jonty cut him off.

'That's it. No more. That's your contract, that's your job. Don't like it? Then you should've never come here in the first place,' Jonty snarled the last few words as he stormed off.

The only thing Danny could do was to flip the bird to his back as he walked off. Fuck his contract, fuck the Pioneer, and fuck Jonty for that matter. He heard someone laugh and he spun around. Gary was securing the R44 post flight and saw their fight.

'How to make friends and influence people, huh?'

'Fuck you too.' Danny snorted and then helped his friend secure the bird's rotors and cabin doors.

They ended up moving the *Baroness* closer to shore than where it had first moored. This made life a hell of a lot easier to unload the sheer amount of goods that they had brought. Danny and Wendy worked together to manoeuvre the giant few hundred feet of hose that was used to pump the diesel from the ship to the multitude of tanks at Mawson. Danny grunted as he used his weight to heave the hose into position while Wendy secured it to the tank.

'You and Jimmy, huh?' he asked her, a wry grin on his face.

'Don't start Danny,' she warned him. 'My knee's not tired yet and even if it was, I've got another one.'

He laughed aloud. 'Is it just me, or do you always so willingly offer to come into contact with what's between a bloke's legs? Christ, I said three words and already you're coming onto me.'

She didn't look at him but he saw the smile on her face. 'Yeah, you won't like the surprise that I'll give you though.' She twisted the lock ring down over the fitting and hopped up easily, away from the connection. 'All good here, how about on your end?'

Danny looked back down the line. No kinks, no twists. 'Looks good to me.'

Wendy unhooked the radio at her belt and held it closer to her mouth than she probably should. '*Baroness*, this is Mawson diesel crew. You are all connected and ready to start pumping.'

'Right.' The answer was steel on stone and Wendy screwed up her face at it.

'He sounds like he'd be the star of any party.' She moved to the side of the tank and went to jump down.

Danny offered her a hand to help her, but she didn't need it, nor did she take it. She leapt from the side of the tank and bent her legs gracefully as they took the impact from the ten feet drop. Danny smiled as he withdrew his hand. Independent feminists would always make points at how they didn't need men to do this or do that. What he liked about Wendy, was that she just didn't give a shit. She was what she was and would happily tell someone where to go, to their face, without any fear of any repercussion. Basically, she reminded him of a younger Louise.

The hose jerked as the diesel was pumped through it and they listened as one of their emptier tanks began to take on the life-giving substance. As the sound of liquid being poured into a large empty metal space filled their ears, they watched as the two skiffs ferried back supplies, while the punt took on board two drums of Av-gas.

'A lot of gear,' he said. 'I suppose they couldn't rely on our supplies; we couldn't feed all of them, not for long anyway.'

Wendy shrugged as she popped a piece of gum into her mouth and began to chew it noisily. 'They'll use us to store it and ferry it over to them when they need it,' she said unemphatically.

'You reckon?' Danny asked her.

'Yeah.' She looked at him like he was an idiot. A face she pulled with ease. 'Why do you reckon they are giving us ten drums of AV-gas, cause we're good blokes?'

She was right, ten drums was a hell of a lot, obviously they wanted the bird in the air. That cost money and fuel. Sadly, the R44 didn't run on diesel, which was cheap and plentiful. Av-gas was top of the line petrol, high octane and refined to higher degree than anything you get off the pump.

When the first tank had taken its fill, Wendy radioed back to kill the pump. They saw the hose jerk in reaction and Wendy broke the seal. They listened to the hiss as the pressure dropped and she gave it a bit of time before she loosened it completely.

While she worked, Craig used their crane to lift the drums of Av-gas from the skiff and place them to the side. Sean guided the chains and then took the punt back out to sea while Craig arranged his pay loads. Jonty stood on the slope and oversaw all, while Marie stood to his side. During the course of his work, Danny felt his eyes meet Marie's. They considered each other in silence, then finally, Danny returned his attention to Wendy. To his surprise, Wendy was staring at him. As a grin spread across her lips, she nodded toward Jonty and Marie.

'You and Marie, huh?'

He pointed a finger at her. 'Nope, not funny.'

This just made her laugh harder. 'Oooohh,' she mocked. 'Don't lay that forceful animal magnetism on me Danny.' She laid her hand back across her forehead. 'I don't think I could handle it.'

Danny shook his head and ignored her. She soon got tired of making fun of someone who wouldn't bite back and returned to her job.

Before long, the diesel had been pumped. The food and sanitary products had been unloaded, as had the Av-gas. Finally, it came to unloading the drill. Based on the same chassis system as their crane, the drill was a sizeable unit and would be the most difficult thing to unload. Once more, the *Baroness*'s exhaust stacks shot black smoke into the air as her enormous diesel engines sprung to life and began to move her about.

The stern of the ship was backed up as close as possible to their mooring point, while the ship used thrusters to angle and position her. It was close but not close enough. Nevertheless, one should never doubt salvage crews, especially when they are funded by the ever-intriguing R.A.G.E. Black rungs were brought out, long and slender, light enough that a single man could carry them. The white letters of the company's name stood stark against the side. Danny watched as they laid them down and laughed.

'Wendy,' he patted her on the back to get her attention. 'Watch this, the drill's about to get drowned here.'

'They wouldn't be that stupid, would they?' she said as she saw what was happening. 'They look like they're ramps to get a dirt bike on the back of a ute.'

'They're doing it.' Danny shook his head as the tracks of the drill's chassis began to roll forward.

Danny's hand crept over his mouth as he cringed and waited for the racks to give way. Further and further the drill went across and the more of it that moved from the rearward gate of the *Baroness* the more weight was spread onto the light tracks. Then Danny's hand fell away as the entire weight of the tracked vehicle was supported by these *things,* and still they did not buckle. Slowly and surely, the drill crossed the gap between boat and moor and before he knew it, the tracks were grinding away at the stone where he had stood only a few hours before.

'I don't fucking believe it,' Danny said as he stood.

Wendy laughed. 'You shouldn't be so quick to judge. Their toys are better than ours.'

'Not wrong,' he grumbled as he stood up again.

He began to move back down to assess what gear he would need to take on the back of the Pioneer, which was a heavier tracked vehicle than the ever-favourite Hägglund. The Pioneer was a slower vehicle but was capable of carrying a hell of a lot more weight, which from the look of it, was exactly what he would need. Behind the drill he noticed a chain that was stretched taught. The closer he came, he was able to hear the sound of steel scraping against steel until he saw it: they were dragging a shipping container behind the drill.

They pulled it as far forward as they could, until the edge of the container was near enough touching the miracle ramps. Then a forklift came into sight and a few men helped manoeuvre the container as they lifted the edge and then guided the drill's driver to move forward again. Once the brick shape had been lifted above the lip of the ramps, the container glided easily across the open space. It wasn't long before they were calling him to bring the Pioneer down, so they could load it on its back.

The rear gates lifted and sealed as the *Baroness* pulled away again. Everything was unloaded now and only the pack up remained. The Pioneer rattled hard as its large diesel fired up. In truth, Danny had neglected the big beast as he doubted that they would have any need of it before the summer came. With the summer brought a new mechanic, and then the big bastard of a thing would be someone else's problem. Now that the Pioneer would not only need to be driven, but driven all the bloody way to Amery and with a load on its back, Danny figured he had a busy night ahead making sure everything was Mickey Mouse.

He sighed as he threw himself up into the large cabin and threw the big bitch into gear. She shuddered as the power went through her clutch and her tracks began to churn. By the time he had driven her the short distance down to the dock, she had warmed up and moved a lot easier. Just like an old truck, they never let you down, they just went about things a little slower. He rapped his fingers on the dash as Craig lowered the container onto the back of the Pioneer and then gave him the thumbs up to say it had been dropped. Danny nodded and leapt out of the cabin to secure his load. Once everything was locked and secured, he hopped back into the cabin and threw the Pioneer into gear again and took her back under cover.

When he hopped out again, he found that Jonty was there waiting for him. Once again there were no pleasantries, only business existed between the two men now.

'Tomorrow morning, five a.m.,' Jonty said as he gestured toward the Pioneer. 'Make sure it's ready tonight and then get some rest. You'll have a big day tomorrow and I don't want any mistakes.'

'Yeah, righto mate,' Danny muttered as he turned his back on Jonty.

'I mean it Daniel,' his voice was low and gruff. 'I don't want any more bullshit from you, not like last time.'

Danny glared at him. There was no response required because Jonty left it at that. The head researcher had started to make his way out of the shed. Danny's face twisted into a snarl as he turned back to the Pioneer. 'I'm sick of that fucker,' he muttered to himself. 'It should have been him that went instead of Charlie.' He closed his hands into fists and stared at them. Maybe it was a good thing that he was being sent away from Mawson. It seemed that every second meeting he had with Jonty now almost came to blows. Was it that Jonty was winding him up? Was it that he was just becoming so quick to anger, so quick to assuming everything?

He thought about the way he'd reacted when he'd thought Wendy had been shot. The way that everything seemed to slow and his vision went funny. He had thought that he had seen a puddle of blood but it was just Wendy's jacket. He thought he had heard her scream, a scream that in his mind had been her begging for her life, whereas in reality she was laughing with joy. He thought about the way he threw his weight against Paul in his moment of terror and then he thought about how Jimmy had reacted.

'Everything is going to shit,' he muttered. If taking this container out to Amery got rid of that fucking ship then so be it. 'So be it.'

25

DANNY SAT IN THE CABIN of the Pioneer as its tracks churned beneath him. Its heavy diesel set out a dull drone that had rattled into his head by the end of the second hour. With only the steady hum of the cabin's heater blower to break up the monotony, Danny had become weary. He was weary of the way the snow danced across his vision, which made it seem like static on an old TV. The only thing he was waiting for was the ripple that seemed to run in an upward direction when the reception was poor. He was weary of feeling alone; having no-one else in the cabin with him on a drive that was made longer by the Pioneer's crawling pace had left him with only his thoughts for company, and currently he didn't find himself to be an enjoyable companion.

More than anything, he was weary of his fear for this place. He had driven nonstop until he had thought that he had found the place where the Charlie incident had occurred. Then he had allowed the Pioneer to slow to a crawl while he sat and looked at the clumps of snow and slush. He remembered the way the blood had seeped into the ice and snow. The way it turned into a red slurry that could have been anything but what it was. He thought about Charlie's crazed face. The way he'd screamed in his claustrophobic outrage. The scars on Danny's face began to itch madly. Then he thought about the ship, and the blood that was frozen to the walls and the floor. Now as he ran his hand across it, it seemed to crumble off and fall to the ground like it was just rubbish that he had left in his freezer for too long.

He was startled by the radio, as the pilot of the Red Brick Hägglund that they had leant the salvage crew told him to keep moving.

It wasn't the fact that Jonty had given them whatever they wanted that annoyed him. It was the fact that he was being treated like a soldier that pissed him off. When they told you to do something, it was an order. There wasn't any asking or any please or thank yous with this mob. It was do this, do it now and have it done yesterday.

Jonty had given him over. Not that he was anyone's to give, but Danny gritted his teeth and moved on. He had serviced the Pioneer in the late hours of the evening. He had changed the fluids that required it and topped up the ones that he thought needed it; it was difficult in the cold like this, as oil got thinner as it got hotter and took up more space, that's why there's two levels on the dipstick of an automatic transmission. But, if they were going to treat him like enlisted trash, then he'd act like it and near enough was good enough when it came to government work.

Once he had finished with the Pioneer, he had been about to start with his tidy up when Jonty had come to see him again. He'd slapped the bright orange guard of the Pioneer as he looked up to it and then told him that both of the camp Hägglunds would be accompanying him out there tomorrow. Each would carry crew in the front compartment while their rear cabins would be loaded with supplies. Danny looked over at the blue Hägglund, which had sat dormant for the last four months while they used the newer red one for most of the heavy lifting. He had shaken his head and sighed as he had thrown the rag he was holding to the ground.

The Blue Brick had taken more work than the Pioneer, having two flat batteries, oil that looked as though it had been refined back in the forties and a busted engine mount. How the hell one of those things could break an engine mount was beyond him, but nevertheless. It had been two in the morning when he had finished. His eyes had near hung out of his head by that stage. As he walked out to shower and sleep, he saw that there was already movement on the *Baroness* as figures moved behind lighted windows and partially blocked out their brilliance. He had figured that he would only get an hour or two if he was lucky, but he managed three hours of stone-motherless-cold unconsciousness before a rap at his door told him they were ready to leave.

Now they were almost there, the Pioneer had laboured up the steep slopes but had trundled along happily enough on the ridge lines, the treacherous slopes that were just endless sweeping hills of white. The Pioneer's tracks had ground away at the ice when they had first reached Amery. They slipped and churned while the cabin jolted and bucked Danny about, but it was the drive from the rearward skids, the ones ladened down by the weight of the container that had driven him forward. Once the forward tracks were up and over the small step, the rear ones followed easily. Once the heaviest and widest vehicle had created the path, the smaller, more agile Hägglunds followed easily and finally the drill which had kept pace with the slow, ambling Pioneer easily. Then they were on Amery again. The flat, desolate ice shelf that the snow skittered across, leaving shallow rivers of powder in the low spots.

It wasn't hard to know exactly where to go. Danny felt as though he could have parked them directly on the spot where the Red Brick was left. It wasn't the fact that he remembered where D-28 had been; the colossal block of ice had moved further away from Amery in the short time since he had seen it last. It was the fact that the memory was engrained in his mind. He remembered the way the cliff looked as he drove the Red Brick up to its edge. He remembered where he had been standing when the R44 first came onto them. He remembered where they had set up camp and slept in the back of the Hägglund. But none of it mattered anymore, it was all for naught.

The closer they came, the better Danny could see, and sure enough the silhouette that was becoming larger and larger, was that of the R44.

Three figures stood stalwart against the horizon. One of them pointed as he walked slowly around a spike that had been driven into the ice. Even at this distance Danny picked Rheinmarsh easily. He was the only one in Mawson that had white hair but not only that, he moved differently to everyone else. Powerful, yet smooth and deliberate.

The man to his rear, which he thought was Thompson the electrical engineer, was making notes as Rheinmarsh was pointing things out. The other was Jonty. Being a glaciologist, Danny figured that wouldn't be able to keep himself away from the situation. How a glaciologist would allow the drilling of an ancient ice shelf was one thing, but to close his eyes to the opportunity was another.

Thompson waved him into a position as they came nearer and the other Hägglunds parked further back.

'What took so long?' Rheinmarsh complained as Danny stepped out of the cabin. 'I was told that the drive only takes five hours, you were at least seven.'

Danny blinked at the demanding tone. He pointed to the Hägglunds. 'Five hours in one of those, with fuel stops.' Then he pointed to the Pioneer, the big lumbering orange hulk. 'Seven hours in those. Your drivers didn't know where to go, so they followed me.'

Rheinmarsh shook his head as he turned away and muttered, 'these delays are unacceptable.' He spun and clapped his hands together. 'Drop the container here, where I am standing.' He ran his arms to express the direction where he wanted it to run.

Danny put up his hands. 'Look. I'll bring the Pioneer around, you just tell me where to be.' He'd been out of the cabin for not even a minute and already he was sick of being there. Jonty said not a word about the way Rheinmarsh spoke to him, not that he'd care, the piece of shit.

The Pioneer fired back into life and the cabin shuddered as Danny reversed the vehicle up thirty feet. He moved into position where Rheinmarsh wanted him and rolled his eyes as the white-haired European stood there moving his arms in that AFL referee motion the entire time. He sighed as he let the heavy diesel fall to an idle, and stepped out into the cold.

By the time he had used the chassis-mounted crane to drop the container, Gary had joined him from inside the R44's cabin. He yawned as he stretched and then came about from the other side of the Pioneer's cab, so not to get crushed by the twenty feet container. 'You look like shit,' he said to Danny through another yawn.

'You are shit,' he grumbled back.

Gary laughed as the crane settled the container down and one of the crew members that he didn't know un-hitched him. No sooner was the crane packed away that he was yelled at for not moving the Pioneer out of the way. He sighed again as angry thoughts flooded his mind but held his tongue as he entered the cabin and shifted the Pioneer again. If driving for seven hours had pissed him off, being spoken to like he was an idiot set him over the edge. Danny entered a dark brood as he folded his arms and leant back against the bright orange hull.

Gary leant next to him. 'Don't stress about it man, we'll head back soon and we can have a shot of rye.'

'Rye?' he asked in disgust.

'Yeah, well can't keep drinking the good stuff. I'll run out. We still have a few months to go don't forget.'

Danny sighed once more as he let his head rest against the steel side. He was right, but Christ it was coming up quick. His end date was the 10th of December, which was when the ship that brought their yearly supplies would disembark again. Hopefully he would be back by New Year's. Hopefully. 'Can't come quick enough,' he mumbled.

They watched as the crew swarmed around the container. The front doors were unlatched, but then he noticed that men had climbed on top of it and were removing large, stainless-steel bolts from various spots. Pneumatic guns rattled as bolts were pulled from the roof, then others rattled as more were pulled from the side. Danny screwed up his face in confusion as the two of them watched. Danny had friends back in Sydney that were into campers and trailers that unfolded into tents and things like that. He was interested slightly as well, but some of the cheaper ones were like fifteen thousand dollars, which he found to be a ghastly amount. If cheap, nasty trailers were fifteen grand he would've hated to see the bill for what was unfolding in front of him.

Each container wall dislodged and was laid flat on the ground. From there, heavy rolls of canvas and the same material that Paul's shirt was made of, were dragged out and lain in sections. Each man knew exactly where everything was and what his job entailed when it came to setting it up. Danny heard short, sharp rips as someone pulled the chord on a petrol generator and then heard the rattle as an air compressor started up. In five minutes, the structure had taken shape. Six, vast, spacious rooms stood in front of him, where before there had just been a shipping container. Each wall was lined with the dark fabric and the cross-hatched material. More generators were being fired up by the second.

Danny couldn't believe the rapidity in which the structure grew. In no time, men were inside and were organising tables and chairs that had been flat-packed into the upper section of the container. Chords were being hung from plastic hooks that were sewn into the fabric, LED strips ran on almost every seam and soon they blared to life. One of the men had walked closer to the cliff's edge with a large black box, while another ran him a power cable from the generator. Danny heard the short, sharp cracks from a ramset gun as the first man secured the box to the ground. Then he opened it up and unfolded a wire-thin satellite dish. Once he had finished, he offered another man, who was sitting inside the structure, the thumbs up. Danny then watched as three laptops were pulled from black, plastic cases and set up on the desk. He nodded aptly as he hammered away on the keyboards. 'Communications are up.'

'Impressive, isn't it?' said a familiar voice. Danny turned and saw Paul Stathis there. He smiled as he smoked a cigarette; once more he was only dressed in his parka and thick, black cargo pants.

'Gift from the same place?' Danny asked as he gestured to the logo on Paul's chest.

He nodded. 'Pretty good. Hopefully they don't want to keep it after this trip, I'll make a house out of it.'

Gary laughed. 'Wouldn't miss watching TV?'

Paul smiled again as he took another drag. 'Either of you have your phone on you?'

Danny reached into his pocket and pulled out his phone, holding it out to Paul. With the smile still plastered across his face, his held out his hands. 'Make a phone call, I'm sure it's been a while since you've spoken to your mother.'

'It has been,' Danny said. 'Are you nuts though? I have trouble with reception on this fucking thing in Sydney, let alone out here.'

'Look,' he said confidently.

Danny considered at his phone and the screen lit up. Four bars and the little 4G symbol sat next to it, yet instead of Telstra which was his standard carrier, it had the same name that was embroidered on Paul's shirt.

'Who the fuck are these guys?' he said, absolutely stunned at what he had just seen.

'I don't know.' Paul shrugged as the smile disappeared from his face again. 'They've got deeper pockets than I do.' He pointed back over to the satellite dish as the cigarette lolled about in his mouth. 'Good little setup, it piggybacks off your satellite array and offers a mobile signal for about forty, fifty feet.' He took the butt out of his mouth and spat. 'Even has a battery pack, so if the generator dies and all the radios go quiet, one of the guys can use their phone to call the *Baroness* and help can at least get on its way out to them.' He put out his cigarette on his boot and put the butt in his pocket. 'Anyway, better get back to it.' With that, he left.

Danny was left there standing next to Gary with his phone in his hand and mouth open. With the structure now complete, Danny was left in a further state of shock when he saw them fit an inflatable door, which was likewise made out of the wonder material, to the opening of the structure. Rubber seals lined its edges and the man who was fitting it needed to push hard to get it to pop into the opening. When he pushed, his hands didn't sink into the material, as Danny would've expected. Even with an inflatable raft, which was made of some pretty tough stuff, you could get your hand to sink if you pushed hard enough. This stuff looked like concrete. Once the door had been pushed into the opening, Danny saw the crew member pull a tab and it swung open just like a normal house door. Then, when he let go, it automatically swung shut and sealed again.

'This is unbelievable,' Danny said. 'Could you imagine this thing at a camping expo?'

'Yeah, I've seen crappy versions of it that fit into a trailer,' Gary said as leant back on the Pioneer. 'The ones that blow up like this thing cost like fifty grand and look like shit in comparison to this.'

'Yeah,' Danny shook his head. 'You know it.'

Rheinmarsh had moved over to the drill operator; if Danny had felt sorry for himself then the poor bastard that had driven the drill out onto the ice shelf would've been ready to commit suicide. The seats in those machines weren't designed for long hauls, neither was the suspension. Danny watched as the poor bugger almost fell out of the machine when the door opened. One hand was on his back and his face looked as pale as the ice he fell on. Rheinmarsh didn't blink; he examined the other men in his crew, near ten of them, and barked an order. Instantly, tools were dropped as was anything else in hand and three men assisted the weak driver into the structure, while a fourth took the wheel. They watched as Rheinmarsh directed the man to the spike into the ground, and then kicked the spike to loosen its hold. With some force, the white-haired European was able to remove the spike and without further ado, the drilling commenced.

It was then that Rheinmarsh turned his attention to Jonty once more. Over the drilling and the other tools, it was impossible to hear what was said. Nevertheless, it was hard to miss the look on his face when he pointed toward them. Jonty looked abashed, his face went red, and they saw him try and stand up for himself. Obviously, something had been said that he disliked but Danny doubted it was about either of them.

Eventually, Rheinmarsh disappeared beyond the inflatable door and Jonty waved them over.

'It's time for us to leave, they don't want us here while they're working.' His voice was almost a sulk and Danny worked out what the problem was. He wanted to stay but Rheinmarsh wouldn't allow it.

'Gee, Jay,' Danny started. 'I thought you would have stayed out here to supervise their work? After all, you are the glaciologist.'

Jonty's eyes narrowed above his pursed lips. 'You know that Mawson and its people are more important than a block of ice.'

'What about what's below it?' Danny returned as he opened the cabin door to the chopper.

Jonty didn't reply, instead he brushed passed and took the front passenger seat in the R44, the seat that Danny had been heading for. In the end, Danny did want to sit in the front, but he wanted sleep more, so he happily took the back seat all to himself.

He doubted that they had even taken off by the time he had fallen asleep. With the cabin doors shut and most of the noise from the drill blocked out by the rising turbine pitch, he felt himself sink deep into the softness of the back seat. His eyes closed beneath the weight of their lids and he felt the heaviness of deep sleep come over him. As soon as the dream began, fear gripped him. The darkness that loomed around him was one thing, but it was the sound that was the worst, almost like monstrous breaths. Low and deep grumbles seemed to shake him in his slumber, seemed to suck him closer and closer with each inhale but deny him any escape with the exhale. He tried to claw himself away, he tried to scream, but the weight of the world above him prevented him.

Then he saw the eyes again. Large and yellow, hate that had grown in them over the past decades poured out. He felt the malice that they held. He felt the hunger in its gut, the desire to leave, to stretch. Then it spoke to him, in a cold, deep voice that started in the centre of his head and ran down his spine to where it speared a stake of fear through his heart.

'I will kill you all.'

And then, there was darkness.

26

THE AFTERNOON THEY ARRIVED back to Mawson, Danny found that a new sort of spirit had worked its way into the hearts of his camp mates. Everyone seemed happier; everyone seemed a little less stressed. Even Jimmy had smiled at him when Danny had passed him in the cold porch. Anne Castelli and Corinth Butler were in the kitchen when Danny made his way into the mess, and to Danny's surprise, the pair of them were humming. Realising that the reason Anne was in the kitchen was because he had managed to shirk yet another one of his chore-roster shifts, Danny sheepishly entered. They had all the eggs out and he figured that today must be the day that they needed to be oiled and flipped again. He stepped to Corinth's side and leant his head on her shoulder.

'I'm sorry Ma,' he said as if he was her child. 'I almost missed another night with you.'

Corinth didn't look at him, her face had gone sullen, but the smile in her eyes betrayed her. 'I know how it is these days,' she said in a remarkably accurate Boston accent. 'Kids don't want to hang around with their mothers. All the new kids come to town and all of a sudden, ole Ma is forgotten and hung out to dry.'

'Oh, come on Ma.' He picked up the accent well enough. 'You know it's not like that.'

'Oh, I know well enough,' she feigned again. 'I'm just happy your father wasn't alive to see this.'

'Christ,' he said defeated as he retreated. 'You do that well enough to be on Broadway.'

Corinth smiled at him. 'I did classes.' She hadn't dropped the accent yet and pronounced the 'a' as 'air': 'cl-air-sses.' 'I always wanted to get out of the kitchen and onto the stage but you know how it is.'

Danny nodded; sure, everyone knew how it was. Everyone had a dream. It was easy enough to do as Corinth had, to take a few first steps along the path of one's dream, to wet their toes. But to take the almighty plunge into the depths of the icy water, that was another thing altogether. To be honest, one of the saddest things in his life would be that he knew very little people that had actually taken that plunge. Who had actually said 'Nope, fuck it, I am giving this everything'? Everyone just seemed to do their job and became caught up in the daily grind. He didn't have to ask why, although he would've liked to. At that moment he would've loved to have been a child again and look up to old Ma and ask why she hadn't just said 'fuck it,' and pursued her dreams because hell, why not?

But he didn't. It was nice to be a child, or childish from time to time. In the end, pretending is just an escape from the reality, a short respite from the cold and bitter truth. Besides, he hated to be patronised. If he had asked, she would've turned to him and smiled and said because she had children of her own, and her job was to keep the money coming in so that they could eat, sleep under a roof and pursue dreams of their own. That was the automatic response. The parental response. He had seen it in the eyes of his father, who had persisted in wearing holey underwear, because they felt 'comfortable.' He had seen it when his father had pored over a new power tool, the way he had lingered on that page in the advert, only to put it aside so that he could pay Danny's school fees. Danny's mind went to his own child, the days were just coming closer and closer. Already, his life had started to revolve around 'it.' Already, the child within him had been forced to take a step back, while the adult laboured to bring in the coin.

He sighed as he turned away; his smile was long gone and only the ghost of a grimace was left to offer his feelings. Corinth had yet to meet his eyes. It was then that he saw that she wasn't oiling and flipping the eggs, but cracking and splitting them. He was almost horrified at the sight, all of that work they had put in… well, them, not him. Nevertheless, all of that work just to throw it away now?

'What are you doing?' he asked, dumbfounded.

When Corinth glanced up and saw his face, she started to laugh.

Anne, who had remained silent till this point, also began to chuckle at the sight of him. 'You'd think we had taken your firstborn out the front of the city hall and stoned her, from the look on your face,' she remarked.

Danny glanced at her, then returned his attention to the egg yolk that Corinth was separating from the white. 'Well, you kind of have.'

Corinth laughed as she tipped the perfect yolk into a bowl that contained many others and poured the whites into another. 'We have ample supply, Danny.' She smiled as she reached for another. 'Didn't you see all of the supplies they brought in from that ship? Almost enough for six months, and our usual supply ship will be only a few months at tops.'

'I thought that most of that food was for the crew out at the ice shelf,' Danny said, confused.

'I imagine most of it is,' she said with a shrug. 'But they brought a lot and last night there was none of them hounding me to make them anything. Anyone that was left at Mawson went back to the ship and I haven't seen heads or tails of them since.'

Danny watched Anne Castelli, who was spreading flour out over a section of stainless benchtop and had started to knead some dough. 'So, you're going to make a cake?' he asked.

'We're going to do more than that Danny.' Anne gave him one of her looks.

'We're going to have a party,' Corinth said excitedly. 'Isn't that great?'

'A party? Really?' His mood had been so dark lately that a party had been the furthest thing from his mind. 'You think now is the time?'

'I think it's the perfect time,' Anne backed up Corinth. 'You small few have been moping around here, making everyone else miserable.

So yes, Danny, I think a party is a fantastic idea to get everyone's mind off that stupid block of ice.'

Danny shrugged. 'You're probably right.'

'I know I'm right, and don't forget that I am the doctor here, so you all have to do what I tell you anyway.' She pointed her long, slender finger in his face.

'Ok, ok.' He held his hands up as he backed away. 'Sure thing, doctor's orders and all that.' He moved to the bench then and picked up a knife. 'How do you want me to help then? I'm rostered on this afternoon so I am all yours.' He smiled at them.

Corinth looked from his face to the knife clutched in his hands. 'Put that down, go and get yourself cleaned up.' She wrinkled her nose. 'I can still smell fuel on you from those machines.' She began to wave her hands at him. 'Then maybe go help Marty, we will be fine in here.'

Danny raised his eyebrows as he placed the knife back on the rack. He sniffed beneath his armpit as he left the kitchen and noticed a slight smell, but who knew. If they didn't want his help then so be it. He showered and put on one of the hoodies that Louise had stained with hair dye and a pair of textured socks in lieu of his Ugg boots; his favourite set of clothes were still yet to be found.

Marty ended up being in the communications room with Bobby. The pair of them were bent over Marty's laptop and were giggling to each other as they scrolled through a list of songs. 'What are you two galoots up to?' They both snapped their heads towards him and then relaxed as they saw who it was.

'Ahh nothing.' Marty waved back at him. 'Just going over the song list for karaoke.'

'Christ,' Danny shook his head. 'This party thing is the real deal huh?' What else were they going to bring out?'

'Oh yeah.' Bobby smiled. 'We've been going through getting everything ready, we've got a projector, speaker and mic to set up. Fair bit of stuff to do by the time Friday rolls around.'

Danny nodded. Ok so he finally knew when the party was going to go ahead. It was easy to lose track of what day was what in Mawson as no day really meant anything different. But after a look at his phone, he saw that it was Wednesday, so the big party would happen two nights from now. 'Man, it's only Wednesday and they're already cooking?' he said incredulously.

Marty looked up at him confused. 'Cakes are ok to cook now,' he said. 'My mum used to do that all the time.'

'Anyway—' Danny was starting to get annoyed by all this party talk '—they said you two needed a hand getting ready.'

'Nah, we're fine,' Bobby said. 'Won't need a hand until Friday.'

'You can sit down and help us go through songs if you want, some people have already started to hand in their requests.'

'No thanks. Have fun,' he remarked as they went back to their computer screen. He moved back out into the hall and decided to go for a walk outside. The party had gone from being an interesting piece of news, to something he found suffocating.

He moved back into the cold porch and ignored Jimmy's happy greeting. Passed by Craig and Sean who were lugging a television screen back to the cold porch's heavy entry door. He agreed to hold the door open for them while they lugged it in, but ignored any further comments they offered about what the television screen was for.

Instead, he went to his four kings and checked their oil levels, he checked the torsion of the rocker covers, for no particular reason but he wanted something to do. He moved underneath and checked for oil leakages and then ran his hands over the hoses that ran the co-generative system to check for coolant leakages. It was all stuff that was good to do, but none of it really needed doing.

The next thing he did to occupy himself was to service the great crane that had seen seldom work since summer, apart from unloading the *Baroness*. Once again, the vehicle was fine and needed little actual work, but nevertheless he ran his eyes over the whole thing and made sure. By the time he had finished, he was exhausted. It had been a tremendously long day that had now, finally, fallen into night. As he sagged down next to the crane, he pulled his phone from his pocket. Instinctively, he checked the reception bar: three bars. He would've been only fifty feet from the communications array and he'd had better reception on Amery. A laugh escaped his mouth as he opened the video call application. He sighed a deep and terrible breath of air as his thumb hovered over Louise's name. Not allowing himself any further distractions, he bit the bullet and called his partner.

He could tell she was tired when she answered. She didn't generally get bags under her eyes, but the eyes themselves looked exhausted. Still, she smiled at him and asked him how his day was and he told her. He told her everything about the ice shelf, he told her about the creature that he had seen and finally, he told her about Charlie.

Louise, to her credit, pulled herself out of bed when she had heard the urgency in his voice. Had made herself a coffee and had sat up to listen. When he told her about the creature, she placed both hands over her mouth as if in horror at what he had described but her reaction to what had happened to Charlie had torn him to shreds. He watched a tear roll down her cheek and a single thought flashed through his mind – *why can't I do that?*

It was like the answer to a long-lost prayer, why did he feel so shit and why was he in such a bad mood when everyone else was happy? The answer was that he needed to sit down and have an honest to God cry. He needed to get everything out of his system, he needed to move on. A weight that was equivalent to the crane that he leant against had been lifted from his chest but still, he didn't think it was all gone.

When she asked him what they had done with Charlie, a question that was as honest and innocent as the child that asked their parent why they hadn't followed their dream, he did cry. His lips became fat with the exhaustion that poured out of him. The tap had been opened and his eyes became bleary. He put the phone down as he blew his nose into one of the rags that he had kept in his pocket and then he rested his head back again and looked up to the roof of the shed.

'They put him in the freezer with the food,' he bawled almost unintelligibly. 'I couldn't handle looking at the cakes, knowing they were making cakes now because they would have to put them in the same room as him.'

Louise, through all of this, did exactly what he needed her to do: listen. But more than that, she cried with him as the pain that he felt moved into her. When the tears had started to slow, she asked him to look at her and that was probably the hardest thing to do.

'Danny,' she said calmly as he continued to cry in his refusal to face her. 'Honey, come on, look at me.'

It took more strength than he had to pick the phone back up. More strength than it had taken to beat the life out of Charlie Muscat. More strength than it had taken to push himself away from that fucking thing in the ship, but he did it.

He gazed into her beautiful eyes which glistened now with the tears that had welled up in them. 'The reason you do anything is for me,' she said calmly. 'If you hadn't done what you did, then I wouldn't be seeing you right now.'

'But you can't touch me,' he sobbed.

'I will again, one day,' she replied softly. 'But for now, seeing you is enough. I'd rather see you, than hear about what had happened from someone else. More than that Danny, I want you to be able to see your daughter.' She put her hand over her mouth.

'Daughter?' he choked. 'You know?'

She started to cry again. 'I knew but I wanted to surprise you, honey. I'm sorry.'

'Don't apologise to me,' he wept. 'Don't. Please.' He held his hand to his face as another convulsion of tears passed through him. 'That's the best news anyone could've given me.' He smiled through the tears.

'Do you want to help me come up with a name?' She sniffed as she wiped away the tears that had started to roll freely down her cheeks.

'You know it.' He laughed while he blinked away the water in his eyes. 'You know it.'

And so, for the next hour they rattled names off to each other, they went through the list of famous people. Louise was especially fond of female adventurers, so Danny listened patiently while sent she went through the list that she had already come up with. Amelia, for the famous pilot. Lara, was everyone's favourite athletic archaeologist.

One that threw him was Freya, after the Norse goddess, but Danny just smiled as he pretended to mull them about in his mind and Louise tried them on for size with his surname. 'Freya Myers, Lara Myers, Amelia Myers.' He had to admit, Amelia wasn't too bad but the rest were rubbish.

Danny put forward a few of his own: Anne, Corinth; he omitted Marie's name for obvious reasons. He ran his hand through the stubble on his chin as he racked his brain. His grandmother had been named Leanna, he liked that one and muttered the full name to himself before he even offered it to Louise. 'Leanna Myers.'

'Huh?' she asked him, her head cocked to one side. 'Say that again.'

Danny repeated himself a little louder and saw the smile appear on her face. 'That's a nice name,' she conceded. 'Really nice.'

Danny said it again. 'Leanna Myers.' His smile softened and they knew it. He began to wonder if every couple had this connection and this feeling of love between them as they decided on the name of their firstborn. Then he laughed as he looked into the eyes of his darling partner.

'I love you Hun,' she said softly.

'I love you too,' he replied as he watched another single tear roll down her cheek.

27

WITH THE WEIGHT OF THE WORLD lifted from his shoulders, Danny slept well that night, free of muscle cramps, free of disturbances. Better yet, he slept free of dreams. Whether good or bad, he was thankful. When he emerged the next day, his outlook on the world seemed different. He didn't feel claustrophobic, as if he was trapped by the weight of everything that he had seen or done. He felt happy, for the first time in weeks.

Sure, he had laughed at jokes and had contributed to the humorous banter between camp mates, but any man knew that meant nothing. A man that wore his heart on his sleeve was an open man, but Danny dwelled. He held everything in and allowed the wounds that he bore on his heart to fester and become fat with gangrenous pus and muck before he had allowed himself to be helped. This often came to the detriment of his relationships, whether sexual or based on nothing more than friendship. His attitude swings were fantastic at driving people away. Yet Louise was different, she managed to see through it, managed to give him space when he needed it and offered a full-on assault on his heart when he became stubborn.

The way she used her words, the way she looked at him, stripped the defences that he had built around his heart to nothing more than what they were: fabric, flesh and bone. As the walls came tumbling down and the wounds that he had carried so close became exposed, she wouldn't kick him in his vulnerability, nor would she make him resent her. Instead, she would brush away the dirt and wash away the grime, until he was once again the man whose child she bore. Only then, would she help him back to his feet and embrace him as her equal and as a half that could never be whole without its partner.

Hence, the feeling of being uplifted coursed through Danny's veins through the following day. It brightened his outlook on life and he imagined that it made him more pleasant to be around. Rather than shun the idea of the party, Danny even became involved, somewhat. As the *Baroness* had been kind enough to offer so much Av-gas, Gary and himself figured that the loss of some wouldn't be a problem. In the late afternoon of that new day, the two flew to Davis, another Australian-led camp, for the sole purpose of fetching a few cases of their locally brewed Nunatak Brewing Company ale.

Danny liked a drop like the next man, as he liked a pull on the butt of a cigarette as well. Both of which were hard habits made easy to boot, once he had arrived on Mawson. The lack of convenience was a startling loss to most, the inability to just walk down to the shops to grab whatever one needed meant they actually had to plan. No matter how many times a plan sheet was reviewed or a packing list subjected to a screening eye, one week or two would pass and the realisation would come that something had been forgotten. In the case of the Davis camp, they took it to the next level and started up their own researcher-funded brewery. Danny was told that everyone joined in cleaning the bottles and everyone on camp got to enjoy it for what it was: a bit of fun.

Sure enough, when they had landed, the man that Bobby had organised it with, a wild-haired middle-aged man with buck teeth, handed them the cases reluctantly. 'You're going to bring the bottles back, aren't you?' he asked, his tone riddled with doubt. 'We can't replace them, you know that.'

Gary and Danny waved away his doubts and said, 'come on man, we know better than to just throw them away.' It was that afternoon that the Nunatak Brewing Company Ale became not only the only beer to be brewed on the continent, but the only beer that either of them knew to be worth a flight beyond the Amery Ice Shelf.

They ran the R44 above the inflatable camp that the *Baroness's* men had set up. They saw the drill bring up large chunks of ice from the coring bit it was using. Large enough to fit two men side by side, Danny didn't think it would take them long to reach whatever it was down below. He just hoped he didn't have to be a part of it anymore.

Gary offered to take them down between the ice shelf and the ever-looming D-28 to see the ship, but once again, Danny declined the offer.

They were welcomed back with shouts of joy from the other men who had yearned for a beer ever since Fort Knox had run dry. The fort was another pet name offered by camp mates for the locked liquor cabinet, which had been raped and pillaged by the men months ago. Sore heads and sorrowful regret had followed that evening and only Gary had held any stock of liquor since that day. While the men cheered at the sight of beer, the women rolled their eyes, content with the punch that Marie Swan had been peddling.

And so, everything was set. Even the karaoke had been set up with Danny's help and the women clucked about what songs they were going to sing. Danny found this interesting as Wendy didn't take part of these conversations; instead she hung around Gary more and more, much to James Sutton's discontent. Nevertheless, the cakes were made, the potato bake had been prepared for the oven and the chicken wings were marinating. All of the things to make every man, woman or child lick their lips and rub their tummies. Even Danny, for that matter.

The morning of the party, Gary was forced to fly back to the ice shelf. He rolled his eyes and argued blankly about the whole request, which Danny could sort of understand. This party had been built up so much that no-one really wanted to leave camp that day, except for Marie. Danny had been sitting at one of the tables sipping coffee alongside his friend, when Bobby had entered the room. The look he gave Danny was one of fear, but even as he spoke, the tone of his excitement slipped through his lips.

'They've finished digging.' Three words to chill a man's heart.

'Already?' Danny couldn't help but ask.

'Well, yeah,' he replied, 'that's what I said.' He continued, 'I thought the shelf was supposed to be six hundred feet thick, but the man said that they weren't there to fornicate with arachnids, whatever that means.'

Gary laughed.

A worried expression covered his face. 'You won't be laughing when they ask you to go out there in a few minutes.'

The concern that Bobby had shown had now washed across the face of the pilot. 'What, today?'

'Yeah.'

'Fuck off,' he exclaimed.

Bobby shrugged. 'Tell them that when they ask. I don't care.' With that Bobby left.

Danny figured that he had asked Jonty to give him a toilet break, as it wasn't often anymore that the radio room could be left alone, not that it ever had. Sure enough, not two minutes passed since Bobby's exit when Jonty and Marie entered the mess and made a beeline for where they were sitting.

'Oh, fuck me drunk.' Gary said as he let his face fall into his hands. 'Kill me now, please Lord.'

Danny began to laugh as Jonty and Marie finally arrived at the table. Jonty spoke almost as if he was the manager of an Italian restaurant ordering a bus boy to clear the tables. 'Gary, I need to you take Marie out to the ice shelf.' He said smarmily in his nasally tone.

'Tomorrow,' Gary said flatly, then reconsidered. 'Sunday. I'll be hung over tomorrow.'

'So why can't you take me today then?' Marie looked flabbergasted; she stood with her arms akimbo.

'Getting myself into a position to be hungover tomorrow,' Gary said as he raised his coffee mug to them.

Jonty snatched the mug from Gary's hand. The force of the action sent the liquid halfway across the table. Gary bellowed at the shock as Jonty held the rim up to his nose and sniffed. 'This is just coffee.'

'Christ, it's only 9am, I haven't started just yet.' But even Danny saw it. He was defeated.

Jonty pointed to the cold porch and demanded that he go, and after a few more choice words of protest, Gary went and left Danny to himself. At first, he laughed at the misfortune that had fallen on his friend, but after a while he felt lonely sitting by himself so he went to the kitchen to find some more company.

Anne Castelli was once again in the kitchen alongside Old Ma, and Danny had the thought to ask her if her childhood dream had been to work in a restaurant, but he decided not to ask.

'How are you all going in here?' he asked as he poured water into his mug from the urn. 'Need a hand?'

They both shook their heads. They seemed tired, and rightly so. They had been working flat out to put this spread on and no-one had done so much to lift a finger to help them, but he supposed if they had offered, they would have been turned down, as he just was.

'No, we're fine,' Corinth said through a yawn. 'Where's your friend? I'll need some of his special stash soon to make a glaze.'

'He's just headed out to the ice shelf, won't be back for a few hours.'

Corinth was abashed. 'What? Now?' She slapped her hand against her leg.

'Yeah sorry,' he said with a frown. 'He had to take Marie out there. They've finished drilling.'

Anne nodded her head. 'Makes sense to me.'

Danny and Corinth looked at her. 'How come?'

'She's a marine biologist, the whole point of the exercise is to excavate to the heat source. If I was in her shoes, you couldn't keep me from getting down there. To be honest, I am surprised she wasn't out there supervising the dig.'

Danny nodded as he took a sip of his freshly brewed coffee. 'I suppose you're right, she thinks this thing might be something new so I suppose she would be excited.'

'Who wouldn't in her shoes?' Corinth said, accepting the situation. She shrugged and went back to covering the chicken wings in sauce.

'It's alright anyway,' Anne continued with her trays of potatoes. 'She'll be back soon; she would only be going out for a biopsy and that won't take her long to get. I would think the longest part would be climbing up through the ice shelf.'

Danny laughed. 'Knowing that crew out there, they probably have a fully functioning elevator equipped with a lobby music and white-gloved gentleman to operate it for them.' This brought confused looks from the women. 'Never mind.' Danny retreated. 'What did you mean by "biopsy"?'

Anne sighed at his ignorance. 'She will take a small sample to bring back here to test.' She shut the oven door and rested her behind on the rim of the bench. 'She has all the equipment she needs here, after all, it's a research station.' She raised her eyebrows and moved off into the freezer.

'Ahh well,' he said as he took another sip from his coffee. *If she's not here, she's not making things worse for me,* he thought and smiled. At least he had that to be happy about.

28

ONCE TWO IN THE AFTERNOON had rolled around, the camp took on a different vibe. No business was business at all, unless it had something to do with the party. Wendy had given up on her rounds of maintenance checks; after all, the pipes wouldn't miss her for an afternoon. Sean Wilson likewise had packed it in for the day, saying that he had a hankering for Marie's well-proclaimed punch.

When Wendy and Danny joined forces to ridicule Sean in this, he held up his hands and said with a smile, 'as long as there's vodka in it, who cares.' To be honest, he had a point. As far as Danny was concerned, most of the people that night wanted to drink too much and feel sorry themselves the next day. Sure, there would be one or two teetotallers that would sit by sober and laugh while everyone else drank themselves into a splendour, but as long as they didn't bring down the mood, all would be well.

While Wendy and Sean headed back up to the Red Shed to get cleaned up, Danny remained in the large workshop to tidy up his tools and diagnostic equipment. Not to be seen as unsocial, Danny didn't want to get started until Gary had returned. There was nothing like having a well earnt beer, but one with a mate was even better.

As the afternoon slowly wasted away, a doubt had started to settle in Danny's stomach. He had said it himself and Anne had agreed; it would only take a few hours for Marie to dart down that hole and retrieve the biopsy and then they would return. Yet, with each minute, the sun moved further across the horizon and less light seemed to be around them at any given point. Danny found himself looking to the sky in search for the slightest speck of the R44.

His mood wasn't improved when the red Hägglund rumbled back into camp. Danny stood in the open bay of the work shop and watched the progress of the tracked vehicle. It ambled along almost at a crawl while its engine revved as if it was in low gear. The pilot, a man that Danny didn't know, steered the Red Brick into the bay beside Danny and killed the engine once it was totally undercover. As the diesel clicked while its block rapidly cooled, the doors popped and Rheinmarsh stepped out of the passenger seat. Once again, Danny was struck by how straight the man was; if there was a curvature to his spine, it must have been repressed like the rest of his body.

Rheinmarsh stood taller than Danny, but was built on a lighter frame. His eyes were as grey as his beard and like the rest of them, his hair was cut short, almost military length. He and his crew were all dressed casually with jackets folded under their arms, all of them draped in the same underclothes that Stathis had worn.

'Any news of the chopper?' Danny asked Rheinmarsh after a moment's silence. Danny was surprised to see them here, but they were none of his business.

The grey eyes considered him for a moment longer and then finally darted away as Rheinmarsh replied, 'I have had no contact with it. It takes five hours travel in this machine.' He gestured to the Hägglund behind him. 'Where will the festivities take place this evening?'

Danny wiped some grease from his hands with a rag and nodded toward the Red Shed. 'Same place we had coffee the other day. So, you didn't see the helicopter?' he tried again.

'No.' Rheinmarsh sighed as the driver finally pushed himself out of the cabin and joined them. 'The helicopter and its crew are no concern of mine. I am only here to dig a hole, which I have done. Where is your communication room?'

Danny nodded to the Red Shed again. 'Same answer as before.

Mostly everyone is inside so you'll find someone to help you further in there.' Danny turned his back on the men and pretended to busy himself with something. The three men from the *Baroness* stood there for some time, then without a further word, they left him in peace.

The anger sat low in his stomach as he wrung the rag in his hands. Black water, thick with grease, bubbled from the weaves in its fabric as his hands pulled and twisted. His teeth gritted and he crinkled his nose, giving the impression of dog raising its hackles. He hated the man for not caring about Gary. He despised men like that, who only cared for the money that lined their pockets. He even hated him for Marie's sake, not that he would ever tell her that.

Nevertheless, Danny's moodiness, his anger and discontent were all washed away by the first sounds of the R44's rotors. He sighed as he packed up his tools and shut up the workshop. Each breath seemed to ebb away at the rage that had formed a tight ball in his stomach. By the time he had arrived at the side of the R44, Gary had already stopped the rotors and had mostly secured them against the winds.

'How did you go?' Danny asked as he came up to his friend's side.

Gary glanced at him over his shoulder, then went back to his job. 'Yeah, alright. That mob doesn't fuck around.'

'No,' Danny replied. 'They don't.'

'Hole's already drilled, no elevator, but a rope ladder with a winch. Too bloody deep to get someone to climb down and back up again, so they helped her up and down with the winch.'

'Did she say anything?' he asked.

Gary laughed. 'Didn't shut up the whole way home.' He shook his head.

'So, what did she say, what was it?'

'I don't fucking know,' he said with some disdain. 'I couldn't hear her.'

Danny considered him, his confusion obvious.

'She did not stop talking, alright.' Gary faced him, his nerves visibly shaken, either that, or he just needed a beer. 'Not once did she press the button for the microphone. So, I didn't catch a syllable.'

'Did you tell her?' he asked the obvious.

'Only seventy-eight fucking times.' He shook like a shiver ran up his spine. 'She wasn't even looking at me when she was speaking, the booey bitch. Hot ones are always messed up in the head, huh?' Gary shrugged turned back to the R44.

Danny frowned. There were only two other people he had seen act that way. One was dead, and one was himself in the small view finder of Marty's camera.

'Well, where did she go?'

Gary leant in so that Danny could hear him. 'I don't know. I think over to Anne's lab.'

He ran a hand up and rubbed at his chin through the fabric of his balaclava while he turned his gaze to the AANBUS labs. He started off for it, but Gary spoke again.

'Having a beer?'

Danny grinned. 'Yeah man, get one out.'

The lab was quiet when he entered. It seemed that not even a soul was inside. The light had been left on however, which would be enough to give anyone the shits down here.

'Marie?' he called out as he took off his balaclava. 'You in here?'

Only silence greeted him. Microscopes sat squat against the bench, while computer screens sat as dark as the night; a single light down in their right-hand corner suggested they were on standby. A low hum emanated from somewhere in the room, and Danny didn't know whether it was the damned fluoro igniters again or the hum of some computer fan.

Nothing appeared to have been touched, nor recently disturbed. He moved to one of the fridges and opened it, but nothing that was inside meant anything to him. Bottles of liquids and plastic containers littered the shelves, so he shut the door and wondered why he had bothered looking in the first place.

As he went back to the main door, he noticed something through the heavy glazed windows on the front of the structure. The skiff from the

Baroness had been deployed and was on its way to the mooring point.

Danny frowned as he squinted, but he figured that he could only see a single soul on board. It wasn't until the boat was almost ashore that Danny saw the three figures heading to the moor. Easily identified, Rheinmarsh and the other two men that he had with him walked with resolute strides as they headed off the skiff. They seemed as though they were pissed off or running late, which made little difference to how Rheinmarsh usually looked.

Danny decided that he couldn't care less about the outsiders, and left the lab. Once back at the Red Shed, he removed his gumboots in the cold porch and was happy to throw his balaclava into his locker. The only thing he needed now was a shower. The music from the mess had already started to pump, but thankfully they hadn't started the karaoke yet; he figured they all needed to get a bit further along the drunk train for that one.

When he finally walked into the mess area, the sounds of System of a Down beat into his head, while the smells of hot and spicy chicken wings, potato bake and roast lamb flooded his nostrils.

Gary headed over to him, smiling. He held out a glass stubby which was unlabelled.

'The mob from Davis isn't half bad.' He held back a hiccup and took a hesitant breath. 'Sits a bit heavy on the old stomach though.'

Danny laughed as he took the stubby from his friend. 'I'll have it while I clean up, I stink like shit.'

'Least it fits the way you look.' Wendy laughed as she walked past, a glass of golden liquid clasped firmly in her hand.

Danny shook his head as he left the mess for the showers and took his first swig of the Nunatak Brew Co's finest ale. Gary was right, it wasn't bad and sort of tasted like a real heavy 150 Lashes. He burped as the heavy fluid ran around his gut.

'Christ,' he said to himself in the shower while he held the bottle out to examine the fluid. 'Any more than three of these would make you feel worse than having a VB.'

Nevertheless, the second one he collected when he returned to the mess went down better and the third even better again… well, let's say the taste was one that grew on a man. It was when he was near the end of his third stubby and Corinth Butler had brought out the bread rolls that Bobby and Marty approached him.

'Hey,' Marty said quietly as he glanced around. The man looked like a child that had done something underhanded. One that wanted to gloat about what he had done, but didn't want to get busted by his parents. 'Old tight rod's crew is going into the ship, want to watch?'

Danny peered down at him and laughed silently. 'What are you talking about, Milonis?'

Bobby answered the question for him. 'He came into communications before and asked if he could have the run of the room for two hours this evening. I said yes, but I would have to be here in case something happened and another base contacted us. He said he would send someone to tell me, I said not good enough.' He ran his hand back and forth in seesaw motion with this retelling. 'So, he cracked the shits and went back to his ship where he said he would have his meeting.'

'So?' Danny failed to see the point of any of this.

'So,' Marty continued this time. 'They are using "our" communications array, so we thought we'd sit in and see what they're up to.'

This time Danny threw his head back and laughed aloud. He bit his tongue as the other two shushed him. 'Yeah, I'm in on that,' he said. And so they left the mess together and headed into the communications room.

The communications room wasn't very big, as with most things these days; as time went on everything got smaller, cost more and did a better job than the older equipment. There were multiple computer screens that all converged around a single seat. A large UHF radio sat to the side of the computer system, on top of an older system that looked as though it was one of the old HAM types.

Food scraps and empty wrappers littered the desk top and Bobby hurriedly tidied up while Marty sat down and hammered away at the console, although not before he gingerly moved a coffee mug away from the mouse, which appeared as though it hadn't been cleaned for a decade.

Bobby mumbled something before he picked it up and moved it, along with all the rubbish he had just picked up, to the top of the UHF.

'Shh, Bobby move,' Marty said as the centre screen came alive with video footage. Marty scanned the screens as he heard Rheinmarsh's voice.

'Enter the lower apartments.' His voice ripped through the communications.

'Shit,' Marty said. 'He can't hear us, can he?'

Bobby shook his head. 'Nah the feed is only for us.'

Danny told them both to shut up as he leant in closer to the screen. It looked as though they were seeing the world from the view of a man's chest.

'Jesus, his crew has body cams?' Marty broke the silence again. 'Who are these guys?'

'Who knows?' Danny mumbled. 'But something tells me nothing would stop Rheinmarsh from opening his Christmas presents.'

They watched as two men walked across the foredeck of the *Nisshin Maru*, the same place where Danny, Charlie and Jonty had stood about month before. One of the men was obviously Kee Peters as the ZKK was slung over a shoulder. The man in front was the structural engineer, Paul Stathis, that Danny had spent his time with. As Paul came into view, they saw that he also had a body camera mounted to his chest.

'See if you can pull up the other feeds,' Danny said and Marty went to typing.

The two men in camera walked beyond the stairs that they had climbed, and instead descended down to the middle deck that was still littered with large chunks of ice.

The other two monitors flickered and came to life before them and they were confronted with three views, each of differing perspectives. As Paul looked back at the first man, whose perspective they had begun with, Danny noticed that one man carried an enormously heavy backpack. The way he walked with his shoulders slumped and the weight forward, showed just how heavy the pack was.

'Who's this other guy?' Bobby asked as he pointed to the man with the heavy pack.

'Mechanic,' Danny mumbled again. 'Who else would you take onto a ship that you needed to get running?' He didn't take his eyes from the screen.

Once the three had descended onto the centre deck, they turned back to the rising apartment tower, where the bridge sat atop. There was another bulkhead door, visible through Paul's camera. They watched as two gloved hands reached forward and grasped the circular steel of the door's valve-like hand-wheel. They heard him grunt as his feet audibly slid on the frozen steel beneath him.

'Peters,' the stone-on-steel of Paul's voice came through and on one of the other monitors they saw him turn to the younger man. 'Put that piece of shit down and help me with this, I can't get a grip.'

Peters adjusted the sling to sit across his chest, which partially obscured one of the cameras, then moved to help Paul.

'Why did you bring that thing anyway?' They heard the other man ask.

Peters grunted along with Paul, but soon they heard the warble as old steel moved. 'It makes me feel safe,' he panted.

'It makes me feel unsafe,' the mechanic replied.

'Then stand behind me. It's here now, I'm sick of hearing about it. Just leave it alone.'

'Enough, just open the door and move to engine room.' Rheinmarsh came over to quell the children.

Stathis threw his shoulder against the steel and they heard the hinges groan under the weight and then there was nothing but darkness in front of them. A chill ran up Danny's spine as he remembered the darkness of the bridge, and how he had struggled to see. What he saw in front of the three men made his experience seem like daylight.

'Lights,' Stathis barked, and three beams cut through the darkness. One by one, they entered the black and stepped cautiously as they went.

'Man, its cold in here,' the mechanic grumbled. 'Even with the skins.'

'Just keep moving.' Stathis's gruff voice came back again.

It was funny, each time Danny spoke to him he had seemed like a nice guy, but he sounded like a cock when he spoke to the rest of the crew.

Maybe they're the cocks? Danny thought as he leant even closer to the screens.

Through the flashlight's beams, they saw that the lower apartments were much like the upper. The steel was slick with ice and once again, Danny remembered how hard it was to even stand on that surface. The steel had rivets pressed into the floor section to make grip easier, but even then, the ice made those treacherous to stand on.

They followed Paul Stathis as he took a left and Marty gasped as the beam of light crossed over a man's face. 'Found a crew member,' Paul grumbled as he continued closer. The man was obviously dead after all this time, but like Ishimura up on the bridge, he was surprisingly intact for his age.

The young man's head lay flat against his shoulder. He sat upright against one of the walls in the corner of an intersection between two corridors. His mouth hung open and his eyes had rolled into the back of his head. As with the officer on the deck, the man was obviously Japanese. As Paul started to bring the light down across his body, it showed the khaki of his military uniform.

'One of the soldiers, you think?' Marty asked, but no-one replied.

As the light fell lower on the dead man's body, they saw that his hands were linked into a red knot at his stomach. Blood had frozen along with flesh and fabric and had locked the man's hands to the wound that he'd died trying to staunch.

'Look,' Peters voice came next and instinctively the three onlookers all moved over to his screen.

His light was shining away from the body and down one of the corridors. Blood ran lines in almost every direction. They could see where the man had tried to push himself along the wall with his hands as bloody streaks covered the walls while a singular red smear ran across the floor.

'Guy was a tough bastard,' Peters said again as he moved forward. The light ran over a place that looked as though it had been the epicentre; blood had pooled on the floor in a frozen slurry while red spatter marred the white walls that surrounded it. Then the light ran over a familiar sight and they heard Peters whistle in excitement. A timber stock of an old rifle became clearer as Peters moved closer.

'Look, a rifle too,' he said ecstatically as he bent to pick it up.

'Oh great, another one,' the mechanic complained.

Through the camera they heard metallic clinking as Peters ran the rifle along the floor in his rush to pick it up. The camera showed the action and that the bolt was closed. Kee's hand went there and they heard him struggle in his effort and then finally the metal moved and slid freely.

'Jesus, pretty tight,' he complained.

'It's been sitting in ice for 70 years, what do you reckon?'

'Not rusted though, hey it's still loaded.' They saw clearly on the screen a brass case eject from the rifle's chamber while more sat ready beneath.

'Steel doesn't rust when it's frozen,' Paul explained. 'That's why the ship is such good condition. If we were in the tropics, it would've sunk from deterioration by now easily enough.'

'The crew is not important. Continue to the engine room.' Rheinmarsh once again pushed them along. 'Peters, leave the rifle where you found it.'

Once more they heard the clang of steel as Peters placed the rifle noisily down.

'Come on,' Paul said gruffly as they moved passed the body.

'What do you think happened to the guy?' the mechanic asked.

'Probably a mutiny. Crew had nowhere to go so they turned on each other.'

'Jesus, Danny,' Marty said, 'was the officer messed up that bad?'

Danny grimaced at the thought. 'You saw the footage. He shot himself.'

Marty placed his face in his hands for a while, as if in shame. Danny left him and didn't say another word about Jin Ishimura, he didn't care to think about that man again.

The three onlookers remained silent while the three men moved further down into the bowels of the ship. It seemed that even Danny was getting cold just by watching the screens.

They moved down a flight of stairs that was covered in blood and the mechanic expressed his discomfort toward the situation. However, a short word from Stathis put him in his place. That held the quiet again until they moved beyond another corridor that was littered with the limbs of at least five men. Arms and legs, flesh torn from the bone, leaving only fabric and the remains of limbs that had obviously been feasted upon.

'Jesus Christ…' the mechanic began and his camera wavered from side to side.

As Stathis turned, they saw the heavy-laden man bray at the sight. He began to lose his balance as he stood up a little too straight and the weight of his pack put him off centre. Kee moved forward to help him, but no helping hand could stop the vomit from pushing past his lips. Stathis and Peters were forced to wait for the mechanic, who still remained nameless, while he brought up the remnants of his lunch.

The three onlookers were thankful that the other two had faced another direction as the view from the mechanic's camera made them very uncomfortable.

'Come on man,' Peters said as he ran his light over the limbs. 'This is pretty fucked up, you have to admit.'

'Mate, they were stuck here until their death,' Paul said flatly. 'What do you think they would've eaten when the food ran out?'

'I'd rather die,' Peters said while his light ran over a bone that had been stripped clean of flesh, sinew and cartilage.

'Some of them must have felt the same way.' Paul dismissed the conversation and then turned to the mechanic, who was still doubled over under the weight of his pack. 'Come on, time to move on.'

'I'm not going,' he cried.

'Like fuck you're not.' Stathis rushed over and manhandled the man to his feet. One of the flashlights dropped and ran across the floor. They saw Peters' camera turn in its direction to retrieve it. As Peters moved toward the light, his camera showed his perspective down the hallway, along the lines of blood and frozen steel. Marty gasped and Bobby screamed at what they saw, before the screen was turned black as Peters kicked the flashlight in his own fright.

The light had reflected on two bright yellow eyes that sat lidless on a face that was as pale as the steel they walked upon.

Danny's head near exploded at what he saw, but it wasn't the yellow eyes, it wasn't even the fact that it didn't have any hair. What terrified him the most, was that before the light was torn from its face, it blinked.

29

'OH, JESUS. FUCK!' Peters screamed as the light spiralled in front of the camera lens. Everyone was left in darkness while the young man suffered an internal fight on whether to shoulder his rifle or bring up the flashlight in his hand. In the end, by the time the light had washed over the place where the eyes had been, there was nothing there. 'Did you guys see that?'

'See what?' Paul barked as on his monitor he had pushed the mechanic further down the hall.

'There… there was something alive down there.' Peters moved his light back and forth over the intersection, then he spun around and shone the light into Paul's eyes. They saw the man squint then turn away.

'What are you doing?' The leader barked as he raised his hands to shield his eyes.

'Man, I'm telling you I saw something down there.'

'So what?'

'Something alive!' Peters shrieked as he washed the light over the hall again. His breath had become ragged and his movements were still sharp with panic.

'Bullshit.' Paul again. 'There have been no new supplies in here since the forties. There's nothing here, so cut the shit.'

'You cut it man.' There was a fumble and the sound of an action being racked. Then the ZKK was visible through Peters' lens.

'Jesus Christ,' Paul muttered as he stormed past him. 'Where? Here?' He pointed to the place where the eyes had been seen.

'Be careful,' Peters hissed, and Danny didn't know if he could watch. He didn't want to see those eyes again.

The three onlookers sat glued to the screen as they now watched Paul's monitor advance on the intersection. He didn't even approach it with caution; his footfalls echoed loudly with each movement. Then the light began to move around the corner; more and more of the path they had moved beyond became visible as Paul advanced. 'See, nothing.' He was right. Nothing was there.

For a little while, Paul held the flashlight down the hall. Nothing seemed to move and nothing drew anyone's attention.

'Continue to the engine room.' Rheinmarsh again.

The sound made all of them jump, even the onlookers.

'Sir, did you see it?' Peters again.

'There was nothing to see Peters,' Stathis had started to move back.

'Guys,' the mechanic sounded.

'I'm fucking telling you I saw something, man.' Peters snarled at Stathis.

'Guys.'

'The video feed is not clear all the time, Reicher and I cannot be sure. Continue to the engine room.'

'Guys.'

'That's bullshit,' Danny said to Marty and Bobby. 'He would've seen as clear as us.' He moved past Marty and dragged the keyboard closer. 'We've got to warn them they aren't alone down there.'

'Hey,' Marty said as Danny pushed passed him and began to press buttons.

'That would be right, fucking camera,' Peters again.

'Guys.'

'Can you hear me?' Danny yelled as he hammered the monitor casing with his open palm. 'You're not alone down there.' He yelled as he pressed buttons.

'Danny, you'll break something. Just stop.'

'Never rely on technology. You need to be better than that,' Stathis growled to Peters as he moved past.

'Danny you're going to break something.'

'Guys!'

'What?' Both Peters and Stathis shone their light onto the mechanic, who had been pushed beyond their advance. He stood hunchbacked under the weight of his pack and looked almost at an upward angle into their light and didn't even blink. 'I feel better now,' he said almost in a sob as a line of blood ran down from his nose. 'Can we leave now?'

The lights remained on him. Neither of the other two moved. 'What's wrong with your nose?' Peters asked, as his camera bumped against the stock of his rifle.

'Huh?' he asked as he peered down at his shirt. 'I'm sorry, I made a mess… ahh, I'll clean it up. I promise I will.'

'What's wrong with this guy?' Danny asked as he pressed a few more buttons to try and take them off mute.

'Hey stop it would you,' Marty cried, and then all the screens went blank. 'Ahh shit. Look what you've done.'

'Fuck!' Danny roared as he moved away. 'Fix it, quickly.'

'Yeah, well if you hadn't of pressed all those fucking buttons, you knob.' Marty hammered away furiously at the keys. 'We've lost audio as well.' Again and again his small hands moved back and forth over the keys, while even Bobby stood there and watched helplessly. Words and windows scrolled back and forth over the triple screen display as Marty hammered away. 'And…' he said in a slow lead up. 'There.'

The screens lit up again. Paul was standing in front of Peters now, his hands outstretched. 'You just stay there, ok? We will get you some help.' Beyond his arms the mechanic was crying as blood freely gushed down the lower half of his face. He wept as he ran his fingers down his cheeks and tore ribbons of flesh from them.

'I need to get out, I need to get out,' he cried through torrents of pain as he tore more of himself away.

'Calm down!' Paul roared at him as he retreated.

'Jesus Christ,' they heard Peters mutter to himself. 'He's gone insane.'

'Let me out!' the mechanic roared as he charged them, his bloody hands stretched out while blood ran rivers down his face and his neck, soaking the front of his undershirt.

Then the lights dropped as the two men were forced to use their hands to defend themselves, as Danny once had. There were muffled grunts and swearing from Peters and Stathis while the mechanic wailed in distress. The sound rippled back off the steel and resonated horribly through the body camera's microphone. Finally, they pushed him off and some light was shed on the situation again, as they saw the mechanic disappear down into the darkness of the corridors as he screamed and ran.

'Ahh shit,' Stathis complained. 'Rheinmarsh, are you getting this?'

The sound of the mechanic's wails went on and on, while the scene from his camera showed nothing in the darkness.

'We are.' The unimpressed tone was clearly audible.

'What do you want us to do?'

'We can't see shit down here,' Peters joined him as he shuffled the rifle against his body.

'Find the mechanic and take him to the engine room. By force if you need to. Do you need more men?'

Stathis spat, 'Negative. We don't want more men tripping over themselves down here. It's bad enough with just three.'

'Are you insane?' Peters hissed. 'Send a fuckin army.'

'Kee,' Stathis grabbed him. 'Don't you go nuts down here. There's nothing there. Now come on, let's find this idiot.'

The two men trudged off down the corridor, following the sounds of the wails and the clanging that the mechanic made as he went.

Danny knew that the two men would make much better time than the crazed mechanic, who was still heavy-laden with whatever was in his backpack. Now that the men had been separated, the sounds fought against each other through the different monitors.

Paul and Peters made little noise but for their short breathes as they hurried along the corridors. Lights ran across frozen white walls and corridors that lead to black holes of darkness, where the lights beams couldn't penetrate. Footfalls echoed as they jogged where they could, and slight scuffs seeped through their monitors when they had to descend another flight of stairs. The mechanic's monitor on the other hand, offered no visual sight but blurs of darkness and shades of pitch. However, the sound that came through the speakers sent a cold chill down Danny's neck as he replicated word for word what Charlie had said.

'I need to get out, I need to get out. I can't breathe in here! I need to get out,' his voice whined a sobbing pitch as he cried and clawed at himself but he now sobbed low enough for the other two not to hear him.

'Fuck me.' They heard one of the other two grumble. 'Where did this idiot go?'

'It must be down here, I heard him fall down some stairs I think.' That voice was definitely Peters.

The mechanic's sobs had become incoherent and words streamed together in long sobs of pain and horror but something was below them. Danny leant closer to hear, but underneath the footfalls from the other two it was almost inaudible.

'Come on,' he puffed. 'This way, he's got to be down here.'

Danny leant in closer and strained his ears. The mechanic's sobs had turned into a high pitch gurgle that rang in his ears but just below it he heard… he couldn't be quite sure, but it sounded like the sound a dog made as it gnawed on a bone.

'What the fuck is that noise? Can you two hear it?' Marty had pushed himself back so that Danny could lean across him again but once Danny moved away, he leant in himself and frowned. Bobby remained a step away, almost frozen in the horror that was plastered across his face. They all jumped again as the mechanic let out a wild scream that distorted in the monitor's speakers. Then he fell silent.

'Here, did you hear that?' Stathis hissed. 'He's down there.'

Once again, the three onlookers sat in silence as they watched the monitor that represented Paul Stathis. They watched as his flashlight's beam bounced off the frozen white of the apartment's walls and the slick steel that he tracked so easily. He rounded a corner and they listened as his breath and the bounce of the camera emphasised his speed. He came to another intersection and he stopped.

As he rounded the corner, the beam of his flashlight picked something up. A man's legs lay across the path of the corridor further up, but his head and his torso were hidden behind the corner. 'Here, I think I found him,' Paul said as he panted.

'You sure?' Peters said a few metres behind him, seemingly less out of breath.

'Yeah, I don't think the Japs wore black cargo pants in the forties.' He huffed again and spat. He moved slower now as he approached the fallen mechanic. Danny moved closer to the other monitor but the gnawing sound had stopped, and the microphone was now picking up Paul's steady footfalls.

'You calmed down now?' Paul asked and the sound came through all three sets of speakers. 'You ready to head to the engine room?'

There was no answer. They watched on the edge of their seats as Paul began to skirt the corner's edge. The mechanic was lying on his face; this much was evident in the large hump that was his backpack that seemed to emerge from the man's back like a growth. From the angle Paul was standing, the camera couldn't pick up the man's head, but there seemed to be something under him. Paul's light shone down and shimmered off a pool of blood that had ebbed its way out from the upper part of the mechanic's torso.

'Jesus,' Paul hissed as he took another step forward. His hand reached out and grasped the fabric of his pack, and they heard the squelch as his boot sunk into the blood. They watched with horror as he pulled the body over and it rolled onto its side with his back toward Paul, and the light picked up more than just the black fabric. 'Oh, fuck me,' he gasped as he let go.

The creature that had been hidden by the mechanic's pack rolled with the body. It had the dead man's hand entirely in its maw, which was not like anything alive. Its body was small and hunched, strands of rotten fabric hung from its pale flesh in loops that could have only been the remains of a seam. Its jaw split in two along the crest of its chin and two small claws emerged at their ends to sink into the mechanic's forearm.

Its mouth twisted and writhed around its prize and finally Danny understood what he had heard beneath the dying sobs of the mechanic. The yellow eyes seemed pupil-less as they were drawn to the light. Then its jaw split as it released its prize and howled a horrible scream in Paul's direction as if to protect its kill.

'Get the fuck off him!' Paul yelled as he moved forward to the creature. As if in slow motion, they saw the creature lean away from the man's strike and then it sprung forward while it screamed and lashed out with a hand that could have been human, if not for the stumps of fingers that had been gnawed down to bone and tendon.

Paul screamed as it latched onto him and he fell backwards. He grunted as he hit the ground and the three onlookers were helpless but to watch as he fought to keep the pale monstrosity from his own face. The two halves of its bottom jaw clicked together in a wild lunge to capture him, but Paul managed to push it further away.

As it opened its jaw again, the onlookers saw straight down its gullet and the lines of teeth and bone that ran along each edge. Spittle, blood and gore flew from its mouth as it screamed in Paul Stathis's face, while it clawed at him with its hands, if you could call them that.

A hideous roar ripped through the speakers and distorted in the air, as the monitors failed to replicate the fullness of the sound. At the same time, the creatures head exploded in a mess of blood, bone and matter and finally, it fell dead from Paul's chest. The sound rang and rang and rang through the steel corridors, and Danny could only imagine how much it would've hurt their ears but Paul didn't complain.

'I fucking told you I saw something,' Peters grumbled as he rushed to Paul's side. He held his ZKK in one hand as he offered Stathis his other. The two men grunted as the younger lifted the older.

'I…' Paul began as Kee stepped back from him. Kee's light was still on but low in his hand that he supported the rifle with. Stathis's camera faced him as he racked the action of the heavy rifle.

'You guys all laughed when I brought this,' he said as he looked down triumphantly at the ZKK. 'Well, who's laughing now huh?' He spat an arched line of spit at the dead creature. 'Who's laugh–'

Paul's camera caught the horror as it burst through the younger man's chest. They saw the bones of his ribs split outward while a long sharpened white point was driven through it. Paul gasped as his flashlight caught the yellow of two eyes, as the creature that towered behind Peters split its jaw and latched onto the younger man's neck. 'Oh Jesus' was all he could say, as the light and the camera captured the blood that ran down Peters' shirt as the rifle fell from his hands and the life left his eyes.

Paul ran. His breath was heavy on the camera's microphone and the light rippled its way across the frozen metal, blood and flesh that littered his way.

Marty, Bobby and Danny didn't say a word as the man ran for his life. His panting breath and the fear in his throat were audible below the screams and clatter that the creature made in its pursuit of him. They watched in horror as another blocked his path. In the split second they saw it, before Paul changed his direction, they saw that its legs had been torn off at the knees. All that remained were sharpened points that clattered against the steel as it scurried on all fours. Paul started to scream as he ran and his light lit up another that hung from the roof and hissed at him as he ran beneath it.

He turned down another corridor and another; his light showed them gore that Danny couldn't comprehend as Paul's escape took him deeper into the apartments. Flesh seemed to run in vines through the corridors the deeper he went and blood seemed to run down the walls like guide rails. The further they ran, the thicker the strands became and to Danny's horror they pulsed as if they had a heartbeat.

Paul fell and the floor rushed up to meet the camera. As it impacted, the feed was cut.

'Do you think they got him?' Marty whispered after a long silence.

'It would only be a matter of time. He's alone,' Danny mumbled as he considered the other monitors. Peters' monitor had been destroyed in the attack that had taken his life, but the mechanic's feed still ran as far as he could tell. There wasn't any light shining in the direction his body had been left and so the image was dark. Danny leant closer and closer, and he noticed that the other two leant with him, as if they all the same idea. But no sound could be heard through the feed of the first man to die, just the dark silence that every dead man was accustomed to.

'Turn it off,' Danny said.

'But...' Marty pleaded with him.

'Turn it off!' he said in a harsher tone.

'Maybe we could help him?' Marty said. 'Maybe we could...'

'He's five hours away by drive, and an hour by flight. Gary is already too drunk to fly and, in any rate, if he's alive, he doesn't have that long,' Danny said solemnly.

The other two remained silent for a short while, then Marty leant forward and shut the system down. He sat back in Bobby's chair after a while and turned to Danny again. 'Should we tell?'

Danny shook his head. 'It's in Rheinmarsh's hands. Stay out of it, man.'

'I just...' Bobby started; tears had started to form in his eyes.

'Keep quiet about it, Bobby,' Danny urged him. 'Don't tell anyone about it. Not tonight anyway, let them enjoy the party, let them get drunk and tomorrow... maybe tomorrow, things will be different.'

Bobby and Marty gaped up at him.

'Ok?' he put it to them.

They both nodded and hung their heads.

Danny didn't know what to do after that, he didn't know whether to turn and leave or stay and offer support. He looked down to his hand and saw that he still grasped one of the glass stubbies. His knuckles were white he was putting that much pressure onto the glass. As if his nerves had been caught slacking off, suddenly his hand rung out in agony from the excess pressure.

'What are we going to do now?' Bobby asked as he searched the other men's faces for the answer.

'I know what I'm doing,' Danny said as he passed the stubby to his other hand. 'Getting drunk.' He lifted the glass bottle to the screens as if in salute and then drained the last of the liquid inside.

30

WHEN DANNY LEFT the sombre mood of the communications room, he staggered. He steadied himself against one of the walls of the corridor that led back down to the mess hall, which bounced with music. As he rested there and felt the heavy breath on his lungs, he looked to the glass bottle in his hand and wondered if the reason why he had stumbled had been the beer that now sloshed freely around in his gut, or the tear that had just run down his cheek. He was heavy-laden with his sorrow for the men he had known, if only for a short while.

As he exhaled again, his breath shuddered in his lungs and he forced a cough. Saliva welled in the back of his gullet and he moved fast. He had barely lifted the lid of the toilet when everything had come rushing up. The second-hand liquor stank of shit as it came from his mouth, but with it came a little of everything. The horror that had settled in him didn't feel so bad, the sorrow in his heart likewise had lifted. But as he looked down into the bowl, the sliminess of its sinew reminded him of the pulsing vine he had seen in Paul's monitor and it came up again and again.

Outside of the cubicle he heard the door open and heavy footsteps welcomed an intruder. By the sound of the inconsistencies between steps, the man was heavy with drink, which narrowed the choices down. He was muttering something under his heavy breath as he stumbled and glossed over the parts he had forgotten. Then as Danny heard the sound that every man would recognise as the drunkard dropped his fly, he hiccupped and Danny began to laugh through the spittle that still ran from his lip to the brown water in the bowl.

As Danny stood and flushed, the drunkard had begun to sing louder.

'But Casey minds the arrows, and ignores the fatal echoes,' Gary shook himself vigorously and then put himself away. 'Of the clicking of the turnstiles and the rattle of his change,' he slurred these last words heavily as he spun around, and his eyes widened at the sight of his friend. 'Hey man, the fuck did you disappear to?' Gary managed as he approached with open arms.

Having somewhat sobered, Danny felt as straight as a die compared to his friend and didn't feel like being embraced by a man who had managed to spread more piss over the walls and floor than what had successfully landed in the trough, not to mention that his fly was still down. He sidestepped Gary's advance and came back around him. 'Wash your hands big feller, then it's time to break out the heavy shit.'

'Fuckin' aye,' Gary agreed as he held his hands under the tap as if waiting for someone to turn them on for him.

'Fuck me,' Danny complained as he spun the faucet and watched as his friend swayed on the spot. 'Maybe no hard shit for you.'

'Ahh bull… shit.' Pausing only to hiccup a second time, Gary stormed out of the bathroom, leaving the tap still running.

Danny took the opportunity to clean himself up. He washed his face and his hands, then stood there for some time as he considered his reflection. His eyes were bloodshot again. He smiled as he saw them and thought about Louise. God, he needed to get out of this place and get back to her. But even that thought chilled him, the 'getting out' was too close to what he had seen and what had happened to him in his unconscious state. Just that thought was enough to make him not want to even look at himself.

He stood up and spat into the basin, leaving another brown stain and then left it all behind.

As he re-entered the mess, the music washed over him again and he felt a flutter in his chest as his heart reacted to the heavy bass. It seemed that Jonty's pick of System of a Down had given way to a fan favourite: Metallica. People stood in groups around the tables of food and drink and chatted merrily. Wendy Phillips gnawed at a chicken wing, leaving red streaks of marinade across her cheeks while she spoke to Sean Wilson. Craig Hollins had a small group around him as he wove his hands in exaggeration to what he was saying.

'I'm telling you. It's this bastard that's going to kill it for everyone!' he shouted as he pointed to the unbranded stubby. 'Brewing his own beer down here. Christ, the government is going to think we are all a bunch of piss heads.'

'And what's wrong with that?' James Sutton asked as he drained the last of his own.

'Nothing's wrong with it, numbskull.' Craig rolled his eyes. 'But you want the government to think that?'

'Are you saying they'll stop our funding?' Anne asked.

'Worse,' Craig said ominously. 'They'll limit the amount of alcohol we can drink.'

'No.' Corinth gasped. 'Surely not,' she said as she tipped some more white wine into Anne's glass, then her own.

'I'm fucking telling you Ma.' Craig pointed his finger in her face. 'What sounds more Australian than having a beer? Telling someone they can't have one.'

'Too right,' James agreed as he tore the top off another.

Danny saw the opportunity and couldn't let it pass. He stepped into the conversation and took the opened stubby from James's hand. 'Come on mate, don't you think you've had enough?'

The look of shock in his eyes as the glass left his hands was worth everything. Then the wash of anger came through as Danny lifted the glass to his own lips and began to drain the bottle. James started to open his mouth but as everyone else laughed, he eyeballed Danny and started to guffaw himself. 'Where have you been?' he asked in turn as he fetched another.

'Just had to look at something, ahh...' He tried to think. 'Marty just wanted to show me some stupid video.'

'One of those ones, aye?' Craig asked as he winked to Anne Castelli.

He had to think of something that no-one present would want to watch. 'Film making,' he said flatly and by everyone's reaction, even Corinth Butler may have been more interested if it had been pornography. Having successfully killed the conversation, Danny scanned the room and saw Jonty at Marty's computer, which was linked to the speakers. Corinth headed over to his side while Danny walked over to the array of food.

'Anything good?' he asked Wendy and Sean as he approached.

Wendy smiled a sauced-up face at him as she sucked the juices from her finger. Sean raised his plastic cup and nodded. 'The punch is unreal, mate.'

'The punch?' Danny asked as he remembered Sean's comments earlier in the day. 'Supercharged?'

'Oh yeah. Want some?'

'Nah mate, I'll stick to beer I think, and when Gaz comes back maybe some whisky.' He ran his eyes up and down the table in search of something to eat and saw the wondrous punch. The bowl was an immense glass dish that looked as though Corinth had brought it over from her own collection. The liquid inside was golden, with chunks of fruit and ice cubes floating around inside of it. He could smell it from where he stood. Instead, he took a bowl of potato bake and a couple of chicken wings and moved back over to the other group.

He smiled and nodded while he ate and drank as Jimmy Sutton began to tell them a tale of how he became an entomologist; a story that no-one cared too much for. While this happened, some movement from the corridors that led to the Dongas caught his eye. Danny raised his head as Marie Swan entered the room, wearing her tight pink sweater which cupped her breasts and some leggings that hinted to the shape of her ass.

Danny took another bite of hot potato bake and washed it down with some more local ale. A smile was plastered across Marie's face, almost set in stone as she disappeared into the kitchen.

Danny forced his attention back to the group and this time made little effort to give Jimmy his attention. He ate and drank, even returned to the table for more of the chicken wings, which were bloody fantastic and could understand why Wendy had made such a pig of herself while she had been devouring them. Halfway through his second helping Marie Swan had emerged from the kitchen with a silver platter in her hand. The conversation had moved from Jimmy's story, over to one from Anne Castelli. This one was of more interest and was about her love-life as a younger woman. Being childless, the woman had actually spent a fair amount of her time partying from what it seemed.

Danny drifted in and out. At one moment he stopped listening while he watched Marie ladle about six cups worth of punch into various cups and place them on the platter.

'Then when I was about twenty-five, I travelled to Barcelona and for a long time I thought I would stay there.' Danny turned his attention back to Anne as his mind drifted to a twenty-something year old Anne and he imagined how she would've looked. The hard part with that was that his mind just kept going straight back to Marie. 'The days were hot, and the nights in many ways were hotter.' She smiled wryly. 'There was this one young man–' colour had begun to rise in her cheeks '–we couldn't keep our hands off each other.'

She leant back and cleared her throat and then looked around as if someone was going to hear her. 'The man was a police inspector and I went to visit him at work one day. He took me into a room which had one of those two-way mirrors, you know? You can see into a room but the other room only sees their reflection. Anyway, while an interview was being conducted in the interview room, we made love in the inspection room.'

Everyone laughed while the colour in Anne's cheeks rose to a bright red. 'I have never felt so alive as those days. I think I just did things for the sake of doing them.'

'Good to be young, huh?' Craig said.

'Exactly.' Anne laughed and placed a hand on his arm. 'To hell with the consequences.'

'Punch anyone?' Marie Swan had nosed her pretty face into the tight group. She smiled at them as she gestured forward with her tray of punch.

'No thanks.' Craig raised his stubby.

'I'll stick with the chardonnay. Thank you, Marie.' Anne smiled.

'I'm going to go harder rather than softer,' Danny said.

'That's what he said.' Craig laughed. 'Let's see if he can follow through after a night full of grog,' he said it loudly and laughed loud enough to make up for the lack of it around the group.

'I'll have a cup, thanks Marie.' Jimmy smiled at her as he took a cup. 'I think I need something to cool me down after Anne's story.'

'Go easy on it, James.' Marie winked. 'There are some other surprises in there.'

Danny watched as Marie moved away from their group and then whisked the tray over to Sean, who took another cup. At that moment, Gary emerged from the hallway to the Dongas with a few bottles of Glenfiddich in his hands.

'About time,' Danny grumbled as he moved out of the group. 'Where have you been?' he said to his friend. 'A man would go to bloat if he stayed on this shit.' He put the empty stubby down and took a plastic cup.

'Never you mind,' Gary grumbled as he gave them each two fingers.

'Mind if I have some?' Wendy moved over to their side with a clean plastic cup in her hand.

'The more the merrier.' Gary poured her in.

At that stage, 'Nothing Else Matters,' had given way to Roxette's 'Fading like a Flower', and Jonty had started to unwind the cables for the microphone. Corinth Butler waited eagerly to the side her face full of excitement.

'Oh Jesus,' Danny said as he drained his cup. 'Think I'll need a double to get me through this.'

'Ok everyone,' Jonty's voice came through clear, while Roxette's faded like the rose she was so fond of. 'I think we are all far enough into our cups to have a bit of fun with this. So how about we start up the karaoke?'

Cheers followed the question. Gary held up his cup, as did Wendy.

Craig whistled loudly while Anne laughed to his side. Even Danny laughed, but Sean Wilson had taken a seat with his back to the rest of them. Danny laughed when he saw this; maybe his internals weren't built for supercharged punch. He giggled at the humour of that and how clever it was, but the humour washed away when he realised that it was one that only a mechanic would understand.

'I don't think there would be any objections if the lady who has worked the hardest for this evening takes the first song?' Jonty asked the mostly pissed crowd.

'Give us a belter Ma!' Marty shouted out and Danny raised his eyebrows. He saw that Marty and Bobby had joined them from the communications room. It was good to see that both were smiling. Bobby gnawed on a chicken wing, while Marty sipped at a cup of punch.

'What are you singing?' Craig shouted out.

'First person to guess the name before she gives it away wins,' Jonty said in his nasally voice.

'What do you win?' Jimmy asked as he took another cup of punch from Marie's tray.

'A kiss from Marie!' Gary bellowed as he drained his cup of Glen. Everyone laughed, even Marie. 'And I'm going to fuckin win it,' he followed up heavily.

Jonty stared at the computer screen and shuddered. 'Ok well here it goes,' he pressed the button and soft music filled their ears. Almost on cue Corinth started to sway back and forth behind the microphone.

Everyone stood to attention and watched as Corinth gave it her everything. The way the music rolled it was easily something from the seventies. 'There'll be no strings to bind your hands, not if my love can't find your heart.'

'Madonna!' Gary shouted out, and Danny near wet himself.

'Nope.' Jonty shook his head as the music continued to roll through their ears and Corinth swayed along.

'There's no need to take a stand, for it was I who chose to start.'

The music took a change in note here and Gary started to click his fingers. 'Fuckin, fuckin,' he said to himself as if the name of the artist was on the tip of his tongue.

As Danny looked over to Gary, he saw Sean Wilson sitting there by himself. His head jerked sporadically from side to side as if in a poor attempt to be in time with the music. 'The guy's hammered,' Danny laughed to himself.

'I see no need to take me home.' Corinth swayed as her voice dipped low with the last word and Sean rose to his feet.

'I'm old enough to face the dawn.' Corinth tilted her head back and belted the last word out as she shut her eyes and Sean staggered forward from the group.

'Just call me angel. Of the morning angel. Just touch my cheek before you....'

Sean's fist slammed into Corinth's cheek just as she had asked, but somehow Danny didn't think that was what she had in mind. She screamed and the sound reverberated through the microphone. The entire group of them gasped as she hit the deck.

Danny's jaw hit his chest as it dropped and the cup of Glen fell from his fingers. Sean just stood there above Corinth and stared down at her. His head jerked suddenly to the left and came back again.

The room remained silent for almost a second after the blow and then Corinth let fly with a cry of agony that cut through everyone's astonishment like an axe through ice. Gary roared in anger as he bull-rushed forward and crash-tackled Sean. The way Gary ran and bellowed, his advance could have not been any more obvious. Nevertheless, Sean did not so much as brace himself for the impact, his head snapping backward as Gary dropped his shoulder into him, and the two men went crashing to the ground in a heap.

'What the fuck do you think you're doing?' Gary roared as he drove a fist down into the man.

'Woah!' Danny yelled as he rushed forward to restrain his friend.

Corinth shrieked as her hand clung to her reddened cheek where she had been struck. Anne and Marie were helping her to her feet.

Danny caught one of Gary's blows mid-swing and pulled him away from Sean. Craig and Jonty moved forward to bring Sean to his feet.

'Settle down Gary,' Danny hissed into his friend's ear as the pilot writhed to get free.

Sean was sobbing hysterically as Craig and Jonty took him to the bench seat near the food. 'Here, sit down Sean,' Jonty said.

'What came over you?' Craig asked. 'You can't hit women like that, man. You know that.'

Corinth shrieked as Marie and Anne consoled her and took her to a chair. Marie put a cup of punch in her hand and helped her to take a sip. 'This will make it better. Come on now.'

'Ok. Ok. Ok,' Gary said as he held his arms out. 'I'm calm, let go of me.' Danny released him.

As Danny got to his feet he looked over to Sean and what he saw gave him pause. He glanced at Marty and Bobby and they had seen the same thing.

Sean was pulling at his collar as the sweat ran down his cheeks. He shook his head sporadically from side to side as his eyes darted from place to place. He sobbed softly to himself as he shuffled uncomfortably on his chair. 'I just need to get out,' he whimpered. 'I've got to get out of here.'

'Hey, hey,' Craig said to him, as Jonty stepped back. 'You'll be ok mate.'

Sean's hands went to Craig's face and Danny saw the way his fingers sunk into the soft flesh of his cheeks. 'I can't fucking stand it.' The man shrieked. 'I have to get out here.'

'Sean, you're hurting me,' Craig said calmly.

Meanwhile the music was still playing and Danny moved toward Sean to try and pry him off. Sean began to thrash as he held Craig's head in his hands. He brought his head well back and then threw himself forward in a headbutt as hard as he could before Danny got there. The crack the two skulls made as they came together was sickening. Craig went down, hard. Sean on the other hand rose to his feet shrieking while blood ran down his face and into his open mouth.

Danny threw his arms around him and tried to throw him to the ground but he was too strong. Sean flung him off as if he was nothing and Danny felt his legs fly into the air. His back hit the tabletop and his body dragged most of the food and the drink along with it to the floor.

Gary bellowed again and rushed the man with a new rage. Sean twisted and screamed and met the charge head on. The two men came together again with a rush of air from lungs, but this time it was Gary that was taken down.

Sean screamed again, and the flesh at the corners of his mouth had begun to split as his jaw opened wider, wider than his flesh could allow. He brought his fists down in hammer throws onto the pilot's face and chest as Gary did all he could to protect himself.

The music continued to play soft tones as Danny got back to his feet while Bobby smashed the bottle of Glen over Sean's head. Sean rocked with the blow but recovered instantly and then turned on Bobby. The fat man shrieked as he tried to run but Sean was too quick for him; he ran him down as Danny rushed to his aid but once again Sean was just too strong.

As Danny wrapped his hands around him, Sean threw an elbow back into his throat. All the strength went out of him and he went to the ground. He coughed and spluttered and he felt his airway close. He saw Sean open his mouth and howl before he drove his face deep into Bobby's shoulder and the screams intensified tenfold.

Danny clawed at his throat as he tried to breathe but nothing would come through. He saw Anne rush to his side. 'Stay calm, it'll open, just stay calm.' She placed a hand on his chest to settle him and it helped; he pulled with his lungs and they rose a little. He felt as though his Adam's apple had been driven out through his ass, but air had started to slip through.

Sean ripped his head back and Anne screamed as a large chunk of flesh came back with his mouth. Danny realised then that Bobby had stopped moving. A large chunk had been torn from the side of the radio operator's neck and his life's blood was pouring out over the floor. Sean got to his feet and ran both hands down his face as he tore flesh from his own cheeks while he roared. His eyes darted from frightened person to lifeless form as he searched for a new target.

Danny had started to get to his feet again, when he saw Sean's eyes fall on him. Anne stepped in front of him, but Danny pushed her aside. He sucked in a breath as he gained his stance. Sean took a step toward him then stopped. His body twitched, and his eyes rolled in their sockets. With both bloody hands he reached back over his head for something as he went to his knees. Then he went down and didn't move.

Corinth stood above him, and her body shuddered as she sobbed. The kitchen knife that had been in her hand was driven all the way up to the hilt in middle of Sean's back. Danny sighed as he gaped down at the wreck that had been Sean. He looked to Bobby and then to Craig, while Gary got his feet. Corinth bent down and jostled the knife to free it, before she pulled it loose.

'You saved me Ma,' Danny said to her. 'You did the right thing.'

Corinth examined the blood on the blade and rolled it over in her hand. The music to the song she had been singing went back into its chorus again as she lifted her head to meet Danny's eyes. Danny took a step back.

'No, Ma. Come on. No,' he pleaded with her but it didn't make a difference.

Her head jerked to the side and she ran a blood-covered hand down over her cheek while she opened her mouth too wide. He watched as the skin stretched then split and more blood began to run down her jowls.

'No Ma. No,' he tried again, and held his hands out in front of him. 'Come on.'

Corinth Butler threw her head back and howled. Then she brought the knife down across her own face, bursting her right eyeball as she did. 'I have to get out,' she croaked through her torn vocal cords. 'Let me out!' And then with a terrifying shriek, she lunged at him as she screamed, 'Free me!'

31

SHE CAME AT HIM like a crazed animal. Her breaths were short, hot grunts of exertion as she swung the blade in her hand. The white of her remaining eye had been muddied, polluted by the blood that spilt forth when her blood vessels burst. She slashed downward in a stabbing motion with the blade but the tip fell well short of Danny's body. She came again, and again, flailing as she charged him. Steel flashed in front of his eyes as she swung it, the small amount of clean steel that was untainted by her blood or Sean's, shone radiantly as it was hurled about.

Danny took a step back, and moved his head to the side to avoid another wild swing. Her one remaining eye ogled him and almost burst out of its socket in her strain. Her teeth gnashed together and she shrieked again as she came at him. She leapt into the air and brought the blade down with both hands. Danny reached out for whatever he could. His hand touched something cool, and he latched onto it and brought it around with everything that he had left.

There was a scream of metal on metal and a soft crunch as the silver platter that Marie had used to hand out her punch rippled under the force of the blow. The tip of the knife had begun to pierce the platter and then with a horrible crack, it snapped halfway up the blade. With the force Corinth had been putting into her blow, the knife had turned in her hand and she ended up cutting herself to ribbons on the piece that had remained stuck in the platter. She barked in rage as she lifted the jagged piece of steel in the air for another swing.

Danny lashed out. He kicked her as hard and as straight as he could in the stomach and she flew backwards. She snarled like a beast as she landed and rolled back over her head and onto her knees. Danny's kick had allowed him a short respite but Corinth instantly gained her feet again and headed straight back into a head-long charge. This time when Danny swung the platter as hard as he could, it caught her across the face mid-stride and Danny felt the shock go up his arm.

Corinth went down with the blow, taking the platter and Danny's hands with it, but as before, she didn't stay down. The remainder of the knife that jutted from the silver platter had driven itself high through her left cheek. Danny fought to free it until he realised that she was biting down on the blade that remained in her mouth. As he twisted and pulled on the platter, the knife's edge worked away at her cheek until finally the blade pulled free from the platter and came loose in Danny's hand.

He saw her hand move and he dropped his knee on her arm. As his weight came down, he heard a horrible snap as her forearm gave way under him and she dropped the knife. The fight had closed in now and with her one good arm she lashed up at him; the right side of his face went hot with pain and his eye closed against it.

'Gary!' he yelled as he fought to hold her other hand. 'Marty! Anyone!' He yelled as he caught her wrist mid-swing, but then failed to hold onto her through the blood on his hands.

'I've got my own problem!' Gary snarled back and Danny looked to his voice.

Gary was on his back, both of his arms locked around Marty's throat as the small, young man thrashed about and gurgled and swiped at Wendy Phillips. Wendy stood back up against the kitchen boundary, in a protective stance in front of Anne Castelli.

'Fuck!' Danny roared as Corinth's fingernails dug into the right side of his face again. The rage was in him again, Old Ma or not. He threw the platter away as the damned backing track to Corinth's song finally ended. His left knee still pinned her arm and his right arm had finally subdued her flailing left. She was helpless now but to thrash and scream under him. He drew back his left hand, curling it into a fist.

'Sorry Ma,' he muttered as he drove his fist down into her forehead. The sound was dull and thick as her head bounced off his fist, into the floor and was then sandwiched between the two. The shock of the hit silenced her, but didn't stop her struggles. Nor did the second or third hit completely subdue her. In the end, he lost count how many times he struck her. He heard screaming and thought it was still her giving her roar of defiance beneath him as he beat the life out of her, but in the end, it was Anne Castelli, who couldn't bear to see Danny kill her friend.

'I can't hold him. I can't hold him.'

As Danny rose from the mess of Ma's corpse, he felt the warmth and stickiness of her blood as it mixed with his. He felt the pain run down from his temple and into his jaw and he clenched his teeth against it. Marty had mostly squirmed his way out of Gary's grasp. The little man didn't seem to have eyes for the pilot that held him back; he only wanted to get at the women. He slipped out from under Gary's arms and lunged forward with his free arm while Gary managed to hold on to the other. Marty screamed in frustration, a low horrible sound that he could not have made when he was sane.

Another one, Danny sobbed inside of himself, before he felt the last of what remained of his conscience disappear for what he was about to do. He didn't apologise this time, nor did he hesitate. He caught Marty as he finally slipped from Gary's grasp and charged at the two ladies. Being so small it was easy to lift him, but once he had him in his hands, he found it a different struggle. His arm span was long enough to hold him out of biting distance but he couldn't escape the flail of his little arms and the fury of his kicks. He threw Marty as hard as he could into the solid tables and chairs, and the sound was horrible as his little body struck the fixtures and bent around them.

As with Corinth however, that didn't stop him. No sooner had Marty hit, he tried to get himself back to his feet. Gary was up by then and drove his foot into the little man's back as he tried to climb the table and pinned him. Marty howled as he leant his neck back and spat and shrieked as he stretched out with his hands to get a hold of the pilot that had him pinned. Danny moved alongside his friend and brought his fist to slam into the little man's forehead. There was a crack as Marty's head snapped down against his back, too far for his neck to handle, and then he collapsed.

Danny sucked in air as he stepped back away from the scene. He held his hands up in front of his face and sobbed. Then his heel hit something hard and immovable and he turned and saw Bobby's lifeless body. His eyes were open and blank, his mouth gaped and some of the blood that had poured from his throat had gotten in there. Danny felt his legs wobble beneath him and then he collapsed.

He fell back and hard, but let himself go. He landed on his ass against one of the walls of the mess. He put his hands to his face and didn't care about the blood on them, he just didn't want to look at any of it anymore. He just didn't want to know. He heard someone slide down beside him and sigh as they did, then he felt a hard hand squeeze his shoulder.

Gary didn't say anything and he was thankful for that. He didn't want to hear anything nor did he want to say anything. He opened his eyes and saw Wendy embracing Anne Castelli over near the boundary to the kitchen and sighed. It was good that they had each other, Danny thought. Then he scanned the room again. There was no-one else.

His eyebrows furrowed as he started to get to his feet.

'Danny, just rest man.' He felt Gary try to hold him back.

'Where's the rest of them?' He asked. Craig was still motionless on the floor, Bobby, Marty, Sean and poor Corinth were gone, but there were three that were unaccounted for. 'Where's Jonty, Marie and Jimmy?'

Wendy left the safety of Anne's embrace and turned back to him, her great concern visible on her face. 'I…'

'Did you see where they went?' he demanded, panic stricken. 'One or more of them could've…' He gestured to Sean.

Gary got to his feet beside him. 'Man, I didn't pay attention to any of them. There was enough going on.'

'Shit!' Danny slammed his fist onto one of the tables.

'Hey, you go check the dorms. I'll check outside.' Gary tried to keep a calm tone.

'Nah,' Danny dismissed it entirely. 'Then what happens to these two if something happens here?'

Gary stared blankly at the two present ladies. They needed to be careful; in a stroke, their numbers had gone from twelve and now they could only confirm four.

'Shit,' Danny swore again. 'Fuck.' There was no other way to do it. 'Gary, you stay here and I'll go look for them,' he said in a solemn tone.

'No,' Anne said as she stepped forward.

'There's no other way Anne.' Danny silenced her. 'I'm not leaving you two alone. So, Gary can stay here and I'll go look for the other three.'

Gary and Anne remained silent; it was Wendy who spoke up. 'I've got a better idea.' She moved away from the kitchen boundary. 'I'll go with you Danny, and Anne can stay with Gary.'

Danny considered her. 'It might not be safe,' he said softly.

'It's not safe here, is it?' She shrugged.

'Fine.' Danny grumbled. 'We'll check the dorms then; Gary stay here with Anne.' They left without another word.

Before they entered the hallway to the dorm, Danny stopped and turned to Wendy. 'Are you alright?'

'Yeah, I'm fine,' she brushed off the question.

'Stop.' He put a hand on her, and stopped her from trying to push past him. 'None of this can be easy. I need to know that you're going to be here.' He gestured to his head in reference to her consciousness. 'I may need your help.'

She looked at him like he was an idiot. 'You're the one that's more of a risk. Are you going to be ok?' she mocked.

That answer was enough for Danny. He opened the door to the Dongas and pushed through.

It didn't take them long to work out that someone was in the dorms. They heard the shrieks and the pounding long before they saw the open dormitory door. Danny didn't like the way the slaps sounded wet and soft and his imagination started to run away from him again.

Beneath it, they heard the grunts of exertion and the intermittent shriek of crazed intent.

Danny and Wendy hugged the walls as they neared the open door. The intermittent poundings seemed to be slowing but then as Danny finally reached the open door, whoever it was uttered a low growl that turned into a roar and Danny heard a further flurry of impacts.

He leant into the doorway. That the room was Jonty's, there was no doubt. The posters of heavy metal bands and demons that lined the walls were a poor representation of the horror that sat in the middle of the room.

What remained of a human being sat slumped against the bed while Jimmy Sutton roared in the mess that was its face. As if in retribution for all the wrongs that had been done to him in the past weeks, Jimmy screamed it all out in this fury that had overcome him. Like with Corinth, his eyes had turned red with the blood that once pumped through his burst vessels. Veins stood out from his neck and scratches ran down his chest from where he had torn his own shirt from his body.

While Danny watched, Jimmy continued to lay into the mess that was in front of him. He threw a wide haymaker, then a hammer-fisted blow down from the top. He latched his hands to both shoulders and drove his head down into the red mess again and again all while he howled in a psychotic rage.

Danny had no choice, he had to take him out. If he left Jimmy alive, there would be no telling how long it would take for him to move on to Wendy or Anne, or even Gary. He had to be dealt with. Now. Danny stood up and moved into the room. He gestured for Wendy to stay where she was and then lunged at Jimmy.

He drove a fist into the back of his head, but Jimmy had lurched to throw another punch at that stage and the blow only grazed him. Danny was then hit with the full fury of the man. Red and black eyes locked onto him and Jimmy roared anew as he threw another wild haymaker which near knocked Danny from his feet. Danny tried to push him away but he was already exhausted from the effort he had used on Sean and Corinth.

A wild fist hammered his jaw, then two hands latched onto his shoulders and Jimmy drove his forehead forward. The world subdued beneath a hideous crack that he felt throughout his whole body and then he was falling.

The torrent of beatings didn't stop there. He felt another fist slam into his body as he fell. Then Jimmy was on him and he didn't have to strength to protect himself, let alone fight the man off him. He pulled his arms up over his hammered face and felt the onslaught of Jimmy's tireless swings crash into them. He was beyond pain now. Each blow sounded like it was hitting a steel door that was three hundred feet away, but the echo rolled through his mind, again and again and again.

Then it was over. He still heard Jimmy's growls and spurts of rage but they weren't above him directly. He rolled and tried to get up but he didn't have the strength.

'Wendy,' he groaned as he fought to maintain his consciousness. 'Wendy, get out of here.' But then he saw her. He saw Jimmy on top of her, but nothing seemed right.

Jimmy was on his back, his arms stretched toward the ceiling. Wendy had her knees up in Jimmy's shoulder blades and she had him suspended in the air, while his entire body thrashed about. Danny saw the chord that she had wrapped around his neck. It bit into his flesh and the blood ran down toward her over the chord and across her strained knuckles. Finally, Jimmy began to tire and eventually, he was gone.

Danny lay there and panted while he watched Wendy roll him off her. He sucked the breath into his lungs as the feeling slowly came back into his body. Wendy got to her feet and rushed towards him. 'Are you ok?' she asked as she rolled him onto his side.

'I need some Panadol,' he complained as he put his hand to his head. 'Fuck, my head.'

She helped sit him up. 'Yeah, he got you pretty good huh.' She laughed as she rubbed his back.

'Fuck off,' he groaned as he considered the body. If it was Jimmy that had beaten the shit out of him, the other body had to be Jonty. Amongst his posters of death cults and demons, his ruined corpse looked like the centrepiece to a ritual sacrifice. He didn't know what had happened for Jonty to be in here, but he knew that he hadn't stayed to help them. If he had, he might still be alive.

Danny groaned as his body ached from head to toe and he rolled to his stomach and then lifted himself to his feet. 'Help me,' he muttered to Wendy, and she let him put an arm around her so that he could lean on her. Together, they limped back to the mess. They had found two out of the three – the only question now, was where had Marie disappeared to?

His head pounded from the alcohol and the beatings, and for the second time that night he felt like he wanted to throw up. They pushed their way into the mess and then stopped at the doorway.

'What now?' Wendy complained as she struggled more and more with the weight he was putting on her.

'Where… have they… gone?' Danny managed to ask before his grip on her slipped and he went to his knees. 'Gary?' he asked as he collapsed to the ground but Gary wasn't there.

'Ahh shit,' Wendy complained as she tried to get him back up but he was done.

'Charlie?' he asked. 'Where are you man?'

'No, no, no,' Wendy said as she knelt next to him. 'Stay with me Danny, come on.'

His vision reeled and swayed, and the dizziness was making him sick in the stomach.

'Charl…' he muttered as he closed his eyes.

'No Danny, stay awake.' She slapped him lightly on the cheek, but it didn't matter. He was exhausted.

'Le…anna,' he managed before he slipped into darkness and the world of the unknown. 'Leanna.'

32

THE LIGHTS STUNG HIS EYES when he first opened them. He tried to lift his hands to shield them, but they wouldn't come. In his weariness he fought to sit up, but even that was beyond him.

'What happened?' he murmured as he tried to peer through slits. 'Where am I?'

There was a figure right next to him; he saw their silhouette, but couldn't make out any other features. He saw a dark hand reach out for him, and fear boiled up inside of him. He strained to bring his arms up, but they wouldn't come, he strained harder and drove his head back into the softness of his pillow. 'Let me out of this,' he mewled. 'Would you just fuck off and let me the fuck out?' The darkness began to swallow him again, and somehow the lights that blinded him didn't seem to matter so much anymore; the sharpness of their sheer white had been subdued and shadows entered the world again. The figure that stood to his side still remained, but their lines had become blurry. Almost as if they were a projection and the film had begun to skip.

He looked around and saw that he was in the infirmary, the little one cordoned off to the side of Anne and Marie's lab. His hands were chained to the steel runners of his bed and as his vision continued further down, large spikes had been driven down through his legs to pin them in place. He tried to scream but his lips wouldn't part. Instead, all he heard was a muffled groan. He tried to thrash his head about, but even that seemed to be locked in some sort of cage. The more he struggled, the more he felt the chains tighten around his wrists, the more he felt the spikes drive further into his flesh. The more he felt the cage close around his head.

As two large lamps ignited down the far end of the room, the world seemed to lose its final battle. The figure that stood to his side faced the lights and Danny heard a scream, although miles and miles away. The shadow lifted its hands as its being succumbed to the heat of the two lamps down the end of the room. Bit by bit, the shadow disappeared until finally, Danny was alone. Alone with his pain and alone with his fear.

He tried to look away from the lamps but he couldn't. He began to cry as the amber light burnt away the lashes from his lids and tears swept over their remains. He blinked and thrashed again as he tried to scream but it was no good.

The world around him seemed to suffer with every second that those lamps remained lit. The bed began to rust and flakes of rotten iron fell from their posts. The floor turned sour and then burnt away, leaving only ash to rise up before him. The ceiling bowed in and crumpled up in a shower of dust and debris and then it was gone, revealing the sky which had turned red and dark as if to signal the knell that had called them all to death.

And all the while the lamps remained on. Burning into his soul as if it had been so, so long since they had fed on even a morsel. But Danny knew. He knew their secret. He knew what they were, even if he didn't want to believe it. He knew.

'*I will be free.*' The voice was deep and booming. If it had been uttered by vocal cords then the earth would've shaken under its power and the life that Danny had known would have crumbled beneath the weight of its words. But they had not come from the throat of some being, they had not uttered words in a language that had never been heard. The words had come from the centre of his mind, as if planted there like a seed to grow, like a cancer to spread. And as the trail of their echo faded in his mind, the only thing that was left, as if nourished by the heat of the lamplight, was utter, utter fear.

He tried to fight, again he tried to move, but the chains and the spikes tightened their grip on him. He tried to move his head and he tried to blink, but the cage had closed around him and the lamps had sucked him in. The closer he came, the more hideous the heat became, and then the smell hit him and he wanted to die. Christ, did he want to die. Because he knew the lights weren't from a lamp, he knew the smell wasn't just in his head and the heat wasn't a fevered dream. The light of the lamps blinked, as if in congratulations, and the earth shook as the monster opened its jaw.

'I... *will kill... you all.*' The words ripped through his mind again and he heard the air escape from the monstrous mouth that was before him. A roar that had not been heard by human ears for 70 years and now it was going to be free again. Now, it was coming. It was coming. It was coming. For him.

He sat up quickly as he sucked air into his lungs. The lights were bright once more and he had to close his eyes quickly against their brilliance. Once more, he tried to bring his hands up to shield himself but they wouldn't come. His eyes closed for a short while as he gathered his senses and slowly, he opened his eyes and checked himself over. He was wearing the same hoodie as he had the night of the party. Those, as well as his track pants, that had once been grey were now covered in blood smear and what looked like shit. He saw that his arms had been bound to the rails of his bed by leather belts. His veins stood upright in the hollow of his bicep, as if he had been straining, and down at his feet stood Gary, Wendy and Anne.

'Why am I tied up?' he asked as calmly as he could, because he saw the fear in their faces. At his words they all seemed to relax, and Gary let out an enormous sigh as he slumped down in a chair off the side.

'Fuck,' he groaned as he sat down. 'We thought you'd gone insane like the others.'

'So,' Danny said with a frown. 'It wasn't a dream?'

'One could only hope,' Anne said solemnly.

All four of them remained silent for a moment as if in mourning for their friends. Then Danny looked from sad face to teary eye. 'Why am I tied up?'

Wendy came and sat on the edge of his bed. 'You collapsed after what happened with Jimmy,' she said softly as she squeezed his arm. 'I… I had to leave you, because the other two were gone.'

'That's right,' Danny said as he nodded his head. 'I remember that now. You two were gone.' He pointed accusingly at Gary and Anne.

'We didn't have much choice,' Anne said in their defence, as she gestured across to the next bed.

Craig Hollins lay in an incapacitated state with an oxygen mask strapped to his face. He looked dead, but then each time the pump heaved air through the mask, his chest rose with it.

'When you two left,' Gary picked up, 'we decided we should check them out.' He gestured to Craig. 'He was still alive. We couldn't leave him there like that.'

Danny nodded. The answer was fair enough.

'Then we had just gotten Craig in here,' Gary continued as if he was out of breath. 'And Wendy comes running in saying you need help. So, we go back.'

'And here I am,' Danny smiled softly. 'But why am I tied up?' he asked for the third time.

'Because even in your unconscious state, you would not shut up,' Anne said flatly.

There was his answer. He knew exactly what she meant as images of the film he had deleted came back to him. He nodded. 'Ahh, that again?'

'Again?' Gary asked.

'Yeah. You know it,' he grumbled and then offered Anne an exhausted smile. 'There you go Anne; you know why I didn't want to tell you now.'

'This?' She looked at him incredulously. 'This is what was wrong?' She moved forward and slapped him hard, the same way she had slapped Jonty.

His head was rocked to the side and his cheek stung from yet another wound. Slowly, he faced her and wham, she slapped him again. He took a breath to calm himself and looked at her without turning his cheek again. 'Are you finished?'

'No, I am not,' she growled at him. 'You knew about this and you said nothing to anyone.'

'That isn't…'

'Because of you, over five people are dead now.'

'Anne…' She slapped him again.

'Don't you say my name. You bastard.' She tried to slap him again but finally Gary restrained her.

'Anne, it's not like that,' he started as he tasted blood in his mouth. 'God, can someone untie me?' He looked expectantly to Wendy, who hesitated. She glanced from his tethers to Anne and Gary and then finally subdued and released him.

Danny sat and rubbed at his wrists where the leather had rubbed against his skin. 'I'll tell you, but you need to believe me,' he started. 'Because whenever I said it to myself, I wouldn't believe me. I couldn't.'

'You can let go of me,' Anne said curtly to Gary, as she wrenched one of her hands free.

'I'm sorry it's taken me so long to reach out, but…' He stopped and thought about what to say. 'After what happened with Charlie, I didn't want to involve anyone else. It was me, Charlie and Jonty, who went onto that ship and for the most part I knew Charlie and I had suffered from what had happened. After I fainted on that ship, I started talking like… them.' He lowered his head. 'Let me out and all that shit. But Jonty and Charlie never told me, they both went weird about everything. I saw it in that video from Marty's camera, that's why I deleted it.'

He considered Anne with weary eyes. 'I know you were only trying to help me,' he said with a solemn look on his face as he continued to rub at his chaffed wrists. 'But Jonty was trying to turn everyone against me.' He paused. 'At least, that's how it looked from where I was sitting, and I didn't want to expose anyone else to what I had seen on that ship.'

'What?' Wendy asked. 'The dead Japanese guy?'

Danny shook his head. 'Sit down and I'll tell you everything I know.'

So, for the second time, he did. As with his retelling to Louise, he felt better for it. He saw a tear trickle down Anne's face when he told them about what happened with Charlie. He saw anger in Gary's face for a man that was now dead and couldn't get any deader. Wendy placed her hands over her mouth when he told them about the video feed from the salvage crew and how he had seen Kee Peters killed, along with their mechanic and Paul Stathis, by what he could only imagine was the existing crew of the whaler.

It shocked him at how ready they all were to accept what he had to tell them. Even when he told them about the creatures on the ship they didn't scoff or laugh or turn their heads away. They just looked at him with sad eyes and concerned expressions on their faces. The only thing he left out, were his dreams. Even he wasn't ready for that, not now.

When he was finished, Anne stood up and moved next to him. She hugged him and then kissed him on his cheek. He felt her lips press against the scars that Charlie had given him and a tear escaped his eye. Then Anne held him at arm's length and Danny saw that she was crying too. 'And?' she said softly.

'No,' he murmured almost inaudibly. 'They're just dreams.'

'Dreams?' Gary said it with a scowl on his face.

'I hate dreams at the moment,' Wendy said as she turned her back. 'I keep having this one where this monster is eating me.'

Danny gaped at her. 'What?'

'Yeah,' she said as she rubbed her eyes. 'It's a real pain in the ass, scares the shit out of me every now and then. I'm treading water and I know there is this big fuck off fish under me.' She made a thoughtful look. 'Nah, not a fish. Like a big fuck off snake. Anyway, I can see its eyes and I know the thing is going to get me but I can't get away.'

'Like the shit I used to dream about when I was on nicotine patches,' Gary said uncomfortably. 'I had the same dream but with a boat's propeller.' He shivered.

'Wendy,' Danny said softly. 'What does it say to you?'

Her eyes met his and then darted away. 'It says that it's going to kill me,' she said softly. 'It's going to kill everyone I loved; everyone I know.'

Her voice trembled at this. 'It told me that it wanted to be free and to free it, otherwise it would kill all of us.'

Danny didn't say a word, he couldn't believe that he wasn't alone with this. He looked at Anne. 'You knew?'

She nodded as she wiped tears away from her eyes. 'Most of you had trouble sleeping, I was worried I was going to run out of pills.' She sniffed. 'It was only a few people that didn't ask for help in one way or another.'

'I didn't,' Gary said with a smile.

'Probably because you were self-medicating,' Anne said in a distasteful tone and Gary fell back into silence.

'Who didn't ask for help?' Danny asked curiously.

'Apart from Gary, just Marie.'

Danny sat upright again. 'Fuck, where is Marie?'

Anne put her hands to her mouth. 'I thought you saw her in the dorms.'

Danny shook his head and then turned to Wendy for reassurance.

'No,' Wendy agreed with him. 'There's been a lot going on, so no wonder we forgot about her.'

Danny forced himself off the sick bed and became unsteady on his feet. Gary steadied him and held him cautiously until he was satisfied that he could stand under his own power again and they began to discuss their plans.

'I'll have to stay to care for Craig,' Anne stated.

'Well, you're not staying here alone,' Danny grumbled as he rubbed at his eyes.

'I'll stay here,' Wendy allowed. 'I don't think I can go back near that place again.'

Danny nodded and said to Gary. 'You all set?'

Gary nodded as he leant his neck from side to side to stretch his muscles and then they left the women in the safety of the lab, while they went off to look for the last remaining camp member.

Danny's guts sunk almost the moment they left the lab. From where he stood, he faced his workshop. One of the doors had been opened, and the Hägglund that Rheinmarsh had driven back was gone. He pointed it out to Gary and they made a line for the workshop.

When they made it there, nothing seemed out of place, except for the missing vehicle of course. He went through and counted his jerry cans and found that not a single one was missing. He ran a hand through the stubble on his chin.

'What's wrong?' Gary asked him as his eyes scanned the workshop.

'Well, whoever took the Hägglund didn't take any fuel. It'll be a long fucking walk when the thing shits itself halfway there.'

Gary looked at him. 'How do you know?'

Danny pointed to the line of jerry cans. 'These are all the cans I've got; they didn't take any.' He pulled out his phone and checked the time: two in the morning. He lifted his head and sighed. No wonder he was so exhausted. 'If Marie took this thing and she left around midnight when the shit hit the fan, she'd be just about out I reckon.'

Gary frowned. 'We better check the Red Shed out properly before we make that assumption; I don't want to go stumbling around the dark out there for her. It could have been those blokes from that ship, which sounds more likely than Marie.'

Danny agreed and they set out toward the Red Shed. Both men were grim as they knew what to expect in there. Danny hated it. He hated the stillness of the place, that only hours before had been the liveliest he had seen it. He hated the blood that had stained the carpet squares, the smell that was in his head, the smell that he expected when he thought about dead bodies. Instead, he smelt the festivities, beer, scotch and food, all of it strewn across the floor.

The two men stood there and stared overwhelmingly at the mess, while the karaoke system continued to play the backing track of some song that Danny couldn't pick. The speakers that were connected to the microphone emitted a low whooshing sound as if wind was brushing against its foils. Danny moved over to the laptop and disconnected the speaker system. He switched the amps off one by one. As soon as he did, he disliked the scene even more. The music was a stark contrast to what he saw, and it freaked him out to hear it playing while Corinth, Sean, Marty and Bobby lay silent. Now that it was off, there was no distraction and he found that all he wanted to do was turn it back on.

Gary moved into the kitchens and swore. Danny saw him switch off a stove that had been left with a pot of dumplings, which had since boiled over. They made the decision then that their first priority was to ensure that the place wouldn't burn down and they moved from power point to light switch, and made sure everything was safe. Luckily enough, the stovetop was the only thing that could've ended in disaster.

They then went and checked the communications room, which was empty and silent. They checked Jonty's office, which had remained locked. Neither of them really cared what Jonty had to hide so they knocked, called Marie's name and after a few attempts with no answer, they left to search somewhere else. The two men also silently agreed not to split up. They moved together, room by room, and searched the entire place, which being the Red Shed took some time.

They broke into each person's Donga. Even if it was their own, they made sure that Marie couldn't have gotten inside to hide. Gary swore and turned his head away when he saw the mess that had become of Jonty. After a time, he stopped and looked Danny in the eye. 'You know, I never picked Jonty to be a metal head.'

Danny had to laugh. 'Yeah, it threw me too, don't worry.'

Gary sighed as the smile disappeared from his face. 'Marie's room, right?' he asked as he leant up against the door jamb.

'You know it,' Danny said solemnly as he tried the handle. Locked. He took a step back and lifted his boot up to slam into its middle. The lock splintered and the jamb gave in under his strength as the door flew inwards. It took Danny's eyes a little while to adjust to the darkness and he blinked rapidly as he stepped inside.

'I can't see a fucking thing,' Gary complained as he bumped into Danny's back.

'Neither can I.' What made the room darker than every other was the fact that Marie's laptop's screen was on and it was so bright that it made everything else look as black as the devil's heart. 'Switch the light on,' Danny said angrily as Gary bumped into him again.

'Yeah, yeah,' Gary mocked as he moved back to the open door and flipped the switch.

Danny's eyes closed against the brilliance of the overhead light and once more he waited for his eyes to adjust.

'Holy shit,' he heard Gary say in awe.

'What?' Danny squinted and closed his eyes again.

'Man,' he said. 'Look at the walls.'

Finally, Danny could open his eyes and part of him wished that he hadn't. His heart sunk in his chest as his eyes darted from place to place where Marie had scrawled all over her walls with pen, texter or pencil, lipstick, and even in places it looked like her own blood. The phrase had been repeated half a hundred times, on the floor written over the carpet, on her bedspread and even scratched into the timber of her coffee table, where he and Charlie had rested their cups of tea a mere month ago.

The teapot was smashed on the ground, and a single shard of porcelain had been left on the counter. Its jagged edge was red with blood and Danny imagined she had run the white porcelain against her snow-white flesh. He imagined the blood burst from beneath the surface as the China split her skin. Then he examined one of the repetitions, one of the ones written in blood, and shuddered as he read it aloud.

'Free me.'

33

THE LETTERS WERE THOSE of a person who was stuck in a cell. Trapped in small box with no way out but death. Danny saw the urgency in their strokes, the pain and the panic. The absolute urgency for the release that the author craved. The basic desire of all life: freedom. He wondered how it felt, to succumb to this. To have your mind slowly taken away and to be left with only the basest of wants. He wondered if they felt it coming on, or did it seep over them like sleep did, the way it just crept up on a soul. He had seen it too many times to think Marie's circumstances unique. Charlie, the mechanic on the whaler, even himself. Something had reached them, but even he couldn't answer that as he couldn't remember. All he remembered was the dream.

That fucking dream. Those eyes in the distance, ever watching, ever knowing, ever wanting. Those eyes that reminded him of a predator in the dark. The body remained just behind the screen of light, but its eyes were always visible, always there to mock. He hated them so much, and even as he stood in Marie's room, he could almost see those bloody things in the wall amongst her letters. As if every word made up a portion of its body and fragments of the scrawlings curled and shifted as he stared at them to become those fucking eyes.

'Do you think she has what the others have?' Gary asked as his eyes continued to scour her room.

'I don't know,' Danny grumbled. 'She didn't act differently,' he said, then recalled the way she had laughed too loud and too hard. The way she had tried to be overenthusiastic to everyone else, but him.

They moved around the small quarters and Danny shook his head as he found more and more blood, more and more words, all of them repeating the same damned thing. He tried to think about everything to do with Marie, everything that had happened over the last month. He knelt down and checked under her bed, and swore as he found his Ugg boots and favourite track pants. He dragged them out from under her bed and held them before him, like a lost treasure that was finally found again. Then as the reality of the current situation came back over him, he let them fall to the ground and he moved on, leaving them there.

When Danny got to her desk, he struggled to see anything below the scattered papers and notes that were strewn across the top. He shuffled through them, and it didn't take him long to work out what they were. Marie Swan had taken the task of translating the ships log that he had found on the whaler. The pieces of paper he moved about were dates and timelines, names, Japanese characters and what they referenced.

'All of this came from that ship,' Danny said as he remembered the video feed from the whaler. 'It all started there, maybe the log has the answers?'

'What's wrong?' Gary asked as he moved over to consider the papers.

'What do you think the chances are she's held something back when she told us about the log's content?'

Gary laughed. 'Pretty fucking high.'

Danny nodded as he sat down at the desk. As he moved some papers, he bumped something hard and light beneath the mess. The computer screen switched from its screensaver, over to a flat dark screen, with a 'play' button in its centre.

'Wonder what this is?' Danny murmured as he found the mouse and started the file.

'This is Doctor Marie Swan at Mawson, the Australian Antarctic Division base. We have found a ship that we believe dates back to the Second World War, buried within the Amery Ice Shelf. Our crew entered the ship and found the internals in untouched condition, unmolested by the environment nor by the hands of man. We uncovered the ship's log and it has been my task over the past weeks to decipher it. Within the ship's log, I found the personal writings of a military officer. These writings were more journalistic than the military report of a commanding officer and offer us a more personal view of what happened during the final days and hours aboard the *Nisshin Maru*.'

'Jesus Christ,' Gary grumbled. 'You think she sent this off outside?'

'Here are the final pages and the final words of the Lieutenant, Jin Ishimura.'

'Shhh.' Danny leant in close, he didn't want to miss a word.

'Discipline, honour, pride. These are the things that are drilled into a young man when he joins the Imperial army, some even before. The Samurai that we descend from were perfect in their honour. Stalwart in the way they held their family lines and traditions. But I wonder how they would've acted, if they sat where I do now.

Having fled the Allied war ships, we moved south to the land of ice but we were not provisioned well enough for the journey. With my men adding extra strain to the *Nisshin Maru*'s already depleted food supplies, it didn't take long before the situation became dire. I almost laugh now when I remember how that monster broke the surface; it seemed as though all of our prayers had been answered. Food enough for all, and if stored well, for a long time. But this was not my prayer. This was not what I wanted for us. This ship should have sunk in the South China Sea. My men and I should have died on the shores of the Philippines. At least there is honour in that. Whereas this...

The monster proved too powerful. Its hide was so hot, that even on the bow we could feel the heat that radiated from its flesh. The water steamed around it and almost hid it. Many of the men even thought that there was nothing there, that there was just a storm front. But they put two harpoons into its hide, and the sound... the sound... As it fled, it dragged the vessel into the fog, and my men screamed as it touched their skin. They came below deck, with what looked like scalds on their faces and hands. Only when the winds picked up, were we able to go on deck again, as the steam was pushed away.

Some of the men thought that the monster feared us and the pain that the harpoons had given it, but this monster is the devil, this Leviathan is pure evil. It drove us through an ice wall, it melted the channel as it pushed through. The wall turned to slush before our eyes and then forced us all below deck as it crumbed over the prow. I now believe this to be where its lair was. We could not surrender and break the chains and hence we followed, protected from the steam and the ice, by the walls of this steel prison.

The ship took superficial damage, but it mattered not as we could not move. The engines still ran and the props still spun, but the vessel would not move. After some time of trying, the air tasted foul from exhaust, so we ordered the engines to shut down.

Three weeks we were trapped down here and the food was gone. We were able to move about on the deck as the steam had stopped. We imagined that the beast had died, because the cold had become worse and worse each and every day. One day, one of my men noticed that one of the harpoon lines that had dragged us here, had become loose. When we retrieved the line, the harpoon was still lodged in a few hundred pounds of flesh. The men were overjoyed and feasted upon the flesh of the beast. I ordered my men to wait until the ship's crew had eaten as they had kept us alive. Most of them listened, and perhaps that is why I am here still, because my men listened to me. Perhaps it would have been better if they did not.

My men had yet to be served when the first crew member fell ill. He screamed and held his head, and began to convulse while his joints spasmed. Then another fell ill and another. It soon became apparent that the meat was tainted. I ordered it thrown overboard, but the chaos had already set in. The crew members began to attack each other, they began to attack my men. We managed to subdue the afflicted, and they were taken to the infirmary.

In two hours, the afflicted outnumbered us and it became impossible to safely hold them. We began to suffer losses. The men turned to beasts; they used their hands and anything else to destroy each other and my men who tried to intervene. We locked them in the lower holds, to kill each other. A day is all it took for the sounds to die. We reopened the holds after another few hours of waiting, and entered. Do not think that these disfigured monstrosities that used to be men, are mindless. They had stopped killing each other and had lain in wait, setting the trap which we walked blindly into. As if indoctrinated in their training, our retreat was closed off, and my men were massacred.

Only two of us remain: myself, and a young man who has become my friend, not just one of my men. Yoshimori Miroku. I could name all my men who died below, but this man kept me alive for two more weeks. We do not use rank anymore, as it cannot help us. We do not record the log anymore, because no-one will read it.

Food ran short and, in his eagerness to please me, he made us a meal with the tainted meat, and did not realise it. He had eaten some as he prepared the meal and shortly after he attempted to kill me. I retreated to the bridge and locked myself in. I do not want to kill my friend, but he has not stopped rapping at the door.

In my time alone, I have meditated. I have considered my ancestors and I have contemplated my position. I have tried to reach back to my roots and my family's traditions, but I am alone on a ship with demons and only my resolve can stand against them. I know Yoshimori is still alive; I can hear him. I may not be able to save him, but I may be able to offer him an honourable death. If not, maybe he can offer me the same. So, I sit and recall the lessons of my youth, and try to find the solace in the beauty of Haiku:

"Blood runs proud on ice.

They still clatter at my door.

I stand resolute.'"

It chilled Danny's bones to listen to this final report of what had happened on that ship. The thing that chilled him more was to hear how the creatures originated. Danny stared at the screen. He had his answer, he knew he had his answer. He turned to Gary to see if he thought the same, but Gary just looked freaked out. As Danny checked the computer screen, he saw an arrow that suggested there was another track. He had come this far; it was time to hear everything. He clicked on the skip button and the track began to play.

Marie's voice was not the smooth and calm seduction that it had always been. She spoke as if she was only talking to herself, fast and concerned, as if someone was listening.

'Eating made them see. It brought them together. Man, and beast.' She laughed. 'Soon I will have the sample, but will they accept it? Will they welcome it? I need to… I need to get there.' She started to sound uncomfortable. 'I need to get it, need to make them one. They need to see; they need to feel what I feel.' She started to cry then and the sounds of her voice became more urgent. 'Ahhhhh, the eyes, the eyes are always watching me. Don't you know I'm trying!' she shrieked. 'Ahhh let me out, let me go. I just want to be free, just let me out. Ahhhh,' she cried in pain. 'Make it stop, the sound, make it stop.' She rapped her hands on the table in frustration. 'Stop it, stop it, stop it. Make it stop!' In the next moment she stopped crying, as if on command, and the voice became secretive again, as if it was another person talking.

'If I let them become one, the dreams will stop. The eyes will stop looking at me, yes they will, I know they will.' She giggled. 'I have to get the sample, have to make them one. Have to make them see, they will see, I will be free.' She began to hush herself, like a mother hushed a child who was throwing a tantrum.

'And once they are one, once they are free with you inside them, I will let you out. Gary told me how. How… And Jonty told me where. Where…' She almost laughed. 'He didn't even know that he had, but he is too ignorant to ever know anything but where to stick his dick. He wanted what they all want, but not me. No, no, no, no. I want to be free. I want to be free. I want to be free!' she pleaded rapidly and uncontrollably.

Then her voice changed. It became deep, not her own. 'As they see, they will know. And man will fall.'

The recording ended.

'I didn't tell her shit?' Gary said in his defence.

Danny ran his hand through the stubble on his chin. The bags under his eyes felt enormous and his stomach felt as though it wanted to release everything again. 'I don't know man, she sounds fucking insane.'

'When was that taken?' Gary asked solemnly.

'Yesterday, two in the morning. Before you took her out to the shelf,' he replied as he checked the properties for the file.

'Fuck me,' Gary said as he adjusted his hoodie on his shoulders. 'She was probably going on like this the entire time she was in the cabin with me and I couldn't hear the bitch.'

'You know it man.' Danny got to his feet. 'I've heard enough. I need to get out of this fucking place.'

Gary nodded as his eyes returned to the walls. 'Yeah, I hear you man. I hear you.'

The two men returned to Anne's office in silence. They walked past the bodies and through the cold porch and didn't stop to change their boots as they never bothered to change them on the way in. Danny, however, did stop to grab his heavy overcoat and his balaclava, as they had forgotten to grab them for him when they had dragged him to the infirmary.

Once they had left, he looked back to the Red Shed and considered for a short time.

'We might have to turn the heating off in there until we work out what to do with the bodies,' he said to Gary. 'When the thing with Charlie happened, I kind of understood what we did but this is something else.'

'Let Anne decide,' Gary croaked back. 'She's the white collar. You and I are only blue, same as Wendy.'

'Yeah,' Danny agreed. He was right, she was the last of the doctors and the intellects. The contractors didn't run Mawson, it was the researchers and hell, she was the closest they had.

They returned to the infirmary and found the two women standing over Craig. He was still unconscious, but it didn't look as though he was in trouble.

'Did you find her?' Anne asked as they came in.

Danny shook his head. 'No but we found other things and it doesn't look good.'

'What?' Wendy asked as her shoulders slumped. 'I don't know if I can take any more of this shit.'

'I think it was Marie who did this. I think it was her that sent everyone crazy,' he said in a solemn tone.

'How do you know that?' Anne questioned.

'Because there is basically an audio confession on her computer. It had the final details of the ship's log, and it explained that the crew went insane when they ate part of whatever fucking creature is under that bloody block of ice. They went mad and killed each other until only he was left.'

'Tell them about the second one,' Gary put in.

'Yeah well, the second one is just bug-shit nuts. She obviously got whatever Charlie had – it was kind of the same.' He tripped over his words trying to work it out in his head. 'Anyway, first things first, Gary took Marie to get a sample of the creature.'

'A biopsy, that's right,' Anne agreed.

'Where is it then?' Danny asked. 'I actually looked for it before the shit hit the fan. I wanted to see it but I didn't find it.'

A cross expression came over Anne's face and she went to one of the fridges. She reefed open the door and rummaged through the bags and bottles. 'Nothing here.' She moved to one of the other common areas and even inspected some of the microscope slides. 'She hasn't entered anything here. There's no slides, there's no data entry. She should have at least done that.'

'I know where it is,' Gary grumbled.

'Where?' Wendy asked.

'In that fucking punch bowl. Why else would someone push punch that hard? I heard her in that tape, she wanted to send everyone apeshit.'

'Fuck,' Danny said as he put his face into his hands. 'Christ, I think your right.'

'She put the biopsy in the punch?' Anne questioned. 'But I'm sure I had some and I didn't go insane.'

'You had wine,' Danny said flatly, 'I remember. We were on Glenfiddich by that stage.' He gestured to Gary. 'And Wendy was too busy feeding her face, let alone having a glass of punch.'

'Shut up,' Wendy dismissed him.

'Where is she?' Anne asked bewildered by this whole thing.

'She's gone.' Danny shrugged. 'As far as I can see, she took the Hägglund that Rheinmarsh brought back and pissed off back to the ice shelf.'

'She'll run out of fuel first. Bitch.' Gary laughed.

'Why would she head back there?' Wendy asked as she leant over Craig.

'"I will set us free,"' Gary repeated her words. The sound of it sent a shiver down Danny's spine. 'Apparently I told her how,' Gary finished as he shrugged.

'Yeah,' Danny agreed. 'She said that Gary told her how and Jonty told her where. Do you think it's to do with the ice shelf?'

Gary nodded but it was Anne that answered.

'Jonty was a glaciologist. It was he who had to crunch most of the data, to see whether the shelf could handle the vibrations of drilling,' Anne said flatly again, as if talking to children. 'He told me this. He said he was confident that the shelf could handle one shaft in a set area, but they had to be accurate; he didn't think the current face would stand another hole drilled so deep or any kind of shock.'

Danny stared at her. 'Well, it sounds like it's getting another one. Or maybe something else?'

'And what does this all mean?' Wendy asked with an ignorant tone.

'Well, if you look at everything we know.' Anne sighed. 'The crew from the *Baroness* are here to drill down to an unknown specimen so that Marie could take a biopsy, to see what it was.' She folded her arms. 'We know there is something down there because of thermal scans.'

'Yeah?' Wendy said slowly.

'Well, I don't know about you, but something that has been dead for seventy years wouldn't show up on a thermal scan,' Anne said bluntly. 'The thing's alive and Marie is going to set it free.'

All Danny could do was laugh. 'Well, at least that will give it what it wants.'

No-one laughed with him.

'We can't let her do that. We have to stop her somehow,' Anne cried.

'I can get us anywhere with the bird,' Gary said.

'Yeah, but the R44 will be useless if we're too late,' Danny grumbled.

They all considered each other for a while, as if searching for the answer that wasn't there. Danny got up and moved away from them to look out through one of the windows.

'There has to be something one of us can do,' Wendy said.

'Maybe you're right.' Danny replied. 'But maybe it's not us that can do something.'

They all looked at him.

'Maybe it's one of them?' He said as he pointed out the window at the *Baroness* as she loomed in the depths, off the coast of Mawson.

34

THE COMMUNICATIONS ROOM sat quiet in its disuse. In the same way that the three monitors that had shown the perspective of the three men inside the whaler, the darkness of the screens replicated the emptiness of their deaths. Danny felt a horrible shiver run up his spine as that thought rolled into him and the clear memory of Peters' death flashed into his mind. He thought about the sharpened limb that had burst through his chest. He thought about the blood that burst forth from the broken banks of his flesh. Like a river in total flood, it'd run down his front as the colour left his face. Then as easy as pressing the power button to shut down one of these computer monitors, the life had left him and the darkness had swallowed him whole, when Paul Stathis had run for his life.

Life was easy to lose, and it scared him how quickly it had left those men in that ship. Kee Peters, a man that was strong and tall. He remembered the natural way the smile had come to his face, even after Jimmy had tried to wipe it off with his fist. Then he remembered the way his jaw had dropped and his smile had twisted in a silent scream as his life had left him.

Danny remembered Paul Stathis, the structural engineer, the way he laughed, joked and smoked. One of the few members of the salvage crew that didn't seem as though he was in the military. Probably the only thing that Danny had to be thankful out of this whole thing was that he hadn't seen his death, although of its occurrence he was certain.

The only thing he wanted was to press the button at the bottom right-hand side of the monitor and bring them all back to life. As if it was that simple. As if once the three monitors in this room had been switched back on, the men that were probably being torn to pieces by whatever lived below, just suddenly blinked and took a breath. Hell, if that was the case, once he had done that he would have to find the proverbial monitors for the rest of them. Corinth, Marty, Bobby and the rest. The hurt was so great in his heart that he didn't even want to think of their names. Like the three on the ship, their monitors would have gone dark as well, wherever they were, and nothing would ever turn them on again.

To his right, Gary sighed and that was all the encouragement he needed to get moving. He picked up the receiver for the UHF that Bobby had covered in his rubbish only hours before. Unsure whether the unit was even turned on, he depressed the microphone's only button and spoke.

'Mawson camp to the *Baroness*. Mawson camp to the *Baroness*, are you on channel? Over.'

He waited a few seconds and repeated himself.

'Mawson camp to the *Baroness*. Mawson camp to the *Baroness*, are you guys hearing this? Over.'

He turned to Gary. 'Fuck, how do you work this thing?'

Gary moved forward and flicked a switch a couple of times and adjusted a knob. 'Try again.'

'Mawson camp to Rheinmarsh. Come in. Over,' he spoke into the mic again.

Gary continued to scan the frequencies and he nodded back at him. 'Keep going, man.'

'Rheinmarsh? Are you there? Come back to me, this is Mawson. Over.'

Danny was about to give up hope, when a reply crackled back over the receiver. 'We hear you Mawson. Over.'

Now that he had established communication, he didn't know what to say. Where did he begin? 'We have a problem here; I mean at Mawson.

Baroness, we need help. Over.'

The reply came back quickly and unempathetic. 'We all have problems, Mawson. Out.' The man's voice was gravelly over the speakers and he knew he wasn't speaking to Rheinmarsh. This was the same voice he had heard Wendy communicate with in the past.

'Where's Rheinmarsh?' He stopped with the courtesies.

There was a pause on the air for a long time and Danny figured he wasn't going to get a reply.

'People are dying here, *Baroness*. Something....' He didn't know how to explain the situation and didn't want to over this broadcast. 'Something's happened.'

'We have our own losses, and our own problems, Mawson. We can't help you. *Baroness* out.' The man tried again to close the conversation.

Danny forgot himself, but it didn't matter. Who cared about breaking into private viewings when people were dead on both sides of the screen. 'I know you have, and our problems are the same, *Baroness*.'

Nothing came back over. Danny waited and waited but nothing came and he figured it wouldn't come. 'Kee Peters,' he said over the microphone softly. 'Paul Stathis.' He waited again. 'Jin Ishimura. You don't know him, but Christ, I do. I feel like we are great old pals. Brothers who have seen the shit go down on the *Nisshin Maru*. Cut the shit *Baroness*, I watched the feed from their cameras. I know about your losses and I'm telling you, we are all going to suffer more if you don't fuckin' answer me and give us some goddamned help.' He let his finger off the mic, and took a breath. He felt a hot flush over his face and a little light-headed, as if he had just taken a long drag for the first time on a stale cigarette.

Danny and Gary stood in silence and waited for a reply that they figured would never come. Almost a minute went by before the radio clicked and the gravelly sound of the man's voice came back over, solemn this time. 'Standby, Mawson.'

Danny wanted to thank him, but didn't bother. He had known guys like that back in Sydney. They reminded him of dogs, they bayed and snarled at first, then limped away with their tails between their legs once they had been defeated in argument. Yet, as they slunk and subdued, if they smelt any form of weakness, including compassion, they would be right back at your throat as if the argument had never happened.

Gary sighed again as he took a seat at Bobby's desk and leant back on his chair. His boots clunked as he threw them up one by one and leant back on the swivel chair and closed his eyes. Sleep would be a good thing right about now, Danny figured. He at least had succumbed to concussion when Jimmy had driven his forehead through his own, but poor Gary and the others must be exhausted. It didn't matter; they needed to stop Marie, they needed to end this before it got any worse and then they could sleep, then they could rest.

'Rheinmarsh,' the radio uttered. Although it was early in the morning, the man didn't have the faintest touch of weariness to his voice.

Danny took a breath and raised the mic to his mouth. 'Rheinmarsh, this is Danny Myers, here at Mawson.' He paused and let off the mic, but Rheinmarsh didn't come back. 'Jonty is dead, a lot of us are dead… and I suppose I am in charge, when it comes to the problems that we are having.'

He let off the mic again and took another breath. He didn't want to say the next part over the air, just in case Marie was listening, but it made no difference in the end so he bit his lip and continued. 'The woman that caused this, she took a biopsy from the creature that is under the ice shelf and she put it in the punch for the party. Those that drank it went insane and tried to kill the others. She's on her way back to the ice shelf; your men need to stop her before she can do anymore damage.' He released the mic again, paused for a second, then depressed the button once more and said, 'over.'

Danny waited in silence again and shook his head. 'These guys sure know how to make a guy wait.' But his friend didn't open his eyes, he just continued to breathe slow and steady. Lucky bastard had fallen asleep; best to leave him that way for the moment.

Then the radio clicked again and Rheinmarsh's voice came back, calm and collected. 'I'd love to help you Mister Myers, but I cannot reach my men that are on the shelf. Over.'

Danny stared at the microphone blankly. 'What do you mean you can't reach them? I saw all the communications gear you guys had, you had better phone reception on that ice shelf than I had in my own house in Sydney. Over.'

'Yes, that's right. But the most expensive phone in the world will not answer itself, will it? Over,' he said in that infuriatingly calm tone.

'You're saying that they're dead?' Danny demanded, almost lost in his disbelief.

Rheinmarsh sighed over the radio and his calm tone began to waver. 'Mister Myers, my second in command, whom you began this pointless conversation with, informs me that you saw the video feed from the team that I sent onto the Japanese Whaler. If that is the case, then you saw what happened to them and you saw what happened to my diesel mechanic. Although it is a sad affair that your team members became aggressive when they took part of the specimen into their bodies, I can assure you that my mechanic did not, yet he still suffered from the madness.'

He paused for a moment and Danny heard his furious breaths over the radio. 'You ask for my help? You already asked for my help when you asked for me to come here. You asked me to drill a hole and in exchange I would have a ship. So far, I have drilled a hole and the men that I sent onto the ship have been killed and I have to assume that their support crew have been as well. So, I am sure, Mister Myers, that you can understand my hesitation when you ask for my help again, when I am faced with the decision of abandoning my men and, worse yet, my prize. *Baroness* out.'

Danny stood there as his words washed over him. The fear, the anger, the concern. The thing beneath the ice had been in his head, there was no doubt about that. He took his phone out and considered the photo of Louise on his background. He thought about her and Leanna. He frowned as thoughts of them swam through his mind and then he picked up the mic again and spoke.

'I'll get it running,' he said solemnly, as the thoughts of those creatures came into his mind. 'I'll get your ship running, but you have to help me and you have to send men with me.'

He stood there and felt his chest close in on him as his eyes returned to the photo on his phone. 'Do you hear me Rheinmarsh?' he snarled into the mic.

The radio clicked and once more, Rheinmarsh sighed. 'Mister Myers, I admire your ambitions, but my mechanic is dead as is my structural engineer. Even if I could get the ship running, there is no guarantee it would make the journey back to Australia. Over.'

'It's floating now, isn't it?' Danny snapped back. 'Were they tools your mechanic had in that backpack?'

'Yes, but he is dead. Over.'

'Don't worry about him. I'm your mechanic now,' he snapped. 'But if I'm going down into that shit fight, I'll need your electrician and another bunch to keep us safe while we work. Alright?'

A short pause, and then he came back. 'And what more would you ask of me if you would do this? Over.'

Danny felt light-headed; he leant back against the UHF. 'The hole you drilled. The specimen below…' he started, once again he didn't know how to answer the man.

'Yes, I know about your researcher's finds, what more do they want me to do with it? Over.' His tone had settled back into annoyance.

'I can't believe I'm saying this,' he said it aloud to no-one, and without pressing the button to the mic. 'I think it's still alive and that woman is going to try and set it free.'

'Mister Myers?' Rheinmarsh began.

'Trust me, I know how ridiculous this sounds, but you and, I bet, a few others that are on that ship with you now have been to that ice shelf. At least one of you would have had the dreams.' As soon as he said it, he knew he had said the wrong thing. 'Ah fuck, look. Rheinmarsh, we need to be ready, ok? I've got a bad feeling about this whole thing and more than just going down into that ship. All that I'm asking, is that you take the *Baroness* to the gap in the ice shelf. That's all I'm asking.'

Once more, there was silence. A long, excruciating silence that doubled the weight on Danny's chest. Then the radio clicked and Rheinmarsh came back over. 'So, you will help me get the whaler running, and in return you want me to move the *Baroness* into the gap between the iceberg and ice shelf. Is that right? Over.'

'Yes. Over.' He thought he had better recommence with the pleasantries.

'And if, by whatever miracle the ice were to shatter, and we were all to survive the collapse of the ice shelf, what would you have me do with this specimen that you believe is alive? Over.'

Danny glanced over at Gary. His friend looked so peaceful in his exhausted sleep. He thought about his other friends... Anne, Craig and Wendy were all that remained to him. Those that had survived the disaster of the party. In his dream the monster from the depths had told him its intentions, it had told him about its plan. 'I will kill you all,' it had said, and Christ, if Marie was its puppet, then it had almost succeeded.

Danny clenched his fist as once more he remembered the gruesome way in which everyone had died, and he raised the mic to his mouth again.

'If all that happens, and this thing is still alive and I'm still alive, and you're still alive...' he allowed the theoretical as he laughed and thought about the odds. 'Then, I want you to help me kill it.'

He was met with another wall of silence and was left to worry about Marie. If she had heard all of this then she could plan. He knew that was a risk. In the end, if he thought about the odds, he had to look at it the way it was. On one side, there was Danny, maybe three or four other men against a ship full of monsters, a woman and some unknown specimen, as Rheinmarsh called it. Somehow, he doubted he would have to worry about his bargain. He doubted that he would survive long enough to get that old ship running, but he had to try. For the sake of everyone at Mawson, for the sake of his partner and his unborn daughter, for the sake of everyone if this damned thing got out and followed through with its promise to bring desolation to man. For the sake of all those things, he had to try. And if he didn't succeed and it did break out, then at least Rheinmarsh stood in its way and it wouldn't have such an open door to escape its tomb. All his plan depended on now, was that Rheinmarsh would agree. He waited for the answer with bated breath while he watched Gary sleep soundlessly at the desk.

'Mister Myers,' the radio crackled again and Danny jumped at the sound. 'I believe we have a deal.'

35

THE RADIO FELL SILENT and for all the strength that Danny could muster in those next few moments, he was unable to look away from the mic. He sat there with the unit in his hand as he waited for another signal. Waited to hear the words that he knew would never come. Sure enough, it had been his idea, but a large part of him hoped that Rheinmarsh would call it off. That he would see the senseless risk to life and refuse the offer. The sad part was that Rheinmarsh didn't have to risk his life, only Danny's and his men and to him that was probably nothing.

Danny let the mic fall to the floor after what seemed like an age. He glanced over to Gary, who still slept at Bobby's desk, and Danny couldn't help but smile. *Rest a little longer man,* he thought. *You don't need to know until it's time to go.*

It was probably the fact that Gary was asleep that enabled him to follow through with his plan. Christ, if there had been the slightest mention of another way, then he would have been all ears, but there hadn't been. Gary slept and Rheinmarsh went along. Two hours is what he had to prepare and then the light would be on them, and the small skiff would ferry those who would accompany him down into the depths, to shore.

He left the communications room and stopped in the hall. He shut the door gently behind him and then rested his back against one of the walls. The sorrow, the panic and the fear came over him like a disease. Overwhelmed, his body slid down the wall and tears spilt forth from his eyes. His body spasmed with the sorrow he felt for his friends, his mouth twisted in the fear he held for what lay ahead, and his hands shook, for he could not think on what to do.

The tears ran down his cheeks and wet the stubble on his chin. He went to wipe them away but stopped when he saw the blood that still stained his gloves. As he sat there and stared at his hands, the tears stopped flowing and his body finally relaxed, as he pondered whose blood it was. In the end, it didn't matter. None of it did and it never would. It may as well have been his blood, for what was to come would surely spill it freely.

Once he had composed himself, he moved back into the mess and scanned the shit that had been strewn across the floor. The funny thing was that through everything that had happened, the punch bowl miraculously had survived. He stood above it as he looked from the pieces of fruit to the blood-red liquid that covered everything and wondered which piece had been the one to start it all. Which had been the piece to start the killing and the chaos.

He took the bowl's weight in his hands and moved to the kitchen with a grimace. It would be an easy out for him to take even one sip, but that wasn't fair to the rest of them, to have to deal with him when he was gone. He watched it all swirl down the drain as he poured the entire contents into the stainless-steel sink. When it was all gone, he threw the bowl in and watched it shatter amongst the fruit that it once held.

He checked the clock and sighed when he saw he had only an hour and a half left to prepare himself. Danny gathered all the glass bottles that had been used. Most of them were the unlabelled ale bottles they had collected from Davis.

'Sorry big fella,' he said to himself as he collected the bottles and thought about how eager the brewer had been to get them back. 'You won't be collecting your ten cent deposit back on these bad boys.'

By the time he had taken the dozen ale bottles out to his workshop and filled them with Av-gas, he only had a bit over an hour left to him.

He tore strips of rag and punched holes through the collection of caps that he had found. He threaded the rag through the caps and then re-seated the seal on the neck. He upended the bottle and smiled when not even a drop leaked out. He stood back and admired his soldiers. A dozen there, all dark and cloudy where the av-gas had mixed with the remnants of the ale.

He opened one of the draws of his large, red tool box. A Bic lighter sat there covered in grease, from the early days since his arrival when he had still smoked. He thumbed the igniter and felt the flint wheel turn in its frame. The sparks flew as the fuel ignited and the flame danced in his hand.

With all the work that he could think of completed, he returned to Anne Castelli and Wendy Phillips, to tell them what had happened. The two women had remained in the lab while himself and Gary returned to the Red Shed. Wendy said she wanted to make sure that Anne was ok, and Anne said she wanted to make sure that Craig was ok. Danny just figured that both of them didn't want to see the mess hall in the state it was in.

He figured they deserved that much; they had seen enough. The one thing he hadn't counted on when he told the two women the news, was for Anne Castelli to strike him again. His head rocked on his shoulders and once more Danny felt weariness come over him. He turned back to her and saw she had cocked her arm for another blow, this time he caught it mid-swing.

'Enough of that,' he growled as he held onto her struggling arm. 'You think I don't know the risks?'

Tears had started to run down her face now and even Wendy looked so forlorn that she barely resembled herself. 'Typical man!' Anne shrieked at him. 'You always think it's your job to get yourself killed. Don't you think we have all seen enough death?' Her face contorted as she fought back the sobs and tried to strike him again, but Danny held her back. 'Don't you think we would all feel safer if you just stayed here?'

If Danny had been in the mood, he would've laughed at the irony. He brought her close to him and embraced her against her struggles. She thought he was doing this to be brave, when really, he wasn't brave at all. He was scared shitless and had spent the last hour trying to find any way to get out of the situation he had put himself in. But as those wisps of ideas died within him, he felt the struggling woman in his arms finally subdue. She buried her face into his shoulder and wept into his hoodie, meanwhile Wendy continued to sulk on her own.

He murmured Wendy's name almost silently and she raised her large brown eyes to look at them. 'Come on,' he gestured and slowly she came to them. He had seen three-people hugs before and had always thought they were awkward but there was nothing wrong about this. It felt good to have their warmth press into him, and Christ knew that he needed it. The only thing missing in the whole world and in this small situation, was that he was hugging the wrong girls, but nothing could change that. One of them wasn't even born yet.

Anne sniffed a wet sob as she pulled away from him and Danny hung his head.

'I need one of you to go wake Gary up and let him know,' he said as he checked his watch. 'I'll need him to fly us out there in about 45 minutes.'

'He's your best friend,' Wendy said glumly. 'You should be the one to tell him.'

He nodded. 'You're right, but you go wake him. I've got something else I need to do. I'll talk to him in the air.' With that, he left the two women; he couldn't bear to look at them anymore.

As he walked alone back to the Red Shed and through the cold porch, he remained silent. All he heard was the crunching of his boots in the ice and the steady thump of his heart beat in his ears. His breath steamed up in front of his face and his eyes were heavy, yet he knew he couldn't sleep. He smiled to himself as he thought about all of those tacky movies, where the hero spends days without sleeping as he fights hordes of monsters. Then throughout all of it, when his body would have been broken and sore and there was no way that any human could continue through that exhaustion, he steps bravely into the fire again to fight the final boss, who puts up an even harder fight. But the hero doesn't waver, the hero doesn't tire, and says before he steps off to kick the living shit out the last bad guy, 'I'll sleep when I'm dead.'

Danny pulled his balaclava up and spat to the ground in an attempt to remove the foulness that had crept up in his mouth. Now it was his time to act the hero, but he already felt tired even though he figured that he hadn't even gotten through the first level yet.

He frowned. Of course he had. Charlie had been the first. Then there was Sean, Corinth, Marty and Jimmy. He thought it might have been hard to hurt those that he had loved, but in the end, they were already gone and he still remained. The frown was replaced by a grimace as the foul taste returned. Soon he would turn his anger and his strength on Marie and he would not feel bad for that.

He steered clear of the communications room when he entered the Red Shed and headed straight for his Donga. He would've given the world for a shower but there wasn't any point and there was one thing that he needed to do that came before most everything else. He sat down in his room and flicked away at the keys on his laptop. In the darkness the bright light of the screen hurt his eyes, but he didn't care anymore. He just didn't care.

'Hey, babe.' Louise yawned as her face took up the screen. 'It's like seven here, what time is it there?'

'Early,' he said softly as he smiled. 'I'm sorry to wake you, honey. I just…' He examined his keys as if the words that he was looking for would be spelled out by the keyboard. 'I just needed to see your face.'

'Well, it's not too pretty at seven in the morning, I know that much.' She shifted in her bed and groaned. 'Oh, gees. Your daughter kept me up most of the night,' she said through partially gritted teeth.

'She'd be getting ready to see you.' Danny smiled at her. 'If she's anything like her mum, then I'm sure she hates being cramped up.'

'If she's anything like her mum, she's feeling pretty fat and lethargic right about now.' She laughed.

'Any day now huh?' Danny mused as he raised his eyebrows.

'Yeah, they said I'd be due around the first of November and that's the end of this week, so I'm not far off, babe.'

'Your Mum and Dad around?'

'Yeah,' she yawned. 'They're sleeping in the baby's room for the moment, but they've been great this last week.'

His smile grew wider. 'That's great. Really good to hear.'

She yawned again and then considered him. 'Danny, what's wrong?'

'Nothing's wrong.' He held up his hands.

'Uh-huh. Then why are you calling me at like four in the morning your time?' She knew, but Danny didn't think she'd push it very far this morning.

'Like I said.' He glanced down to the keyboard once more. 'I just needed to see your face.'

She gave him a concerned look for some time and then smiled. 'Alright, well I'm sorry to cut you short but I can hear Mum calling for me.'

'Hey,' he said feigning his smile. 'That's fine, go have something to eat, you're looking thin.'

'Piss off,' she muttered as her smile broadened.

'Hey Lou,' he said before she could leave. 'You know I love you, right?'

She stopped and then turned back to him again. 'Of course I do. Are you sure you're alright?'

He smiled genuinely again. 'Yeah, you know it.' With that he cut the transmission before his eyes could fill up with tears. He stood in the darkness of his room. He thought about how dark it would be in the ship, like the way he had seen in the computer monitors, and he thought about how his eyes were becoming accustomed to the lack of light.

He walked the entire way back to the cold porch, without turning on a single switch, or reaching into his pockets for his phone. Part of the reason was to prove to himself that he could do it, the other part was so that he didn't have to see their bodies again.

When he left the cold porch, he saw that Gary was already outside. Wendy sat to the side of the helipad on a small crate of tools and watched as Gary unfastened the rotor blades. Danny slowly made his way down to his workshop where he collected the crate of Av-gas Molotovs and then shut the place up before joining them at the helipad.

'And you're some right cock smoker, aren't you?' Gary grunted at him, interrupting his conversation with Wendy to insult him.

'Is that why you've been so friendly lately?' he asked. 'Not the right way to go about it, if you're trying to seduce me.'

'Fuck off,' Gary friend dismissed, and then pointed at Wendy. 'She told me that you reckon you're going to go onto that old death trap.'

'That's right,' he said flatly.

'Even after all the shit you told me?'

'Gary, I don't want a lecture, mate. I don't have a choice, you know that.'

'You have a choice alright,' he growled. 'Tell them you're not going.'

'No,' he replied just as flat as before. 'I've made my decision mate, and I'm going to stick with it.'

'So that's it hey?' He laughed in his disbelief. 'Well, I'll tell you what. I'm not going to fly you out there.'

'Yeah, you are.' He put down the Molotovs and approached his friend. 'You're going to do it, for the same reason I am.' He poked his finger hard into Gary's chest. 'Because we fuckin' got to.' He glared into his mate's eyes. 'I've tried to protect all of you from the shit that I saw on that ship, and now I'm the last one. So yeah. I'm going to fuckin' go down there and I'm going to get that piece of shit running, so they can fuck it off out of here.'

Gary nodded sarcastically. 'Yeah and all those things don't come into your equation?'

'Nah,' he laughed, 'they don't.'

'They didn't for the other mob that went down there and look what happened to them. On top of that, you've also forgotten how many people can fit in the R44. You're too eager to get out there and get yourself killed.'

Danny smiled as he pulled his balaclava away from his face. 'Two things make all the difference here mate,' he said as he patted his friend's cheek. 'First of all, I wasn't there the first time, so already they were at a great disadvantage. Second of all, they didn't know what to expect and I do. Finally, I know your flying record remember? Something tells me flying overweight wouldn't worry you too much.'

Gary didn't reply to that, but the look in his eyes were reply enough. He was defeated. He nodded slightly to his friend, and lowered his eyes before he went to leave. Danny stopped him before he could and took his friend in short embrace that consisted of two back pats. Gary laughed. 'Get off me you big fag.'

'You love it, don't lie,' Danny sniffed.

'Yeah well,' Gary held him at arm's length. 'Don't you get in trouble down there, ok? Otherwise I'll have to come down there myself.'

'And we wouldn't want that.' He smiled back.

'Fuck no.' Gary turned as he said it. 'Here they come.'

Danny gazed out to the *Baroness*. The water behind the massive ice breaker had begun to churn as her propellers came to life. The enormous anchor she had dropped was being winched back onto the deck as the skiff churned its way toward them. Once more Danny squinted as he tried to make out the figures on the boat, but as the sun began to rise in the morning sky, his eyes struggled to make out the features of the men's faces. Four including the coxswain, two to protect him, and one more engineer.

As the skiff pulled up to their moor, Danny, Gary and Wendy made their way to help. Thompson was the first off the skiff, and the only one that Danny recognised. He held out his hand and Danny shook it.

'Thompson, yeah?' he asked as they pumped their hands up and down.

The man nodded. 'Yeah. I went with Rheinmarsh the first time. I'm the electrician.' He raised his eyebrows and then frowned.

'Second most important, hey?' Danny tried to joke, but no-one laughed. The next man to get off the skiff was tall, grey haired and stern. There was a cold look about the man, and he moved with a certain calm. A pistol was holstered at his hip and Danny's eyes were drawn to it. 'Didn't think we'd be going down with any heat.' He held out his hand and the elder man shook it. 'Danny Myers,' he introduced himself.

'Reicher,' the elder man barked as he looked Danny up and down. 'We spoke on the radio, before you convinced Rheinmarsh to go ahead with this fuckin idea.'

Danny nodded. *How to make friends and influence people*, he thought. The poor bastard was about as happy as Danny was to be going down there. At least it was Danny's idea; this man was not his friend.

The final man to climb out of the skiff before it roared away, was slender, well-toned and carried a long length of bar. In one section he had wrapped a piece of electrical tape around, to act as a handle. Danny shook his hand and met his brown eyes as he introduced himself. The young man offered back a crooked smile that seemed to age his entire face.

'Ryan Carmichael.' As soon as he offered his name, the smile disappeared and the lines that had traced his brow and the corners of his eyes receded back into the smooth skin of the youth.

'You all ready?' Gary asked as he considered his passengers.

All of them nodded and together, they walked in silence back to the R44. Before Danny jumped into the cockpit, he hugged Wendy again and gave her a kiss on the cheek. 'Look after them, ok?' he whispered in her ear as the rotors began to power up. 'You're the strongest now, even Gary's more of a girl than you.'

She laughed as she pecked him on the lips. 'Be safe, dickhead. I'll see you soon.'

'Yeah,' he said as he took a step back from her. 'You know it.'

He climbed into the cockpit and watched as Wendy covered her face against the silt and snow that was thrown up into the air as the overweight R44 hoisted itself off the ground. He watched her get smaller, and then disappear into the white as Gary turned the bird into the wind to aid his downforce, and took them off to face what lay below the cold, dark decks of that damned ship.

36

AS THEY LIFTED HIGHER into the sky and the light began to illuminate the ice below, the warmth left Danny's heart. He seemed to see the environment as if for the first time, the way the ice clung to the surface of the rocks and glistened in the morning sun. There seemed to be a tide line the entire length of the coast where the land was low enough to meet the sea, where the snow and ice seemed to stop and the salty kisses of the Pacific began. He saw the way the nunataks rose up like prehistoric monsters from their beds of ice. Frozen in time to peer out across the icy plains, never to roam them again.

In his eagerness to tear the Band-Aid from his wound, all he had thought about was the darkness of the ship. Due to this he'd failed to think about packing a set of sunglasses and it wasn't long before the reflection of the sun's morning rays off the ice below became too much for him to look at. For the rest of the flight he kept his eyes closed, dreaming of days that had yet to come. He imagined holding his newborn daughter in his arms. He imagined pushing her on a swing as she screamed in joy and hung her head back to look at him as the momentum took her away. He imagined holding his partner and kissing her again, and slowly the warmth came back to him.

'Coming up on Amery now.' Gary's voice lacked the humorous tone that it had been rich with the first time he had met them there. Even as Danny looked at his face, lines that had never been there before coursed deep crevasses into the flesh near his eyes and Danny was sure the grey hairs that speckled his scalp had not been there the previous day. 'We should be seeing the camp any moment.' The audio equipment in the R44 had a habit of making a man's voice seem distant even though he wasn't more than a metre away. In this case, the distance of Gary's voice couldn't hide the dread that Danny felt through his words. The dread that washed through him and became contagious in the small cabin.

'Here, there it… oh Jesus, no,' Carmichael groaned through his headset as he leant into the glass window of his rear seat. Gary's head seemed to follow the site as the R44 continued along its course.

'What the fuck happened?' Thompson groaned.

'Take us down,' Reicher barked and wordlessly Gary took them in.

As the nose came about, Danny saw their missing Hägglund parked on the ice. His eyes locked on it as he examined the Blue Brick, the Red and then the Pioneer, all of which sat dormant. He half expected to see lights illuminating the work ground and men scouring the ice shelf, but there was nothing. Obscured by the lip of the shelf on which they sat, the sun had yet to rise high enough to breach the wall of ice and the world still seemed dark below them. Still, Danny saw the dormant drill, frozen like the other steel tyrants that sat to its side. Through the gloom he saw the red beacon flash from the small communications array that had been set up to piggy back off the signal from Mawson.

'I thought they'd be drilling,' Danny muttered, and didn't bother to depress his microphone switch. 'What happened here?'

As Gary circled the camp to get to his landing position, the front of the shipping container camper was brought into view. The fabric of the structure stood proud in its frame one second, then rolled with the wind in the next. Each moment seemed to be a fight between the air in its lungs and the air that wanted to lie it flat. Across the white of the PVC beam, a red smear stood stark in the low light and Danny groaned.

'Keep the rotors turning,' Reicher barked as the skids touched the ground. 'Carmichael, with me.'

The cabin door popped and the noise in the cabin seemed to triple for a second as snow rushed in through the gap. The two men stepped out onto the ice shelf and began to advance on the fluttering structure.

Their heads low as they walked with caution, Danny watched them from the safety of the cockpit, as the rotors continued to throw up flurries of snow to conceal their movement. Reicher stormed through the snow while Carmichael took staggered steps behind him, the piece of pig iron low in his hands. Then they paused.

Carmichael moved up to Reicher's left, while Reicher drew his sidearm and shuffled his feet apart. Danny could see Reicher's mouth moving as he hollered something, but beneath the *whup, whup, whup* of the rotors and the rattle of the engine, he had no chance of hearing. Suddenly a man burst out of the partially collapsed shelter and Danny gasped.

He ran flat out at Reicher in an almost crablike way, like a vehicle with a twisted chassis would crab its way up a highway. His arms remained low at his side, and his head seemed locked in a position as if his ear had been welded to his shoulder, and he screamed. Even from the safety of the R44, Danny could see the red on his face, and the rage in his eyes. His upper body rocked with each furious stride as Reicher calmly brought up his arm.

The sidearm cracked three times. To Danny, they seemed little more than pops inside the cabin of the R44, yet Carmichael jumped. With each shot, a blood cloud appeared behind the runner and the air was misted with the life that it held. The runner's pace staggered and he went to his knees. As if the runner had lost the use of them, his arms remained at his side. Slowly, it raised its head from its slanted position and cocked it back as if in search for the sun that normally graced the heavens. That was when Danny saw clearly for the first time that the redness of its flesh was not the pigment of its skin, but the rawness of meat recently exposed. Where its jaw had once been, only its tongue and gullet remained below a single row of white gleaming teeth.

Blood ran from the hole where its mouth had been and covered the slickness of its thermal shirt. Its eyes locked on Reicher and it sprayed blood and snot as it leant forward, as if in a scream that Danny couldn't hear. Reicher took another step forward, raised his sidearm and fired once more. A red mark of pity appeared between the runner's eyes, and another cloud of mist appeared in the air before its body crumpled to the ground and he remained still.

'Fuck me drunk,' Danny muttered and then depressed the button for his mic. 'Should we get out and help him?' He considered Gary, whose flesh had gone white and his eyes were large behind the lenses of his glasses.

'No, stay here.' It was Thompson that answered him. 'This is what Reicher is here for; let him do his job.'

Danny frowned. 'He's here to kill people?' he asked.

Thompson gave him one of those 'here we go again' types of expressions and sighed. 'He's here to protect you and me. We need to do our job, and he is here to make sure that happens.'

Danny's frown embedded itself deeper into his face but he didn't reply. How could he? To be honest, he was thankful that they would be going there with at least one gun, but at the same time he remembered the way the others had been when they were ambushed. He remembered the way they'd talked amongst themselves, the noise they'd made. Christ, they would've brought the whole horde down on themselves with that racket. This time, they needed to be quiet, almost stealthy.

Danny nodded to himself as he looked back out the windscreen and watched Reicher enter the structure. He would talk to them before they went down. He would make sure that they were all on the same page.

The R44 continued to rock gently as its rotors idled above them. They waited for what seemed like an age as Reicher and Carmichael rooted around inside the half-collapsed structure, and Danny had started to become anxious. The way the failing support moved was giving him motion sickness. Over and over again, the structure stood up as the pressure inside it increased, then crumbled to the ground as all the air rushed out of one of its wounds. He grimaced as he watched this sequence happen for what seemed to him like the hundredth time and he snapped.

'Fuck this,' Danny muttered to himself as he took off his headset. He popped the cabin door and was met with an onrush of ice and silt. Ignoring Gary's attempts to keep him in the cabin, his eyes formed slits against the flurry as he pushed out into the cold; he couldn't sit still any longer. He slammed the cabin door shut and began to trudge toward the structure.

The further he went from the R44, the lesser the sound of its idling engine and rotors became. Instead, it was replaced by the roaring of the generator's motor and the burring of the air pump that had picked up a bearing noise. Closer still he came and more sounds flooded his ears; the flapping of the PVC had a wetness to it and beneath it, the air rushed against the frayed edges of the slit in its hide.

Danny grimaced as he stepped past the corpse of the runner and then brushed beneath the blood-smeared curtain that was supposed to keep the inhabitants safe.

As soon as he stepped through, he was struck by the smell of sweat and shit. It hung heavy in the air and seemed to choke the life out of him. Danny gagged, but managed to hold his stomach's contents down. He rolled his balaclava down and held his hands to his face to stifle the smell. The plastic floor of the habitat was smeared red with blood.

Danny stood as in shock as the scene washed over him. The bright red to the deep dark clots of mess that had been strewn up the walls and spread by the hands of the dying. Corpses lay twisted in misshapen forms that could barely be thought of as men the way Danny saw them. One corpse's mouth was frozen open in a roar of pain. One man's thumb was still lodged in the pit of his left eye, while his right eye had likewise been pushed inward. The one whose thumb had remained inside the other, had expired during the act when a blade had been driven down through the crown of his head, where it still remained.

Danny's mouth hung open, looking from horror to horror, when he noticed Reicher and Carmichael staring at him.

'I told you to stay put,' Reicher snarled as he stormed toward him. Blood splashed with each heavy footfall and speckled the dark leather of his boots.

Reicher laid hands on him, but Danny fought to stay put. 'It's alright,' he tried. 'I need to move. I need to do something. Just let me help.'

Reicher struggled to throw him out at first, but as Danny spoke his attempts got weaker and finally stopped. They considered each other until Reicher nodded and turned away. 'Looks like these boys went out last night to save your little lady,' he growled in his stony voice as he walked away. 'They have a communications log here, it says they were contacted by a Marie Swan from Mawson at oh-three-hundred-hours, who had run out of fuel.'

'Sounds about right,' Danny muttered as he took a deep breath and stepped further into the habitat.

'You knew?' Reicher asked with a hint of accusation.

'I knew that she'd run out of fuel,' Danny admitted. 'I only learnt that she had fled maybe three hours after she had, she would've already been out by then.'

Reicher considered him, then nodded, accepting his story. He grunted as he reconsidered the communications log. 'Still doesn't explain what happened.'

Danny looked around at the rage, the horror, the death, and he knew. His eyes swept from bloody wrecked bodies, to hands that had lost their strength and amongst it, he saw a glimmer of polished metal.

He bent down and ignored the blood that stuck to his hands as he grasped the container. He hadn't recognised the thermos as Marie's but there were easily a hundred of these things around Mawson for people to use. Like coffee cups, people latched onto their favourite thermos and wrote their name on it, or failed to clean it properly because they could taste the difference, but this one was new. He unscrewed the cap and didn't even have to look inside it to know what it contained. The sweetness of the aroma filled his nostrils and he wanted to be sick. He fastened the lid again and let the thermos fall to the floor.

'She killed them,' he said flatly.

'You told Rheinmarsh that she poisoned your team,' the snarl seemed to be fixed on his face and the more Danny spoke to him, the less it affected him.

'Yeah, same shit that's in that thermos,' he spat as he kicked the container across the room in his frustration. 'She must have taken some before she left. Poor bastards.'

'They saved her ass, so she poisoned them?' Carmichael questioned. 'What sort of people are you lot?'

'Hey,' Danny snapped, 'this is not us.' He stuck his finger in Carmichael's face. 'It's that fucking thing down there that's caused all this shit. Not us.'

'Some of these guys were my friends,' Carmichael said solemnly.

Danny let his hands fall to his side. The anger that had risen inside of him had washed away to almost nothing. 'Yeah,' he said softly. 'I've lost friends too.'

Reicher shuffled over to the table and then stood up. 'Time to leave. There's nothing here of use.' He pushed past Danny on his way to the entrance flap. 'Carmichael, give me a hand.'

Danny exited the habitat just after Reicher; he had no wish to stay in there any longer. He stood on the ice shelf with his balaclava rolled up on his head, thankful for the fresh air. He stood in the cold and the wind as he watched Reicher and Carmichael drag the body of the runner into the habitat. When they emerged, they looked ill and their hands were covered in blood and mess. Carmichael knelt next to a small channel that the wind had created in the ice and where some snow had collected, and used the soft powder to try and clean his hands. All that he managed to do was create a mess of pink and blackened snow and spread the shit halfway up his arms. Danny spat to try remove the foul taste that had settled in his mouth and a shiver ran up his spine.

When it appeared that they were done, Danny returned to the cabin of the R44 and settled back into his seat next to Gary. The pilot looked at him with tired eyes as the idle of the chopper rocked him gently. 'What happened?' Gary had to ask.

Danny shook his head and frowned. That was all the answer he was going to get off him. His stomach rolled again, and Danny had to laugh. The shit had only just begun and already he was fighting back the urge to lay up his guts. Christ, it hadn't even been twenty-four hours since he'd seen the horrors on the monitors, it hadn't even been twelve hours, now that he thought about it. He had nothing left to throw up but bile and acid. As if in realisation of this, his stomach burnt fire within him.

He popped the door again and spat out the side as Reicher moved to the pilot's side. When Danny sat upright again, he saw that Reicher had knelt down next to the skids and was rummaging in the equipment stored there. Although Danny didn't see what the elder man had retrieved, it didn't take him long to work it out. He saw the lighter in his left hand and a beer bottle in his right as he walked back to the habitat.

The flame from the lighter guttered in the wind and Reicher moved his body to shield it. Soon flames were climbing from his hands as the rag ignited and he tossed the flaming bottle in through the flap. Reicher didn't stand to watch the habitat go up; he was like one of those battle-hardened movie heroes that didn't flinch from an explosion that happened behind them as they walked away. He was already most of the way back to the R44 when the flames had started to lick at the flap and curl its edges up from the corners. There was no satisfying explosion, no burst of flames that Danny saw, not even a 'flump' as the flames caught. All of it was washed out by the steady *whup, whup* of the rotors and the rocking of the engine's idle.

By the time Gary had taken them into the air again, the PVC shell had crumbled to nothing. The flames had caught everything inside of the shelter and had turned it all to a blackened mess, but how long the fire could stand against the cold and the wind was anyone's guess. Danny figured it wouldn't be long. As the sun finally crept over the lip of the ice shelf and cast its light back over the vastness of Amery, they descended into the darkness. D-28 loomed to Danny's left, a hulking goliath that lingered at the place of its birth, while Amery, the eternal wall, sat to his right.

As they descended to the *Nisshin Maru* below, something on Amery's face caught his eye. He peered through the shadows at the line that ran down. He gestured to Gary and the pilot noticed it too. He moved the R44 closer until finally, they could make it out. A ladder, even equipped with a cage, had been pinned to the face. Down and down and down it went and they followed it in the bird. Danny watched it with disbelief as the iron continued straight as a die until finally, they saw the ship and the destination for the ladder's fall.

He turned back and looked at the three men in the rear of the R44 as he depressed the button for his mic. 'If we ever get out of this fucking place, you guys are going to give me a job.'

Thompson laughed at that. 'If we ever get out, you can take mine.'

'Fuck that,' Danny muttered as he sat back in his chair.

The deck of the *Nisshin Maru* emerged out of the darkness and the fog that had settled below them. Just the sight of it lodged settled a stone in his stomach. All of the warmth went out of the air the further down they went and Danny noticed a progression with each breath that he took, steam had started to flow from his mouth. The prow of the ship stuck out like a broken dagger's point, while the windows of the apartments loomed above, still white with ice, like cataracts in an old dog's eye.

Gary settled the skids on his side down across the railings, as he had all that time ago, and Reicher's door burst open. This time, no flurry of snow or silt burst through the gap, just an unbearable cold like a wall of lead. Danny saw the reaction of the men in the back of the R44 and knew how they felt, nevertheless, they all clambered out and unloaded the storage tray on their side. When they shut the door, Gary lifted the bird again and moved away from the ship; he paused there for a second as the three men looked up at them.

Gary's mouth was open and he moved it like he was gasping for air, but Danny knew he was just looking for the words to say.

'It's alright man,' he said over the mic. 'This evening, we'll knock over the rest of that case huh?'

Gary smiled and nodded. 'Yeah, and we'll ransom the rest of the empties to that wanker at Davis.'

Danny laughed and Gary moved the R44 back to position.

'You be safe,' Gary said quietly. 'You come out of there.'

Danny's eyes fell on him as the skids settled on the railing again, and he opened his door and braced himself against the cold onrush. 'You know it, man.' He removed his headset and stepped down off the skid and onto the deck of the old Whaler once again.

37

THE ICE CRUMBLED beneath his boots as he stepped down onto the foredeck. As he slammed the cabin door shut, the rotors of the R44 hammered down on him and Gary took the bird away. He watched his friend take the ascent, as the downforce buffeted the rising fog and sent it into spirals of chaos. Then, as the R44 climbed, Danny lost sight of his friend, leaving only the echo of the rotors and the lapping of the water at the ship's prow.

The four men stood where three had stood before, looking up at the apartments and the bridge, where Jin Ishimura's body still remained. Danny thought about the line of Haiku, in the conclusion of Ishimura's journal: *I stand resolute.* He grimaced as the ghostliness of the ship towered above him, and he couldn't help but think about how long the ship had survived. How long those creatures had sustained themselves. How long they all sat in stasis and now, it came down to him. It came time for him to test his resolve in the darkness and to face his fears.

Danny moved forward, yet he didn't climb the stairs as they had in the beginning. He moved to Starboard, and descended the metal steps as he had watched Stathis and Peters on the tape. He heard the others move behind him and the clinking of the Molotovs as they rattled in their crate. As he came about the apartments, the hatch stood open before him. He held his arm up and they all stopped.

'It's time to get ready,' he muttered to them.

Thompson placed the crate of Molotovs down on the steps and began to hand them out. Although the glass bottles were sure to be invaluable in their defence if it came to it, they were awkward to carry. Luckily, the pockets in their cargo pants were large enough to carry a stubby each, and soon the remaining stock was divvied out. Danny managed to store three in his own pockets and held one. Each other man carried two. Reicher handed out small flashlights to the other three while he mounted one under the muzzle of his pistol.

Danny sighed as he looked to the faces of each of the men. 'Alright, so first point of call, we need to get the backpack from the mechanic, and then we need to head to the engine room.'

'How do we know where they are?' Thompson asked.

'I've got a pretty good idea on the tools, the rest we will have to work out once we pick them up.' Danny moved from foot to foot. 'Alright,' he gasped. 'Let's do this shit.' *I can't stay brave forever,* he finished in his head as he took the first step into the apartments and was plunged into darkness.

The beam of his flashlight scoured the hallway in front of him, while his feet pawed the ground, as if in test before taking the plunge.

Reicher moved up to his side with his pistol extended before him. He leant in and whispered a growl into his ear, 'You keep your light low, show me where I'm walking. I'll light high. You just tell me where to go.' Then he stepped forward and took point.

The relief Danny felt was enormous, as if the weight of the entire ship had been lifted from his chest and he was finally able to breathe again. Still, his breath sounded constricted in his ears as each pant echoed in the emptiness of the hall, along with the shuffles of their feet and the sloshing of the Av-gas.

Reicher came to an intersection and stopped, he glanced back at Danny with a questioning look. Danny remembered the first scenes of the video easily; he gestured to the right and Reicher nodded. When he approached the intersection, he ran his body hard up against an edge, and used the corridor as cover while he checked around the left corner. Once he was satisfied it was clear, he pivoted and moved into the centre to check the right side, and finally advanced.

It wasn't long before they descended the first set of stairs and the world seemed to darken even further with their descent. Their footfalls echoed off the rails and Danny grimaced as the sound seemed to walk down the corridor and then ripple back up to them in waves. He stopped and touched the back of Reicher's shirt.

'We need to take this slower; we are being too loud,' he whispered through gritted teeth. Reicher considered him, then finally nodded and moved on.

They maintained a similar pace but each man took more effort to gently place their feet, which greatly reduced the sound of their advance. Another corridor came that Danny recognised and he urged Reicher on. Once more, corners were checked and the muzzle of the pistol remained the most forward part of their team, as the light scoured the path.

It didn't take them long to find the blood. In the video it had looked much like the mess that Danny had seen up on the bridge, but this seemed thicker somehow, almost congealed as it clung to the wall beneath its layer of ice. Danny frowned as he remembered what came next. Despite his knowledge, he still jumped and his heart skipped a beat when Reicher's light washed over the corpse of the soldier. Reicher's beam lingered on the man before it moved on to the rifle that had been placed back down by Peters.

'Carmichael,' Reicher whispered as he moved beyond the rifle and then highlighted it again with his light. There was no reply for the man on the rear but as Danny kept pace with their leader, he heard behind him the slide of timber against metal and then the rack of a rifle's action.

That's two guns now, Danny thought, feeling a little better about the whole thing. Soon they would find the backpack and alongside that would be the two corpses and more importantly the heavy ZKK that Peters' carried. *It's all downhill from here.* Even in his mind, it sounded like a sigh. Nothing good was to come.

They came to the corridor that had a T section in its centre and Danny stopped them. Wanting to remain completely silent, he made sure Reicher was watching him as he placed a finger below each of his eyes and then pointed toward the intersection. Reicher followed his gesture and then returned his gaze back to Danny. To emphasise his point, Danny ran a finger across his throat. Reicher watched him slowly, blinked, and then returned to his advance. In due caution he raised the pistol slightly higher than it was before and thumbed the safety off. As he advanced on the corridor, Reicher hugged left and leant outward to keep as much of his body out of the line as possible. He remained that way for a short while and Danny watched with bated breath, as the pistol moved here and there and cast its light across the corners.

Eventually, Reicher leant back, spat to the floor and wiped his face. Then he gestured for them all to follow and they continued past.

Danny told himself not to look. He told himself more than once, but even as the words ran through his mind again as he came up on the intersection, he directed his light down the corridor and froze. The mass of bodies that he had seen through the monitor back in the safety of the communications room overwhelmed him. Everything became real for him in that moment and despite his own warning, and his caution to Reicher, he began to panic.

His breath quickened and his heart raced. His stomach rolled as his eyes widened and he pressed himself back against the frozen, steel wall.

'Reicher!' Thompson hissed as the electrician rushed to Danny's side. 'Shhhhhh.' Danny felt a gloved hand clamp over his mouth, stifling the scream that was forming in his throat. All that Danny could do was breathe hard through his nostrils in a hope to push his hand away. Every other part of his body had gone stiff. Reicher came back to them and stood directly in front of Danny to block his view. He leant in close.

'Are you going to get through this?'

Danny sucked a gush of air through his nose and made eye contact with the elder man. Even in the dark, his eyes were bright and solid. He struggled a nod against the pressure of Thompson's grasp. Reicher considered him for a moment longer, then nodded. As he did, Thompson's grasp on the lower half of Danny's face relaxed and he felt the stale air touch his mouth again.

'You alright?' the electrician whispered in his ear.

Danny made eye contact and nodded before he dropped his gaze and fell back in line behind Reicher. The further they walked from that corridor, the more he relaxed. They had moved past the point where the mechanic had freaked out, now they just had to find him. Danny remembered another set of stairs, and as they approached another T intersection Danny couldn't remember which way they had turned. Reicher stopped and Danny met his eyes, swallowed and shook his head.

For the second time in a few minutes, Reicher looked back to him. 'You don't know where you're going?' he hissed.

'If you'd seen the video, you'd know it was hard to follow. Especially at this part, it had gone to shit,' he whispered back. 'We need to go down another set of stairs, it can't be much further than here, let's just move on maybe… to the left and if we don't find stairs soon, we can turn back, ok? No splitting up though.'

Reicher glared at him. 'No splitting up,' he repeated in a mock gesture of accord and moved to clear the intersection.

Until this point, they had not seen a creature and for that, Danny was thankful. The concern that had grown within his stomach and clenched fingers around the nape of his neck, was that he didn't know where they were. For all he knew, they could be behind them, they could be approaching as he even thought about it. Panic seized him again and he spun around with his eyes wide and shone his torch in Thompson's face. The man closed his eyes in surprise and his mouth opened as he threw his hands up to shield himself.

'What are you doing?' he snarled as he shifted to the side and Danny tried to shine the light further on. Carmichael stood at the edge of the beam. Danny could see the reflection in his eyes and the way the steel of his rifle glinted in the darkness.

Behind him, the light shone onwards, revealing nothing but frozen white walls that glistened in the torchlight. 'Are you fuckin' right?' Thompson pushed him.

'Enough,' Reicher snarled and Danny felt two strong hands grasp his shoulders before he was spun around. 'What is your problem?'

The older man hissed in his face. 'Because this is not the time to fuck around.'

'I just wanted to check behind us,' he mumbled. 'I had the feeling that something was creeping up on us.'

Reicher pointed at Carmichael. 'That's his job, you let him worry about that.' He pushed Danny and he thudded into the wall behind him. 'You just do your job, let us do ours.'

He turned back and continued down the left path. Danny scowled as he followed them, there was no 'us' when it came to their little team. They were a team and he was the mechanic, just as it was last time, but Danny would be damned if he was going to freak out like the last one.

They rounded a corner that Danny didn't recognise and Reicher stopped in his tracks. He held his left hand up to stop them, while he kept the muzzle of his pistol trained ahead of him. Danny leant forward to see what was there and his eyes widened.

The corridor in front of them had been completely blocked by what looked like a wall of what had once been flesh. A slime seemed to cover the entire surface. In some places it was thick and green, whereas in others it was thin enough to see the clamminess of the flesh that lay beneath. Reicher held his light steady and as Danny held his breath, he saw the mass of flesh settle in an exhale that rippled along the walls in a low and horrible shudder.

Still, they stood there. Even as Danny wished to run, he remained to follow Reicher's lead. It looked as though he was waiting for something, then as the seconds passed by, the wall of flesh seemed to suck air in from an unknown orifice, in a long, raspy stream. It was alive, whatever it was, and it was asleep.

Reicher gestured for them to go back. Slowly, Danny moved back behind the safety of the corner and exhaled the breath that had remained forgotten in his throat. Reicher moved back slowly and then passed the rest of them to take up position at the point again. They treaded carefully the entire way back to the last T intersection where they paused and Reicher wiped a line of sweat away from his brow.

Danny hated this. There was nothing he could do but remain silent and follow closely behind Reicher's light. Once more the man led them forward. His light swayed back and forth with each step he took, while his feet made soft scrapes along the icy, steel floor. He held the pistol in his hand low to his side like a gun slinger and adjusted the beam of light around with swift movements of his wrist. Each time he neared a corner he raised the pistol and kept it before him, as he leant around out of cover. He was almost military-like in his movements, compared to the swagger that came into his step when he knew he was safe from the sides.

Soon they found the second set of stairs and descended even slower than the first. The sounds of their footfalls weren't even audible below the steadiness of their breaths. The air they breathed became fouler on their second descent, poisoned by the bodies that lay in the dark. The air seemed to rot without the sunlight it was denied and felt dirtier with each step Danny took. The ice that covered the walls sucked all the moisture from the air and although every breath that Danny took gave him life, it drained away his warmth.

He shivered as they rounded another corner and he felt the chill settle in his bones as they turned again and again and again. Reicher didn't stop when he saw the legs of the man before them. At first, it was only the soles of his boots that became visible in the light that emitted below the muzzle of his pistol. Then the black pants came into sight and then the hole that had been punched through the centre of his back.

Kee Peters lay lifeless in the centre of the corridor. The butt of his ZKK stuck out from under his midsection and Danny struggled to pull it free. As he moved closer to the rifle he shuddered when he saw part of the frame through the hole in the young man's chest.

'Here,' Reicher muttered as he holstered his pistol. Thompson shone his own light on the dead man, while Reicher pulled him over onto his side. Peters' mouth dropped open as his eyes rolled back into his head and a line of blood dribbled down the side of his face. Luckily, his head rolled to the side and concealed the wound on his neck that Danny remembered. He grimaced as he retrieved the heavy rifle from beneath the man and sighed as he felt the wetness of his blood that covered the stock. It made the movement of his hands slow and sticky.

Danny hesitated over the rifle and then thought about the sizeable backpack that he had to pick up. He frowned as he handed the ZKK to Thompson, who took it willingly. The mechanic was only a few paces further up. His head had near been torn from his shoulders by the creature that had been devouring him. His entire lower jaw was gone, as was most of his throat. The front of his thermal wear was covered in gore because of what that thing had done to him. Danny tried not to linger, but it was hard not to see the aftermath of what had happened. It had been bad enough watching it on a screen, let alone seeing it all in the flesh.

Reicher helped him remove the pack and then Danny struggled to heave it up onto himself. He remembered the way the deceased had leant forward beneath the weight of his pack and Christ, he could understand why. The pack would have weighed nearly 30 kilos. Perhaps when the mechanic had fallen or during his death throes, something had moved and was now jabbing through the padding and into his back; there was no way the man could've stood it. Danny swore as he let the pack fall from his back as a spasm ran up his spine. The pack hit the floor with a loud, heavy thump, which echoed up and down the corridor and hammered back at them even louder than it had been at the beginning.

Danny ignored it; he knew he'd made a mistake but nothing could change that now. He knelt and quickly unzipped the main compartment, pushed his hand inside and retrieved a long, breaker bar that had been the culprit for his discomfort. He removed it and refastened the zip before straining himself to heave the pack to his back once more.

The echoes that were created by the impact of the pack had died but the ship had not fallen silent. Reicher gave him a murderous look as above them, the ship seemed to tremble. Metal groaned and the clang of iron echoed from above. There was a shriek and a roar, and Danny turned back to Thompson.

'What is that?' Thompson cried, adding more echoes to the mix.

'Shhhh,' Danny returned the favour by clamping his hand down on Thompson's face. In the light that was offered from the residue of Carmichael's beam, Danny saw blood spread from his glove over the electrician's face but he seemed not to notice.

'Come on,' Reicher growled. 'We have the tools, let's get to the engine room.' As he continued down the hall, the groans and the clanks from above them transitioned into the thuds of heavy footfalls. Danny thought about the breathing wall of flesh that they had seen and his stomach rolled again. The things he had seen on the monitors had been men, he had no doubt about that now. If Sean, Marty, even Corinth had been left to feed on themselves and others in hibernation, then they would've become something similar if they hadn't killed each other first. Nevertheless, the thing that hammered its way through the apartments above them sounded too heavy to be one of them and Danny didn't want to find out what it was. From the pace that Reicher had taken as he resumed their search, he didn't want to find out either. So, Danny leant forward under the brunt of his burden, and took Reicher's advice. He let them worry about the others, while he followed the man in front.

38

HIS BREATH WAS HOT in his throat while the weight of the cold seemed to press down on him from all angles. They finally moved away from the heavy clanging that came from up above them. The further they travelled into the bowels of the ship, the further away the heavy footfalls seemed to be. Yet, that didn't settle Danny's heart, which still uttered a tremolo in his chest, nor did it offer to slow his breaths, which remained shallow.

His shoulders had begun to ache beneath the weight of the pack, but pain was a good thing. Pain meant the flesh was alive, pain meant that blood still coursed through his veins and for as long as he remained aboard this damned ship, he would be thankful for every ache, groan or twinge of pain that ran over his body. The alternative was the deep, dark, depths that they walked into, and he couldn't handle that.

He couldn't bear to concentrate on the cold that seemed worse than anything he had ever experienced on Mawson. It was as if they had taken the enormous walk-in freezer, and thrown it out into the ice for him to live in. No winds, no snow storm, or freak howler would have ever made him feel this cold.

Nor could he stomach their footfalls that echoed all around them. So many times, Danny had thought that they were being followed, rather hunted by one of those creatures that had torn apart the last crew. But all it had been was their own footfalls running back up the corridor towards them. It seemed their pace was slow and steady, in all of their attempts to remain silent in their descent and as the echoes rolled away, the pace was immortalised like a thousand drums beating an army to war.

Yet, the worst part of it all, wasn't the cold nor the incessant beating of their own steps, but the suggestions of what lay beyond their line of light. Reicher held his light at arm's length, so if an ambusher were to stand before him, his pistol was already raised to defend them.

Danny, who walked slightly behind and to his left, held his light low, so to illuminate any trip hazards the crew might come across. While the beams from Thompson and Carmichael only served to add shadows to the mix, anything above Reicher's head height became a mere suggestion. The ceiling was lit well enough that if anything moved, they would catch it, but it was as if there was a layer of smog above them, three inches thick. Anything so large as a human body could not conceal itself, but there was something above them, something that ran the course of the corridors like a choking vine that overran a garden.

Danny had seen it through Paul's monitor and he had seen it for himself only for a second as they descended yet again. As Reicher came to a flight of stairs, his light ran over the place where the roof should've fallen before them, but instead they saw something that could only be described as flesh. It seemed to cover the ceiling not in sheets, but in course, thickened veins that pulsed as the light shone over them. A horrid sinewy substance emitted from them and covered the steps with their filth. Each team member was forced to walk through it and how none of them fell was a mystery to Danny. Yet no-one seemed to consider them, no-one even asked a question, and so Danny held his tongue. In the end it wasn't as though there was nothing else to worry about.

Nevertheless, as Reicher paused to assess his heading or to consider a junction, Danny would raise his light to see where the fleshy vines would go, he would follow their path as they wound themselves over the conduit that held the wiring for the lights and whatever else they could wrap themselves around.

As they moved lower and entered a corridor that seemed run forever,

Danny noticed that the vines seemed to descend with them. While Danny, Thompson and Carmichael followed the steady pace of Reicher's swagger, the choking veins wrapped themselves around heavy pipes that had replaced the small conduit above their head. The further they went, the thicker the veins seemed to grow, as if like a root system from some giant tree. Danny began to wonder how thick they would become.

He shook his head, as if to rid himself of the thought before the seed could take root in his mind and stretch its own coursing, throbbing arms throughout his brain. He tried to settle his breaths as he studied the light over the swaying hump of Reicher's left shoulder. Soon he found that his breaths held in his lungs for longer and his heart no longer rattled its chains in the centre of his head. However, with the longer corridor came a different fear for the same reason.

Whether it was wise or not, Danny no longer feared the vines. He put this down to the fact that he had spent some time actually looking at them. The problem they faced now as they presumably moved into the midsection of the ship, was that the corridor was so long that the beams of their flashlights couldn't penetrate the entire length. Danny tried to adjust the focus of his light at the end of his flashlight, but the ones that Reicher had handed out were fixed. As each of them took a step their lights moved, which sent shadows casting up the walls and outward before them.

'Shit,' Danny muttered to himself as he clenched the breaker bar in his hand a bit tighter. Reicher stopped at this and faced him. The older man offered him a look that asked what he'd said but Danny shook his head. He pointed in front and muttered below his breath, 'Can't see the end, freaks me out.'

Reicher didn't hold his gaze, he returned to the front and raised his pistol a little higher before he continued to move on. The shadows danced before them as if to tempt the angle of their light. They swirled forward along a wall, and then darted back as the sway of a man's stride took his light back over that section to eradicate them. It seemed that his light couldn't be everywhere at once; as he moved left, the darkness advance to his right and vice versa as he tried to hold it back.

Meanwhile the corridor in front of them remained a black cyst that boiled as the light washed over it, but failed to penetrate. The darkness moved within, as if to suggest bodies that it concealed, ambushers, hunters. All of those that could see them and the brightness of their light from the safety of the shadows, even though they stood before them.

Once more Danny thought he saw movement before them and his heart skipped a beat, but Reicher never slowed, never paused nor faltered. He continued his slow advance toward the stern. They came to another intersection and once more Reicher raised his pistol. He shuffled around the corner and once satisfied there was no threat, he moved in the new direction.

Danny was surprised by how little he considered this decision, as once they had found what remained of the mechanic, Danny had stopped offering his directions. Since that time, Reicher had pondered carefully over every turn, had shone the light down each side and listened. Once, Thompson had begun to talk to Carmichael during Reicher's pondering session and the older man had moved his light, which meant his pistol as well, onto the electrician's face and had growled four words through barely parted lips: 'Shut the fuck up.' Needless to say, whenever they came to an intersection from then on, they all gave him a bit of space.

Yet this time, Reicher moved without hesitation. He didn't even offer the other choice a second glance. Like those behind him, Danny followed without question and soon he realised why Reicher had been so sure. As they had turned, so had the large pipes above them. Danny saw more coming back from the other way as well and he figured it couldn't be long until his trade was put to the test.

Sure enough, they stepped through a bulkhead, whereas the pipes above them ran directly through the walls. They stepped out into a large, open room that seemed darker just by its sheer size than the corridors. Reicher held his hand up to stop and the rest followed suit.

For a time he stood there, his pistol aimed to the floor. Danny's breath blew plumes of steam up beyond his nose, as if he was smoking a large cigar, while Reicher held his head forward and the steam rose up around his face and trickled through the shortness of his hair. Finally, Reicher lifted his head.

'I think we're alone,' he whispered. 'I can't hear anything.'

'You don't think we were before?' Danny asked a little louder, feeling somewhat relaxed on the other side of the bulkhead.

Reicher shook his head. 'I've felt like we've been watched the entire time we've been on this ship. So, no.' He strode over into the darkness; his pistol swayed at his side and sent his light in a skittering effect across the floor. It amazed Danny that the man didn't light his own way but perhaps there was a reason why. Reicher took only a few more strides before he stopped and placed his hand on a rough metal wall. Through the ambience of the light from the rest of their flashlights Danny could see him fine. He saw the older man turn back to him and nod.

'Here,' he said, his voice low.

Danny moved closer to him and cocked his ear as if to be let in on a secret, but Reicher just continued to stare at him. 'What?' he asked finally and Reicher leant back on the wall.

'Time for you to do your job.' He lifted his pistol and shone his light up over the wall he leant on. The wall itself, was not a wall at all. It was the largest engine that Danny had ever seen. The wall was rough from its castings, and oil seeped in thick glugs of blackened shit from where the castings had been joined. The plant itself stood easily over twenty feet tall; its cylinder heads loomed way above him, almost outside the line of his light.

'Holy shit,' Danny mumbled to himself as he stood back and looked up at the behemoth. Although the engine was gargantuan, it still was just an engine and an old one at that. Danny put his flashlight in-between his legs while he slowly unhooked each arm from his pack, and supported its weight as he lowered it to the ground. The other three men watched him as he did so, their faces stern in memory of Danny dropping the pack. Finally unburdened, Danny began to walk around the enormous motor in his first inspection. If he was expected to get it running, he needed to check its condition.

The exhaust hats ran in one long column off to the side and then joined in a pipe that ran off through a wall, no doubt to be dumped into the atmosphere. Other large pipes that glistened with the ice that covered them ran out through a manifold and disappeared through another section of wall.

'Water for cooling,' Danny muttered to himself as he looked at what seemed to be an ancient, giant thermostat housing. He moved forward to the front case of the engine and saw something that closely resembled the front of one of his four kings. He laughed as he shook his head and ran his light across the water pump that was roughly his height. Ice covered the front face of the plant. He ran his light further down the intake for the coolant and saw the joins were frozen over, especially where the water had leaked.

'All of it will need to be defrosted before we try and start it,' Danny muttered as Reicher followed close by. They walked around the feed side of the plant and looked up again. On the side of the plant's block section was mounted an enormous box. Large steel pipes ran up from it and disappeared over the top of the engine. The steel line that ran into the box was old. The fact that it didn't leak mattered more to Danny than anything, but the pressure came from the other side of the box, not from the weak side so once again Danny didn't care.

'Pump looks fine,' he mumbled to Reicher as he moved on. As they moved to the back of the block, Danny scanned his light up above him while he tapped his breaker bar on his leg. He would've whistled but he didn't want to make any noise until he absolutely had to. Safety in the thirties or forties obviously hadn't been what it was today, as Danny was able to walk right alongside the engine block and could even see the teeth of the fly wheel in a large uncovered section between the block, and generator section. The parts Danny would need to rely on sat directly above him. He ran his hand through the stubble on his jaw and shook his head. The starter motors looked like any old starter motor from any old truck, just larger than he had ever seen. The thing that made him rub his chin was that there was two of them.

'What's wrong?' Reicher asked as he added his light to Danny's.

'There's two starter motors,' he said flatly in a half whisper.

'And?' Reicher questioned.

'Well, that's more Thompson's problem than mine. I don't know if they are geared differently, so for instance let's say the top one has an ultra-low ratio to get the block moving because it's so big and heavy, but not fast enough to fire. Maybe the one below has a higher ratio and comes on only once the first has reached the speed,' he shrugged. 'We will only know when we try and if it doesn't work.' He pointed to the cables that joined to each motor. 'Thompson will need to look at those wires and make sure they aren't too far gone.'

Danny continued down the block section, but he didn't care about the motor anymore, he needed to follow the wires. He ran his light along them. The cables were about as thick as both of his legs combined. He shook his head as he thought about how much power those starters must draw. Along the block they went and then off, suspended above him along some hangers and then into a pipe that ran forward of the face of the plant and through the walls. Another set of wires, much smaller than the main power cables, ran the other direction and led Danny to a boxed-off section that sat high above him, atop a long, switched back set of stairs.

Danny shone his light on it as he stood there. 'That's where the controls will be.' He shone the light up above him. 'Someone will have to stay there when we all go topside.'

'Why?' Reicher put a hand on his shoulder.

'To control it,' Danny grumbled. 'Here, look.' He ran his light along a large steel rod that ran along the block. It remained higher than the power cables, but was connected to the block by a few large spindles, as if to support its weight. It ran all the way to well before the pump section, where another steel pipe came in from the ceiling to connect to a manifold. 'That's your air intake,' Danny said as he moved back and shone his light on an enormous section that held a large semi-circular guide. 'That rod will open and close the butterfly.' He ran his light back down the length of the rod and saw that it connected to linkages that connected it to the upper compartment above the stairs.

'Start it from there, run the throttle. The only thing I don't know about is drive.'

'Drive?' Reicher repeated, renewing his hushed tones.

Danny's eyebrows raised as he realised he had begun to talk too loudly. He leant close to Reicher and whispered. 'Way I see it, this ship got here under its own power. Once it was turned off, all someone needed to do was to turn it back on. They never spoke about a break down, never.'

'So, turn it back on,' Reicher sneered at him.

Danny smiled. 'It's not that simple.' He raised his light to the starters. 'Any idea how much power it would take for those starters to turn this big bitch over?'

Reicher didn't answer him.

'Shit loads.' He lowered the light again. 'Don't know about you, but each winter you notice the car at home gets a bit harder to start? Sometimes it doesn't even have enough to crank over.'

Reicher grunted at this.

'Yeah, well, try having seventy fucking years of winter and no charge in-between.'

'So, the batteries are flat? Is that what you are trying to say?' Reicher grumbled at him.

'Of course they're flat,' Danny hissed at him. 'Batteries aren't that good these days, let alone the shit they would've had back then.'

'You took us down here, saying you'd be able to start this tug,' Reicher said coldly and Danny saw the light beneath his pistol move a little closer to him.

'I'll get it running,' he growled. 'But we need to charge the batteries before we can turn the main plant over.'

Reicher's light wavered for a moment, just shy of Danny's thigh, and then fell back to the floor as Reicher turned away. 'Come with me.' He led them back to where Thompson and Carmichael sat and waited for result of their inspection. Reicher knelt nearby the other two and Danny squatted on his backpack.

'We need to charge the batteries,' Reicher repeated.

'We will have to find some sub-generators,' Thompson added.

'Sub-generators?' Reicher asked. 'If everyone is so knowledgeable about all this shit, then please feel free to tell everyone else so we don't fucking wander around down here for hours on end.'

Thompson gave him a sour expression and continued. 'It's just like an old car,' he whispered. 'Engine dies, you lose charge but the batteries will continue to run the lights and everything else until it runs flat, correct?' Everyone else nodded and grumbled in agreeance. 'Well, that's fine when you can ask your next-door neighbour for a jump but out in the middle of the ocean there is no jump, no push, no hills, no nothing. So, you need other generators to be able to charge the batteries while the main plant is out.'

Danny nodded, as he thought about his kings and his ice queen back at Mawson. 'Makes sense.'

Reicher's eyes went from face to face. 'So, what are we doing then?' This major admission from the older man, who had no idea on what to do next, was enough to make Danny laugh out loud but Danny spared him the humiliation.

'Come on,' Danny said to all of them as he raised himself to his feet and heaved the weighty pack to his shoulder again. He led them to the feed side of the block again while he walked in a crooked shape with all the weight of the pack only on one shoulder. Once they had all gathered beneath the twin starters, he shone the light up to them. 'You want to make sure those connections are all good?' he asked Thompson. 'I'll find the gennies and get them started. Once you get done, try and find some blow torches and put some heat on the water pump at the front, no doubt that'll all be iced up.'

Thompson gestured to the pack. 'What's in this? I haven't got any tools.' Danny sighed as he strained and lowered the pack to the ground again.

He unzipped it and shone a light down inside and shook his head when he saw. There was all sorts of shit inside the pack, no wonder it was so heavy. Spanner sets, and socket sets. One socket was four inches across and used a one-inch drive. There were four more extensions for leverage, a blow torch with a spare bottle, a roll of solder, a timing light, even an oil filter wrench for Christ's sake. He shook his head as he retrieved a small case that contained an adjustable wrench and a half-inch drive socket set. He put a couple of screwdrivers in his pocket and stood up.

'You keep the rest here, I'll be right with this.'

Thompson nodded as he zipped up the rest of the pack and shone his light on the heavy cables. 'They'll go direct to the batteries, follow them and then from there you should be able to find the gennies.'

'Carmichael,' Reicher grumbled as he checked his pistol. 'Remain here with Thompson, I'll go with him.'

Danny looked at the older man as he gripped the case in his left hand and held both his flashlight and the breaker bar in his right hand. He didn't say a word as Reicher turned and followed the cables to the front face of the engine. He glanced back at Thompson as he left, but the electrician was already moving to start his inspection – it was time for him to do his bit and so it was for Danny too.

39

THE PLANT LOOMED UP BEHIND THEM, a monster in the dark pit of its room. The cold seemed to sink deep into the metal casting and Danny felt it soak through clothes, bone and deep into his soul. Once again, he followed as Reicher walked beneath the steel conduits. Danny lifted his right arm and shone his light down the cold, white lengths of pipe to where they disappeared through the steel wall. Just below was a hatch, fastened shut against the heavy frame. Reicher holstered his pistol as he reached the door and clasped the hatch wheel. He strained in the shimmering light as the metal groaned behind the frame. The light rippled off the ice and blinded the older man as Danny watched him squint as veins stood out from his neck in his labour. The wheel shifted an inch, there was a howl of metal, and then finally it began to turn freely and Reicher's jaw relaxed.

He offered Danny a scowl as he heaved the door open. It was open no more than a millimetre when a foul aroma came through to hammer their senses. Danny stepped back and buried his nose in his arm. His eyes started to water and he gasped.

'Fuck me,' he coughed as he jogged away from the door.

Reicher grimaced as he heaved the door open the rest of the way, and fetched a rag from his pocket to place over his face. 'Come on,' he growled through his rag. 'We haven't got time to fuck around.'

Danny fought back a retch and tried to find his own rag to cover his own mouth. From his back pocket, he found a hand rag he had used once he had finished making the Molotovs. It reeked of fuel and was stained with old grease but nevertheless, it was better than the stench that had surprised him. He frowned as he tied the rag around his face so that it would sit beneath his nose and cover his mouth. He collected his gear and followed Reicher through the door.

The smell of Av-gas was sickening and the more he continued to breathe through it the more it became horribly sweet. Nevertheless, beneath it all the pungent aroma of the stale air came through. As if left to rot in the bowels of this ship, the air felt as though it carried the age of death with it – the smell of plague, puss, and corruption. Even their lights seemed to penetrate only half the distance that they had before the hatch and as Danny walked, he saw specks of dust or silt float through air, illuminated a stark white by the brilliance of his light. The specks started to cling to him after a while; the further they walked the more Danny noticed the specks settle on Reicher's shoulder like specks of dandruff. He looked down to his shoulder and saw the same, he brushed them aside but they didn't just move, they spread out over the fabric of his jumper like they had melted and failed to hold their form. Danny checked his hand and saw that the substance had covered the palm of his glove. He clenched his fist and then opened it again, watching as the substance stretched out from the tips of his fingers to centre of his palm. It stretched out and out and then snapped, before it settled back and began to decay before his eyes and drift into the air once more.

Danny shook his hand to speed the process, as he shuddered and frowned beneath his face mask, while Reicher continued through the thick air and horrible stench. Beneath the conduit, his head bobbed back and forth with each step, while the Molotovs in his pockets sloshed with his stride.

As they continued, Danny noticed that the odd vines that choked the corridors before the main engine room had started to reappear. The more he thought about it, he realised that they were headed back in that direction from where they had come, although they had remained centre to the ship's frame, and had not climbed any stairs. He ran his light down their length and although it was difficult to see much further beyond Reicher, he saw an intersection in front of them that would lead to a fork in their road. The steel conduit that Reicher had followed to lead them here continued straight. On the other hand, the vines that fascinated Danny so much wove their way around the conduit then broke left where they became thick and hung low from the ceiling, lacking anything to cling to. Reicher didn't stop; he continued forward along the lines, while Danny paused mid-intersection to gaze down the choked way.

Reicher's footsteps continued to echo in his ears as the older man continued down the hall. Danny squinted as he leant closer to the dark, and held the light out in front of him. Unsure whether it was fatigue seeping into him, he thought he could see a shape, almost like two legs standing in the middle of the corridor beneath the vines and the choking grasp, but the dark was too thick and the more he looked the less he saw. Danny blinked rapidly as he felt some of the floating sediment go into his eyes. He swore to himself and then peered down the corridor again but whatever he'd thought he'd seen was gone.

Dismissing the vision, he saw that Reicher was about twenty feet in front of him; Danny's light only barely brushed the back of his thermal shirt. Danny hurried to catch up, and at the sound of his hurried footsteps, Reicher stopped. He glowered at Danny as he approached and Danny saw the handkerchief suck to his lips as he took a breath. With a shake of his head, the older man continued down after the conduit.

It didn't take them long to find the batteries. The room was smaller than what Danny had thought it would be, but in the end, batteries were different back then to what they were now. The batteries sat squat on the floor; they came up to Danny's hip and were lined four in a row, and each row sat in a corner of the room to make sixteen batteries total. Above the door they had entered from, the heavy cables broke up and streamed down to connect to every terminal that protruded from the large squat blocks. Danny scanned his light from terminal to terminal. Corrosion was minimal; the cold once again had kept the acid levels low and with the lack of heat or humidity, the batteries had done little sweating over the past seventy years.

Reicher went to rub one of the terminals with his hand, to brush the ice away.

'Stop,' Danny hissed. The sudden disruption of the silence scared even himself, and Reicher turned to him cautiously. 'Notice there are no earths?' Danny pointed at each terminal where the starter's large cables had joined. 'The body is the earth; you touch the terminal and there's power then it'll earth through you.'

'And you think there's power?' Reicher's voice was almost sardonic.

Danny ignored him and continued to shine his light around. He thought about all the things that would run on electricity within the ship; most of those wouldn't require massive amperage and hence wouldn't need to run off a bridged terminal. He looked around again and saw single thick wires, off all different shades and sizes, run off to escape the room in the various conduits that led to the epicentre. Ones that no doubt ran the lighting. The kitchen would also require power. He ran his hand along his jaw and then saw another common trend that was just like the starter wires. If starting the main engine required all the amperage that they had, they ran a wire from each of the batteries to combine the amperage together. With that, each battery would require charging and as he continued his inspection, he noticed all of the terminals had another wire in common. He followed them up the wall, before they disappeared in a large cluster through another conduit on the left of where they had entered.

'This way,' Danny said as he dropped the light below the conduit to illuminate another hatch. This time he moved forward and after placing his tools and his light on the ground, struggled with the hatch-wheel. He remembered the first one of these he had faced when they had stepped on this ship all that time ago. He remembered how hard it had been to turn the wheel while his feet slid out in every direction. This time, the wheel gave way under his strength and the metal groaned with age as Danny forced the wheel over. Reicher moved to his side and lifted his pistol as Danny pulled the door open. He pulled it just a fraction, while Reicher raised his pistol. Then, as the older one moved, Danny moved with him until the door was open and the corridor was clear.

When the door stood open, Reicher remained and didn't push through. His eyes darted up, down, left to right, while his handkerchief continued to suck to his face and then push away with his exhale. Danny moved around the door and shuddered when he saw the reason why. The entire corridor was chock-full of those vines. Danny could see where they had followed the conduit but then being unable to break through the steel of the structure, the vine had continued to push forward and nearly completely covered the door way. Danny picked up his tools again, took a breath, repositioned the rag on his face with his shoulder and then pushed through the vines. The feeling of them pressed against him made him sick. It was as if he had been touched by a cold cadaver. The flesh was slimy with a substance that was thick and horrid. The liquid clung to him as he tried to push past, while the smell that the rag had held back came flooding forward to sit in his sinus and his stomach. He fought back a retch as he continued to push through and slowly, the vines parted to allow him. He heard Reicher move behind him and heard his disgust as he pushed deeper and deeper.

The initial blockade was the worst of it. Nevertheless, the build-up had created obstacles all the way down the corridor, making it difficult to pick any line forward. The steam rose thick from his mouth as he worked hard to step over, then crawl under while they became thicker and thicker with each foot that he progressed. For a long time, he lost sight of the conduit that he followed, but with no obvious intersections, Danny continued.

After another twenty feet the vines had become so thick that they could not support themselves any longer; they pulsed sporadically on the floor and cleared the roof so that Danny could see the conduit once more.

Ahead, he saw a 'T' junction with a door in its centre, which sat to Danny's right. The vines crowded the doorway as three sets all fought to push through it. Above it, the conduit took a hard right and disappeared in through the wall above the hatch. Danny sighed as he neared the doorway, directing his light down each of the remaining corridors.

He couldn't see anything. No doubt the corridor he had seen before they had reached the battery room was the one to his left, but that thought had to wait. He tried to peer through the doorway, but layer upon layer of fleshy vines blocked his path. He sighed again and looked back to Reicher.

If he wasn't exhausted, Danny would've laughed at the sight of the older man. He squatted against one of the walls, his chest rising and falling with each heavy breath that he took. His face was covered in the sinewy slime that the vines excreted, the handkerchief was soaked with the substance and lay around his collar, useless to breathe through. The expression on his face warned of murder if anyone were to touch or talk to him.

'We've got to push through here,' Danny said as he panted through the petrol-soaked rag.

'Well, push through.' Reicher sounded just as exhausted.

'I can't, there's no room.'

Reicher growled as he raised himself to his feet and holstered his pistol. 'Then get the fuck out of the way.' Danny moved behind Reicher as he heard a slosh of liquid. In surprise Danny turned around in time to be blinded by a flash of flint and the dance of a naked flame. He shut his eyes and spun away as there was the sound of breaking glass and the ever dreadful 'flump' as the flames caught the fuel. The brightness of the fire and the dazzling heat was matched by a hideous shriek that seemed to come from everywhere as the vines writhed in the fire. Large lumps of flesh fell to the floor, as the meaty ropes thrashed against the door and themselves until one by one, they snapped at the intersection and retreated through the doorway.

Danny watched in horror as the vines toward the bottom became black with corruption and pain. The scream seemed to triple in his head as they gave a final death throw, and collapsed to the floor.

'There.' Reicher spat as he put his lighter into his pocket and stomped on one of the vines that was still twitching in the embers. Most of the fuel had burnt out and only small patches lay like smouldering candles on the floor as their bright orange flames danced above a bed of blue and blistering white paint. Reicher gestured toward the door and Danny stepped through into the darkness once more.

The room that he had stepped into was larger than he'd thought it would be, but in saying that, he had no idea how large it was. From where he stood in the doorway, his light couldn't penetrate any further than twenty feet before him, and in that distance all he could see was the remnants of the charred flesh the vines had left in their retreat and lines of blood and sinew. The conduit lay open on this side of the door and once more Danny followed the path that the wires traced across the walls and then along overhead hooks. As his light washed over the dull grey of the metal box, he sighed.

Before him stood an ancient generator beside its three brothers.

Danny forgot about the darkness on the other side of his goal and rushed forward to the machines that lay dormant. All four of them were the same, spaced neatly apart, about five metres between each machine in a diamond pattern. He placed his tools on the ground and shone his light over the first motor while he went to rub his chin. He paused before he did so and saw that the white sticky substance on his glove was gone. He sighed again as he returned his light to the machine and rubbed at the stubble on his jaw.

He opened the fuel cap and sniffed. 'Diesel,' he muttered, no doubt about that.

'Is that a good thing?' Reicher asked.

'Makes sense,' he muttered in reply. 'They are just harder to crank or pull start because of their compression.' He went to the other side of the engine and nodded. 'Here–' he pointed to another smaller tank that led to what looked like a carburettor '–like an old tractor. You retard them and then you can start them on petrol and then as the cylinders warm, you pull this big old lever and it switches over to diesel'. He laughed softly. 'Fuck, haven't seen something this old for a long time.'

'Welcome to the forties,' Reicher grumbled as he leant his back against the wall.

Danny unscrewed the cap off the smaller tank and sniffed inside. Barely any smell whatsoever came out. Danny frowned as he considered the tank. One of the Molotovs in his pocket sloshed around with his movement. He pulled the bottle and popped the lid. 'Only a little to get you cranking,' he muttered to himself as he poured a quarter of the bottle into the tank.

'What are you doing?' Reicher sighed.

'Petrol's too old. Av-gas will give it a good kick in the ass,' he whispered as he retightened the cap. He moved to the front of the generator, and pulled the giant lever toward him. He watched linkages shift and groan while rods pushed in and engaged into the hybrid cylinder head. Danny stepped back and considered the engine; he inspected the crank case and noticed a large square plug in the centre of where the crank would be.

He squatted down next to the front of the engine to inspect the crank case. 'That'd be about an inch across.' None of the tools that he brought would be any good. He tapped his toe on the floor as he clicked his teeth and scanned the room. Surely, if a tool was so important to be used to start the backup generators, it would have a secure place within the room. Sure enough, above Reicher and to his right, a crank handle hung from two hooks.

Danny smiled as he approached it and retrieved it. The crank slid into its plug as old tools that were well worn often did.

'Here goes,' he mumbled as he threw his weight into the crank handle and the air rushed out of him as the generator turned and then seized. 'Fuck.' He stood again and felt the pain run up his back.

'What's happened?' Reicher sat up and shone his light in Danny's eyes, which meant the pistol was aimed at his face.

He waved the light away as he placed a hand to the small of his back to massage his aching muscles. 'I had the retarding lever in the wrong spot,' he groaned as he grabbed the lever and pushed it back toward the cylinder head. Linkages moved in the other direction and the rods extracted themselves. He gave the priming pump a few squirts for good luck and then threw his weight into the crank again. This time, the handle moved much easier and the he felt the generator turn over. He pushed and cranked again; he heard the puff of air being pushed out the exhaust. Again, he cranked, and again, and then finally he felt it kick in his hands and the motor rattled to life.

Danny laughed as the motor cranked and rocked in front of him. He pulled the crank handle out and watched the motor tick for a little while before he reached for the retarding handle again.

'That's the first step, now for the next,' he muttered as he began to pull the lever out toward him. The note of the engine changed and it rattled and popped and carried on the further he pulled the lever. It coughed like it was about to stall and then it settled into a rattle that could only be an old diesel in idle.

Danny smiled to himself as he moved to the side of the generator. He levered up the throttle and let the diesel run at a good couple of thousand revs. With the first generator running, he moved to the second. Having learnt his mistakes from the first engine, it took him half the time to get that one running on diesel. By the time he had the third running, he noticed that he only had a fraction of av-gas left in his bottle. He didn't want to sacrifice anymore, so he tried what he could to get the last one running.

In the meantime, he knew that the first, second and third generators would be charging the battery packs. It would take some time before power would come back, he knew that, but it shouldn't be too much longer before the lights came back on and if they didn't, then they were done. No lights meant no batteries, and no batteries meant no crank.

He poured the last of his av-gas into the small petrol tank and retarded the cylinder head. He gave the priming pump a few squirts and then put his back into the crank again. Over and over and over he cranked as he swore each time. He gave the primer another few squirts and then put his back into it again. By now his back screamed in agony with each movement but he had to keep going. He gave it one more push and then when it didn't start, he gave it another. He paused to give the primer one final squirt, then he pushed it again and the motor kicked.

He panted and he rested his head against its trembling case and kissed the casting of its block. 'You beautiful piece of shit,' he sighed as he stood and stretched his back again.

He allowed the cylinders to warm as he held onto the retarding lever.

As he waited, he raised his head. Something in the room had changed. He frowned as he turned and looked over to Reicher but the older man was just leaning on the wall as he was before. His arms were crossed and his pistol was in its holster on his hip.

Danny considered the genny and frowned. *If his pistol was still in his holster, then how could I see him?* the thought ran through his mind; neither of them had their light on. Danny raised his head once more and a faint smile spread across his face. 'Come on, baby,' he mumbled as he pulled the retarding lever toward him and the engine coughed and spluttered as its cylinder head ran dry of petrol and was flooded with diesel. 'Come on baby.'

As the generator coughed its diesel death rattle, Danny moved around and thumbed up the revs. No sooner had he shifted the lever, the light globes that had sat dormant and dark behind their cages of steel began to emit a faint glow. Danny laughed as he turned back to Reicher, the smile on his face cut short in its widening grin as he saw Reicher pull his sidearm, raise it and fire.

40

THE REPORT OF THE PISTOL in the confines of that room near split his head wide open. Worse yet, it rolled and bounced back at Danny from wall to wall. He closed his eyes and held his hands to his ears, as if to fasten the barn doors after the horses had fled. In his short-lived excitement for the lights and his sudden shock, Danny's first impressions had been that he was shot. He waited for a flood of pain to wash over him… waited for the slow march of shock that brought with it the dead cold, but it never came. Behind the lids of his eyes, the world had become a red blur. Muffled by his hands, he heard the pop of three more pistol shots and finally, Danny realised that he was not Reicher's target. Almost at once his confusion and his shock ran to fear and cold daggers of dread latched themselves into his spine to send rivulets of terror into his nervous system.

As he opened his eyes, he began to turn. Reicher fired twice more and he had begun to yell something. However, beneath the ringing pitch of his ears and his hands that tried to stem their suffering, Danny had no hope of hearing.

Danny became increasingly aware of movement to his right and above him. His eyes were helpless, drawn to the motion. His hands fell from his face and even though Reicher fired again, the reports barely even touched his ears as his mind and body was filled with the scream that came rushing from his mouth.

The first impression that struck Danny was the creature was some sort of spider. A spider that was trying to make itself as inconspicuous as possible in the upper right-hand corner of the ceiling. Although no spider had ever scared him like this monster had.

Limbs pushed over each other, clawing at the steel walls to push itself deeper into the corner and away from the noise and the light. Its flesh was pale, ill, and it seemed to be covered in a clear sinew that dripped with its movements.

Danny couldn't tell if there were six, eight, or ten legs, the way they slithered and recoiled with every report that rippled in the steel. But to his horror, he saw that some were partially covered by the remains of what could have only been uniforms, meaning that this thing had to be a conglomeration of at least three or four of the *Nisshin Maru's* crewman. Worse yet were the eyes. No longer human, at least four sets glowered down at them, emotionally dead – no fear, no pain, just the abhorrent darkness in them. As one of the limbs slipped more of its abdomen became visible, and Danny saw two large stumps that protruded from its lower body. Black with corruption and shrivelled around their base, Danny had no doubt this was where the organic vines had attached to beast, before they had burnt them.

A shot from Reicher's pistol slammed home into one of the blackened stumps and the beast screamed. It was then that Danny saw that the creature had more than one face. Twisted remnants of what once were human, the mouths hung open in horror as their black eyes stared blankly down at him. From each of those open maws, came a dissonant choir of groans and cries that could only come from beings that had seen hell and had gone mad from it. The voices flowed over each other and sent a horrible ripple of fear coursing up Danny's spine.

As Danny's own scream died in his throat, the horrible sound that came from the creature was still in the air. It grew louder and louder and louder, until Danny was forced to place his hand over his ears once more. He watched in horror and through muffled groans, as the monsters flesh began to shift. The choir of screams intensified, as the pale flesh tore and remoulded itself anew. The faces and their horrible moaning mouths faded to the point that Danny could barely see them. Finally, as the pale flesh split in places and the bones that moved beneath burst through like newly formed mountains breaking the earth's crust, the faces came forward again, spaced evenly along the creature's newly formed spine. The remnants of the black stumps fell from the body like dead limbs from a gum. They hit the ground like sacks of dead meat while blood, sinew and slime stretched down from the mass to mark their fall. Large red welts marked the body of the beast from where they had fallen, but even as Danny watched they turned yellow, then grey, as the sinew washed over the wounds.

One of the other vines had started to thrash against the walls of the generator room and the screaming intensified as the burnt end began to rapidly scab over.

'Get the fuck out of here!' Reicher screamed and the words finally reached Danny's ears as the older man fired twice more into the mass of the body above them. Blood spurted and the screams wavered in their pitch as Danny saw one of the many eyes that lined the ridge of the creature's back close forever. At this newfound pain, the creature leapt from the wall and landed with such an immense crash, that the echo rebounded constantly against the steel of the *Nisshin Maru*.

Reicher moved in front of Danny and held his pistol at arm's length. Danny tried to get himself moving but he was frozen to the spot.

The high-pitched screams silenced all at once. Instead, a low grumble began to rise into a roar as the monster before them raised itself to stand on the swelling meat that had at first reminded Danny of spider's legs, they were that thin. The flesh had now grown taut over the muscle mass that seemed to grow from nowhere.

The beast towered above as it rose and faced them. Its chest rippled over the mess of ribcages and sternums that made up its front while four massive clawed limbs stretched out at either side. The arms that came from upper part of the mangled torso were thick and veined as they flexed in their newfound strength. The flesh split around the bulging mass and the smell that hissed out from underneath brought tears to Danny's eyes while each limb swelled and swelled to the thickness of Danny's chest.

More flesh shifted high on its torso as muscles and bones expanded beneath. Then as if in decay, layer upon layer of skin turned grey and fell from the beast in clumps that almost rotted to nothing before it even hit the floor. Then he saw it, the face that had grown and formed beneath the decay.

Reborn, six eyes ran in an almost curved fashion around the squatness of its mouth. Hard bone tipped its jaw in the place of its chin as it raised its face to the light as if to smell the rotten air for the first time. As the light reflected on its many eyes, Danny saw that they moved individually from their partners as they scoured the room and its clawed arms twisted in their joints.

'Move. Now,' Reicher growled as the creature cast a shadow over them. As he spoke, eye after eye moved in their direction, as if each came to awareness at a different time.

It shifted again and the floor trembled a hideous echo of power as one of its massive legs came down upon it. Its lower jaw split in two at its chin, exposing rows of teeth, some of them human but others were long and yellowed fangs. As all of the eyes came upon him, the lower jaws gnashed together in a horrible clapping sound, spraying stinking saliva outwards with each clap.

Danny wanted to run, but his feet remained fixed to the floor, his mouth open in unending horror. He saw that each of those eyes were all focused on him alone.

The lower jaws split once more and the creature bellowed a sound that was new and hideous. A scream from another world that was now more animal than man. The air rippled as it shrieked, and Danny was hit full in the face by the wind, saliva and the smell of rotting corpses. It fell forward on its foreclaws as its roar ended in a wet growl, while blood and slime ran over its jaws and pooled heavily on the floor.

Danny broke and ran.

The ringing in his ears was gone. His feet slapped the steel and he pushed through the door. He didn't even stop to think about which way to go; he headed straight. The memory of the intersection he had seen on his way to the battery room was fresh in his mind. He looked back and saw that Reicher was right behind him. His face had gone almost as pale as the monster that towered behind him. As Reicher cleared the door, he stopped to reach for the heavy iron door, but the monster had already leapt into motion so he abandoned it. Together, they pushed beyond the heavy vines that still crowded the corridor and broke into a run through the darkness for their lives and for safety. The sounds of their breath and the soles of their boots pounding against the steel were drowned out by the primal grunts and pants of the beast.

The ship's hull rocked as the creature's enormous strength slammed into the door frame, and Danny almost fell. Reicher caught him and then together they were running again as steel groaned and the monster roared again.

With the heavy part of the vines behind them and only thin remnants trailing above them, they picked up the pace. An intersection loomed in the light in front, a single bulb glowing where the vines had not choked it out.

They were almost there when the sound of metallic groans turned to screams and Danny ran harder. Each step was a milestone, each inch gained was a breath of life, but with each gain the metal tore further and soon even the shrieks of the tearing steel were replaced by the rapid thudding of the monster's advance.

As the light touched his skin, Danny breathed easier, as if the light was a safe zone and he was unable to be harmed under its halo. Reicher, on the other hand, pushed past him and continued straight, rather than taking the right that Danny had thought led to the engine room. Danny stood there, as if tied between following the gun or following his gut. His eyes scoured the right side and he thought it seemed familiar but everything looked the same in this ship. He returned his gaze to Reicher and saw that he had almost disappeared into another dark spot of the corridor. The pounding rocked the ship's hull again and Danny looked over his shoulder and almost fainted at how fast the monster was gaining.

It pushed the walls of the steel corridors outward as it ran toward him. Its jaw open and wide, it snarled and spat and tore flesh from itself on the steel beams that it bent and buckled in its war path. Panicked, Danny followed Reicher. His breath became hot in his throat as he gasped for air and he began a low scream of horror as the monster pushed through the intersection behind him. It had come so close that he could smell the breath beating the air behind him but he didn't dare to look back. All he could do was focus on what was in front, the darkness where he hoped there was nothing for him to trip on.

In a lit section well in front of him, he saw another hatch. It was open and Reicher was standing in its frame. He was moving his mouth and waving his hand in a beckoning gesture, while someone stood beside him, unmoving in the brilliant light. At that point, Danny figured that his mind had finally snapped in all of this, as the man whose face he recognised was dead, he was sure of that. Nevertheless, the panting and the snarling came closer behind him and the air felt damp from its spittle. Danny kept pumping his legs and soon he could hear Reicher's words above it.

He leapt and dove for the door, for safety and life.

Reicher moved to let him in and as soon as he passed the door, the other two threw their shoulders into its heavy mass and slammed it shut before the monster impacted it from the other side.

Reicher was thrown completely off his feet by the impact, while the other man was only pushed back slightly. Danny leapt up and rushed to the door and threw his shoulder against it with the figure that he'd thought was dead. The hatch sealed miraculously and Danny threw the hatch wheel over to lock it. No sooner had he done that, the door groaned and pushed in slightly under the second impact of the beast.

'The door won't hold,' Paul Stathis said.

In the hours since the video feed had scarred Danny's mind, Paul had aged twenty years. Greys speckled his hair and large bags hung under his eyes. A gash stood open on his cheek, while another tore the front of his thermal shirt to reveal the hard body beneath.

'You were gone, I saw it,' Danny muttered

'No time,' Paul said as he moved further into the room behind them. Danny turned to see a storage room that was perhaps thirty feet deep.

Racks of supplies, clothes and blankets were stacked to one side, whereas on the other, odd-looking weaponry sat in racks. Rifles leant against the wall, their timber stocks dull in their age, while the ice that covered their parkerised barrels glistened in the light. A timber stocked short-barrelled weapon with a magazine port in its side lay on the ground in front, while a machine gun sat with its banana-shaped magazine on a crate to the side.

'Where there are soldiers, there are guns,' Reicher said as he picked up the short-barrelled weapon and moved over to crates that held ammunition and stacks upon stacks of magazines.

There was another crash from the other side of the door and its frame buckled further.

'The door won't hold for long,' Stathis barked as he lifted the machine gun that reminded Danny of an old Bren and rested its frame on a large crate. Reicher likewise had found a magazine to suit his submachine gun and had inserted it into the frame. The small room was filled with the sounds of old weaponry being racked for the first time in decades. As with the ship, the weaponry all seemed to be fine; there was no rust, just a thin layer of ice.

Another heavy blow from behind him sent Danny scrambling to find his own. He found another submachine gun in a crate with its muzzle down and picked it up. He looked over and saw the thin curved magazine sticking out of Reicher's model and he dug through the crate to his side until he found a few. In his inspection, he saw the curve went forward so he positioned it right, and rammed the magazine home into the frame. He knelt next to Reicher behind a heavy crate while Stathis squatted behind the large frame of the look-a-like Bren, and he reached forward and pulled back on a lever to cock the weapon.

Danny realised that he hadn't taken that step. He saw a lever on the right side of the metal tube and a track that was cut out behind it. He grabbed and pulled the bolt back against the spring until it clicked. The door buckled again under a massive impact and the sound of it made Danny jump almost out of his skin. He looked up, saw the door had held this time, and then returned his eyes to his weapon to see the bolt open and the tip of the magazine inside. A small bullet casing sat there, and the old brass sat dull against the old steel, while it waited to be fired and fulfil its purpose in life.

The impact came again and the door groaned heavily as its middle stretched out. 'Fuck this,' Danny muttered as he placed his cocked weapon on the crate. He pulled one of his Molotovs from his pocket and held it in his hands. The impact came again and the door groaned a tired old wheeze under the power of the monster. Reicher considered the Molotov and pulled one of his own.

The impact came again and steel screamed as the door started to give way. Steel tore in its frame and peeled back into the room. Through the gap they saw the snarling maw of the beast as it tried to hook its jaw in through the gap.

'Light them,' Reicher said as he held his zippo under the Molotov and thumbed the flint wheel. Flame danced in his hand and then soon the rag blazed afire. Danny held his over and soon his own rag was blazing as well.

'Get ready,' Stathis growled as he steadied his cheek against the stock of the heavy weapon.

Behind the door they heard the rapid thuds as the monster approached. Danny counted down in his head.

'Three.' More thuds, it wouldn't be long.

'Two.' *It's almost on us, it's almost here*, Danny thought.

'One,' he said as he hurled the bottle to the door. A scream of metal shrieked at his ears, as the door finally gave way under the monster's immense weight. Its face burst into the room as the door collapsed beneath it and the glass bottle shattered at its feet.

There was a soft flump as the fuel caught and the flames rose up to the flesh above it. The monster opened its gape and shrieked a horrible sound as the fire licked at its flesh and the pale white turned black with corruption. It thrashed its head about and the steel supports caved in around it. Then Reicher threw his own Molotov and the glass exploded in a burst of fire and pain on its face. The sound was dreadful. Danny heard not only through his ears but inside of his head, as the beast's flesh fell from it in sheets of rotting, melting hide.

Then Stathis stood and the small room trembled and shimmered with the fire from the machine in his hands. Even the sound of the monster's wails was drowned by the fire of the heavy weapon. Slow and methodical, the reports made Reicher's pistol seem so insignificant as they bounced back into Danny's face. The flesh erupted in a volley of blood, sinew and slime as meat gave way to fire and bone gave way to metal. Then Reicher raised his own weapon as did Danny, and they added their own bursts to the mix.

The monster thrashed as it tried to move forward into the flames and the piercing gunfire. The heavy machine gun fell silent, and Stathis moved to reload, while Danny was forced to step back as one the monster's massive arms crashed through the crate before him. The sharpened claw at its vanguard ground the steel beneath it as it tried to drag itself forward. The submachine gun rattled in Danny's hands as he held it forward and unloaded the magazine into its open mouth. Teeth burst into the chunks of shrapnel that flew back into his face, as the bullets ripped through the jaws. Then Stathis racked his weapon and the world was drowned in the heavy thunder once more.

As if only angered, the monster reeled and threw itself forward. Danny saw this coming and tried to leap out of the way but his foot slipped and he went down. The monster moved above him, almost blinded by the onslaught, and moved toward the noise, fire and pain that still harassed it. Danny clambered to his feet as it moved away and threw another magazine into his weapon. He racked the slide as Reicher began to scream and the heavy thudding paused again.

The black eyes that ran down the monster's spine glared at him as he neared. The mouths of the faces of the crew that had become this thing opened in horror as Danny raised his weapon and raked the fire down its back in a long, bloody streak. As the weapon rattled, Danny saw each impact as they sporadically tore through flesh and bone. Eyes burst one by one as Danny brought the weapon down the monster's spine, until finally they were all gone. All that remained were twisted, horrible mouths that gaped for air as the blood from their own eye sockets ran into them and drowned them. One of them coughed, sending a spray of blood as it tried to scream again, but the torrent was too strong.

The creature lurched to the side and Danny was forced to step back to avoid being crushed. From in front of the beast, Reicher had stopped screaming and Stathis roared as the heavy weapon sprang into action again to tear through the staggering beast. Danny rushed out of the way, his own weapon empty and useless to him. He dove to the corner of the room and watched as the old Japanese weaponry ripped the beast to pieces. The body rippled as bullets pounded into its flank and its back legs went out from under it. The firing paused as Stathis shifted and then he lit it up again as the monster tried to lift itself.

The floor had become covered in the monster's lifeblood to the point that it lapped up over Danny's hand. Still the creature tried to stand as Stathis fired into it. Danny stood up, and pulled his final Molotov and lit it.

'Move back!' Danny screamed as he lit the rag and then he saw Reicher beneath it. His legs had been mauled beneath his waist and he lay there lifeless, his face as pale as the monster's flesh that had killed him. Reicher's eyes were wide and they stared straight at Danny, straight into his soul as if urging him to throw the Molotov, almost pleading. The glass left his hand and shattered against the ruined flank and the world was filled with bright dancing flames once again as the monster shrieked and rolled onto its side.

Its legs flailed in the air, as did its claws. Each voice came out in a horrible scream; some were high-pitched, insane in their hysterical dying, while others were low, as if a gurgle while blood filled their throats. One by one, they fell silent, as first the back legs stopped moving. The room became quieter still as the small, useless claws at the monster's waist fell motionless, and then the massive uppers. Danny stood there as the flames cast shadows across the walls, as if they were the ghosts of the poor men that had made this beast leaving the world for good. Then as the flames guttered and finally died out, the monster slumped and died before him.

41

THE ROOM FELL SILENT with the dying of the beast, apart from the ringing in Danny's ears and the sound of the tremolo that was his heart. Each breath was rife with death, as the sweaty smoke from cordite mixed with the remnants of the burnt Av-gas. His heart seemed to pulse with pain from the roaring agony that had started along with the gunfire. Being trapped in this floating tomb, the gunfire was horrific to the ears; even the metal seemed to ripple against the sharpness of its report. The echoes came back with the ring of steel and rasp of ricochet as the ship seemed to contort behind the heavy smoke.

Yet through the haze, it wasn't the deformed body of the monster that drew his eyes. Not the twisted flesh, or the rippled muscles that ran up its limbs, but the blackened face of the man that he had entered with. Reicher's mouth hung open in a horrible blackened, scream of pain. Danny knew the man was dead before he had thrown the Molotov yet the way his flesh had succumbed to the fires made him sick. It was as if the stroke from the fire's fingers had put life back into him. His lips curled into a sneer, then as the fire continued to consume the flesh, a ghastly snarl was revealed, leaving Reicher twisted in a silent scream. The flesh on his jaw rippled then moved as the muscles contracted and then let go as they tore loose. His eyes rolled, then fixated as they bulged from his head, before they burst and sizzled in the heat. His hair caught fire as his nostrils flared then melted away to leave his corpse scarred and horrific.

'Hey,' Paul shifted the weight of the machine gun in his hands, as he moved around the charred corpse. 'You alright?' He slapped Danny on the shoulder.

Danny couldn't take his eyes from Reicher's twisted face. 'Yeah,' he said, in words that didn't even feel like his own. Somewhere in the room, something had startled to rattle. He frowned as he blinked and finally tore his eyes away from the mess before him to see what it was but for the life of him, he couldn't work it out. Finally, he looked to Stathis's face as the man reached out for him. There was a soft frown on his face, and his eyes were full of either pity or concern, as he placed his own hand over Danny's and the rattling stopped.

Danny stared down at the submachine gun in his hands. With each tremor that ran from the tips of his fingers up his wrists, the charging handle rattled against its tubular guide. Even under the gentle pressure from Paul's grasp, his hand still shook sporadically. He looked up to the man's face, as his breaths quickened in his chest and his face contorted.

'I don't know why it's doing that.' This time, the voice was definitely not his own. The sound was high and it teetered on the edge of breaking. It sounded to Danny like the voice of a child that had nowhere to go. Paul placed his hand around the back of Danny's neck and pulled his face down onto his shoulder. He clapped Danny on the back, the same way his father used to, before death had separated them.

Danny felt the trembles move from his hand, up his arm and finally, as the tears welled up in his eyes and broke their banks, his whole body shook.

He cried into Paul's shoulder and allowed himself to be embraced. He tried to imagine Reicher embracing him this way and couldn't. The thought brought a smile to his face and through the tears he began to laugh. The man that held him was hard, but he was also kind; Reicher had been iron, hard and inflexible. Danny tried to think of what he was, but no word came to his mind; he wasn't as hard as the man that had died, nor the one that held him. Yet he had the spine to come down here but that wasn't him. Now that he thought about it, none of it was. Everything he did now, he did for Louise and Leanna. They were who he was and the thought of them would get him through this.

He grimaced as he pulled away and he forced himself to think about them. Christ, the last time he had seen Louise, she had looked ready to burst. He needed to get out of here, he needed to see her again. Even if it was through video, he needed to see his daughter's face.

'You alright?' Paul asked again.

'Yeah,' he sniffed. 'You know it.' Danny headed for the door but he stopped before he reached it. Scattered along the floor, amongst the fury of the monster that had driven its clawed arm through the crate that sat before him, were rounds of ammunition. A few long stick magazines lay in the rubble and Danny stopped to collect them. Likewise, he noticed that Stathis had retrieved a few more of the heavy banana-shaped magazines for his machine gun. Danny was forced to wait as Paul tore strips of cloth from his sleeves to fashion a sling for the heavy weapon.

The door frame had almost shattered beneath the strength of the monster. Heavy steel lay warped across the floor and the bulkhead was in ruins, but as Danny stepped through into the corridor that had been his escape, a chill ran up his spine. The corridor that had once been an almost exact rectangle, higher than it was wide, had been pushed outward the entire length. Each and every light that had hung down from the ceiling to light a man's way, had been torn from their fixtures. The only thing now that illuminated the hall, were the odd sparks that raked down across his vision.

Beneath the ringing in his ears and the pounding in his head, the sounds of his footfalls were softened. In the low light it was difficult to see, but as they neared the intersection and the light from the junctions washed in, Danny saw the layer of slime and sinew that coated the ground. It moved to allow his foot entry and then sucked at the sides of his sole as he tried to walk on. The grimace reinforced itself on his face as he adjusted his grip on the timber stock of the automatic weapon.

They took a left turn at the lit intersection, but not before Danny inspected the conduit that had been buckled along with the roof. The steel piping was not torn but only pushed upward and out of the way. He wondered how much slack the cables had to begin with. If the starter wires had been damaged or the flow of current had been interrupted, there would be no way for them to start the ship, unless they could find spools of heavy gauged copper wire and splice them somehow.

He sighed as he sniffed back another nose full of snot that had remained from his outburst. He felt more relaxed now that he was in the light. Again, he followed the heavy conduit that held the starter wires and didn't dare to look at the vines that had trailed into the illuminated corridor.

As he stepped through the already opened hatch and into the engine room, he paused. The lights now revealed the enormous plant that sat in the middle of the room and towered above them. The room itself was quiet, despite the work that occupied the other two men. Carmichael had been given the task of defrosting the water pump. He glanced over his shoulder while he wagged the open flame of his blow torch over the front of the casing and squinted as his eyes fell on Stathis. His mouth opened then closed.

Danny shook his head subtly as they passed the young man and continued to Thompson, who was finalising some wire replacements on the lower of the two starter motors. He too raised an eyebrow at the sight of Stathis. 'Leave with a hard case and return with an engineer?' he muttered. 'What happened? We thought we heard gun…'

'You don't want to know.' Danny sighed. 'All I'll say is Reicher is gone. If it wasn't for Paul, I wouldn't be here either.'

Thompson looked Stathis up and down with a frown on his face.

Stathis cleared his throat as he shifted the weight of the machine gun on his hip. 'How many of you are there?'

'Four,' Danny muttered. 'Reicher, and me–'

'Thompson and Carmichael, yeah I get it,' Stathis finished for him,

Danny turned to him. 'Hey, what the fuck happened to you?'

Stathis shot him a look and then continued down the room. 'It's a long story.'

'I saw the video feed. One of our guys tapped into your wire so a few of us saw it,' Danny confided. 'I saw Peters go down. I saw what happened to the mechanic, but yours just went out.'

Paul remained silent, as if contemplating what to say next. 'I broke the camera, from there I managed to lock myself in a room. They're strong, don't get me wrong, but if you saw the ones that I had seen, they can't open doors too well.'

Danny shook his head as his attention switched to Thompson. 'How's your end looking? I just want to get this thing started.'

Stathis stopped at this. 'Fuck that. Let's get out of this fucking place.'

Danny shook his head. 'I can't, I need to do this.'

Stathis met his eyes, and Danny could almost see the choice roll over in his mind. Should he leave or should he stay?

'Help me, please.' Danny tried to make his decision to leave even harder.

'Why do you want to stay?' he asked, then pointed to Thompson. 'What has this lot got over you?' Thompson shook his head and returned to the lower of the two starter motors.

Danny frowned again and Christ, he felt tired. 'It's a long story.' He offered him a weary smile and shrugged.

Stathis considered him for some time, something that reminded Danny instantly of Reicher. Then he sighed as he pulled a cigarette from his pocket and lit it. 'Tell me what to do,' the hard man said, through the cigarette perched between his lips.

Danny looked up at the control platform and sighed. 'Wait here.'

He moved toward the stairs, and felt naked in the openness of the large engine room. He couldn't help but peer over his shoulder, as he moved upward and on. He climbed up the switched back flights, one by one, and noted the narrowness of the stairway. As he said, someone would have to stay down here to control the motor while a man above reported down the commands. Of course, they would seal the room at every entrance point to protect the individual, but if it came down to it, they would need to protect themselves. With the stairway so narrow, only one man could move upward at a time; that may give him a hope.

The platform was open topped and had a small chair bolted to the steel in its centre. In front of the chair was a small, relatively simple console with a few gauges. Danny checked over the needles that surprisingly still worked; even back then the Japs seemed to make good gear. Voltage was the first gauge that he saw; the needle was in the lower quarter but that still may be enough to start it. He rubbed his sleeve against the glass of the second gauge and then peered to see through the foggy glass.

From what he could tell, this gauge represented fuel pressure. The needle rested against the stopper below the zero and Danny ran his hand through the stubble on his jaw. He didn't know whether that meant there was no fuel pressure, or if it just sat that way when the engine was off, like in a car. His shoulders slumped – when he thought about it, he knew that wasn't the case. He checked the voltage reading again and he knew that in all this time, they wouldn't have enough power there to continuously turn the great engine over. The massive mechanical pump would surely draw the fuel up as it cranked, but Danny didn't like the odds of there being enough power to crank the engine for enough time for that to happen.

'Fuck,' he said aloud as he went back to the stairs. 'Fuck it.'

'What?' Stathis looked up to him.

Danny ripped down the stairs as he held his weapon to his side and continued to swear under his breath. 'I should have known it wasn't going to be that simple,' he muttered as if in answer.

'What?' Stathis repeated.

Danny sighed when he reached the bottom of the stairs. 'Fuel pump has no pressure.' He ran a hand over his face, ignoring the slime and the grit that had accumulated on his gloved hand.

'So, what we do then?' Stathis urged him on.

Danny was in his own mind, thinking about trucks' fuel systems and filtration methods. 'There has to be a lift pump, or a priming system. Fuck knows what they had seventy years ago, may as well had a bloke sucking on the hose until the diesel touched his lips, who fucking knows?' He kicked at a tool that Thompson had left lying on the ground and sent it skittering across the floor to clang against the wall.

'Settle down,' Thompson said sternly as he moved away from the block to retrieve the tool.

'Fuck off.' Danny waved him away as he moved to the pump housing.

The steel lines that ran up to the monstrous cylinder heads were in good condition; he doubted that the leak had come from there. As he traced their lines back down to the feed pump, he found the problem sooner than he thought he would. Thompson had replaced the rubber feed hose that connected the pump to the steel lines than ran through the ship's body. As with a truck, you couldn't run steel lines the entire way, as engines wanted to move in their torque ranges, steel would split. Just another thing that should have been thought of: the rubber perished over the years and needed to be replaced. 'That's why there's no pressure,' Danny said as he pointed at it. 'It was lost when the feed hose perished.'

'Uh-huh.' Stathis pretended to understand.

'I could've told you that,' Thompson grunted as he returned to tighten one of the bolts that secured the starter to the engine block. 'I figured that we would need to change it, lucky there was spare hose lying around.' He gestured his head to a rack of various tools and spare parts that were dusted white with ice. 'The hose isn't the best, but it'll be close enough for government work.' He said this through gritted teeth as he put pressure to the final bolt. He panted as he released the pressure and pointed to the hose. The replacement hose was in a poor state, but Danny agreed that it was better than the one Thompson had removed. 'You two will need to prime it.'

'Alright,' Danny said as he lowered his head. 'But, if we're going to be down that end priming the hose, I'll need you to stay ready on this end to bleed the air.' He pointed up at the diesel line that Thompson had already replaced.

'I've never bled a line before,' Thompson said almost beneath his breath.

Danny sighed. Once more he pointed to the hose. 'Keep a close eye on it, you've left enough slack in the line that you should hopefully notice some sort of change when the pressure starts to build. If you can't notice anything, break the seal slightly. You'll hear air start to hiss out if I have started to raise the pressure.'

Thompson nodded, his eyes stern in his concentration.

'Let me build pressure up, then break the seal. Let the air come out until you see a bit of diesel and then seal it again. Once you've closed it off, give me ten seconds to build pressure back up again and then bleed it again.'

Danny saw that Thompson had actually started to write some notes. Danny gave him time to write everything down as he peered over his shoulder at what was written. After a while, the electrician raised his head. 'How many times will we bleed it?'

'After the initial bleed, let's say another three times. I just want to get rid of as much of the air as possible.'

Thompson scribbled something illegible. 'So, four?'

Danny nodded at this and repeated the number. As he raised his free hand to his jaw to scratch at the stubble on his chin, he faced Stathis again and raised his eyebrows. 'You a betting man?'

Stathis flicked his half-smoked cigarette into the corner and spat after it; Danny followed it with his eyes. 'Only when the odds are certain.'

'Odds are shit,' Danny muttered.

'How's the pay off?'

'Fucked, but it will get us out of here.'

'Sure, I'll play.' Stathis adjusted the heavy weapon on its sling and gestured for Danny to lead. 'Where to?'

Danny pointed up to the steel pipe that had connected to the rubber hose that Thompson had replaced. 'Wherever that goes.'

Stathis grunted in response and Danny led the way. Neither of them said a word to Thompson as they passed. The electrician, on the other hand, smile as he waved the rag he was using to clean the grime from his hands. 'Be safe,' he grunted as the two continued away from him, beneath the trail of the fuel line.

The steel pipe took them in the opposite direction to the batteries. As he walked, his mind rolled the possibilities and the obvious parts in his head. He figured that a ship of this size would carry a hell of a lot of fuel to carry it on its voyages, and they wouldn't keep all that weight up high in the vessel as it would make it unstable. In this case, it made sense to

Danny that they would store most of their fuel low in the ship. At the same time, he doubted this line would take him down that far.

A foul taste had crept into Danny's mouth and he ran his tongue over the furriness that had become his teeth. He maintained a slow pace in the brilliant light, as he still didn't trust that they were completely alone. He followed the line in through a wall that took him to a hatch that had already been opened. Danny stepped through and Stathis awkwardly got the heavy weapon through with him. At least this time he didn't have to shine a light above his head. The lights in this section of the ship were perfect and every corridor seemed to glisten anew, while the lights reflected off the thin layers of ice that clung to the walls.

The pair walked in silence. Even the sounds of their boots against the iron walk didn't seem to bother Danny, until he heard something low almost behind him, a word or two or three. He stopped and turned back to Stathis. The hard man stopped and raised his eyebrows at him as if in question.

'What did you say?' Danny asked in a whisper but the only response he got was a frown and a shake of the head. Danny stared at him for a while longer, before he continued down the corridor.

The steel pipe continued overhead. Unlike the conduit that held the wiring for the lights, the steel for the fuel was painted brown. A blue pipe ran next to it, but that one he didn't care about. He followed a junction where the blue pipe broke off and disappeared down to his left, down a corridor that for one reason or another, was poorly lit. The brown, however, continued straight down a well-lit corridor that had only darkness to either side.

Danny despised the darkness of the corridors that he passed. Everything played on his mind beyond the shadows. The darkness seemed to swirl and the light failed to penetrate even an inch into the abyss, as the globes weren't placed in the centre of the junctions. Danny laughed to himself; it was funny how it was only at times like these that someone would notice a small fault like that. A question that seemed obvious when you looked at it in Danny's perspective, whereas back in the thirties, all they thought about was putting a light every ten feet or so, and if that happened to be in a junction, then great. However, if it didn't, so be it.

'Free me.' The long rasp of the trailing whisper cut through him like a blade through his heart. He tried to take a breath but it caught in his throat. Frozen to the spot, Danny couldn't move an inch. It wasn't until Stathis put a hand on his shoulder that he felt a jolt go through him and he was able to breathe again.

He turned to Stathis, eyes wide. 'Tell me you heard that?'

Stathis' eyes became slits as he squinted at him.

'Now.' The whisper came again, long and pained in its ragged tone.

'That!' Danny pointed as if to the sky, where the voice seemed to come from. He scoured the area for a speaker, but there wasn't any.

He considered Stathis, who likewise had started to search, training the muzzle of his weapon down a corridor of darkness.

'That, I heard,' Stathis muttered as he panned the muzzle slowly across the darkened pane.

Danny's grip tightened on his own weapon as he raised it to his shoulder, but nothing came. Nothing stirred in the dark except for their imagination. His mouth had gone dry as he started to move again. Now that their footfalls had begun to ring softly in their ears, Danny noticed another sound. A slow rumble that rose to a point, paused, and then fell back to its point of origin. Each dragging rumble took five seconds to climb, and then another five to fall. The hairs on the back of his neck stood on end and his arms erupted in gooseflesh.

He peered back over his shoulder at Stathis as they held their slow pace. The hard man met his eyes, wrinkled his nose and breathed hard through it. The notion was clear to Danny; he thought it was the sound of breathing. Slow and methodical, ragged and rumbling, the sound didn't come from any corridor.

No matter how far they went down the hall, the sound didn't change, it didn't get louder, nor did it become softer. It just remained at that damned pitch, as it dragged gravel over steel on its intake and rattled at the chords of hell on its exhale. The sound of it drove through him but Danny couldn't say that it came from somewhere outside.

The more he walked, the clearer it became. It was breathing inside of his head, and just the idea of that sparked a terror inside of his heart that threatened to unhinge his knees and crumple his soul, beneath the heavy weight of that hideous, hideous sound.

42

DANNY'S WORLD SEEMED TO DARKEN, as if all the light from the world had started to drain. His vision blurred and his hearing became faint beneath the steady rasp of those incessant breaths. It came to the point that Danny felt as though he was a passenger in his own body. He felt himself move and he heard the sounds the soles of his boots made against the frozen steel, but everything seemed to come to him a second or two after the fact. As if the computer that was his brain had failed to buffer the video feeds from his eyes.

He dropped his head as he walked and saw the progress his feet made. First his left moved on and then his right, as the walls closed in on him from every side. The roof came down to meet him and the floor rushed up beneath his steps and he felt his breaths become heavy in his panic. In an attempt to escape, he turned to Stathis, but the light had vanished behind him and nothing seemed to be there but the glooming darkness. He stretched his hand into the black and clawed for anything, for something. All he found was the cold, icy feeling of the steel that had closed in behind him. Again, he spun and tried to run from it and ran straight into another wall, a wall that hadn't been there in the instant before he'd looked down.

His weapon clattered to the ground as he fell to his knees. His breaths had become so short and rapid in his panic that small specks of light had begun to explode before his eyes in horrible starbursts.

He pressed his arms against the walls to either side but felt the steel push into his back and his stomach at the same time. He tried to gain his feet, but as he rose, he slammed his head into the ceiling that had fallen to block his exit. The last light exited the world as it all closed in on him and Danny began to scream.

'Let me out of this place! Oh fuck, I have to get out here!' He started to thrash as the walls edged in even closer toward him. 'Oh Jesus, not like this. Come on, I have to get out.'

A pain shot through his shoulder as the wall to his left edged in even closer and he was forced to shift onto his ass. He wrapped his hands around his shins as he curled up into the smallest ball he could. His knees dug into his cheeks and his arms pulled his legs closer into his body as he shrieked in fear. 'Let me out, let me out, let me out!'

As the walls rushed in to take up the space that he had made, he took a breath and felt his body shudder as he released it. The next breath he took he felt his back press against steel again. He held it as long as he could, while he pushed outward with his legs and his arms but eventually, he had to let the air go. The next breath he took, he wasn't able to expand himself to same place as before and he felt the cold of the steel around him start to sink into his flesh. Tighter and tighter, more and more it squeezed the life out of him, until finally Danny cried out and spent his last breath on the words that had been on the tip of his tongue the entire time.

'Free me!' He let it out in a horrible rasp as his vocal cords shredded under his hysterical cry and the world closed in on him to put him out, like the last guttering candle on a powerless night.

Danny felt a hand close around his shoulder and he jerked away from its touch. He raised the weapon in his hand and held it before him like a threatening talisman. His eyes were wide but unfocused and his breaths came in short bursts that offered him no air. The blur before him stepped away and he saw one hand raise in a calming gesture.

'Woah Danny, it's me.' The voice came to him from a distance, almost faint as his vision began to wane again. He blinked and rubbed his face against the cuff of his collar while he raised the muzzle of his weapon closer to the blur before him. When he opened his eyes again it was Paul Stathis before him.

Paul's eyes were wide as they darted from Danny's face to the muzzle of submachine gun that trembled before him. 'Don't shoot,' he said softly as he tried a smile that didn't suit his face, nor the situation.

Danny let out a rush of air as he lowered the weapon and turned away. Even in this cold environment, the sweat had poured of him. He ran a trembling hand across his face in his fear and felt the sweat line his palm.

'You alright?' Stathis' voice came again behind him. The clarity in which he was able to hear these words, settled Danny somewhat. He took a deep breath and listened to the way it sounded to his ears. The long, wretched gasps that had drowned his mind before were gone and he felt like he was himself again.

'Yeah, yeah,' Danny muttered as he brushed the sweat off the palm of his hand. 'Just something put the wind up me.'

'Tell me about it,' Stathis muttered. 'Anyway, are you good now or do you need a minute?'

'Nah,' Danny said as he raised his head to search for the brown pipe and paused. When the hideous breathing had rattled him, he'd been partway down a long corridor. Now he stood in a large room on an elevated platform. Large, powerful overhead lights hung down to illuminate the tank that sat squat below them. The brown pipe that he had followed before his cloudiness descended from the ceiling before him and connected to a large housing that sat to the front of the tank. Even from his position above the system, Danny could see a socket for a handle that looked just like a hydraulic socket for a bottle jack, and next to it looked like a glass dial with a gauge. Whether he had known what he was doing or not, he had found the priming system for the main pump.

He rolled his tongue around in his mouth as he considered it. This had to be the feed tank, but the tank was nowhere near big enough to run the ship. As he ran his eyes over the rear of the tank he saw more pipes; they ran off the tank and descended further down into the depths of the ship through the floor and beyond.

'So, what now?' Stathis asked as he leant his weapon on the rail of the platform.

Danny pointed down the large housing where the brown pipe connected to the tank. 'See that?' He leant further over. 'That's the priming pump.' He ran one of his hands through the stubble on his chin as he thought about how the fuel system would have to work. Sometimes in race cars when a car is put under intense cornering force, the fuel can slosh about in the main tank. To prevent the main fuel pump being starved of fuel, many operators use a surge tank, which is a fraction of the size of the main tank and is designed to be full the entire time. The main pump draws its fuel from the surge tank while another lift pump carries the fuel from the main tank up to the surge; this had to be something similar. It was the only explanation that he had for what he saw and it made sense to work against the vast distances of pipes these pumps needed to pressurise.

'If I'm right, that tank there should be chock-full with diesel. All we have to do is manually prime the fuel line through that housing.' He gestured toward the housing where the brown pipe connected. 'Once I feel the pressure build up, we can head back and start her up.'

'Sounds simple enough,' Stathis said as he shifted his weight.

'Simple enough if Thompson's still there,' Danny muttered beneath his breath as he moved beyond Stathis to the stairs that led down to the surge tank. Stathis went to follow him but Danny gestured him back. 'You may as well wait here; you get a good view from up here. Just keep an eye on me.'

Stathis shrugged and dropped the weight of his weapon down on the railing once more. Danny descended the stairs alone; he allowed his weapon to hang low at his side as he strode in long determined steps to the primer housing. The first thing he needed to find was the primer handle. He swore at himself as he inspected the diameter of the socket, as the breaker bar he had left in the generator room probably would have fit. Yet, it was what it was and he didn't have it any more, so he was forced to explore the room.

Danny rummaged through shelving that had held shit that no-one had cared about for seventy years. He searched behind crates and onto other machinery for any hope to find it. Again he found himself assuming the same as he had with crank handle for the generators – if something was that important, surely it would have to be kept somewhere obvious. If that was so, he still couldn't find it, and he couldn't use the lighting as an excuse anymore. The room was well lit and no matter how many times he scoured the walls with his eyes, high nor low he couldn't find the priming arm anywhere.

The more Danny searched the more agitated he became; all he needed now was for Stathis to hurry him up and his temper would begin to boil over. He stepped beyond a crate that had been smashed across the ground, and saw a corner of the room where the lights didn't reach. He frowned in his frustration as he hastily stepped over the wreckage of the crate to reach the shadows. As his foot came down it slid forward and Danny gasped in his surprise. He came down on the remains of the crate and the timber cracked beneath him, the sound of it made his heart skip a beat and Danny swore aloud.

'What was that?' Stathis asked.

Danny groaned as he lifted himself to his feet again and swore aloud for a second time. 'Nothing, just slipped on…' he didn't finish his sentence as he looked down to find the answer for it. The light penetrated just far enough beyond the shattered crate to shimmer off the slime and sinew that covered the floor. The breath caught in Danny's throat and his heart stopped as he saw a figure rise before him in the darkness. His hands moved for his weapon but in his fall, it had slid away from him. He wanted to lower his eyes to find it, but they were locked on the moving shadow before him. He opened his mouth and shut it again as he kicked back with his feet. As he shifted back, the highest point of the shadow twitched while the rest froze and Danny heard a slight metallic sound to his right as his leg bumped his weapon. Slowly he reached to his side as the shadow moved toward him.

His eyes widened as the tip of its head broke through the barrier of darkness and entered the light before him. Its flesh was a pallid grey and slick with something that looked like sweat. Its eyes were black bowls that shrunk to yellow vertical slits that radiated in the light as they adapted to its brilliance. Where its nose had been, two holes remained and the faint white outline of cartilage pressed out against its flesh. Its lower jaw parted and the saliva spread and left strands between the joints. The sound that came from the movement of its lips and jaws was wet and horrid, like the sound of dead meat being torn from the bone. Further and further, they spread apart as Danny saw rows upon rows of teeth. Its eyes narrowed even further as two limbs raised themselves above its head and it took a final step into the light to reveal the sharpened points that existed where its wrist had once been. It leant forward and roared at him as a smell of ancient rot and decay hit Danny full in the face and his hand fell on the cool, metal barrel of his weapon as it lunged.

If there had been any part of the monster's body that light had not touched, the flames that shot from the submachine gun's muzzle left nothing in the shade. The frame of the weapon rocked hard in his hands as the roar ripped through the room. Flesh exploded in the monster's mid-section as it staggered in mid-charge. Danny raked the weapon upward as the fire continued to singe the air and the roar of the cordite hammered his ears. He watched the flesh ripple and part as the fire-driven metal ripped through the monster and he was staggered by the awesome power that he held in his hands.

Flesh vanished to reveal the gleaming white beneath and then the white was shattered to a thousand pieces. Blood misted the air and still the bolt rattled back and forth in its tube, as the power seemed endless and absolute. It couldn't end, it was eternal.

Then, as the monster fell to its knees and the fire caught it full in the face, Danny watched as parts of the jaw and teeth were torn from the bone and sent across the room in a tumult of bloody chaos and gore. Still the weapon continued to fire, continued to dismantle, while its angry roar ripped back at him from the walls the surrounded him. Then finally, as the monster fell back, the bolt fell forward and the silence consumed him once again.

His ears rung bloody murder once again as he scrambled to his feet. Blood covered his hands, his clothes and his face, but Danny didn't notice. His breath was heavy in his chest as he rammed one of his last two magazines into the receiver and racked the charging handle.

'Are you alright?' Stathis called down from his elevated platform.

Danny looked up to him, still speechless. He saw the concern on the hard man's face but he also saw that the man was ready. He was behind the heavy weapon; the butt was to his shoulder and his head slightly raised from the stock. 'Let's get this line primed and get the hell out of here,' Danny half yelled to him, his ears still ringing.

He turned back to the shadows and took a few steps toward the dark, when the sound of heavy, fast falling footsteps made him spin to his left. Another one of those monsters emerged from the darkness in full sprint. Its entire lower jaw was gone. Still, it snuffled and slobbered as it ran toward him while its armless upper body rocked awkwardly in its pace.

Danny raised his weapon to his shoulder and once again the submachine gun rocked into life. Once, twice, three times the weapon fired and each time the round hit the chest of the charging beast, but it was too close. The monster hammered into Danny at full pace and sent them both sprawling. His weapon skittered away from him, while the monster wasted no time clambering to its knees and renewing its assault. It thrashed its head around while the yellow eyes remained focused only on him.

Danny screamed as he pushed himself away. The monster took three staggered steps toward him and then a fierce thunder filled the room.

Slow and methodical, the sound was cut short as three reports exacted three heavy impacts on the beast. The power of Stathis' weapon put the monster back on its ass. It sat there stunned, while the eyes remained locked on Danny in an almost desperate urge.

Danny pushed himself further away, panic in his chest once more. The snuffling was replaced by a heavy, wet gurgle but the eyes continued to follow him as he moved. Danny rolled onto his side, latched onto his own weapon and then turned it on the crippled beast. He aimed down the metal tube as his hand clenched around the stock. The weapon rattled off a single round, and was then silent while the air hung heavy with the blood from the creature's opened skull. It fell forward and didn't move again.

Danny got to his feet and moved into the shadows. Their weapons were going to keep them alive, but they were too loud. He thought about the heavy movement that had come from above them when he had dropped the mechanic's backpack and a chill ran up his spine. He had less than two magazines remaining to him; he didn't know how many creatures he could defend himself against with that, but something told him it wasn't enough.

'Time to get moving. We can't stay here much longer,' Stathis called out from above.

'No shit,' Danny called back. 'I need to find the priming arm.'

'Well get fucking finding,' Stathis snarled as he shouldered his weapon by lowering his body behind it.

Danny followed the direction of his aim and flinched as the weapon thudded a short burst behind him. At the end of the room was a bulkhead. The hatch was opened slightly but was jammed against a stack of crates that had been thrown across the room in some past impact. A creature was trying to pry itself through the gap of the door but had become lodged. Danny watched as one of the heavy projectiles thundered off the steel next to its head, scarring the metal. In the next burst, the aim was corrected and the body of the creature fell limp in the gap.

Danny breathed easier when he saw the life flee from the monster's eyes, but no sooner had the body collapsed in the opening had the door clanged from an impact on the other side and Danny saw the crates shift slightly.

'Get looking!' Stathis roared and Danny moved into the darkness.

He could barely see a thing. In his panicked search he tripped over and fell heavily onto a crate. His weapon clattered against the ground and then something fell and rung hollowly as it bounced on the steel floor.

Danny's eyes widened as he moved his hands blindly across the floor.

First, he found his weapon, but he kept moving and finally he brushed smooth steel and smiled at the beautiful sound it made when it rolled away from him. He followed the sound with his eyes and watched a long tube roll into the light and rest against the corpse of the crippled creature.

Danny leapt to his feet and latched onto it with his free hand. He sprinted back to the priming system and slid the arm into the jack-like socket. At first it moved so easy that Danny thought for sure that the system was broken. But as he pumped, he felt a slight increase in resistance.

Soon, below the layer of ice on the glass dial, the needle began to climb.

43

HIS BACK HAD BEGUN TO ACHE, as had his shoulders. He threw the lever up and dragged it down against the hydraulic strain again and again. His eyes darted from the slow progress of the pressure needle to his weapon at his side. It wouldn't be long until the system was pressurised, he knew that. But it also wouldn't be long until the creatures hit the door hard enough to burst through. It seemed that each millimetre the needle climbed, the door had opened a further three. With each motion that his body took, the panic inside of him rose while the storm behind the bulkhead stirred and lashed out.

'We can't stay here!' Stathis called out the obvious as another creature fought to push through the widening gap in the bulkhead.

Danny watched in tormented silence as he continued to pump. The creature writhed, pushing its stumps against the steel while its jaw snapped and clacked. Their eyes were the worst, the way they locked onto him, the way they yearned for him like it was their only desire to reach him.

With each pump, the creature worked its way further through the bulkhead, while others rammed the obstacle hard from behind. Danny's eyes went from the door, to the creature, to his weapon, to the needle, and then back again. A panicked circuit that was rushed further with each pass.

The pain in his back intensified as the needle began to waver.

Each pump saw the pressure rise, then slowly fall back to its original spot. He thought about bleeding brakes, he thought about all the times he had pressurised lines back on the mainline. Once the fluid started to flow out, the person on the hose would clamp it off. The person priming would feel the pressure rise, and then as the line was bled, the pressure would fall as the oxygen was purged from the system. If Thompson was still there, if Thompson was still alive, then surely, he would see this soon.

The creature that was part way through the door slipped through.

As soon as it felt the hatch's grip on its body fail, its efforts to reach Danny tripled. It pumped its legs as if in a run as it fell.

Danny kept pumping. He lifted and dragged the steel bar down as the creature stumbled towards him and struggled to regain its feet. His eyes widened as it got closer and closer and his hands clenched harder on the steel pipe.

Stathis caught the creature in the mid-section with the first volley. The heavy report only came twice, yet still the carnage before Danny's eyes was abhorrent. The first round caught the creature low in the right of the hip, there was a sickening crack as its structure caved in and the entire right leg fell useless to the floor. The second hit higher and more centre, blowing the creature's guts and entrails out through its back. A horrible smell filled the air as the creature screamed. Danny continued to pump as he breathed in the poisoned smell of death, while the creature thrashed and bit at its own stomach, at the pain that had sunk into it.

As Danny lifted the handle and drove his weight down on it again, he felt the tension rise in the last third of his throw. The feeling of the resistance pushing back up against him almost made him slip off the handle. He lifted again and pushed down hard, the handle dragged down softly as he strained and gritted his teeth against the build-up.

As the needle rose in the gauge, the creature turned away from the mess that was its guts and began to crawl its way toward Danny. Its stumps of limbs clacked against the floor while its remaining leg hung useless behind it. Its lower jaw parted down its centre in a horrific scream as it dragged itself toward him, leaving a slick of entrails and blackened mess behind it.

The heavy report came only once this time as Danny forced his weight down hard on the handle again.

The projectile hammered the creature in the hollow of its neck. The creature convulsed and threw its head back, a trail of blood spraying above it. As Danny pushed down and felt the handle stop against the sudden climax of pressure, the creature gave him one last longing look, and fell forward in its death.

'Is that it? Is it primed?' Stathis called from above.

'Not yet!' Danny yelled through gritted teeth; the bar had stopped in its motion in its first quarter of travel and Danny strained to hold it there. His eye focused on the needle, which stood up around the seventy-five per cent portion of the reading that he couldn't understand. 'Come on Thompson, you motherfucker. Bleed!' he growled as he forced the lever down. Then finally, the handle edged further down and Danny's eyebrows raised. Down further again and then all the way down. As the handle drifted further down, the needle wavered and then followed suit.

'Yes,' he urged as he pumped faster than he had before to help drive the oxygen out of the line. The pressure rose quickly this time as the line had already filled, and as with their previous agreement, Danny counted the seconds as they passed.

Within the first four seconds, he pumped hard and fast while the low pressure allowed him speed to move quickly. At the halfway point, the hatch shifted heavily in its frame as three more creatures tried to force their way through at once. One of them bit savagely at the one above it, while the other two screamed and tore each other to shreds with their flailing limbs.

The handle slowed as the pressure rose and by the time Danny had reached the count of eight, his back had begun to scream.

'Ten!' he roared as he lifted the handle and pulled down hard against the strain. The handle dropped an inch and then stopped against the back pressure. Danny growled through his teeth as he held it there while he watched the lower creature wrap its lower jaws around the face of the one that thrashed above it. 'Come on, come on,' he muttered as his whole body screamed in pain. The handle shifted down, and then finally sunk all the way to the bottom again.

'That's two.' He called up to Stathis, who was swearing to himself as he looked down the sights of his heavy weapon at the chaos that had started at the door.

'Hurry the fuck up,' Stathis replied in an urgent tone.

Danny didn't reply; he was exhausted. The pressure rose even quicker the third time and it seemed that Danny hung on for an age as he waited for Thompson to bleed the line. He couldn't bring himself to look at the gauge any more, the door was what concerned him now.

The creature that had wrapped its lower jaws around the face of the other had torn the monster's head clean from its shoulders. As blood that was as dark as the devil's soul ran down its chest, it glared at Danny and screamed, renewing its efforts to reach him.

Danny hissed as the handle slowly reached the bottom of its travel on the third bleed and began to rapidly pump it again. The pressure rose fast again, but the further they went, the more Danny knew that they weren't going to be fast enough.

Heavy reports came again, slow and methodical, and the bloody scream ended in the monster's throat. It slumped in the doorway. Behind it, more creatures tried to push over it, under it, through it. The crates that held the door shut, ground as they slid further on the steel floor and the steel hinges groaned as the hatch surrendered another half inch.

The handle stopped in its travel again and the veins stood proud on Danny's neck. 'Fuck, Thompson come on!' He shouted, as he redoubled the grip on the steel handle. The palms of his hands were lined with sweat as his flesh slid on the smooth surface. Danny gritted his teeth as his tired hands struggled to clench down on the surface. The hatch was hammered again and again. The handle almost sighed as the pressure fell away beneath it and it fell lower through its travel.

'Yes!' Danny screamed as he began to pump wildly again. As if in realisation of his near success, the creatures pushed harder and more rapidly against the door.

'We need to leave now!' Stathis screamed, as the steel hinges groaned again and more creatures fought to burst through.

'I just… need to…. pressure.' Danny was exhausted; he couldn't talk and pump at the same time any more. He drove the handle up and down, rapidly at first as the low pressure allowed but he slowed much faster this final time and the pressure rose slower than ever.

'We need to leave!' Stathis yelled again as a heavy crack ran up the crate that held the door shut. 'We don't have the time, we need to go.'

'Need…' Danny sucked air into his lungs as a bead of sweat ran down the bridge of his nose. He stole a glance at the pressure gauge, fifty per cent. *Only a few more*, he thought as he pumped a few more times. *Only a few more*. He lifted the handle again and screamed along with his arms, his legs, his back and his neck as he brought the handle down for the final time.

As if in answer, the hatch burst open.

Danny stood frozen as the monsters piled through the door toward him. The screams of what sounded like a thousand of them ripped through his ears as each fought to claw its way above the one in front, to get to him. Their shoulders slammed into the frame of the door, as they all tried to force their way through. They pushed and bounced into each other as some fell, only to be trampled by the surging horde they were no longer a part of.

The heavy weapon that Stathis grasped ripped into a continuous motion of fire that buffeted at the tumult, but failed to drown it out. Danny watched as the ones in front were cut down mid-stride, consumed by the mass that washed forth.

Four fell, then another five, as the heavy weapon hammered into them again and again but they just kept coming. They spread out and upward. They leapt onto the surge tank, they bounded over the crates, they leapt up to the ceiling, and still they fell under the withering fire of the heavy weaponry.

Danny leant forward and grasped his own weapon as the gap between him and the horde vanished. He saw one creature, a single soul in the moving mass of death, leap at him. He saw the life, the hatred, the want to kill and devour in its eyes, overflowing from the yellow slits on its face. And then it was gone, washed away to nothing, poured out like water on the ground in an instant, as the heavy thunder clapped as if to flip a switch.

Danny broke and finally, ran for his life.

As he neared the stairs, the heavy thundering above his stopped and the world was drowned in the horrendous screams and primal cries of the mass that remained. He raised his head as he climbed and saw that Paul was gone. The creatures had begun to climb the railings and some were already above him. Danny lowered his head and charged forward. His feet rung off each step while the monsters crashed into the walls behind him and flowed over themselves to get to him. He climbed one flight and then turned back to face the next.

One clung to the railing of the landing above him. Its lower jaw parted in a scream as he rushed towards it. He centred the muzzle of his weapon and squeezed a burst off as he rose. The creature's head exploded in a flurry of red mist and grit and its body fell back over the edge, down into the masses. Danny took the last flight and faced the final landing, where Paul had stood.

Two of them leapt up before him and rushed through the door in pursuit of Stathis. Another leapt up behind them and screamed as Danny raked the muzzle of his weapon across its chest in a bloody ripple of fire and metal.

Below the top landing was a mess. Creatures clung to almost every part of the damned ship. They moved so quickly it was hard to see how many there actually were. They flowed over each other, up the stairs behind him, up the railings, up the walls. He burst through the bulkhead, knowing that he couldn't stop to seal them in. His feet hammered the floor as he sprinted for his life to the engine room, to end this horror.

In front of him, the two that had vanished ahead in chase of Stathis, screamed as they fought to push past a partly closed hatch. They roared as they thrashed against the door. Beyond them he saw the white steel move back under their power and then recoil hard against them. Paul was just behind the door, fighting to hold them back.

As Danny ran, he centred the muzzle of his weapon and fired a continuous stream of lead at them. He yelled as he fired, streams of sparks ripping over the walls to either side as the muzzle swayed in his pace. Blood burst from holes punched through their backs. Metal whined as ricochets bounced from wall to door, and Danny even heard the scream of a bullet as it whistled back past his ear.

The creatures collapsed forward as the fire trapped them against its source and the door. Danny watched in his place as the door fell open and the creatures fell in a heap in the doorway. Above them, Stathis continued to run down the hall, the brown pipe that had led them here a beacon of hope above his head. He leapt over the corpses and continued his pace as Stathis ran an awkward waddle with the heavy weapon still in his hands.

Danny's breath became heavier in his chest the further he ran, a hot fire that spread down to his guts and burnt a blistering iron into his side. He dropped the weapon and heard it clatter to the ground behind him as the hallway swelled and broiled closer and closer. He sucked air into his lungs as his pace slowed and slowed. In front of him, he saw three people; they waved at him and encouraged him to hurry up and he thought, 'I've already done this. I've already run away from that monster and I've already made it.' They had fought the beast in the armoury and they had lost Reicher. This time, he didn't think he would make it.

He stole a glance over his shoulder at the brimming horde that pursued him; he saw the leader fall and watched as it was swallowed by the mass that ran over it, the mass that had gained and was only ten metres behind him and closing fast. He couldn't look anymore, almost defeated as the stitch that burnt in his side twisted a hot agony into him. Danny let a hand fall to his side as he tried to suck air, but his body was gassed. He wasn't going to outrun it this time, he wasn't going to make it to the door in time.

A quick study of the faces of those that crowded in the doorway told him that they knew that as well. Thompson sat and watched. His hand on the edge of the door, a frown on his face. Carmichael waved at him frantically, his eyes wide with fear at what he saw. Stathis, on the other hand, was moving. He was standing, and heading through the doorway toward him. Danny almost couldn't believe what he was seeing. Stathis held his weapon out before him with a handle that sat above its fore-end. He strode forward away from the door and shrugged off Thompson who tried to hold him back.

The sounds all seemed washed out by the roar that rose up behind him and the movements seemed to happen slow. He glanced at Paul as he passed and the two exchanged a glance in the final moment. The smile that was on the hard man's face was a sad one, but kind. Then the heavy rattle sprang into life as the weapon at his side set into motion. Danny burst through the bulkhead and gasped for air as he spun around.

The corridor was yellow fire in front of Stathis. The reports hammered back at them, as if amplified by the steel surroundings. The sight beyond the man was horrible, floor to ceiling filled by the creatures as they broiled over each other to get at him. The ones in front fell under the power of his fire, but more and more and more seemed to come.

Stathis laid down a continuous stream, it never faltered, it never failed. As Thompson and Carmichael pushed the hatch closed, and Danny moved to get a final look, he saw the creatures run Stathis down. His body twisted as he fell and the weapon tilted up as the fire from its barrel shot out. Then they were over him and still surging as the heavy reports fell silent, drowned out finally by the screams and death cries. Drowned out, as the hatch closed and even those sounds became muffled and washed out behind the layers and safety of the thick, impenetrable steel.

44

THE HATCH THUMPED against its solid frame, while Thompson and Carmichael struggled to close the dog-wheel. All Danny could do was sit there and look at the place where Stathis had been. His mouth hung open in his disbelief as the writhing horde slammed into the door. He heard their movements as if through a body of water. Drowned, watery and distant as they pushed and battered themselves against the heavy steel. Their frantic and urgent cries, as they roared their frustration and beat out their utter need to kill. Danny closed his eyes, but even behind the lids of darkness that shrouded him, he could still see the yellow slits burning into him. He could see the way they piled over Stathis, as if he wasn't even there.

Thompson and Carmichael likewise stood at the door, as if helpless to know what to do without Reicher or Stathis. With the two hard men gone, this left Thompson in charge. But Thompson was like Danny, a tradesman, not military-bred; he was an electrical engineer. Carmichael on the other hand, struggled to fit into either of these categories. The young man's hand trembled as he collected his Japanese rifle from the wall where he had leant it. The old webbing clattered against the timber stock as the tremor in his hand transferred down the fabric. With the rifle in both hands, he let out a breath that threatened to take his soul with it, as it rattled with his dismay.

'What…' he tried. 'What do we do now?' The youngest of the three stammered.

Thompson let his chin rest against his chest as he walked away. He didn't say a word as he took his short steps away from them.

'Thompson?' Carmichael sobbed, wiping away a line of snot from his upper lip. 'What do we do now?'

Thompson swayed heavily with each step that he took.

'Thompson? Thomps–'

'I don't fucking know!' he snapped as he whipped his heard around in a snarl that was reminiscent of the creatures they had just locked out. 'Just give me a minute to think.'

Carmichael recoiled at the outburst and walked off out of view behind the towering engine. Danny followed him with his eyes while he remained on his ass before the bulkhead. The thrashing of the creatures on the other side still continued, but the ferocity had died down somewhat since they had lost sight of their prey. As Carmichael disappeared behind the large iron block, Danny's eyes remained on the plant. He thought about his ice queen, and his four kings. He thought about the dreams.

He frowned as he clambered to his feet. Gritting his teeth, he ran a hand through the stubble on his chin and purposefully strode to the pump housing.

Thompson had sealed off the new hose and the smell of diesel was heavy in the air. Danny saw the puddle that had grown beneath the housing as he came about the block, an unavoidable occurrence when bleeding happened, as the air rushed out, sometimes it brought fluid with it as well but the puddle was too big for that. He wondered how many pumps had been wasted on Thompson's inefficiency. How many seconds more could they have had? How many minutes?

The frown on his face turned from determination to rage in an instant and his teeth strained in his gums as he bit down hard with frustration. For a while he stood there, with his fists clenched and his eyes wide as he glared at Thompson's back. Then his grip relaxed as his own shoulders slumped, as he watched the electrician walk in circles with his face in his hands. *He's beating himself up enough as it is, he doesn't need you to do it for him.* Often people needed an excuse to blame someone, as if it would make everything just that little bit better. He found that when you worked out who that person was, they already felt guilty enough and it didn't matter how much more you put on their shoulders, it didn't change anything, nor did it improve the situation.

Danny sighed as the diesel fumes washed over him and he glanced back to the pump housing. As he turned, something fell from the pump and pattered gently on the floor at his feet. His eyebrows furrowed as he looked down to see what it was but all that lay below him was the puddle of diesel. Danny watched the pump housing as a small bead of diesel grew while it trembled. It gathered its mass beneath the connection from the rubber hose to the pump hosing. It gathered and gathered until it was too heavy to support its own weight, and came crashing down to add to the mess at his feet.

Thompson may have changed the hose, but that didn't change the fact that the new hose was just as old as the first.

We were lucky it even held the pressure, he admitted deep down below. What they needed to do was start the engine, before all that was left of the pressure they had built was a puddle on the ground.

They had power, now they had the fuel. It was time to kick her in the guts and see if she would start. Danny's eyes went to the twin starters and he examined the cabling. Thompson had already repaired it. He saw the new shielding around the heavy gauged wire and saw the scraps of the old shit down on the ground below. All he needed to do now was to follow the small actuator to the switch so he could try.

He left Thompson to worry in the palms of his hands and Carmichael, wherever he had gone. He moved to the stairwell and sighed as he started to climb it. Three switched back landings, just as there had been in the room that had held the surge tank. Each step echoed in the vastness of the engine room yet no-one called out to him. He peered down at Thompson before he turned and climbed the second. The electrician still walked in circles with his face in his hands.

Danny climbed the second set. The engine rose up from the ground before him. It was an absolute monster. Part of him was a little excited as he had never seen an engine this large run before.

As he climbed the flight, he took in things about its design that he had never seen before. Unlike anything else he had worked on, the timing chain sat on the outside on the main block. The links were almost as thick as his arm and they stretched way up from the crank sprocket to the cam shaft which sat to the side of the block, a design which somewhat reminded him of a slant six. The sprockets sat dormant while the chain still hung taut after all these years.

The third flight of stairs stood before him and Danny saw the small control box. 'Fuck, this has to work,' he said to himself as he climbed them. 'This has to be it. I have to get out of here.' A chill ran up his spine, as the words left his mouth and he reminded himself of Charlie. But it was true, he looked to his feet as he climbed the last few steps and he repeated the words that had chilled him. 'I have to get out of here.'

The control box was smaller than he thought it would be, but he figured there wasn't much to control. A small board was fixed to a box section and on it were a few levers and buttons. To its side were more levers that stood upright from the ground, large and heavy to pull the linkages and cables that they operated. Danny had no doubt that the large levers operated the transmission and the clutch. They reminded him instantly of the retarding lever on the old generators that presumably still ran, given that they had light.

He ran his fingers over the buttons that sat beneath the Japanese markings that held no meaning to him. His hands hovered over them for some time as he thought about what they and the levers meant. If he tried to start the motor while the clutch was engaged, then not only would the starters need to crank the motor, but the transmission and prop shaft as well. He moved to the three levers, and inspected the symbols that sat before each of them.

There were lines marked before each lever, showing the path that they took and what each marker represented. None of it made any sense. The first lever had three positions, each of them marked out with a character that was barely recognisable under a layer of ice that had formed over it.

The second lever only had two positions; their markings were much the same. The final lever didn't seem to have any marked position, there was just a line that became thicker the further it rose from the bottom.

He ran his hand through the stubble on his chin while he thought about it. One of them was a clutch, he figured that much. The other, probably controlled the direction in which the transmission turned the prop, while the other could have been anything. He bit his lip as he scratched at the ice that sat on the characters that were etched next to the first lever, as if that would help him read Japanese. He ran his fingernail over the crumbling surface and a large chunk popped loose. He pushed it away and noticed something below it. A line was further etched along the side of the middle symbol; he rubbed his palm over it to clear it up. A yellow circle sat next to the middle symbol of the first lever.

He frowned as he considered it, then moved on to the second lever and its symbols. Without removing any ice, he could see the yellow circle next to the lower symbol. He reached out with his hand, and grasped the handle of the first lever. He squeezed the grip to allow it to move and pushed it all the way forward. At first it groaned as the old steel resisted his movement, but after a while it shifted and went with his hand. He felt linkages pull and shift with him as the lever moved up and hitched in one position. Danny repositioned himself and pushed again and the lever went with him and then finally stopped at the end of its travel.

'Ok,' he said to himself. 'That's all the way forward, now let's move back one.' He squeezed the handle again and shifted the lever back to its centre position. To his left, beneath a layer of ice, two small amber lights glowed on the control panel.

Danny moved to the second lever and clutched the handle, squeezing as he pushed it forward and the linkages groaned beneath him. A low thump sounded below him as the lever stopped and Danny saw that both of the lights had turned off. A frown spread across his face as he tapped the lights and broke away the ice that had formed. Characters sat above each of them, none of them meant anything to him but he didn't like how the lights had disappeared; that didn't feel like a good thing.

Danny moved back to the first handle and tried to pull it back, but it wouldn't move. Instead, he pushed hard and tried to move it forward but it resisted him, as if it was blocked by something. He considered the second lever and nodded. 'So,' he said as he moved back. 'You're the clutch.'

He gripped the handle and squeezed the gate lifter as he shifted it back. The linkages groaned and something sighed as he moved the lever. Over to his left, two amber lights shone once more.

'Ok,' he muttered as he moved over to the third. 'Third one's the charm.' He clutched the lever and squeezed the gate. Up and up and up, he shifted the lever until it stopped. Nothing. He frowned as he released the gate and scratched at his head. He squeezed the gate again and brought it slowly back toward him. All the way, slow and steady, but still no light. He examined the line, saw how it thickened the further it went away from him. He was reminded of his old Victa lawn mower and thought all the picture was missing was the turtle and the rabbit. 'Fuck it,' he muttered as he squeezed the gate again and pushed it all the way.

He moved over the control panel, and stared intensely at the lights. He pointed at the first, and shook his head. 'Neutral safety?' he questioned, as he focused on the second. 'Maybe the clutch for the alternator?' He scratched at his head. 'Fuck.' He looked at the only two buttons that existed on the panel; there were two starters and he figured one button for each.

'Here goes nothing,' he muttered as he pushed them both at once.

The room was filled with the hum of electricity and the smell of diesel as the massive plant turned over. It didn't happen so ferociously as a car's engine; the first starter spooled slowly, bringing the massive plant to speed but the second tripped and clacked like it was shorting.

Danny frowned as he looked down and saw the chain rotate. The heavy sprockets shifted slowly as the plant turned over inch by inch. He thought he could hear something and he squinted as he scanned the immense room. Whatever it was, wasn't mechanical. It came again and again, and he looked away from the slowly rotating chain, down to the starter side. Thompson stood there, waving his arms. His eyes were wide and he mouthed something that looked like *hop* or *top*.

Stop! his mind confirmed and he released the buttons. Instantly the hum reverted and whined back slowly as the chain slowed to a crawl and then finally came to a halt. The room smelt of oil and the hiss of air sounded in pipes as one of the massive cylinders vented itself into exhaust.

'Stop, you idiot.' Thompson roared up and Danny turned to him. 'You don't know how these starters work; you might have broken them.'

'Well, tell me then!' he shouted back.

Thompson looked back over his shoulder as the commotion on the other side of the bulkhead sparked up again. Danny heard the clanks and shudders as limbs were thrown against the heavy steel. The electrician shuddered as he walked over to the starters. 'They aren't geared the same, so don't try and run both together.'

Danny stared blankly down at Thompson as he recalled the first thought he'd had about the starters. With everything that had happened, he had forgotten all about the possibility that they could have been geared differently.

Thompson pointed at them, not that Danny could see from his position. 'The gears that engage to the fly wheel are different sizes.' He shifted closer and pointed again. 'The bottom one is to get it moving, then use the top one to pick up the pace.'

'How do you work that out?' Danny shouted back down, after he considered both of the buttons.

Thompson gave him a withering look. 'Do you want to try it or do you want to come down here and argue?'

A heavy thud came from the hatch and both men glanced at it.

Danny decided it was time to give it a go and pushed the left button first. As soon as he did, Thompson held up his hand in a stop motion and Danny released it. The motor whined and clacked twice before he let up on it and then it spooled back down to nothing again. Thompson glared up at him and Danny smiled. 'Sorry, wrong one.'

He moved his finger over the second button and pressed it. Once again, the motor turned over, the electrical hum filled the room and the chain began to spin. Slow at first, but then it picked up speed and settled in it. Danny watched Thompson and saw the electrician wave at him. Danny sighed and pressed the second button.

The humming became more intense. The rotation of the chain picked up its pace and the motor began to whine. He released the first button and the speed increased even further. The hum climbed and climbed, and Danny's ears began to ring.

'Come on you big bitch,' he said as he pushed down harder on the crank button, as if that did anything. 'Start, you big fucker.'

The chain turned and turned and turned and then the room shook as the motor fired. The platform rumbled with the vibration and the chain's links became a single stream of steel and iron. The engine chuffed and sighed as the exhaust vented but before even that sound finished it chuffed and chuffed again. The block trembled with its own power as the tappet knocking and the sighs of venting exhaust came quicker and quicker.

Thompson held up his hands in his stop motion again and Danny released the button, but the motor didn't slow. The electrical hum peaked and then subsided to nothing beneath the whir of the timing chain and the racket of its tappets. Then, a smile came over Thompson's face as he threw his arms up in the air. He opened his mouth and it looked as though he was screaming but Danny couldn't hear a damned thing under the racket of the main engine as it revved hard for the first time in seventy odd years.

45

DANNY'S THOUGHTS WERE SWALLOWED by the rumble of the diesel and for some time, he stood there with a soft smile on his face while he watched the rotation of the timing sprocket as the giant turned over and over. It was as if the ship trembled in its elation, as the ancient plant surged on its mounts. The rails for the stairway noticeably vibrated on their pedestals. The walls rippled gently against their rivets and even under his boots Danny felt the ticks and murmurs that any old engine had. He felt it within himself and he heard it inside of his head, like it was the ship's own heart that tremored on every second beat.

As the motor cranked over, the air started to change and for the first time since he had boarded the ship, he had forgotten how cold he was. The motor chuffed as exhaust was vented and the diesel rattled as its revs continued to climb. Danny moved to the levers; he stepped past the first two and squeezed the gate on the third. As he pulled the lever toward him, the racket seemed to purge from the engine and the motor slowed its rotations. As the sprocket spun, slower and slower, the noise that had buffeted his ears dissipated with it. Danny shifted the lever slowly toward himself and stopped it three quarters of the way down.

The heavy sprocket pushed through the air as it whirred around; it seemed seconds could pass between each rotation of the heavy chain, timed with the chuff of the exhaust release and the incessant hammering of the tappets. Danny snapped his head around as he noticed something and saw that Thompson had climbed the stairs to his left. The electrician stood at the top of the stairwell, noticeably excited. He moved his mouth, but his words were washed away by the roaring air that bristled as the sprocket spun.

Danny shook his head and leant a little closer to him. He flinched when Thompson slapped him on the back and then smiled when he leant in to congratulate him.

'Not hard to work on well-built gear!' he yelled back and Thompson nodded with a vacant expression on his face, making it obvious that he hadn't heard what Danny had said. Danny returned the nod and moved back to the levers. A frown came over his face as he searched around the controls for any communication devices; there were things that could have been used but he wasn't sure. The more he looked the more the worry must have spread over his face, because it wasn't long before he felt Thompson's hand settle on his shoulder again.

He considered the electrician and the expression on his face was that of concern. Danny cupped his hands around his mouth as Thompson leant in.

'We need to be able to communicate!' he roared into Thompson's ear. The electrician turned and looked at him with a puzzled expression and Danny sighed when he figured that he would have to elaborate. Once more he cupped his hands around his mouth and moved closer to Thompson's ear.

'The motor and transmission are controlled through this panel,' he pointed to the levers. 'The ship is steered from up on the bridge. Whoever goes up needs to be able to communicate to whoever stays down here.' This time when Thompson pulled away, his expression was gaunt and serious. He wasn't sure on the electrician's own thought process, but he was pretty confident on his own and there was no fucking way Danny was going to stay down in this hell for any second that he didn't have to. His part of the bargain was done.

Thompson cupped his hands around his mouth and leant in. 'Teach me the controls,' he roared into Danny's ear. Danny watched Carmichael as the young man looked up at the engine, his Japanese war rifle slung over his shoulder. Danny gestured down to the young man, but Thompson shook his head. He leant in close again and raised his voice. 'He's just a kid, take him up. Just do me a favour and help steer the ship until Rheinmarsh can get a few other guys on board to help.'

Once he was finished speaking, he stepped back to see Danny's reaction. He looked tired, as if he had aged a decade in the past fifteen minutes. Danny nodded and dropped his eyes to the controls again and shook his head. 'We still need to be able to talk to each other.'

Thompson waved away the words. 'That I can get around. Show me the controls.'

Danny shrugged as he moved over to the controls and thought about the best way to explain it. He figured the man had driven a car before and basically, this was the same thing, the only thing you didn't have to worry about on a ship was a brake pedal. He pointed to the third lever, the one on the far right. He faced Thompson and held both of his fists out, as if he stood on a bike. He rotated his wrist back on his right hand a few times, in an imaginary rev. Thompson's eyebrows furrowed for a second and then he pointed to his right foot.

Danny looked down at his boot, then back up to Thompson's face. 'What is this idiot talking about?' He said it aloud but low enough so the other man couldn't hear. Thompson held both of his fists out in the same manner Danny had. He twisted his right wrist back twice, then pointed to his foot and tapped it on the floor twice. Danny shook his head.

Thompson's shoulders slumped and his eyes rolled. He leant in close and yelled a single word into his ear. 'Throttle.'

Danny nodded, he pointed at his boot, tapped it twice and shrugged. The anger flared in the electrician's brow and he leant in. 'Fucking accelerator pedal in a fucking car. Forget charades, just tell me.'

Danny had to laugh at his own stupidity. He pointed back to the third lever and raised his eyebrows. He offered Thompson a thumbs up and the electrician nodded. He moved to the second lever, and pointed at the three stages of the gate. Thompson followed his finger and furrowed his eyebrows. Danny leant in close. 'Transmission, forward, neutral, reverse.'

Thompson nodded and then his eyebrows furrowed as he leant in close again. 'Is forward up or down?' Danny shrugged. 'Is neutral in the middle?' At this Danny nodded, and he thought about telling him about the neutral safety light but figured it didn't matter.

He came to the final lever, the one on the far left. He emphasised again the gate path on the side, how there were only two positions. He leant in close and yelled the word into Thompson's ear. 'Clutch.'

Thompson nodded a slow and over exaggerated sign of understanding. Danny frowned as he studied the controls for a final time. 'Fuck it,' he said aloud again. 'Not my problem anymore.'

Danny noticed the air had started to smell of oil and soot, a smell he was used to but not in enclosed spaces. The engine had only been running for a matter of minutes and already he could taste the exhaust on his tongue. After an hour or so the smell in here would be overwhelming, but he figured the trade-off was that it would be warm. Already the massive block had a hint of heat sync and warmth had started to radiate out from its massive core. The more the engine idled the hotter it would become, the thinner its oil would get and then he figured the shit would really hit the fan in here.

Danny moved beyond Thompson and started down the stairs. He was ready to get out of here but he stopped and turned back. He closed his right fist and stuck out his thumb and pinkie, he held it to his ear like a phone and this time there was no confusion in his mime. Thompson nodded and pointed down at the backpack that they had collected from the original mechanic. He then pushed past Danny and led the way there.

Carmichael moved over to them as Thompson unzipped the main pocket and began to rummage through the bits and pieces. Danny considered the young man and thought that he had only really noticed just how young he was. The kid couldn't have been much more than seventeen years old. The stubble on his face could barely be called that, more the fuzz that you found on peach. Danny frowned as something patted against his chest and he looked down as he caught it.

Thompson had slapped a radio in his hand. Danny held it in his open palms and when he looked back up to Thompson, the man had a set of earmuffs on. A single wire ran down his left shoulder to his belt, where another radio was hooked. The electrician pushed a stick microphone down to sit in front of his mouth, and played with its angle for a second before he considered Danny and offered him a wink. Carmichael's eyes went from Danny to Thompson; it was easy to see that the poor boy was confused.

Danny held his hand out and Thompson shook it. A frown creased his lips once more as he released his grip and placed a hand on Carmichael's shoulder.

Carmichael's brow was furrowed as Danny turned him away from Thompson but the young man offered no resistance. They walked together across the floor of the engine room, the place it had seemed to take eternity to find. Thompson followed them as they went and not a man of them spoke a single word. When they reached the hatch, Danny was the one to open it, but Thompson stood close by with Peters' ZKK in his hands. As the hatch-wheel released and Danny was able to open the door, Thompson raised the rifle in preparation for an attack, but one never came. With the lights now on, they didn't have to worry about flashlights, and it took only quick glances to see that the corridors were empty.

Although the air in the corridor was stale and old, it smelt like a fresh summer breeze in comparison to the heavy oil and exhaust that had started to fill the engine room. Danny stepped into the corridor and Carmichael followed him. When Danny turned back, the bulk head was already closing behind them and Carmichael shouted out. Danny put his hands on his shoulders and pulled him away as the heavy steel closed against its frame and Thompson sealed the dog-wheel, barring himself inside.

As the door closed, the immense racket from the engine almost ceased entirely. It took a few moments for Danny's ears to adjust and he didn't want to move until his hearing had settled – after all they weren't out of danger yet, far from it. Carmichael on the other hand, moved straight back to the hatch wheel and tried to reopen it.

'Hey,' Danny tried to whisper and failed. 'Leave him, man.'

Carmichael's face had turned red with the effort he was putting into the hatch-wheel. 'Can't,' was the only word that hissed between his gritted teeth.

'We need him to run the transmission and operate the throttle from down here.' He held up the radio. 'Don't worry. We will still be able to contact him.'

Carmichael offered the hatch-wheel one last distinct push, before he gave up on it. He panted as he rested his head against the door. 'I don't like the idea of splitting up, especially with those fucking things down here.'

'I know man,' Danny said as he scanned their surroundings. He didn't like standing where they were; it hadn't been long since they had closed the door on Stathis, and surely there were other corridors which would loop them back to that place. 'Come on,' he finally managed in a whisper. 'We need to get out of here and get top side again.'

Beneath the hum and clatter of the monstrous plant, it was impossible to hear much movement on the lower decks. Danny figured that this could work in their favour if they happened to make any noise, but they remained vigilant.

They moved in silence until Danny shivered as he walked under those fleshy vines and he saw Carmichael swallow as he eyed them. His mouth went dry as he thought about that thing, and he lowered his head to move on below it. Thankful for the vibration and the low hum, Danny moved quickly while his steps were drowned out. But as soon as they found the stairwell that led them back up to where the bodies of Peters and the mechanic lay, the world subsided into silence once more.

Seeing the corridors they'd crept down in full light was a different concern. The darkness may have concealed the creatures that had ambushed them lower in the vessel, but it also concealed the horrors that were spread throughout the lower deck. Things that in the past were only suggestions in the faint flashlight pencil beams, were now unveiled in their full grotesque appearance.

Blood that had aged and gone black with time sat beneath a frozen layer in puddles on the ground. In places it had been smeared across the walls and even over the ceiling, staining them a colour so dark that if it had any odour then Danny would have thought it to be shit. Bones scattered certain areas, sometimes they were even left in small piles where a creature had feasted on one of its old crew members. Strands of rotted fabric that had torn during the carnage that Jin Ishimura had described, hung loose from rivet heads and swayed gently as they passed.

The sight of Peters' body was the worst. His flesh had gone pallid in the cold and his blood had become a thick slurry. Danny could smell him; the shit in his pants, the piss that had run down his legs, and the horrid gas from his guts that had been nicked when the creature's forearm had driven through his abdomen. Danny held his hand over his mouth as he struggled to get past without stepping either in the mess or one of the men. His stomach rolled and he felt cold again, as he moved to put them behind him.

They climbed another set of stairs, where new horrors awaited them. The corridor where the mechanic had lost his mind came and went. Danny didn't even offer it a glance, he didn't think he could handle it. The one thing that had come to his mind, shortly after they had crossed Kee Peters body, were the heavy footstep that had echoed from above them when he had dropped the backpack. He then thought about the thick-backed monstrosity that had filled the corridor to his rear when they had tried to find the path down. He had no wish to face any other monster; he had seen enough, he had done enough.

On and on they moved. The air became warmer by the minute and Danny thought for a second that he even heard the lap of a wave against the hull. Still, they walked in corridors of endless steel and old pulsating light until he was sure that they were close. Danny came around another corner and saw a set of stairs. He sighed as he started to climb them but paused halfway up.

'What?' Carmichael whispered behind him as he stopped short of running up Danny's ass.

'Look at the walls,' he said softly as he raised his hand to point. The light from the pallid globes seemed washed out on the walls in front of him. The brightness was still there but the light seemed fuller, more natural. Danny took the steps two at time as he climbed; he was so close he could feel it, he couldn't care less about the creature now.

He breathed in heavily through his nose and smelt the freshness of the air. He rounded the corridor at the top of the flight of stairs at a jog and didn't care how much noise he made. Beneath his heavy footfalls and the rush of his breath, he heard the ocean and he could almost feel the sun. Then he heard Carmichael's footfalls and something else. The ghost of his smile vanished as the frown spread across his lips.

He heard the water erupt as something heavy fell into it. His brow furrowed as he took another step forward and another and finally, he stepped onto the deck of the *Nisshin Maru* and into the light. He jumped as something exploded next to the ship and sent a tower of water up into the air as the deck shuddered beneath his feet. Steel groaned as ice splintered and water hammered down on the deck. And somewhere, deep inside of himself, he heard the voice, he heard the tremor, he heard its triumph.

'I am free.'

46

THE DECK ROCKED BENEATH HIM as water rocketed up into the air. The blast had hit just between where the ship had sat up against Amery. Danny felt himself lose his balance and soon the deck rushed up to meet him as he fell to his side. Light exploded in his head as his skull slammed against the steel and his eyes rolled around in their sockets. Water churned around the heavy steel of the hull and Danny looked up as the ship listed away from the ice shelf, finally detached from the thing that had pinned it there.

He watched, almost stunned, as water and chunks of ice splattered over the vast mid-section of the *Nisshin Maru* and then settled back to nothing. Before him, a dark line ran up the ice shelf's face and a thunderous crack rippled across the water, hit the cold face of D-28 and ran back to him. The sound was ice buckling under heavy, heavy weight. Jagged lines ran up the face, just the way Danny had seen cracks run along a windscreen flat. The course of it seemed to have a mind of its own, the way it jigged left and doubled back and down to the right. Off shoots ran like burst veins further up and the wall itself seemed to shudder as it detached. Then, with a horrible sound of rushing water, crumbling ice and a snap as if a tree's limb had given way, the face fell down onto them.

He watched as chunks the size of warehouses tumbled forward. Like a man that had finally made the decision to jump and end his own life, they tilted forward and fell end over end soundlessly until they crashed onto a jutted section of ice below and shattered into a thousand pieces, hitting like enormous buckshot into the depths. Danny watched helplessly as the remains of the dig site were thrown over the edge and cast shadows above them. He tried to move but his legs seemed like they didn't belong to him anymore. His mouth fell slack as he stared at his coming doom like a deer in the lights of an oncoming car. All he could do was hold his hand up before him, as if to shield his eyes from a bright light.

Someone grabbed and pulled at him. His eyebrows furrowed as he was pulled to his feet and his first impression was that it was the creatures that got him. Danny opened his mouth to scream but nothing came out but for a wheeze of surprise.

'Come on man, we need to move.' The voice sounded in his ears as he was dragged away from the hatch and up a set of stairs. Danny felt his heels rap against the steps as he was dragged from behind. The man's arms were looped under his armpits while his arms hung hopelessly by his side. There was nothing he could do but watch as the carnage erupted behind him, as he was dragged to the side of the forward apartments and into the safety of the shadow they cast below.

Water ripped upward as ice smashed down into it. Steel groaned and screamed as the hard ice broke upon it and scattered across the deck into small pebbles that rolled and slid in all angles. The darkness came. Everything above them was tumbling ice and falling death. The sound as it hit was rain on tin rooves, it was machine gun fire into heavy steel, it was the crumple of metal, it was the crashing of the wave.

Danny's back hit the foredeck as the man let him fall. Again his head rapped against the steel beneath it and pain shot down his neck into his shoulders. A groan escaped him as he closed his eyes and rolled onto his side and his ears began to ring, sending him into a swirling silence. He expected to feel the weight of the water crash down on him, the cold penetrate into him as the ship was taken down, but it never came, it never came.

Instead, he opened his eyes and saw sunlight. Danny rolled onto his stomach as the world continued to swirl. Then, as he placed both of his hands to the deck before him, it began to steady, and as he rose his hearing came back to him. The water rushed off the decks and back to the ocean, and the hull thrashed in the choppy waters as the ship found its balance and settled itself again. Danny looked to the man that had saved him, the young face, the peach fuzz that seemed to stand out from his cheek in the natural light.

'Thank you,' Danny said in a soft voice to Carmichael. He took an unsteady step. The young man held his hands out, but Danny waved him away. 'You've done enough.' He panted as if he was out of breath. 'We need to get up to the bridge,' he managed to say as he took another step and then another, until finally his hands closed on the railing of the stairwell. The same one he'd climbed with Jonty and Charlie, all that time ago.

As he began to climb, he felt Carmichael's hand fall onto his back and he welcomed the support. Each step seemed to drain more and more out of him, but at least he knew the ship wasn't sinking. He felt the way it rolled about, the ease in which it handled the waves, and he knew it was fine, but with each step he took, he was taken further back toward the end of the apartments and he saw the carnage the crumbling ice had wrought. The rear apartments had been torn to shreds in the collapse. Half of it was gone, and that which remained exposed rooms that had not seen the light for seventy years. Scraps of furniture lay twisted on the edge, an inch away from falling from their perch. Rags that had once been curtains or bed sheets twisted in the winds and beat their agony as they were torn to shreds by the jagged steel they clung to.

Down below, the mid-section had suffered some damage but little in comparison to the higher points. Ice still littered the decks, but most of it had broken on the steel and pushed off the other side to plunge further into the water. The most notable damage was the destruction of the midway H frame, which had once stood proud in the air. Now it hung, almost detached, to the portside as it wavered out above the water.

As Danny reached the landing, he paused to take a breath and looked out over the carnage. The steam from his lungs beat at his eyes and

Danny squinted against it, his attention drawn to a flashing light. He lowered his head and he leant on the railing at the landing's edge. He had never seen flashing lights on this ship before, but who knew what he would see now that the power had been restored. He pointed at it and called to Carmichael. 'What the hell is that?'

The young man joined him at the railing's edge and held a hand against his brow to cut the glare. 'It's a dish or something,' he said, uninterested.

Danny frowned as he squinted and copied Carmichael's gesture. The dish was attached to a large clump of ice that had crashed onto the deck of the ship. It was mangled by an impact, but still the light that sat to its side flashed with a steady motion, as it had next to the site tent on the top of the shelf. The letters that represented its company's name stood proud against the darkness of its surface. R.A.G.E. Danny laughed as he worked out what it was. The cellular transmitter had survived the fall. If it was like everything else that bloody company had made, he was not surprised in the slightest.

He continued up the flight of stairs, pulling more with his arm than lifting with his legs as he swayed with the motion of ship. The next landing came easier and as he moved to the hatch that still remained open, his legs felt firm beneath him. His stomach wrenched as he stepped inside the upper apartments, but this time there was no darkness and nothing to fear. The hallway was lit by two overhead globes that sat behind their cage of steel, but the artificial light was washed out and almost eradicated by the light that poured through the doorway to the bridge itself.

As Danny stepped into the room where Jin Ishimura now lay crumpled in an awkward frozen lump on the floor, he saw that all the glass that had once been frozen over and had shielded the room from the outside light, had shattered against a spray of falling ice. Nothing stood between the bridge and the outside world, but a few strips of steel where the glass had been framed.

Danny's breath shuddered in his chest as he tried to ease it out, but from where he stood, he gazed out across the ocean and back at the place where the ship had once been pinned.

The face of the Amery Ice Shelf had once again been changed. Tonnes upon tonnes of ice had fallen down, cracked and shattered by the explosion that he still couldn't explain. Just beyond where he thought the ship had once been, a section of ice was discoloured against the rest. Rather than a grey of white, this seemed blue, and as Danny watched its shade seemed to change by the second.

An air horn sounded in the distance, and the roll of its blast made Danny jump. His heart hammered in his chest and he looked to his left and saw the *Baroness*, in all of her glory. All at once, Danny felt as though it was over, as though at any minute he would be taken from the ship and allowed to go back to Mawson where he could be safe. He thought about Anne Castelli, about Wendy and Craig. Most of all, he thought about Gary, his mate. How good it would be to see them again.

'Carmichael,' he said with a new found excitement. 'Help me find the horn.'

'Yeah,' the young man agreed, even he struggled to contain himself.

Together they searched, and thankfully the ship being as old as it was, it didn't take long to notice the looped chain that hung from a section of ceiling. Being a truck mechanic, Danny was instantly drawn to it by the familiarity of the vehicles he knew so well. It felt comfortable in his hand and the sound that seemed to erupt from nowhere and everywhere felt so damned good that he had to laugh. The air horn was deep and solid. In comparison to the trucks that he was accustomed to, the *Nisshin Maru*'s bellow was ancient and stalwart. He let it roar across the waters for a few seconds and silenced it as he raised the radio to his lips.

'You alive, Thompson?' he asked as a child's smile lit up his face.

The response came back quicker than he thought it would. 'Yeah, fuck.' The poor bastard sounded panicked out of his mind. Behind his voice, the racket of the engine was audible besides some other clanging and commotion. 'What is happening up there?'

'Never mind, you ready to get us moving?'

'Yeah.' The panic was still in his tone but Danny figured he could wait a little longer.

'Give me forward propulsion, with a quarter speed,' Danny bellowed into the radio again as he began his search for the steering apparatus. Hydraulics were an easy thing for Danny to recognise, and although the units no doubt would have traced their lines all throughout the ship's skeleton, it wasn't hard to see the valve that controlled the steering. The unit was a large, solid block that was bolted to the centre of the bridge. Other units were placed to either side, and somewhere down to the right was the corpse of the creature that had made Danny faint during his first venture inside.

'Myers,' Thompson's voice came back over the radio as Danny placed his hands on the wheel.

He sighed as he plucked the unit from his belt. 'What's up?'

'I'm having trouble engaging the first lever.'

Danny closed his eyes to try and remember what purpose that lever performed.

'Every time I try to push it forward it keeps bouncing back.'

'Sounds like the clutch unit,' Danny muttered before he pressed opened the channel. 'We aren't here to fuck spiders mate. Keep pressure on it and ease it in, it'll be ok.'

He returned the radio to his belt and placed both hands on the wheel. At first, like most other things on the ship, the wheel offered quite a bit of resistance but the more Danny pushed, the more it moved, and soon the hydraulic equaliser turned freely and hummed with the cycle of its fluid.

'First lever engaged.' The radio crackled as Danny wheeled the equaliser to the far ends of its cycle. He peered down at the water's edge, and focused on a point close to the ship's bow. 'Engaging drive now.'

It was hard to tell at first if he had power to the propeller, as the nose of the bow bucked upward and dipped low as it bobbed. But after a while, the point he focused on moved considerably to the right of where the bow was. The nose dipped down and when it came up again it had moved even further. Danny smiled as the *Baroness* let rip with her horn once again and he adjusted the steering to take the *Nisshin Maru* to her side.

'Carmichael,' he said to the young man who stood with his back to him as he watched the *Baroness* churn up the waters in front of him. The young man faced him slowly, his lips spread in a faint smile. 'See if you can find a way to communicate with them. I need to keep this line open with Thompson.'

'Sure,' was the reply as Carmichael moved back around to Danny's side of the control units and leant his rifle up against the console.

The *Baroness* was a good way into the gap where between the D-28 iceberg and what remained of the Amery Ice Shelf. Her nose pointed toward the narrow section, where the ice shelf met the iceberg, so Danny turned the *Nisshin Maru* in the opposite direction. He swung the wheel hard until he heard a soft whine from the hydraulics and he backed it off slightly. Slowly but surely, the ship began to come about and as it went Danny backed off on the rudder so that he didn't have to correct.

'*Baroness, Baroness,* do you read me?' Carmichael's spoke into a microphone that was secured to a console. 'Fuck this thing,' he muttered as he started to play with some knobs.

Danny left him to it as he watched the *Baroness in her movements*. He liked his line and it wouldn't be hard for the *Baroness's* pilot to pull up alongside, provided they were someone that was at least more skilled than Danny at piloting a ship.

'Thompson, you there?' he put over the radio as a triumphant cry escaped Carmichael's mouth.

'Yeah mate.' The sound crackled back. Beneath his voice he heard the clanging and cracking again, but he could also hear the motor and it sounded alright.

'Cut propulsion, just pull the clutch, that'll be enough,' he said as he frowned.

'I reckon I've–' Carmichael started, but Danny cut him off.

'I need to hear this, just wait,' he said sharply as he held the radio close to his ear.

'Propulsion is cut,' Thompson came back in a pant. Beneath him he heard the hollow clanging and something else that made him shiver.

'What's that sound?' he asked Thompson through the radio.

After a short pause, the electrician came back defeated. 'They've started to break through the bulkhead.' His tone was flat and sorrowful.

Danny hissed through his teeth in his frustration as he gripped the wheel. 'Can you get out?' He asked after giving the question some thought. If Thompson left, there would be no-one to control the ship; if he remained, he would die.

'Nah.' The word was flat and final. 'I've checked all the doors, they're at each one.'

Danny loosened his grip on the mic, then brought it back up. 'We'll come back down–' he started but Thompson cut over him.

'You'll stay there. I'll tell you when you've got your last chance to change your setting and then I'll take a few of these fuckers out. Reicher was a hard bastard, but he was a friend of mine. I owe him that much.'

Danny glanced at Carmichael who had listened to every word of the conversation. 'Any luck?' he prompted him. The young man jumped at the question and returned his attention to his console. Danny raised his mic and depressed the button again. 'Alright,' he said softly. 'Sit tight and keep in touch.'

Thompson came back in the affirmative and signed off. The ship continued to list toward the *Baroness* but the speed was ebbing out of her rapidly. Carmichael took his opportunity in the silence and began to hail the *Baroness* again, however this time, the console clicked before he spoke.

'*Baroness*, do you read me. This is Carmichael.' Nothing at first, just silence. '*Baroness*, this is Carmichael, can you hear me?' Nothing again.

'Is there a switch to operate the mic?' Danny asked him, thinking about his own experience with handheld radios.

'I don't know.' Carmichael started to flick switches.

Danny heard one or two clicks and then a voice came over the speakers that rattled in their bracket as ice and dust fell from their diaphragms.

'You hear me? Come back Whaler.' The accent was Rheinmarsh, of that there was no doubt. 'Sound your horn twice if you can hear me.'

Danny reached up and rapped the horn in two quick bursts. The sounds ripped through the silence and echoed across the water's edge.

'Very good,' Rheinmarsh came back. 'Stay there, Whaler. We will come to you.'

Danny smiled as he leant on the steering apparatus.

Carmichael turned to meet his eyes. 'I think we've done it,' the young man said as he leant against the console. Steam rose from his mouth with each word and Danny had to remind himself that it was still bloody cold where he stood.

'Yeah,' he said as he turned to the *Baroness* again. 'You know it.' They watched as the *Baroness* moved to the point where the ice had continued to darken in its colour. As he followed the progress of the ship, Danny's brow furrowed once more as he wondered why the ice wall had taken damage in that way.

Carmichael continued to talk about how there were times down below that he didn't think that they would get out, but Danny wasn't listening. The words flowed over him but failed to sink in as he watched black lines appear again in the ice wall. This time however, there were no sounds of fracturing ice, there was nothing to offer any warning at all apart from the darkening blue and the black lines of death.

Danny clutched the wheel hard with his left as he brought the radio up to his mouth. The blue line of shade had started to move along the ice wall. It moved directly toward them and turned black where the *Baroness* cruised, like a shadow had fallen over it.

'Thompson. Reverse prop, full speed!' he said the words calm but the panic was already in him.

'What?' The voice came back and when Danny repeated himself, he failed to hold his calm.

'Fucking reverse!' He screamed into the radio. 'Now goddamn it. Now!'

The section of wall where the *Baroness* was had now turned black and water ran from sections in sheets as the ice melted before his eyes. 'Quick, tell them to turn hard starboard.' Danny barked.

Carmichael's eyes had turned white and Danny didn't realise that he hadn't seen what was happening. 'Now, fuck ya!' He screamed at him as the *Nisshin Maru* began to crawl backwards at a glacial pace.

Before Carmichael could get to the console, Rheinmarsh's voice came over the speakers. 'Whaler, hold your position. We will come to you,' he sounded cross but Danny couldn't care less.

'Rheinmarsh,' Carmichael tried. 'Turn hard star—' The rest of his words were lost as his mouth dropped open.

Danny struggled to comprehend what he saw. Ice fell to the water in massive sheets and turned to slush as its captive came forward. The ice parted under its power and its heat, as the water at the surface began to bubble. Up and up and up its body stretched as it continued to push outward from the ice and even from where Danny stood, he had to raise his eyes to look at it.

Taller than the *Nisshin Maru*, and just as broad as the *Baroness*, its body was lined with hard, glistening scales that were the colour of old plate steel. Its snout was rounded and darker than the rest of its body but paled as its face ran back to the many horned fins that stood out from its skull. Its eyes were the worst. They were the eyes that had haunted him in his dreams, the ones that had pretended to be the lamps, the ones that had hovered below him in the depths. Those large amber pits that burnt with hate and desperation.

Danny screamed as its mouth opened and its eyes fell on the *Baroness*.

The roar that followed was one that rippled the water and shuddered the steel against its rivets, as even the air trembled before its might. But it wasn't the roar that Danny couldn't bear, it wasn't even the sight. It was the voice that echoed in his mind, the one that raped him each time it spoke and forced its way inside of him to control his thoughts. The voice that he couldn't bear anymore, the one that pushed through him so easily.

'I will kill you all.'

47

THE WIND GUSHED through the open face of the apartments and howled against the steel framework that had once held the plate glass. Danny's hair was pushed back away from his brow and the force of it was that strong that he was pushed back a step. If the force of the gust of air that came from the creature's mouth in its roar was one thing, the smell was another. Rank with ancient decay and rot, the air that carried its breath seemed thicker and Danny choked on it as his lungs rejected it. Even the water that boiled where it met the creature, pushed down and away from the streaming air as it rushed out of its mouth. Steam rose up and swirled through the air in large spirals as if to conceal the beast. But the further it rose, the more it became caught up in the mighty rushing roar and to be swept across the face of the water.

'Oh, Christ,' he heard the words as he managed to hold onto the steering apparatus. It felt like it had been an age since he had blinked but he couldn't bring himself to look away, if only for an instant.

The amber eyes that burnt through the mist and the haze grew more intense as the creature leered its head back and finally, the roar came to a vicious end. At the distance they were, it looked as though the monster moved in slow motion, but the size of it made up for its lack of speed. Its mouth opened wider as its head retracted around its writhing body. A red tongue lashed around rows and rows of razor teeth that lined the monster's mouth in an arc of jagged edges and needle points.

Saliva coated the yellow rotted spikes as even they shifted in its maw to create a fearsome sight of razor-edged death that would've been at least fifty yards across.

'Oh Jesus, no,' Danny murmured as the creature coiled itself like a snake ready to strike. Saliva dripped like an acidic froth from the tips of its jagged teeth. Worse yet, he saw the intentions of the creature in his own mind as if broadcasted into him by some alien device. All at once, he knew what was to happen to the *Baroness*, and as the attack played out in his mind, it was the aftermath that concerned him the most. The waves that came, the sluggish reaction of the *Nisshin Maru*. If he didn't act now, the wave would hit her abreast and she would capsize. The thought struck him like déjà vu and without thinking, he raised the radio to his lips as he began to swing the wheel.

'Thompson, give me forward prop, half speed.' He spoke the words in the calmest tone he had ever spoken, and let go of the mic once he had finished. He didn't need to wait for Thompson's reply; a large part of him, the only part that mattered, knew that it would work, and it did. As if the ship had become an extension of him, he felt the propulsion drive through her as the massive propeller churned through the water to edge them forward. He managed to blink as he spun the apparatus and the nose of the old ship began to come about. As he opened his eyes he was drawn once again to the immense creature before them as its mouth opened wider and wider until it roared again.

The amber eyes had become obscured by something and they no longer seemed as fierce as they had. Then Danny saw that a third eyelid had moved up from the place where his own tear duct would be. As the dull, earthy lid slid up to protect its eye, the monster struck out.

As if in a frightened death cry, the air horn of the *Baroness* sounded just before impact. The blast rung out as the wall of jagged bones hammered into her flank. The impact sent a visible shockwave out that almost knocked Danny from his position. Danny saw steel crumple under the impact and the *Baroness* shifted heavily in the middle where she was struck. She seemed to bend inward at that point as the monster struck her hard at a hard angle.

She was driven down into the water and that was where Danny lost her, as the water surged upward and outward as if to try and escape the fate that the ship had not been able to. The wave grew and grew and grew as it rushed outward in an enormous ripple. It grew so tall that the creature itself was obscured and the horrible sound of ripping steel and the failing air horn was drowned out by the rushing of the water, until it was as if they had never existed.

Danny watched with gritted teeth as the wave powered above them. As the front end came about finally to the point where he was dead on, he centred the steering apparatus and lowered his head.

'Carmichael,' he said loud enough to be heard. Out of the corner of his eyes he saw the young man look over to him. His mouth still hung open in the same position it had fallen to when the creature tore out of the ice. His eyes were disbelieving but none of that mattered. Danny knew that now. 'Hang onto something,' he said to the young man as he wedged his foot against the steering apparatus. 'There's not much further to go,' he said with a faint smile.

The young man blinked as he said it, but nodded. Danny braced himself as the nose of the ship dipped slightly as it reached the wave's sucking point and the young man closed his eyes. Danny, on the other hand, kept his eyes focused on the tip of the bow. There was a part of the railing where the ice had caved in the tubular steel, and it stood out to him for some reason. He smiled as he realised why. That was the place where Gary had rested the skids of the R44 each time he had come down. That was the place where he had first stepped onto this damn ship and his smile softened as the vision that was planted in his brain continued to play out.

The tip of the bow penetrated the wave and the dark water turned white where it broke. The nose of the ship climbed hard and Danny felt everything want to slide as the apartments leant further and further back. He took a breath as he doubled his grip on the steering apparatus and the water rushed toward him and that was all he could hear, the rushing and the screaming of the water as it rolled over and over in a viscous torrent. The bow vanished into the darkness and it flowed like a surreal plague over the deck in a rushing, hungry froth of ice-cold death. Closer and closer, the entire fore deck was gone and he felt his feet start to slide. He managed another breath as the noise became unbearable and then it breached the windows and he was struck so hard by a wall of ice that he almost slipped.

The impact threw him back to arm's length and the shock of the cold was so intense that all he wanted to do was breathe. His eyes widened as the world went dark and his body screamed along with his mind for air. *Open your mouth and breathe!* his mind screamed at him, but deep down inside of him there was another voice. A woman's, soft and calming; the tone sent a tingle of heat up his spine.

'Just a little longer babe.' Her voice came through his mind. *Just a little further.'*

'Breathe, now!' his own voice this time, weak and frail.

'Not yet, you're stronger than this.' Hers, the source of his strength, the reason why he was here. *'You are strong.'*

Danny closed his eyes in the darkness and redoubled his grip on the steering apparatus as his feet tensed against the steering apparatus. The cold didn't seem to matter so much anymore, he didn't seem to feel it. He didn't even need to breathe, he felt as though he could stand there for an eternity, he'd never felt so at peace.

He opened his eyes under the depths of the water and before him he saw a light. It seemed as though it was a mile away in the darkness before him, but even as the seconds ticked by it grew larger and larger and the speed in which it grew, doubled and then tripled. The water pummelled his ears again as it began to rush and then suddenly, they were out of the water and his mouth opened as cold air rushed into his lungs.

He blinked rapidly to clear his eyes while his hands remained clenched to the wheel of the apparatus. He sucked air into his lungs as finally his eyes began to clear and for a moment, a seed of doubt was planted into him as through the glassless windows before him, all he could see was sky. The breath caught in his throat as his eyes widened again. Steel groaned and suddenly, he felt as though he was falling.

He went from clinging to the wheel to pushing against it, to stop himself from being sucked over it. The sky swirled through the windows as the front end came down; he saw a glimpse of ice wall and the grey plate of the monster's scale and then all he could see was water. Dark and unrelenting, worse than the eyes of the monster. Worse than his dreams had ever been.

'Hold on.' He raised his voice to be heard over the sound of the water that rushed around their feet, as it tried to escape the bridge. He never heard a reply from Carmichael, and he didn't need one – as with the wave, he knew what was to come.

Danny braced his legs as the bow exploded into the water before him again. Darkness turned to white froth before his eyes as the floor came up beneath him. He pushed down hard with his legs while his arms held his upper body away from the apparatus. Spray hammered through the window to sting at his eyes and his ears were assaulted once more by the roar of the ocean and the groan of the old ship. Then he looked up as the deck settled beneath him and the impact of the wall of water against his body never came. He saw the water swirl in white rivers as it ran across the foredeck and disappeared over the gunnels. The water was white foam to either side of the ship and every metal surface glistened in the daylight, almost renewed in its baptism.

Once again, Danny allowed himself to breathe in relief as the nose of the bow climbed into the air again as the ship rocked on the water. He glanced at the sky briefly and the amber of the sun before the nose crashed down again and sent up a lesser spray then before. As the ship settled in the troubled water, Danny's relief turned sour in his mouth. The forward half of the *Baroness* stood up from the water, while the monster tore steel from its side, completely detached from the rear of the ship, which now stood directly up in the air as its propellers spun a slow methodical pulse. The water was littered with chunks of debris, timber and fabric, and worst yet, the bodies of men that had been wearing life jackets. The jackets had kept them afloat, but the crushing water and the cold had sucked the life from them in a matter of seconds.

In a new flurry of rage, the creature sunk its teeth into the forward section and steel crumbled beneath the power of its jaw. Like it was nothing more than tissue paper, the hull of the *Baroness* split open for the creature and water poured in through its breach.

Danny watched for what seemed like an eternity as any life that could have remained on that vessel was extinguished. Air bubbled up through the holes that were created in the ice breaker's hull, while the water that swirled around the immense body of the monster boiled and churned with the heat that came off it.

Carmichael had survived the pass through of the wave, as Danny had expected, and the young man stood dripping wet before the radio unit. Fear and devastation poured from his face in thick tears as he witnessed the death of his fellow crew, and Danny felt for him. 'Cut prop,' he panted to Thompson.

The young man flicked the radio switch to activate his microphone and he leant in. '*Baroness, Baroness,*' he cried through his thick tears. 'Come on, some of you have to be alive in there.' He thumbed the switch off and listened for any reply but nothing came. Only static filled the air in a warbled tone from the water that had gotten into the speaker. '*Baroness?*' He tried again, then after a short pause. 'Rheinmarsh? Anyone?' No reply came from the speaker. Not that he expected any to come again, but Danny was shocked when the *Baroness* responded in the only way it had left.

The air horn rung out across the water, still strong and powerful as the water tracked higher and higher up its apartments. Danny's eyes widened as the sound ripped in through the glassless windows. 'Christ,' he said softly to himself. Someone was still alive.

Carmichael turned to him in desperation, his eyes although wide, still brimmed with tears. 'We need to help them, whoever is left.'

Danny watched as the goliath threw its head back and roared again in its rage. The air horn sounded again and its blast echoed across the water as the creature's third eyelid cast up again and it threw its head down to finish its prey.

Danny's jaw was set in stone. His teeth gritted as he clenched the steel of the steering wheel. He had seen what was to come, but this, someone surviving that, none of it was there. Maybe they could make it, maybe it was all a lie.

Carmichael flipped his switch once more and cried into the *Nisshin Maru*'s mic again. 'Hold on. We are coming. We will be there any second now.' He heard the desperation in the young man's voice and as he raised his own radio, he repeated the single thought through his mind again. *It was all a lie.*

Danny opened his mouth but no words came out. A pain had settled in his stomach and he felt all the strength in the world run out of him. He held the mic down for a second as Carmichael continued to cry out to the flailing *Baroness*, but then the pain became too much and he had to let it go. His legs buckled but he managed to hold himself up. A gasp escaped his lips and he tasted blood on his tongue.

He lowered his head and his eyes fixed on the intrusion, the one thing that shouldn't have been there. Jin Ishimura's blade stood proud from his gut. Even after seventy years of sitting in the damned cold and darkness, the Japanese steel was sharp enough to punch straight through him. Blood lined the steel and ran across its blade in odd rivers that almost looked like the pattern of Damascus folds. Danny coughed and saw his blood spatter against the steering apparatus. His legs buckled under him again and this time he couldn't hold himself up.

As he fell to the ground and his head clanged against the floor, he saw a slender hand raise the pistol that had last been used to take Ishimura's life. Carmichael spun around at the sound of Danny's collapse. Danny wouldn't have thought it possible, but his eyes widened even further as he saw Danny lying on the ground. As the pistol was turned onto Carmichael, Danny saw a single tear leave his left eye and run down his cheek before his entire face was turned to red mist and shit, while the pistol's report sounded like an earthquake against the walls of the bridge.

Carmichael's body fell in a lifeless heap to the floor. The red mist lingered in the air after his body had collapsed and then slowly, the drops fell to the floor and dissipated to nothing more.

Danny's chest rattled as he took a breath and his hand closed around the blade. The steel bit into the flesh on his hand and he bared his teeth at the pain. It seemed to start inside of him and radiate up his chest, into his neck and through his mind while it went down into his legs and out his toes. Someone knelt next to him and he felt a soft hand touch his cheek.

'Oh Danny,' she said and he met her eyes. 'You had to get involved.' Marie Swan looked as beautiful as ever as she knelt above him and stroked his face with her slender fingers. Her large doe eyes gazed down at him almost sympathetically as she shushed him to sleep. 'Go on now,' she soothed. 'Let it come over you. Let the wave come. You were never going to get out of this. You were never good enough.'

She said the words like a mother tutted and worried over her child who had hurt themselves tremendously. Then she left him there, in the shadows of the bridge. As her footsteps rung out and then finally vanished, the darkness started to fall. The cold came up his back and it became harder for him to breathe. He tried to think about Louise, but as he coughed again the lines of her face vanished from his mind. Then finally, as the darkness fell over him and he lost his awareness, the *Baroness* sounded her horn one last time, so that he might not forget her and the help that he would never give.

48

DARKNESS CONSUMED HIM. In this little world of his, nothing could touch him. Not the pain or the suffering, the loss or his failures. He was alone. Not even the harsh light of the burning sun could touch him where he was, nor the cold that radiated up from the dead hull beneath him. He felt none of it. He could no longer hear the thud of the diesel that churned away below him, nor could he smell the salt or feel the push of the waves against the hull. All the things that had concerned him, everything that he'd tried to do, none of it mattered now and none of it ever would. There was nothing left for him now, nothing more that a man who waited for his death could achieve. Nothing, but to wait for the slow march of bliss to wash over him, to silence the scream of pain, to soothe the ache of burden. All that he wished, was that it would hurry up and claim him.

'Danny.'

The single word rocketed through his mind and deep down he felt something. The black swirled with an amber tinge and a fire burnt down within him. *No,* he thought. *Just let me go. I can't do this anymore, I'm not strong enough.* The amber light wavered before his eyes and slowly the darkness ebbed forward and consumed it all again. The fires and the pain subsided into nothing and the world went silent once more.

'Danny.'

Again, it came, and he felt himself stir like a bear stretching after a winter's hibernation. The amber swirl fluttered before his eyes, and this time its colours were more vibrant. Stars danced behind the darkness; they bobbed and swayed before him and made him feel as if he was falling.

'Danny.'

Again, it came, and he was sure it was her. It had to be her. He knew somehow that her time had come, she had been too close the last time they had spoken, she had looked ready to burst. If it was her time, then why was it his stomach that now felt afire. *Why?* he asked himself. *Why won't they let me go?* He sobbed internally, while the amber flecks flared red with anger. His bones ached with a frozen fire that started in his joints and rippled through his flesh.

'Danny, can you hear me?'

The voice came again and the urgency that the words carried settled into him. His stomach was a leaden pit of molten metal that ripped away at everything. Air rushed into his body with what felt like his first breath in an age; his mouth felt dry as sand. The breeze kissed his naked face and he heard it whistle through the glassless windows and caress the stubble on his chin. He felt the eternal cold beneath him as it soaked into his body, only to be washed away by the pain that ran through him.

'Danny, for fuck's sake! We don't have much time.'

He jolted and his eyes opened. Wind whistled through the bridge, carrying a flurry of snow and ice along with it. His eyes opened and he grimaced as his lids ground back; he felt as though his eyes were full of sand and each movement was an agony. His mouth was a dry, desolate desert, and when he opened it to groan, only a gurgle of pain escaped his cracked lips.

'Carmichael, anyone? Is anyone left?'

The voice belonged to Thompson; below his voice he heard the roars of the creatures that had been trying to break through the bulkhead. He heard a groan of steel and the panic in the man's voice as he tried to raise someone. Danny lowered his hand to the radio at his hip, he brought up the mic and dropped it. He blinked slowly as his hand sluggishly went for the receiver again.

'For Christ's sake, can anyone hear me?'

He picked up the receiver again and for the first time, he noticed the tremble in his hand. Danny blinked slowly again as he coughed and splattered the mic with his blood. He watched the way the small droplets formed on the lined, black plastic. The way they stood proud against the smooth surface, and he shuddered at the sight. He closed his eyes and depressed the button.

'Thompson,' he managed to croak before another cough racked him and he spat up more blood.

'Who's that?' Thompson came back, the roars and cries of desperation almost drowning him out. 'Fuck it, it doesn't matter. They are almost through, I don't have long, if you want something done with these controls, tell me now!'

Danny opened his eyes and studied the blade that still protruded from his stomach. He didn't look at it with surprise or with horror, but more the way a driver who was halfway through a five-thousand-kilometre trip looked at a flat tyre when he had already used his last spare. A groan escaped him as he sat up and he felt the hilt of the blade grind against the floor behind him; the vibration sent a quiver of pain all the way through his body. He grimaced at the feeling while he reached up for the steering apparatus once more.

'Danny,' Thompson's voice came again. 'If that's you, then you need to give me an answer. I don't have long.'

'Neither do I,' Danny spat without bothering with the mic as he looped one hand around the steel wheel and clenched hard. He screamed as he dragged himself up and he felt the steel of the blade rub against the console's wall. Finally, he got his feet under him and his legs trembled as they raised him. Blood ran from his mouth and his head had begun to hammer with each and every heartbeat.

As he rested his chest on the steering apparatus, he looked up and out through the gaping windows, grimacing as his eyes fell on the Leviathan once more. Jagged steel painted red and black hung from its mouth, like a strip of meat torn from a carcass. The bow of the *Baroness* was barely visible at the stem of its immense body. Steam and bubbling water frothed over the remains of its hull, while the writhing, slithering body of the monster that had destroyed it, wrapped itself around the shattered hull. The amber eyes burnt down at the sight of its kill and as it opened its mouth to roar in triumph, the strip of steel fell to the sea, lost along with the rest of it.

'It's now or never Danny,' Thompson came again. 'They're through.' Danny heard the scream of steel over the transmission and rattle of their feet and their sharpened joints against the plate of steps.

Danny raised the mic to his mouth. 'Full ahead,' he said as his left leg buckled beneath him. He struggled to rise again as the wheel rotated under his weight. He swore at the wheel as blood ran down his chin and he rose to his feet again.

'It's done.' Thompson came back and the screams of the howling creatures became louder and louder.

Danny flinched in pain as he reached for his receiver. 'Thompson,' he called for one last time. 'Thanks.'

There was no reply from Thompson, nor would there be from anyone else down there. His eyes fell on the Leviathan and he smelt the rot as the wave of air ripped through the cabin once more. The sound shuddered as it travelled through the air and once again a ripple was sent across the waters. Danny sneered as the wave of power came over him and the smell of ancient dying filled the air. He spat as he spun the wheel and slowly the ship started to turn.

The bow bounced as it skipped over the waves that had been made by the movement of the massive beast. Each time it sank down and the spray spat up to either side, the further the bow moved across the ice wall when it sprang back up. Danny spun the wheel back the other way to correct and to slow the movement and finally, the bow of the *Nisshin Maru* sat steady beneath the horror of the *Baroness*'s remains.

'Alright,' he muttered as he locked the apparatus in place and sagged to the floor. He would've liked to have rested his back against the console, but with the hilt of the Samurai sword still wedged into his lower back he was forced to rest his side up against it. He breathed heavily from exhaustion as he let his hand fall to his side. As his wrist fell against his pant leg, it touched something hard in his pocket. He frowned as he moved his hand to it and then let his head rest back against the console as he saw it was his smart phone.

As he traced his thumb across the glass screen. Blood smeared along its face but he was beyond caring. The phone unlocked and when he saw his home screen, he was shocked to see that he had reception. In the top left-hand side of the screen, he had four solid bars and the four letters stood next to them, as they had up on the ice shelf. R.A.G.E. His brow furrowed as he considered the reception, and then he remembered the satellite array they had installed. The one that had fallen along with the rest of the ice and had landed on the mid-section of the ship. A soft smile came across his face, as his eyes fell from the reception to the face of Louise.

He focused on the way her hair fell about her shoulders, the way the curve of her nose made her eyes look even bigger. Then he saw the roundness of her stomach and his mind was taken to Leanna, his daughter who may be drawing her first breath at any minute. The smile vanished from his face as he thought about everything that he would miss: her first steps, her first words. The good times and the bad, hell anything would be better than where he was now, but that wasn't her fault and he wouldn't let her live wondering.

The phone's screen switched as he selected the application and he was left looking at a very sorry image of himself. He saw the blood in his stubble and large bags under his eyes. 'Christ,' he laughed at his image. 'I've aged a decade.' He put the phone down and tried to clean himself up, but with the blood on his hands, he feared that he only made the image worse. As he raised the phone to his face again, he smiled. 'I'm sure she won't mind, I'm sure Louise will raise her better than that.'

His thumb hovered over the record button as the ship ploughed through another wave. He took a breath and hit the red circle.

'Hey kiddo,' he said softly as the smile became more natural. 'I'm sorry,' he started and then paused as he dropped his eyes from the camera. 'There's a lot that I'm sorry for, but firstly for the way I look. Know that you were always the first thing on my mind when times were hard. You and your mother were the only things that kept me going through all of this and I thank you for that.'

His eyes began to well up as he spoke and a tear ran down his cheek and cut a clean line through the grime and blood. In the distance, the Leviathan roared again in triumph. Danny closed his eyes at the sound.

'I'm sorry I'm not going to get to meet you, and I'm sorry I won't be there.' Another tear and then another. 'This is no-one's fault so don't take it on your own shoulders because that just isn't right and don't blame your mum, because that's just not fair.' He sniffed back a nose full of tears and emotion as he wiped his face dry.

'I want you to live your life, knowing that your Dad loves you more than anything. I'd like nothing more than to see your smile and to hold your hand, but I know you'll be fine. You always will be, because I'll be watching over you.'

The smile vanished from his face and his eyes were red with emotion. In the screen he saw something behind him and his eyes were drawn to it.

He rubbed a hand beneath his nose again as he sniffed once more and he raised his eyebrows. 'Hey, you know I always try and show you something cool with each of these videos, so how about one more?' He grimaced as he moved his head to allow the screen of his phone to pick up the wall behind him.

'You see that?' he said as he saw the lines of white and red radiate out from the red centre. 'That is the rising sun of Japan,' he said as the smile returned to his face. 'A good friend of mine once told me that this sign was used to celebrate a child birth, but it also meant terror to those in the Pacific back in the forties. So, if this flag celebrates you and your life, you make sure that you're sweet and kind, and a damned terror to anyone who stands in your way.' He said it with a smile. 'Alright?'

He took a breath and it shuddered in his chest. He turned his head and had to refrain from coughing. He let the camera roll as he finally felt the urge subside and he took another tentative breath. 'I love you, kiddo. You know that. I'll always be here for you, just close your eyes and know it.'

He stopped the recording and pressed the menu button. He saw the link that he needed and selected the option, a small window appeared with an age-old question: 'Would you like to upload the video to your cloud? Yes, or No?'

Danny pressed the 'Yes' icon and the words were replaced by a small swirling circle. Around and around the circle went, like a dog chasing its tail, and then finally the circle disappeared and was replaced by three words: 'File successfully uploaded.'

Danny smiled as he let his phone fall to the ground. He wouldn't need it anymore; he was ok with that. He didn't even look at it as he struggled again to his feet, he didn't even think about it as he took his first staggered steps toward the corridor that sat behind the bridge. All that mattered now, was that he needed to end this and make his daughter proud.

49

SALT SPRAY PEPPERED HIS FACE as he staggered onto the top landing. White foam spat up into the air as the *Nisshin Maru* picked up momentum. Each small wave, a ripple from the movement of the monstrosity that had destroyed the *Baroness,* was a force for the old whaler to break through. The bow sunk down and the water parted under the power and weight of the old ship, and spray was sent as high as the top of the two remaining 'H' frames, as she powered toward her endgame.

Danny was exhausted. He rested against the railings on top of the landing as he looked out over the bow. The blade that had done him in still protruded through his gut. He closed his hand around it and started to push, but the pain was too much. With his effort, he felt his consciousness start to slip and the life drain from his head. He panted as he released his grip and spat over the edge. At the moment, he mainly felt uncomfortable. Of course, he was in pain, but he didn't think he was bleeding as much as he could be. The blade would have to stay in, only for a while.

Each step took everything he had. To hold onto the railing with one hand, while his feet descended the slippery steps, was like learning to walk again. His vision doubled then tripled as he descended the flight of stairs to the rear of the apartments.

He saw Marie.

Still dressed in the same tight-fitting, high-necked sweater that clung to her body so well, Marie Swan was heading across the main deck to the rear apartments. Her outward appearance had not changed, yet Danny saw her in a new light and his face twisted in rage as his fist clenched over the railing. A rattle formed in his chest with his next breath. As he exhaled, he promised himself one thing as he watched the ground between them increase. He would kill her before he was done, even if it killed him, he would watch her die.

He began to lower himself down the final set of stairs toward the foredeck while his breath was a hot labour in his throat. The bow rose up, then all of the weight seemed to go out of it and down it fell again. Then, the deck seemed to come up from beneath him and his legs buckled as a tower of spray shot up the side of the ship and rained down on him. Danny's legs went out from under him and he fell forward the rest of the way. His eyes opened wide, more from the anticipation of the pain then from the shock, and when the blade hit the steel and its shaft bent beneath his weight, he cried out in agony as the world spun in waves of darkness and speckled light. It bent and bent to ninety degrees as Danny's weight put more and more strain on the shaft, and then finally it snapped beneath him.

It felt as though a pressure valve had been released and all of the built-up pain and angst just fell out of him. His eyes opened and the world seemed surreal. Everything happened as if on a television; he felt detached, removed from his surroundings.

When his hands touched the deck, he didn't feel the steel beneath his palm. He pushed himself to his knees and didn't feel the pain that should have erupted in his stomach. The front of his hoodie was drenched with his blood as it had continued to run from him. Even his pants were now soaked with what could only have been his own blood, but he couldn't feel any of it.

He got one foot under him and then the other. A grimace came over his face as he swayed to his feet and he blinked slowly as if it was all that he could do. The sound of the waves seemed distant, and the spray of the water seemed delayed, but the only thing that seemed to hammer in the back of his head, was the slow beat of his own heart. Some water hit his face and the smallest drop entered his mouth, which hung open in a daze. Danny blinked as another sense came back to him, and blinked again as the dirty salt taste spread across his tongue to lather his gums. He leant forward and spat a glob of red mess across the white sparseness of the foredeck.

The deck twisted beneath him again, and the ship tilted hard to the starboard side. Danny almost fell; he slammed into the railing and peered down at the swirling darkness beneath him. His jaw remained slack and his eyes semi-focused, as the hull of the *Nisshin Maru* leant over and over. Just at the point where Danny felt that he was going to fall in, it stopped and began to right itself. As the hull came back with a fierce snap, he was thrown back against the wall of the apartments as water splashed over the decks and flushed his entire front with a chilling cold and the salt spray.

He blinked and when he opened his eyes, the world didn't seem as far away. His skin prickled at the cold that rushed over it and his gut roared with anger as the salt worked into it. He wanted to double over, he wanted to cry and let himself die. But the other part of him smiled as the pain rushed back over him; he wasn't dead yet.

He clenched his fists and gritted his teeth against the pain and raised himself to his feet as the roar of the Leviathan ripped through the air and the water began to broil around the hull. Danny glanced behind him, toward the rear of the ship, where Marie had sauntered off. Her time would come, but not yet. The water burst to his side and a large coil of the Leviathan's body rolled out of the water. The grey plate scales glimmered in the sun and hissed as steam rose from their edges. Along its back edge, long webbed spikes stood on end, as if in torment of the light. Then, as the bulk of its weight fell into the water again, they fell back to lay flat again against the folds of its fins.

Danny snarled as he saw it and braced himself as the body crashed into the starboard side. For a moment, he felt the intense heat wash over his body and it seemed like the first time in an age that he actually felt too hot in his clothes. Steam rose from the fabric of his hoodie as it dried in an instant, only to be soaked by the blood that seeped from his gut.

This time, the *Nisshin Maru* was sent reeling in the other direction.

Danny felt himself leaning harder and harder onto the wall of the apartments as he pushed himself forward. The water to his side vanished, and soon even the heat was gone. D-28 towered well and truly overhead and that was the only way that he could tell that they had stopped completely.

He heard the rush of water but it didn't sound right. The ship rolled back to an upright position, but too slow, as if it was controlled. Danny lifted himself off the wall as he felt his weight spread over his two feet again and he peered over the edge. The reason why the ship was no longer moving, was that it was no longer in the water. Twenty metres of air was between the bottom of the hull and the boiling water beneath. The steam rose and stank of rot and salt, as the Leviathan's body writhed in the depths and lifted the *Nisshin Maru* even higher.

'I've got something you'll fuckin like,' Danny muttered. 'Yeah, I've got something you'll remember, you big bitch.' He started to laugh as he moved forward onto the foredeck and over the ridges for the winch cables. The starboard harpoon gun had been spared the thrashing that the portside had suffered against the ice, and the body of the cannon was in fine condition. Danny moved to its pedestal mount and examined the device. At the rear of the cannon a large breech was sealed shut. The device looked basic enough and Danny latched onto the handle at the top of the breech. He pushed hard and just like everything else on this damned ship, it resisted him at first and then slid open like it had only gone into storage the day before.

With the breech open, Danny saw a hole of about four inches at its rear. He would need a charge and a harpoon to load the cannon and then he would give the monster something to remember. He looked back to the winch drums which sat at the bottom of the forward apartments. Between each drum was a crate, heavy steel with a solid ridge around its edge. Danny moved for it and stumbled when he was most of the way there.

'It'll be unlocked,' he said to himself as he fell onto the box and gritted his teeth as the pain shot through him again. 'It has to be, they wouldn't have had time to seal it before they were dragged through the ice.'

He pushed his palms to either edge of the lid and heaved against the weight. It didn't move an inch. Exhaustion had ebbed most of his strength away and now even breathing was a massive effort. He ran his hands around the edge of the lip and finally found a hook that had kept the unit locked. He thumbed the release and then found another on the other side. This time when he used the heels of his hands to raise the lid, the hinges parted with a tired scream.

The inside of the lid had a rubber seal similar to a refrigerator, which ran along its closing edge. Years of exposure to the ice had made it brittle and in many places the rubber had cracked and crumbled away, yet the inside of the box was still dry. Danny hoisted himself to the rim of the box and peered inside. Like a child who had discovered his father's gun, he gaped in awe at the jagged edges of the harpoons as they sat in their storage rack. Almost five foot long with a heavy solid shaft, the harpoon's edges glinted in the light as if to suggest their sharpness, despite the years. To the back of the box was a plastic sealed section that contained large brass cartridges. The rim of them looked about four inches in diameter.

Danny tore open the bag and took out two of them. He shoved them down into his pockets, where the Molotovs had clattered barely an hour before. To their side, he saw heavy metal cones. He took one to be safe and then retrieved a single, heavy harpoon.

As he clambered to his feet, relying solely on the harpoon to get him there, Danny realised that the world around the ship had dissolved. A wall of steam had risen around the hull, and obscured anything beyond. He looked up and saw that he could barely even make sense of the sky; it was as though he was in the middle of cloud. Drops of water fell from the sky and seared against the cold of the deck when they exploded. Danny took a step, and found that his legs wanted to buckle. He snarled as he redoubled his grip on the shaft of the harpoon and used it as a walking stick. Another step, and the body of the cannon sat before him, the open mouth of its breech waiting for the charge.

At the bow, the steam parted as the snout of the Leviathan came through. Danny took another lunging step as he raised his head to look at the beast. The heat had become tremendous as the short snout of the beast moved forward over the bow. A hot jet of rushing, rotting air shot forth out of its nostrils as it exhaled and Danny felt all the moisture leave his skin.

'Yeah, come on you bitch,' he snarled as he took another step. 'I've got what you want right here.' He slammed the haft of the harpoon down on the deck as he lunged again and the Leviathan reacted to the sound. It recoiled slightly and cocked its head so that one of its great, burning amber eyes could consider him. The world seemed to turn an orange tinge under the luminescence of its eye and the edge of the harpoon looked like dancing fire.

'See this?' Danny roared as he held the harpoon up. 'Remind you of anything?'

The eye focused on him and he felt his entire body freeze up. He felt as though insects had gotten into his head and they were crawling over his brain and up his spine. Danny closed his eyes and shook his head as he began to scream. Inside of him he heard the thing thinking, he heard its thoughts and its hatred and at that moment if he could've died, he would've been happy to, for he saw how insane the monster was. Seventy years of awareness. Seventy long years of wanting to move but being trapped in a mountain of ice while all it could think of was to get out, to get out, to get free.

Even though his eyes were shut, he saw the eye emblazoned into his eyelid. The fire that ran out from the slitted pupil, the way it swirled and danced on the darkened field. The fire that had settled in the middle of its mind, the fire that wanted it to kill, to kill, to kill.

The air around him changed and the smell of rot increased tenfold. Danny opened his eyes and saw that the orange tinge was gone. The open maw of the monster moved down to claim him. He saw up close the rotted flesh, the yellowed spikes of teeth that stood proud in their gums above the rows and rows and rows of spares that waited to fold up like a shark's jaw. Darkness waited at the end and he saw the shards of steel that had once belonged to the hull of the *Baroness*, which had snared in-between two of the yellowed teeth. The air rushed over him as the Leviathan reached in to seize him and finally, Danny felt that he could move.

He threw himself down as the Leviathan's lower jaw came over the bow and crashed into the deck at his rear. He heard steel scream and splinter as its maw closed around the forward apartments and tore out its frontal face.

Danny took his chance. His scrambled toward the cannon while chunks of steel thundered down to the deck to his side. He reached the pedestal and heaved himself up with the haft of the harpoon and finally he was there, at the breech once more.

He checked inside and saw instantly the place where the metal cone sat. He pushed it in and then retrieved the heavy brass charge from his pocket. He pushed with his hands but something seemed to be holding the rim of the case back. He pushed and pushed, but he was too weak to seat it. Then he saw the harpoon shift to his side as the hull of the ship rocked on the writhing body of the monster, and he seized it again. He raised the harpoon and pushed hard with the haft on the rim of the charge and finally he saw it shift and seat into the breech. He rammed the breech closed and then almost collapsed as he moved to the front of the cannon.

Steel and shrapnel clattered against the deck as the Leviathan growled above him and ripped its head to the rear. Danny saw the steering apparatus come crashing to the deck along with the remnants of other consoles. In the mess that was left above, the rising sun of Japan shone in the light, open to the world. Below it, he saw a hand hang limp over the edge of what remained of the bridge. Danny grimaced and rammed the haft of the harpoon home into the cannon's muzzle. He felt it slide and then engage against the metal cone.

As the monster threw its head up in the air and released everything that it had taken, chunks of steel, and even the wrecked body of Jin Ishimura, were flung into the air above him. Jin rose and finally stopped as everything tumbled over itself in its flight. Then as it all slowly began to fall, the jaws of the beast hammered shut over him and his body was gone forever.

'Alright you mad bitch, I'm ready for you,' Danny panted through a mouth full of blood as he moved to the rear of the cannon and pushed his shoulder into its brace. A handle stuck out from its rear that had a small lever toward its end. It was positioned just so that it was comfortable to hold with his right hand. Danny saw there was another lever below him, attached to the pedestal mount. He wound the pedestal lever over and felt the cannon's weight come onto his shoulder. He pushed back and found that he could pivot it and turn it on its axis. He placed his right hand on the handle to help him guide it and then he grasped the trigger.

'Hey!' he shouted up to the monster as it devoured the steel and the body of the old Samurai soldier. Danny saw the creature react and slowly, as it faced him, the world turned orange again. He heard steel crumble as its jaws worked together. The heat began to rise again as the grey plate of its scales came closer. Then finally, it was there again above him. He felt the insects in his brain crawl over his scalp and up his spine and all he wanted to do was to close his eyes while the fire ran out from the slitted pupil.

'I will kill you all,' the mad Leviathan roared in Danny's mind. His ears screamed with a ringing pitch and his neck twinged almost to lock his ear to his shoulder. Danny screamed as he forced his eyes open and pressed his shoulders into the cannon's brace. The sharpened edge of the harpoon glinted in the orange light as the cannon swung around and up.

'Just try it,' he muttered as he squeezed the lever up in his right hand and the cannon erupted before him.

50

THE CANNON RECOILED SO HARD that he was almost thrown back into the railing. Instead, his knees unfolded and he collapsed onto the shoulder brace, while he looked up in awe. The harpoon glinted off the amber light as it hurtled through the air. Tendrils of flame and unburnt powder wisped in the atmosphere behind it. Over and over, it twirled in a spiral of sharpened steel and hardened haft until finally it disappeared into the eye of the beast. The orange light that had irradiated the deck vanished instantly as the Leviathan's third eyelid rose. Blood exploded outward over the rim of the eyelid as the monster threw its head back and uttered an absolutely horrible cry of pain that Danny heard in the middle of his mind, as well as with his ears. Back and back and down its head went, away from the bow out over the sea. The *Nisshin Maru* shifted violently on its body and then a weightlessness came over Danny as the deck fell out from underneath him.

Danny held for dear life to the pedestal of the cannon as he leant over the railing to peer at the boiling water below, but even that escaped his sight for the steam that continued to rise made it impossible for him to see. He squinted and tried again, but as the steam drifted over his flesh it burnt the areas it touched and Danny was forced to pull back.

The further the ship fell the worse the steam became. It drifted over the deck and swirled downward with the vacuum the enormous mass made as it dropped through the air. Danny screamed as his flesh was near burnt from his face and he pulled the hood of his hoodie up over his head. He tried to hold on to the railings at the same time, but he needed both of his hands to shield his face and so he went blind as he tried to walk away from the cannon's pedestal, so that he wouldn't brain himself on it if he fell. With the movement of the ship, he stumbled forward, his hands shrunk up into sleeves and his fists clenched around the ends. He held his hands to his face as he screamed at the pain and the terror and he allowed himself to fall, for if he was already down, he had no further to go.

Air whistled through the fabric and buffeted his head as sweat began to run down his back and dampen his armpits. He didn't know why he was screaming anymore, whether it was for the pain of his burning flesh, the terror of the fall, or if it was the monster in his head screaming its insane cry of agony. Nonetheless he screamed as he buried his wrapped fists into his eyes and lay in a foetal position on the foredeck. He screamed as his voice broke, and his shrill rasps became a ragged cry. He screamed as he lifted his head and let it drop to the steel below as if that would help anything. He screamed as the Leviathan finally vanished below the depths and the scream in the middle of his mind vanished with it.

Danny fell quiet and drew a shaky breath, taking in the silence. Nothing made a noise apart from the wind that buffeted his hood as it rushed upward and then sucked downwards on top of him, but that was ok. He took another breath of stifling hot air as he prepared himself for what came after the fall. He short exhaled and then sucked in hard again as the bow plunged into the depths and ocean came rushing over the railings.

Danny felt like he was hit by a wall of red-hot iron. His entire body erupted in agony as the boiling water rushed over him. He screamed into his hands again as the steel of the foredeck slid beneath his body. Faster and faster, he was pushed, until something hard slammed into his back and his foetal position broke. His arms shot outward at the pain in his back and the hood flew back off his head to reveal his face. His body was pushed and thrown off the hard surface and along the deck again;

the heat was unbearable and his mind began to break, but the more water rushed over him, the cooler it became. Then he slammed into a something solid and thin and his body twisted around it. His hands clasped something that could only be the railing as he bent over it and clung to it for dear life.

Cooler waters now rushed over him. Cooler and then cold, beautifully cold, but with the relief from the heat came the kiss of salt into flesh and once more he gritted his teeth as his wounds began to scream at the pain. He wanted to scream but he needed to breathe to do that. He wanted nothing more than to open his mouth and suck in air but he couldn't. His eyes felt like they were about to burst from their sockets and every vein on his body stood out from his reddened flesh as he yearned for air.

Then the sound came as the bow broke out from the depths and rose into the air again. Danny opened his mouth and gasped fresh, salty air as the water rushed off the deck again to return to the ocean that had failed to claim the ship, yet again.

He opened his eyes as he clung to the railing and sucked air into his wretched body. He knew he was still on the ship, but where, he had no idea. He looked back to the right and saw the stern and half smashed rear apartments. Way behind the ship now, a wall of steam rose up into the air, and beneath it, the water churned and ran over itself in its boiling rage. He watched the ferocious water as he took another breath and then another, and sighed finally as he was sure it was getting further away.

He groaned as he hoisted himself up, using the railing as support. To his left were the stairs that led to the foredeck and the forward apartments themselves and beyond, D-28, the immense iceberg that had caged the Leviathan for almost a century. With the steering apparatus gone, there was no way to steer the ship. With Thompson overrun below, there was no way to cut the drive. The ship was doomed to run directly into the ice wall. What happened then, he didn't know, but he planned to be at the rear of the ship by then.

The ice that had littered the mid-section of the ship was gone, as was the communications array; everything was gone. The ship still bounced over the water and spray was sent up to either side but Danny didn't seem to notice it. One step at a time, he shifted his hand along the starboard side railing. His breaths were short and ragged now, his gut a ball of steel and pain. The ship swayed in front of him and his vision blurred then snapped back with a heightened sense of clarity. His mouth hung open and his feet dragged along the deck with every step he took.

The stairs that led upward to the aft loomed before him and when he reached them it took every bit of concentration that he had just to raise his foot high enough to climb the first step. By the time he raised himself up the final step, his breaths had quickened and become heavy. His chest heaved as he sucked air into his lungs, but it didn't seem to do anything.

He peered down at his hands, the flesh was red from the scalding it had received and in places, blisters had begun to rise. The more he looked at his open palm, the more he noticed the tremble that had set in. He tried to clench his fist but only managed a loose ball. His strength had left him, and there was little that he could do.

The ship suddenly lurched to the portside and Danny was thrown into the wall of the rear apartments. He raised his eyebrows in concern, and saw that the waters in front of them were littered with enormous chunks of floating ice. The ice was pushed away by the momentum of the *Nisshin Maru* and the ship's course was pushed further to the portside, so that its collision with D-28 wasn't going to be directly head on. To his front, he heard the sound of something heavy roll and roll and then crash into something. The sound of steel buckling and crumpling filled his ears, and if Danny hadn't been in the middle of a body of water, he would've sworn that he'd just heard a car crash.

He clambered to his feet again, and as the ship steadied itself in the water, he took a half-staggered step toward the sound. With each movement he took forward, he saw more and more of the aft. He saw a steel frame that looked as though it pivoted in the centre, while it was designed to cradle something large at its lower point. In the centre of the aft, a large hatch was open and a crane sat to its side. The ship shifted in the water again and the rolling sound of the heavy steel came from its depths again. Danny's eyebrows furrowed as he took another step toward the open hatch and stepped out entirely onto the aft. He saw movement to his right and he turned to it, his arms still by his side and his mouth open in exhaustion.

Marie Swan came at him with a slow and steady pace. Her face was blistered from the steam and her neck was red with blood where some had burst. Most of her hair had fallen from her head to reveal a scalded scalp where the skin had burst to reveal the brilliant white of her skull beneath. Her left cheek had mostly melted and her face was twisted in a forever smile that had stretched too far. Her teeth clattered together as she stepped toward him and her brilliant eyes seemed too large as she raised her arms and the bar in her hands.

Danny tried to raise a hand to defend himself but he couldn't; he just didn't have the strength. Instead, as she brought the iron down in a wild arc, he moved his head to the side in a poor attempt at a dodge and bore the brunt of the impact on his right shoulder. The blow drove him to his knees before her and he glared up in pain as she laughed.

'You should've stayed in the bathroom Danny,' she said softly, in a ruined voice that was made even more horrific by the loss of her lips. 'I wanted so badly for us to be together,' she said as she lowered her face to his. The flesh under her eyes hung down so that he could see the insides of her lids. Her nose had partially melted and sat somewhat to the side, but the left side of her face seemed almost untouched compared to the right.

'How I would love for us to be back there now, so that you could have a second chance.' The untouched side of her face smiled, while the melted half glared with exposed teeth and jaw. 'Do you want to kiss me now?' she asked him. 'Do you still want to fuck me like the rest of them?' she teased as she let him look at her ruined face. 'This is all your fault,' she whispered. 'You just couldn't keep out of it. You and Charlie, had to keep digging.' Her face twisted into a grimace of hate and malice.

'Well,' she said finally in dismissal as she raised herself to her feet before him. 'None of that matters now. See for yourself.' She pointed out over the railing of the aft at the wall of steam that rose up over the ocean. 'She's coming for you,' she said mockingly, and Danny saw that she was right.

Beneath the wall of steam, a large mass headed toward them. It was gaining on the ship ever so slowly but when they hit the wall everything would happen quickly. The old ship wouldn't survive another scrap with that monster, Danny knew that much, and he was too far from the harpoon cannons to be able to fend the beast off again. If he had the strength he would choke the life out of the bitch before him, before the beast took him down to the depths. If he had the strength, he would watch her die before he followed.

'Give it up Danny,' she laughed at him. 'You're spent and there's nothing left for you to do.' She stepped back and raised the bar above her head. 'Nothing left to do, but die.' As she said the last words, her face twisted again and she started to bring the bar down.

At the beginning of her swing, the ship lurched again and this time the steel screamed as the hull was thrown in a new direction. Way behind him, the bow lifted into the air and came crashing down again and Marie stumbled. Danny took his chance; he lowered his head and threw himself forward. He drove the shoulder that she had caved in, into her stomach and the impact pushed her back. As she stumbled backwards, her eyes opened wide and she let go of the bar. Behind her, the ocean exploded in a wall of steam and boiling water as the Leviathan raised itself in a final charge. Marie took another step back, as her arms waved through the air.

'No!' she cried as her balance left her and her body leant dangerously back over the open hatch.

Danny stumbled with her as he watched the monster close the ground. Its mouth opened and the one remaining eye locked onto him. The roar came as it lunged forward for the final time. Danny felt something latch onto his front and saw that Marie had grabbed him to stop herself from falling. His head snapped back on his neck as she dragged him with her. The darkness came rushing up and then the world outside was gone – the air, the Leviathan and the ocean was left outside as they tumbled down together into the black.

Danny grabbed onto her shoulders as she screamed in his face. Over her shoulder, the steel grate came up hard behind her and with a cry of agony, they crashed to the ground. Danny landed on Marie. If he hadn't, he didn't think he would've been able to rise. Her eyes rolled into the back of her head with the impact as the air left her lungs. She gasped as she squirmed to get out from beneath him but what remained of Jin Ishimura's blade pinned them together.

To his right, he heard the sound of the heavy rolling steel again and they both turned to the sound. Danny remembered the one thing that Gary had said in their meeting where Marie had discussed the ship's log in detail. The Japanese had used depth charges to escape the Americans, just as Marie had used a depth charge to release the monster from the ice. As the ship ground against the ice, the depth charge rolled viciously toward them. The weight of its casing propelled it forward and Danny saw the chunks of steel that had been torn from its outer edge, as it came crashing toward them.

'Hey,' he whispered to Marie, 'one thing you'd never work out.' He said it with his mouth so close to her ear so she was forced to listen to him as the rolling explosive came down on them. 'You were never good enough,' he snarled as he dragged her body around and held her head out in the depth charge's path. She screamed as it came and fought, thrashing at him with her arms and her legs, but it made no difference. Her skull cracked beneath the weight of the depth charge and her body fell limp.

Danny collapsed at that point; he was spent. He sat there and breathed heavily as he rolled himself onto his side. He looked up at the sky and squinted at the brightness of the day outside. He heard the water rushing around the hull and he felt the churn of the diesel and the massive props beneath him. He was so exhausted that he didn't even react when the daylight slowly became night outside as the Leviathan came down on the rear of the ship. He heard the roar of it in its final blast of glory before it tore the ship that had trapped it to shreds. He was so exhausted that he didn't even fight the beast as its voice slipped into his mind again, and without speaking it showed him everything that it would take from him, everything that it would do to those that he loved. He saw the Sydney Harbour Bridge, trashed to the depths, fire along the shores and the city in ruins. He saw bodies on the harbour walk, flesh melted from their bones and the clothes burnt to cinders. He saw warships torn to shreds and the men fighting as the water rushed in through the holes in their hulls, and he saw his partner there, crying as he never returned to her as she raised their child by herself.

The light vanished overhead as the shadow fell over him. Then the steam rushed forward and finally the ship was thrown upward and to the side as the massive jaws closed on its stern.

Danny was thrown against a rack, and he gasped as the haft of the Japanese blade was driven out through his diaphragm. The monster surged and raised the rear of the ship into the air.

As the life rapidly began to leave him, he saw the same depth charge that had claimed Marie come rolling down to crush him in his final moments. Again, he saw the damaged shell and the hint of the explosives that lay beneath. He glanced to his rear and saw the racks and racks of depths charges up above him and he knew what he had to do.

As the weight of the charge came crashing down, he calmly reached for his pocket. Where his phone had once sat, now sat a brass cartridge about four inches in diameter. He pulled it from his pocket and looked down at the jagged steel of the broken Samurai sword that had punched through his guts. With the last breath that he held in his lungs, he placed the priming edge of the cartridge against the jagged point of the sword, and then the weight of the rolling explosive crashed into him and detonated the charge.

He never felt the weight, nor did he feel pain in his last moment before the charge exploded in his hand. All he felt was pressure on his chest as the world went bright with the flash. He smelt the sulphur and smiled as the visions in his head stumbled and wavered.

As his mind cleared, he was allowed one final thought, before the depth charge ignited. He thought about Louise and he thought about Leanna grown up, although he had never met her. He smiled at the thought of them, laughing as they held hands as they walked down some street, down some city, ignorant of what had happened to him. He smiled as the depth charge ignited and started a chain reaction.

He thought of one final thing, before everything went black and nothing remained.

You can't have them.

EPILOGUE

THE RAVENS CAWED as the morning light came over the lawn. Their calls repeated as if it were an echo, over and over, as it drew out at the end. Each spring morning, they started up that racket and each morning they did, Leanna Myers woke up to it. She sighed as she rolled onto her back and threw her hands under her pillow, unwilling to get up so early this day. Although what waited ahead was sure to be good, she felt that she deserved to sleep in this day. After all, it was her eighteenth birthday.

School had just about finished; the world was about to open to her and tonight she would have her first 'legal' taste of alcohol. She stretched her arms out over her head and yawned as she shut her eyes again in a smile. The birthday was one thing, though what she really looked forward was her party, but that wasn't until Saturday and today was only Wednesday. Sure, she had no exams until next week and today she could pretty well write off and do just about nothing, which she thought was apt for a day such as this.

She rolled onto her side as her jaw clicked beneath the gape of another yawn and her dark hair covered her eyes. Blowing at the strands, she tried to focus on the open window through her locks. She sighed as she brushed her hair away and resigned to sit up. The world through her window had already taken the leap of faith into the day, and she saw birds in the trees that lined the suburban street. A couple were walking their dog, a great boof-headed Kelpie that refused to heel and walk by their side. The world was awake and up and moving, so she figured it was about time for hers to do the same.

Smells of bacon and fresh bread had already started to waft beneath the crack of her fastened bedroom door and her stomach rumbled. She stretched again as she rose to her feet and doubled over to touch her toes. She felt an odd stiffness in her lower back that popped as she touched her left large toe with her right index finger. Her brow furrowed as she rose again and rubbed at her hips. She caught a glimpse of herself in the mirror above her dresser.

Leanna was a slender young woman. Her long thick, brunette hair, a gift from her mother, hung down over her shoulders in knotted strands, as it screamed to be brushed. Freckles dotted her cheeks, like dark stars on a pale sky, they sat as a border to the deep pools of her piercing blue eyes. She screwed up her face at herself in the mirror and stuck out her tongue. Then she flipped herself the bird with both hands and even cocked her thumbs out for good luck before she bounced to the door and headed down for breakfast.

Leanna yawned again as she entered the kitchen of her mother's modest house. Louise Bastianich stood at the kitchen window, a steaming mug off coffee suspended below her chin as she day dreamed out the window. Leanna's birthdays had always been a bittersweet affair for her mother, that much she knew. Although the day represented the birth of her only child, the day also meant the loss of her first love and the man who was Leanna's father. Throughout her childhood, Leanna could remember many times where her mother had been so happy for her as she watched her play with her presents and then, almost for no reason at all, she would start crying.

'What's wrong mum?' she had asked one year or another.

Her mother, as beautiful as she was, just smiled at her and wiped the tears away as she said, 'I'll tell you when you're older.'

Older had come and gone, and soon enough Leanna had wrangled the truth out of her. She had never known too much about her father. She knew that he was a good guy and that he'd been working in Antarctica of all places, when he had died. She knew that her mother had really loved him and when she found out, it had really hit her hard. Finding out that her birthday just so happened to be the day that good old Daddy had died, filled in some of the blanks, but not all. To Leanna, her father was someone that she'd never met. Sure, she supposed she kind of loved him, as much as a person could love someone that they had never known. She couldn't really blame him for not being there; it wasn't his fault that he had kicked the proverbial bucket. Nevertheless, each birthday she knew to give her mother space, if she wanted it.

She smiled softly as she pulled one of the stools out from under the kitchen bench and slid herself onto it so that her bare feet could swing in the air. 'Morning mum,' she drawled in a silly tone.

Louise blinked at the sound and took a sip of her coffee before she looked at her daughter. 'Happy birthday, lazy bones,' she said with a wry smile that did a poor job of hiding the fact that she had been crying.

Leanna fought back a sigh. She considered briefly asking her mother if she was alright and figured that if she wanted to talk, in her own way, she would. 'I'm not lazy,' she protested as she kicked her feet freely back and forth. 'It's my birthday, I'm allowed to sleep in.'

'Uh-huh,' her mother replied as she poured some juice into a glass and placed it before her daughter. 'Haven't seen the rule book where that's written.'

Leanna picked up the glass and drained a quarter of it in a big gulp. The orange juice was freshly squeezed, thick with pulp. She loved it when her mother juiced fresh oranges, even if the machine was as noisy as all hell in the morning, the result was worth it. 'Never you mind about that rule book,' she said as she wiped the pulp away from her upper lip.

Her mother tutted as she watched her. 'For a beautiful young woman, I still ask myself every day, whether or not you should have been a boy.' Louise shook her head as she turned her back and began to plate the toast, bacon and eggs for her.

Leanna laughed at this comment, although it had not been the first time she had heard it. Even as she was growing up, her mother thought it was a great idea to have Leanna's hair cut short; at times she was even mistaken for a boy. That was of course before puberty hit.

She considered her mother; even in her age, she was still a beauty. Her dark hair never knotted, and face free of freckles made Leanna question where her own had come from. She showed little signs of aging.

Leanna pondered on the word "beautiful" that her mum had used to describe her. She didn't see beauty when she looked in the mirror, but she did notice the eyes of boys follow her. Eyes that never lingered long on a face before they dropped down to assess the rest. She didn't care too much for boys currently; if her mum had aged so well, she supposed that she had plenty of time to worry about these things later.

Leanna's stomach growled again. When her food was placed before her, she wasted no time hooking in and her mother, who was accustomed to her eating like a pig out of a trough, resided herself to reading a letter that had come in yesterday afternoon's mail run.

It was unusual to get anything like that these days, through mail. Generally everything was done via email or web chat. This intrigued Leanna a little bit as it had been some years since she had even seen a printed advertisement. Printing on paper was super expensive, she knew that much; she had to buy a book once for school because it wasn't available online and she was thankful for her scholarship as the damned thing had been ten times the price of any online publications she had paid for.

'What are you reading?' she asked her mother through a mouthful of toast and egg; a line of yolk managed to escape her mouth and ran down the line of her chin.

Her mother glanced up at her, and furrowed her brow as she tutted and tossed her a napkin. 'Thank God this company has never seen this side of you, because I'm sure they'd think twice about what they do for you.'

Leanna screwed up her face and pushed food through her teeth just to disgust her mother even further. She laughed when it worked. Leanna finished her mouthful, wiped away the line of yolk on her cheek and then placed her knife and fork down at either side of the food, as she had been taught, time and time again. 'What is it mother?' she mocked.

'Here,' Louise said as she handed it over. 'The company that's given you the scholarship all these years, wishes you a happy birthday, and has invited you to do an internship with them.'

Leanna picked up the paper and instantly marvelled at the quality of the parchment between her fingers. It was real thick paper, textured too. She moved on to the letter itself. She didn't really read it; the company logo was something that had been a part of her life for as long as she could remember. They had been going on about internships and career opportunities for the last three years now that she could remember. She studied the letters that made up the company's name: R.A.G.E, the four letters that seemed droll but cool at the same time.

She skimmed over the words as her stomach urged her to continue eating, so she skipped to the signee before she put the letter down.

'Hans Rheinmarsh,' she said the name before she stuffed her mouth full of bacon. Her mother looked up at the name, her eyebrows raised in question. Leanna shook her head while she finished her food. 'Just the guy's name, very German isn't it?'

Her mother frowned and shrugged her shoulders as she moved over to the sink to begin washing up. Not another word was said that morning about the letter or the company that Rheinmarsh represented. She knew that her dad had something to do with them, her mother had said in passing once; the letters had started only a few months after her birth and her father's death. Letters that consoled and congratulated. Letters that offered support that a then single mother took up. The company had funded Leanna's education and from time to time someone even came out to see them, but it had thankfully been many years since that had happened.

When Leanna had finished her breakfast and had cleaned her face and her teeth, her mother called her back into the kitchen. She looked sad, and something told her that her mother had been crying again. 'Are you ok?' she asked as she hugged her mum.

'Of course, honey,' she said softly, the words she always said when she had asked. 'You've grown into such a lovely young lady; how could I not be happy?'

Leanna smiled as she sat next to her mother.

Her mother took both of her hands in her own and cupped them. She took a breath and Leanna noticed for the first time that were signs of aging. Grey hairs had started to speckle the thick brown hair, and the lines of crow's feet had appeared on her face. Even her skin looked old and tired. She had never seen her look like this before, and she cocked her head as she noticed more tears leave her mother's eye.

'Come on,' she asked. 'What's wrong?'

Her mother dropped her eyes as pulled an old USB stick from her pocket and handed it to her. Leanna knew what it was but she didn't know why her mum was giving her one – computers hadn't been able to read USB sticks for almost a decade now.

She rolled it over in her hand and raised her eyes to her mother. 'What's this?'

'It's something that you should've watched a long, long time ago,' her mother replied as another tear ran down her cheek.

Leanna didn't reply to that, she didn't know how. She opened her mouth and closed it again, as she rolled it over in her hand again.

'Your father, was so excited to meet you,' she laughed softly. 'He never really said it, but I could tell that he was terrified of you.'

'Terrified?' she managed. 'How could he be terrified? He never met me.'

'It was the idea of how much his life was going to change. He didn't know what to do, he was stuck at the bottom of the world and he couldn't get back.' She sighed. 'We talked every few days, you know he had left to go to Antarctica before we even found out I was pregnant?'

'Really?' She raised her eyebrows.

'That's right, he was supposed to be there for a year and we found out a little over a month into his stay.' She sat back into her chair. 'He wanted to come home but we needed the money, and if he was to come back early, we probably would've been in an even worse position. So, he stayed.' Her eyes welled up and Leanna hugged her as the tears came in torrents.

Leanna embraced her mum as she felt her tears wet her shoulder and finally, she pulled away and apologised as she blew her nose.

'Don't be sorry, it's sad.'

'Yes, but this is your day and I don't want to be sad for you.'

She wanted to say that she was used to it, but held her tongue. That comment would hurt her mother, whether malice was meant or not, and she didn't want that.

'Anyway, one of his friends that was there with him, told him that he should make videos. That way he could get over his fears and get used to talking to his child and Danny got right into it.' She smiled. 'He made a heap for you and he always tried to show you something different. He used to tell me all about it when we talked.'

'You haven't seen them?'

'No, they weren't for me,' she said as the smile went away from her face. 'They were between you and him and I don't want to ruin that. I've probably ruined it enough as it is by holding onto them so long before I handed them to you but, I just…' She wiped away more tears as she sobbed. 'I just didn't know when would be the right time. I thought when I got over it, the loss of him, maybe you'd be ready then. But… that day never came for me. So, I hope I haven't kept it from you for too long.'

Leanna didn't say anything. She didn't know of any words to make her feel better or to help the way that she felt. So, instead she hugged her mother again and held her until the tears that had come flooding forward once more, finally subsided.

'If you want to watch them, please go to your room. I don't think I can watch them with you.'

Leanna got up and looked at the USB drive again and thought about how she was going to watch them when she couldn't insert the drive into her computer. She started to walk toward her room when her mother called her back.

'I'm sorry, I'm so emotional this morning,' she said as she blew her nose. 'You'll need this too. Don't think your mum is that bad with technology, do you?' She handed Leanna a package. Leanna unwrapped it and laughed when she saw a Belkin adapter USB to HDMI-IV.

Alone in her room, Leanna sat staring at the USB and the adaptor.

She sat on her bed with her knees under her chin as she wrapped her hands around her shins. She had never seen a photo of her father, now apparently the USB drive that sat on her bed contained a whole bunch of videos from him to her. She couldn't answer how she felt about that, she wasn't even sure whether or not she wanted to watch them.

She stewed about it for an hour. She laid down, tried to read a book, sat up and stared at the USB again. She put it in her drawer and then laid back down but found that she couldn't stop staring at the drawer she had hid it in. Finally, she conceded and tore open the adaptor packaging and connected the device to her laptop.

A folder popped up on her home screen almost instantly after she connected the device. The name of the USB, she could see by the icon that it contained files. She doubled clicked on the icon and it opened up. There sat a whole bunch of videos, all titled the same thing with numbers to their side: Kiddo. She smiled softly as she hovered the cursor over the first of these, and she sighed as she double clicked and the media browser opened the file.

An image of a man came up on the screen before her. He opened his mouth and shut it again, as he obviously thought about what to say. The stubble on his chin was blonde, verging on grey. He looked so damned cold as he sat there in front of a machine with his beanie rolled up on his head. His nose was crooked and the hair on his upper lip looked wet from the snot that had run down from it. But when she looked at his eyes, the piercing blue that they were, she placed a hand over her mouth. As a single tear ran down her cheek, her father smiled softly and spoke the first words that she had ever heard him say.

'Hey kiddo.'